The Plagiarism Allegation in English Literature
from Butler to Sterne

The Plagiarism Allegation in English Literature from Butler to Sterne

Richard Terry
Northumbria University

PR
438
P54T47
2010

web

palgrave
macmillan

First published 2010 by
PALGRAVE MACMILLAN

Palgrave Macmillan in the UK is an imprint of Macmillan Publishers Limited, registered in England, company number 785998, of Houndmills, Basingstoke, Hampshire RG21 6XS.

Palgrave Macmillan in the US is a division of St Martin's Press LLC, 175 Fifth Avenue, New York, NY 10010.

Palgrave Macmillan is the global academic imprint of the above companies and has companies and representatives throughout the world.

Palgrave® and Macmillan® are registered trademarks in the United States, the United Kingdom, Europe and other countries.

ISBN 978–0–230–27267–5   hardback

This book is printed on paper suitable for recycling and made from fully managed and sustained forest sources. Logging, pulping and manufacturing processes are expected to conform to the environmental regulations of the country of origin.

A catalogue record for this book is available from the British Library.

Library of Congress Cataloging-in-Publication Data

Terry, Richard (Richard G.)
  The plagiarism allegation in English literature from Butler to
  Sterne / Richard Terry.
      p. cm.
  ISBN 978–0–230–27267–5 (hardback)
  1. English literature—17th century—History and criticism.
  2. Plagiarism—Great Britain—History—17th century.   3. English drama—
  18th century—History and criticism.   4. Plagiarism—Great Britain—History—
  18th century.   5. Great Britain—Intellectual life—17th century.
  6. Great Britain—Intellectual life—18th century.   7. Literature and society—
  Great Britain—History.   8. Originality in literature.   9. Imitation in literature.
  I. Title.
  PR438.P54T47 2010
  820.9'004—dc22

                                                             2010023947

Printed and bound in the United States of America

To Carol, Hannah and James

Contents

Acknowledgements

I began working on literary plagiarism over ten years ago and am deeply grateful for the help given along the road by friends, associates and institutions. My interest was triggered by an invitation to speak at a conference organized by Paulina Kewes on 'Plagiarism in history and theory' at the Institute of English Studies in November 1999. I have delivered papers relating to the project at various venues since then, and the book has benefited from many helpful pointers and criticisms. I am grateful for Claude Rawson for equipping me with a useful reference on Pope, and to Simon Stern and Vike Plock for the opportunity to see work of theirs before publication. The latter stages of the book were supported by a sabbatical granted to me by the University of Sunderland, matched by a period of research leave awarded by the Arts and Humanities Research Council.

The book incorporates some material published in different form elsewhere. Chapter 1 contains material published previously as '"Plagiarism": A Literary Concept in England to 1775', *English* 56 (Spring 2007): 1–16, and Chapter 5 is based on my article 'Pope and Plagiarism', *Modern Language Review* 100 (July 2005): 593–608. In addition, some ideas contained in the book were rehearsed at an earlier stage of formulation in '"In pleasing memory of all he stole": Plagiarism and Literary Detraction 1747–1785', in Paulina Kewes (ed.) *Plagiarism in Early Modern England* (Palgrave Macmillan, 2003), pp. 181–200. I am grateful to the publishers and editors for permission to reproduce this material.

Introduction

'Plagiarism' is one of those words that simultaneously identifies a concept and conveys an attitude towards it: in this case, a strongly disapprobative one. Swift referred to it as a 'hard' word, meaning harsh or censorious in its application.[1] In this sense, it works rather like the word 'noise', which means nothing more than 'sound', except that it is viewed in a disapproving way as a disturbance or intrusion. This doubleness in the construction of plagiarism is evident in the *OED* 2 definition:

> **plagiarism** 1. The action or practice of plagiarizing; the wrongful appropriation or purloining, and publication as one's own, of the ideas, or the expression of the ideas ... of another.[2]

It has sometimes been asked whether the practice of plagiarism has always been deemed a bad thing, but such an issue is actually foreclosed by the very definition of the word 'plagiarism'. Plagiarism is the term we apply to instances of appropriation that we consider 'wrongful': the language simply makes it impracticable to consider plagiarism in any light other than a negative one.

That the word 'plagiarism' should always be used to convey reproach tells us little, of course, about what sorts of linguistic appropriation might deserve to be reproached. Indeed, it is precisely what the *OED* definition leaves out, as relates to the period 1660–1780, that this book attempts to fill in. It will try to clarify just what kinds of appropriation were subject to rebuke and why. What will become evident is that writings considered plagiaristic at one historical moment were not necessarily considered so at others, as changing attitudes to the practice of appropriation dispensed their particular incriminations or exonerations. And even where certain writings seem to have fallen under an enduring cloud of plagiarism, this should not make us conclude that the grounds of their inculpation have always remained the same.

In a forthright essay on the immorality of plagiarism, Christopher Ricks claims that while the adjudication of plagiarism cases might prove a taxing process in practice, the actual definition of the term, on the basis of which all such judgements must be made, remains a 'simple' one.[3] However, if there is one thing that seems not to be straightforward, it is the meaning of 'plagiarism'. For a start, we have to cope with the *OED*'s omission of any guidance as to what might justify a conviction of the 'wrongfulness' of an appropriation: all we are in fact told is that once an appropriation has been deemed (by whatever criteria) improper, the term 'plagiarism' would be the correct one to apply. Over and above this, we have to contend with marked historical variations in the dictionary definition of the term. It should be noted that the two centuries from 1600 onwards are the ones in which 'plagiarism', in a narrow lexicographical sense, was born. They encompass its earliest occurrence as a lemma in a dictionary in England (1611) as well as the earliest definition (1775) that bears a clear ancestral resemblance to the current *OED* one cited above.[4]

Changes in the lexicographical definition of 'plagiarism' will be discussed at a later stage, but it might be useful here to spell out some broad developments in the word's meaning from 1600 onwards. A caveat requisite to the exercise is that lexicographical trends reflect only imperfectly, and normally at a significant chronological remove, actual habits of usage. They retain, however, an indicative value. For the whole of the seventeenth century, the prevalent acceptation of plagiarism relates it to theft, and is strongly influenced by Martial's original metaphoric association of the act of reciting other people's poems with the activities of a 'plagiarius' or abductor of slaves.[5] Crucially constitutive of the idea of plagiarism at this time is that it entails theft of a work in its entirety, in the sense of a work being presented to an audience as if it were the creation of someone other than its actual originator. An author damaged by an act of plagiarism, as the offence was understood at this time, found himself actually stripped of the very title of ownership of a work and being forced to witness the credit of his labour being diverted to another party. The sort of epithets that collocate with 'the plagiarist' around this time tend to be those reflecting the 'boldness', 'audacity' or 'flagrancy' of the offence, with the plagiarist sometimes being seen as glorying in the absence of any legal redress for his victim. Also consistent with this concept of plagiarism is that the original author is joined as an equal victim of an incident of plagiarism by the wronged reader, who has been duped into consuming a work under false pretences.

During the eighteenth century, lexicographers slowly embraced the idea that plagiarism might concern something less brash than the seizure of an entire work: it might also manifest itself in the petty appropriations of ideas or expressions. This shift is significant in as much as plagiarism for the first time becomes viewed as an artistic malpractice rather than an offence pertaining to how a work is put before an audience. It breaches an ethics of composition. Moreover, because the offence relates not to works in their entirety but to elements within a work, plagiarism becomes associated for the first time with secrecy: the plagiarist offends by suppressing his appropriations beneath public notice. We can see this development in John Ash's *New and Complete Dictionary* of 1775, which defines a plagiarist as 'one that clandestinely borrows the thoughts or expressions of another'. Notable here is not just the emollient attitude suggested by 'borrows' (as opposed to steals), but the way that the expression transfers the opprobrium of plagiarism from the act itself to its manner of execution. What is objectionable is not so much the appropriation itself as its skulking, clandestine nature. What this new understanding allows is that a plagiarism accusation can in principle be defused by an admission of debt, for it is the lack of acknowledgement, rather than the fact of textual borrowing as such, that constitutes the offence.

The idea that plagiarism was, in effect, a compositional technique made it possible for the first time to propose extenuations for it from the realm of aesthetics. Thus, an act of plagiarism could be seen as pardonable because the plagiarist had improved artistically on the original source or had assimilated the appropriated material so harmoniously that it deserved no longer to be seen as foreign matter. And once aesthetics began to provide these sorts of palliation, it became inevitable that it would provide a corresponding set of incriminations. As such, it became possible for a critic such as Percival Stockdale, for example, to allege plagiarism simply on the grounds that an author's assimilation of borrowed material was clumsy or incoherent, regardless of whether this material, on the basis of a different set of criteria, could be viewed as having been stolen.[6] Plagiarism became seen as less a moral failing than a creative impairment.

The purpose of the preceding paragraphs is not so much to convince the reader of the rectitude of my arguments (there will be time for that later) as merely to suggest that it skimps on the complexities of the matter to claim that the definition of 'plagiarism' is either simple or historically invariable. Were that the case, the entire enterprise undertaken here would be rendered obsolete and void. However, while the matter of definition is tormenting enough, the questions addressed by this book concern not so much the semantics of plagiarism as its pragmatics. This book is distinctive in the crowded field of plagiarism studies in not being directly about plagiarism but about its allegation.[7] It has not formed part of my project to unearth buried plagiarisms from an earlier age or to sit in judgement on the more scandalous cases. Nor is it even assumed here that any correlation need exist between plagiarism allegations and actual occurrences of plagiarism, plagiarism accusations being viewed here as speech events answering only to themselves and their own particular motives. My book instead explores allegations of plagiarism as part of a wider rhetoric of literary detraction, concentrating on the motives and circumstances that prompt them.

My governing assumption is that an understanding of how 'plagiarism' was used in the past involves precisely the same thinking as understanding the historical usage of any appraisive term. In some part, this inevitably remains a matter of the *meaning* of the term, the particular criteria that need to be met, and have needed to be met, for an invocation of the term to be apposite. In the case of the now prevalent sense of 'plagiarism', these have to do with the fact of borrowing by one author from another, with the deliberateness of this borrowing and with its perceived wrongfulness. But it would be misinformed to suppose that even if the meaning of the term 'plagiarism' in the eighteenth century were identical with that in our own day, this would mean that the pattern of usage of 'plagiarism', or the working life of the concept of plagiarism, could then be assumed to be constant across time. Understanding how a word functions in history demands that we attend not just to its meaning but to the contexts that govern whether, or with what degree of qualification, that meaning will be applied to a given set of facts.[8]

Let me demonstrate the point with another appraisive term. A bank robber, having shot dead two security guards, flees, swag on shoulder, across the rooftops, leaping daringly between the dizzying heights. The making of these vertiginous leaps equates with what, in a strongly appraisive word, we might call 'courage': fearlessness in the face of an understood risk. Yet the word 'courageous', given the larger circumstance, is one that positively discommends itself. A thief, a murderer, a fugitive from the law: less 'courageous', we might think the manner of flight, than 'reckless' or (more probably) 'desperate'. This is not to question that those criteria apply, in virtue of which 'courageous' might seem to be an apposite term; the point is rather that the social condition for the application of that meaning, that it be invoked only in the context of strong approbation of an agent's actions, has failed to be met. To invoke the term 'courageous' in connection with the course of events would accordingly be to commit a linguistic error.

Historicizing plagiarism, then, involves looking at when its meaning is invoked and what incites, qualifies or deters its invocation. The critical question is what work is actually being done when an allegation of plagiarism is made. Why should Dryden and Pope, the satiric writers of the highest eminence in their time, have been subject to such virulent plagiarism allegations? Why should Shakespeare, whose extensive plundering of source material was being investigated during the eighteenth century, have been almost entirely exempted from such allegations? And why did William Lauder go to the length of actually forging source materials for *Paradise Lost* in order to stick the brand of plagiarism on Milton?

Chapter 7 explores a more general question of the same sort: why should it have been the case that so many women writers seem to have run the gauntlet of plagiarism allegations and why, equally, do there appear to have been so few plagiarism accusations levelled by women against men? There exists some evidence that during the literary period covered by this book, the plagiarism slur actively conspired with other forms of misogynistic belittling of women's writing. The slur had the effect of challenging women's entitlement to be seen as authentic originators of their own productions, as legitimate bearers and custodians of their own literary property. Samuel Johnson argued that plagiarism allegations were typically directed upwards, discharged enviously and querulously by lesser writers at the greater reputation enjoyed by superior writers. However, the allegations aimed at women writers seem to suggest an opposite trajectory, with those enjoying cultural power using the charge as a means of disqualifying others from gaining access to the same eminence. This issue is, as always, not what 'plagiarism' means, but what it means for the stigma of plagiarism to be applied in any particular instance.

It might be as well to come clean at the outset that a general conclusion of my study is that plagiarism accusations are often as much deserving of censure, as a form of malfeasance in their own right, as the actual perpetration of plagiarism. I have been suspicious throughout of arguments that seem to me to lend a forced dignity to the aspersion, as in the claim that has gained some ground recently that the notion of plagiarism is a necessary pre-determinant of the concept of literature in general. It was fear of exposure as plagiarists, so the argument runs, that imposed on writers operating before the advent of copyright protection an acceptance of the inviolability of literary property, this principle being a necessary precondition of the reification of literature as a concept. The idea that the allegation acts as a sort of benign cultural watchdog, tutoring authors in modern literary ethics, is one that I challenge in Chapter 2.[9]

A further key contention of my study is that plagiarism cannot be historicized adequately without taking into account the boundary pressure exerted by other concepts that are either contiguous or antonymous. Both the levelling of the accusation and the defence constructed against it are qualified by the way that plagiarism relates at any particular time to a spectrum of bordering concepts. Take the idea of 'sufficiency', for example. Around the turn of the eighteenth century, the label of sufficiency seemed to sum up one particular hostile view of original creativity: it encapsulated the notion that intellectual self-subsistence, the reliance of modern authors purely on their own creative reserves, represented a form of cultural insularity and chauvinism, an ill-informed disrespect for the creative achievements of other authors, especially of the great classical authors. The most vivid portrayal of the idea of sufficiency is in Swift's fable of the spider and the bee in his *Battle of the Books* (1704), in which the spider is shown spinning his web-trap out of his own entrails in contrast to the bee, who forages liberally through the flowers of the field.

Swift knew perfectly well that the promiscuous sipping of the bee could also offer an analogy for plagiarism, but for the most part he distances himself from this insinuation and is content to champion the bee's method of composition over that of the surly, self-sufficient spider. It would be altogether wrong to suggest that Swift had a propitiatory attitude towards plagiarism, and he was certainly outraged when in 1705 William Wotton purported to bring to light plagiarisms in his own work, publicizing an allegation that Swift considered to be of the utmost literary gravity. Yet Swift's antipathy to the principle of creative sufficiency, while not tempering his hostility to plagiarism, had the effect of constraining his ability to voice that hostility. To denounce plagiarism is necessarily to uphold some positive principle against which the act of plagiarism offends. But Swift's desire to contradict Wotton's aspersion by aggressively asserting the originality of his own methods inevitably clashed with his opposition to just that sort of creative self-determination that had become stigmatized under the term 'sufficiency'. For a while plagiarism and sufficiency rub up against each other as concepts: the *meaning* of plagiarism may not be modified by this process, but the act of invoking that meaning is certainly rendered more complicated.

Other concepts and practices also abut on the space of plagiarism. The earlier decades under investigation here coincide with a literary period during which the imitation of (largely) classical originals enjoyed considerable standing as a mainstream literary practice. The virtues of this practice were certainly subject to debate, but imitation was not in general seen as incompatible with a high level of literary achievement. Yet, during the mid-eighteenth century, imitation becomes increasingly scorned as part of the movement by which originality (susceptible to being defined in a number of distinct ways) is elevated into a major criterion of literary merit. This trend is one to which no writer falls victim so graphically as Pope. While Pope was subject in his lifetime to a chorus of accusations of plagiarism, these mostly responded to his perceived conduct towards contemporaries, including his collaborators. Many can also be dismissed as simply needling and opportunistic, rather than as representing some objective revelation about Pope's working methods. It is only after the poet's death that the notion of Pope's widespread use of literary models betraying an inherent plagiarism becomes elevated into a critical commonplace: that his whole technique is imbued with the servile spirit of the copier.

What has led to this state of affairs is a change in the relation between imitation and plagiarism. In the early eighteenth century, plagiarism is viewed as a reproachable sub-category of a largely honoured literary practice: imitation. It occurs where imitation is perhaps taken too far or where certain proprieties are omitted. However, 50 years later, as a result of the influence of works like Edward Young's *Conjectures on Original Composition* (1759), as the standing of imitation dwindles, 'plagiarism' begins to be used in a way that is almost synonymous with imitation itself, or with what could be seen as reproachable in imitation as a general method. Not only is a higher premium placed on originality, but the bar of originality also gets raised, such that reliance on models can now be viewed as essentially incompatible with true creativity. It is as the bar of originality gets hoisted upwards that Pope's oeuvre increasingly falls under the incrimination of plagiarism.

Just as we need to note how the concept of plagiarism is encroached upon and shaped by related categories, such as 'sufficiency' and 'originality', we also need to be aware of conceptual *lacunae*, where the eighteenth-century understanding of plagiarism was modified by the very absence of a concept that we perhaps today take for granted. One concept that has been discussed recently as an antithetical or countervailing category to plagiarism is allusion. Christopher Ricks has suggested that allusion should be considered as plagiarism's honest sibling: whereas plagiarism depends on a concealment of debt, the literary appropriation that constitutes an allusion depends instead on the reader's recognition of the source of a borrowing. The most direct way, so Ricks suggests, of rebutting an allegation of plagiarism would be to relabel the offending text as an allusion: 'the defence that the poet is alluding is one that, should it be made good, must exculpate the poet'.[10] This argument certainly rings true of our own day and of how the conceptual space around literature is currently carved up, but the elementary dichotomy between plagiarism and allusion may not have been as meaningful in earlier literary periods as Ricks claims. It was not necessarily axiomatic to eighteenth-century readers, for example, that their encounter with literary works in verse and prose would be enriched by the discovery of covert references to other texts, or that the distinctive mode of existence of a literary work was one that actively solicited recognition of its relation to a range of other works.

The danger of allowing a rubric of allusion to explain cases of supposed plagiarism can be seen from the example of Sterne, a writer widely believed in his day to be a paragon of literary originality. When, after Sterne's death, it was brought to light that *Tristram Shandy* in particular was dotted with pilferings from other writers, the novelist's admirers were hard put to tender any ready exculpation. For Sterne to have been publicly garlanded as a writer of unusual powers of originality while secretly helping himself to the words of other authors seemed particularly shocking. Nobody in the 1790s seems to have appreciated that Sterne might be let off the hook of plagiarism if only his borrowings were instead relabelled as allusions. The idea seems not to have presented itself. Instead, Sterne's supporters sought to preserve his reputation not by contesting the nature of his borrowings but by arguing that originality (the principle that Sterne's surreptitious activities seemed to breach) was not to be equated with a mere avoidance of borrowing so much as an undefined creative power and inimitability.

The book concludes with my chapter on Sterne, the 'plagiarist as genius'. His case is one of the most illuminating about the shifting and fluid nature of plagiarism during the eighteenth century. Hailed as a singular creative genius during his lifetime, Sterne's reputation was shattered after his death when scholars like John Ferriar uncovered the trail of his textual borrowings. What was so disconcerting about these pilferings was not just the scale of them but their highly miscellaneous nature: drawn from religious sermons, works of history, science and philosophy, and even midwifery textbooks. Most of Sterne's borrowings derive from texts with which he could not have been seen as being in professional competition, yet many readers and critics were happy to seize on the plagiarism indictment as clinching evidence of the low morals habitual to a clergyman who had left his wife and nakedly prof-iteered from the publication of his sermons. Yet, at the lowest ebb of Sterne's literary reputation, an unlikely salvation was at hand. For even as it was being mounted, the case against him was being overtaken by a larger intellectual debate about what constituted 'originality', the tendency of which was both to relocate issues relating to literary theft to an aesthetic rather than a moral plane, and also to effect a rapprochement between the two seemingly antithetical practices of originality and borrowing. Thus it is that in the early nineteenth cen-tury Sir Walter Scott could pronounce Sterne to be at the same time both an inveterate plagiarist and a creative genius. The vicissitudes of Sterne's reputation reflect the way that plagiarism, as well as the oppos-ing category of originality, are made and unmade during the period covered by my study. This restless process of reconstitution is what this book is about.

1
'Plagiarism': The Emergence of a Literary Concept

I

It would be hard to imagine any culture in which authors were not inclined to feel some chagrin at seeing the credit for their writings being appropriated by others. As long ago as classical Greece, we can find lively discussion of the practical distinction between acceptable and culpable forms of literary borrowing, and writers who were discovered to have gained unjustifiable help from the creativity of others were liable for public exposure.[1] The trespass of illegitimate literary borrowing posed itself then, as it does now, as both a moral and an aesthetic issue: literary theft constitutes a moral infringement, but derivative writing has also been vulnerable (at least in Western cultures) to being criticized as a failure of craft, as bad art. The word that nowadays labels literary borrowing of this morally or aesthetically questionable kind is 'plagiarism', and the purpose of this opening chapter is to consider the shifting semantic ground that was occupied by this term from its importation into England at the end of the sixteenth century through to the final quarter of the eighteenth century.[2] The process will inevitably involve some discussion of general attitudes towards literary theft and derivativeness, but these will be pursued in the current chapter only insofar as they arise from invocations of the actual word 'plagiarism' or in relation to the very specific ideas that were associated with the term at the moment of its coinage.

II

The word 'plagiarism' arises from the Latin 'plagiarius', meaning a 'kidnapper' or, more specifically, an abductor of slaves. Its first application in a figurative sense to an author who falsely appropriates the writings of another appears in the Roman poet Martial's *Epigrams* I. 52:

> Quintianus, I commend you my little books – that is, however, if I can call them mine when your poet friend recites them. If they complain of harsh enslavement, come forward to claim their freedom and give bail as required. And when he calls himself their owner, say they are mine, discharged from my hand. If you shout this three or four times, you will make the kidnapper [plagiario] ashamed of himself.[3]

The representation of literary theft in these lines is intricately conceitful, but in places the conceit seems muddled or at least inconsistent. Martial depicts himself fretting over the fact that Fidentius has been reciting his (Martial's) verses under his own name, without acknowledging their true authorship.[4] The poet asks Quintianus to expose the plagiarist in public, so that Martial's true ownership of the poems might be reaffirmed. In the injury done to them by the plagiarist, Martial sees his works as having been 'enslaved' by Fidentius and accordingly requests that Quintianus intervene to 'claim their freedom'. At one level, Martial is at pains to assert that the poems are his own, not Fidentius's, but another reproach lies in his insistence that the works in question have already been manumitted or 'discharged' from his own hand and so enjoy a literary status equivalent to that of a freed man. The argument here is complex and it should be noted that Martial does his best to have things both ways. He admonishes the plagiarist because the enslaved writings already belong to an original author, while also using the opposite argument that the works cannot be seized by the plagiarist because they are free, in the sense of having already been enfranchised into the public realm.

This is the sole epigram in which Martial uses the word 'plagiarius', thus invoking the specific conceit of enslavement, but it is one of several in which he waxes indignant at the theft of his poems. 'Theft' in this context invariably means another author reciting Martial's verses as if they were his own, though in one epigram the poet seems to be annoyed that a rival has inserted his poems into a bound volume of verses.[5] The anger felt by Martial concerns the process by which his works pass (by whatever means) into the public domain, for the particular offence committed by the plagiarist is that of falsely claiming ownership of a work at the very point at which it becomes public: works that had already been published were, for this reason, seen as proof against the offence. In *Epigrams* I. 66, for example, Martial taunts a 'greedy purloiner of my books' with the disheartening news that an effective act of plagiarism can only involve writings still in a pre-publication state: 'private, unpublished work, poems known only to the parent of the virgin sheet'.[6]

'Plagiarism' begins, then, as an offence against a writer's foetal crea-tivity ('known only to the parent'), and something of the outrage of plagiarism is the sense of a literary womb having being rifled, and an unrealized thing having had its natural passage into the world cruelly intercepted. Yet, for all this, it is not the sense of dispossession per se against which Martial is protesting; what pains him is a feeling of hav-ing been cheated from the material remuneration that should have followed from a voluntary decision to cede ownership to another author. Nowadays, we tend to think that the affront of plagiarism is that it alienates an original author from a commodity that should properly be seen as inalienable: that is, his creativity. However, nowhere does Martial see his creativity as inalienable. Several poems, indeed, indicate that he is only too willing to sell his poems, provid-ing the price is right: 'If you want [my books] called yours, buy out my ownership.'[7]

III

Martial understands plagiarism as a particular kind of literary affront. It involves the unlicensed seizure of a work at the point at which it enters the public domain; the metaphors used to express this seizure are those of kidnapping and enslavement; and yet the whole con-ception of the offence is nuanced by a pragmatic acceptance of the potentially alienable nature of individual creativity. The point at which this conception of plagiarism translates into English culture is hard to fix, but seems to occur in the second half of the sixteenth century.[8] It is around this time that Martial's epigrams become cher-ished by a number of English poets. The earliest instance in English poetry of a writer evincing something of the spirit of Martial's concept comes in John Heywood's epigram 'Of bought wit' in his *Proverbs and Epigrams* of 1562: 'Wit is neuer good, till it be bought:/Thy wit is dere bought, and yet starke nought.'[9] These lines do not, of course, encap-sulate a notion of literary theft as such, but they suggest authorial rivalries being played out in a culture in which writings can be traded between practitioners. In this sense, the epigram seems consistent in outlook with those of Martial.

In 1577 Timothe Kendall's *Flowers of Epigrammes* introduces the first verse translation into English of some of Martial's epigrams relating to plagiarism. These include a rendering of *Epigrams* I. 72, which begins:

> Thou deemst thou art a Poet fine,
> And wouldst be thought so *Fidentine*,
> By bookes, and *Epigrams* of myne.
> So *Ægle* of her self is thought,
> To be well toothed, though stark nought
> Hauying of horne & bone teeth bought.[10]

A version of the same poem also appears in Sir John Harington's *Epigrams* (1618) as one of three epigrams specifically about literary theft, all more or less modelled on Martial.[11] Kendall's epigram sees the plagiarist as suffering from a creative impairment which he seeks to remedy by using plagiarism as a sort of prosthetic, in the same way that Ægle supplies her bare gums with false teeth.

One of the more important figures in the history of literary plagiarism in England is Ben Jonson, whose writings evince an unusual degree of interest in the subject and were themselves to be tainted by numerous plagiarism accusations.[12] Jonson's collection of epigrams contains one based on Martial's *Epigrams* I. 63, 'To Prowl the Plagiary':

> Forbear to tempt me, Prowl, I will not show
> A line unto thee, till the world it know;
> Or that I have by, two good sufficient men,
> To be the wealthy witness of my pen:
> For all thou hear'st, thou swear'st thyself didst do.
> Thy wit lives by it, Prowl, and belly too.
> Which, if thou leave not soon (though I am loath)
> I must a libel make, and cozen both.[13]

The resentment being vented concerns Prowl's habit of attributing to himself poems composed by other hands, the exact same offence of which Martial accuses Fidentius. Moreover, Jonson, like Martial, identifies plagiarism as an injury that afflicts works in their nascent state, before they have fully emerged into the public domain. Prowl's stratagem is to issue under his own name all poems that he happens to hear being recited, to frustrate which the narrator proposes to invite 'two good sufficient men', like witnesses of a royal birth, to vouch for his authentic parentage of his own works. If Prowl continues in the deceit, Jonson threatens to publish a 'libel', presumably an exposure, which will strip the plagiarist of his pretensions to wit, as well as of his means to a livelihood.

IV

There is one aspect of the offence of plagiarism, as delineated by Martial, that has been implied in my discussion but which I now want to bring into full relief. This is that the theft committed relates to the *entirety* of a work, rather than to its constituent parts. Martial never complains that individual expressions, lines of verse or particular ideas have been purloined, and this particular reproach is also absent from Martial's seventeenth-century imitators, such as Kendall and Jonson quoted above. As a general rule (though one not perfectly observed), the specific idea of 'plagiarism' is reserved for the act of dispossessing an author of an entire work or body of works through false attribution. The word tends not to refer to what we might understand as micro-plagiarism, or plagiarism of the component parts of works. Something of a marker for this usage of 'plagiarism' is the word 'all'. In Ben Jonson's play *Poetaster* (1601), for example, when some plagiarized verses are read out, they are denounced as '*all* borrowed', and in the same author's epigram 'To Prowl the Plagiary', the plagiarist's avarice is captured in the line 'For *all* thou hear'st, thou swear'st thyself didst do' (emphasis added).[14] Plagiarism, here, is stealing in bulk.

The same understanding of plagiarism is evident in a well-known passage of Sir Thomas Browne's *Pseudodoxia Epidemica* (1646), where Browne argues that the plagiaristic tendencies evident in writers of his own day were no less visible in those of the classical world. The notable ancients themselves were far from being above

> subscribing their names unto other mens endeavours, and meerely transcribing almost all they have written. The Latines transcribing the Greekes, the Greekes and Latines each other. Thus hath Justine borrowed all from Trogus Pompeius, and Julius Solinus in a manner transcribed Plinie. [...] Thus Eratosthenes wholy translated Timotheus *de Insulis*, not reserving the very Preface. The same doth Strabo report of Eudorus and Ariston in a Treatise entituled *de Nilo*. Clemens Alexandrius hath observed many examples hereof among the Greekes, and Plinie speaketh very plainely in his Preface, that conferring his Authors, and comparing their workes together, hee

generally found those that went before *verbatim* transcribed, by those that followed after, and their originalls never so much as mentioned. [...] Thus may we perceive the Ancients were but men, even like our selves. The practise of transcription in our dayes was no monster in theirs: Plagiarie had not its nativitie with printing, but began in times when thefts were difficult, and the paucity of bookes scarce wanted that invention.[15]

The general point that classical writers had pilfered freely from one another, such that even an august poem like Virgil's *Aeneid* could be seen as a veiled plagiarism from Homer's *Odyssey*, was a stock notion and is voiced by several other seventeenth-century authors, including Butler and Dryden.[16] What stands out in Browne's rhetoric is his stress on the *totality* of the thefts perpetrated by plagiarists: 'transcribing almost all they have written [...] borrowed all from [...] wholy translated [...] *verbatim* transcribed'. For Browne, 'Plagiarie' equates to the seizure of another author's work in its entirety or near-entirety. It is essentially an act of false attribution, which involves an author putting his name to works composed by other hands.

Because plagiarism was seen as an offence pertaining to how a work was published or put before an audience, rather than to how it was composed, there existed a case for seeing its principal victim as the unwitting reader rather than the plundered author. Thus it is that Gerard Langbaine in his Preface to *Momus Triumphans* (1688), a work in which he identifies and rebukes numerous plagiarisms by living authors from dead ones, outlines his concern to protect 'that Fame [or posthumous reputation] of these ancient Authors', yet also to prevent 'Readers being impos'd on by the Plagiary, as the Patrons of several of our Plays have been by our Modern Poets'.[17] To the same year of 1688 we can also date the composition of the anonymous *A Journal from Parnassus*, in which authors are depicted bringing grievances for settlement before an imaginary literary tribunal. When the issue of plagiarism is raised, however, those who are permitted to lodge their complaint are not authors, but instead a delegation of readers, who protest that:

The extraordinary pleasures & satisfaction we have receiv'd in our frequent Conversation with your learned & elegant Works has of late been mightily disturb'd by the many avocations we have mett with from a Company of fullsome impudent Plagiaries that without fear or witt daily endeavour to impose upon us their sophisticated ware under the deceitfull title of a new Poem, which generally has nothing new but it's Name: [...] But our greatest grievance is that after all this toil & trouble, we find our time & our labour lost, & the Author's mighty Promise dwindled into a stale repetition or corruption of other men's Works. To that pass is the Poetry of this Age come, that our Writers are not contented to quote a Line or two of an Author in their Title-Page, but they must steal two or three hundred in their Book, & them so miserably cloath'd, so poorly disguis'd that the meanest capacity may see through the thin Cheat, & perceive that in all their Writings there is nothing their own but what they have made so by corrupt translation. In short, what part of their Book is free from Deceit?[18]

The offence committed is squarely that of plagiarism: authors have been caught out illicitly appropriating the words of others. Yet to assert so much scarcely does justice to the real outrage alluded to here, and to the full indignation felt by the party of readers, for instrumental in the plagiarism is the whole hypocritical apparatus of the book's presentation. The work is advertised, and its title worded, so as to generate an expectation of new matter and so that the prospective reader is caressed with the usual cozening salutations. And yet the plagiarism is brazen, and 'so miserably cloath'd' that the least perspicacious reader can immediately see through it. 'Plagiarism', as narrowly understood, is perhaps only part of what is protested against here, which is in total the expansive insincerity that marks the relation of the makers and sellers of books to their reading public.

What might surprise modern readers about these early usages of 'plagiarism' is their complete lack of abstraction or dubitability. Nowadays, we are resigned to the need to tease apart a plagiarism per se from an allusion or a licit borrowing, or to differentiate between an idea that falls under individual ownership and one that exists in general circulation.[19] We are even tolerant of the notion that an act of plagiarism might be redeemable on aesthetic grounds, as an embellishment, albeit a disreputable one. In the seventeenth century, however, these indeterminacies tend not to exist. 'Plagiarism' meant stealing from another author by arranging that his work appear under the plagiarist's own name: no palliation for such an offence comes readily to mind. This sense of the physical incontrovertibility of the act of plagiarism is reinforced by the fact that it seems that the word could be used to denote, with uncompromising literalism, the actual theft of books. In *The Life and Death of Mrs Mary Frith* (1662), for example, Mal Cutpurse describes the practice of stealing books from stalls:

> I was grown of late acquainted with a new sort of Thieves called the *Heavers*, more fitly *Plagiaries*, whose Employment was stealing of *Shop Books*.[20]

'Shop Books' were not of the kind that were sold by booksellers, but were account books for which the traders would pay money to have them returned, or which the shop apprentice might be obliged to buy back if his negligence had been instrumental in the theft happening in the first place. Plagiarism here is nothing so abstract as a violation of intellectual copyright: it is the bearing away of physical property.

Because, in the seventeenth century, plagiarism meant the unauthorized publication of another writer's work under the plagiarist's own name, the concept stood more closely than nowadays to literary piracy (as this was in the process of being understood).[21] Indeed, it might be useful, as part of mapping the semantic territory occupied by early invocations of 'plagiarism', to tease apart three distinct kinds of literary transgression current during the century. The first of these is the copying by one author of ideas, statements or expressions from a work originated by another; the second occurs where one author appropriates a work generated by another not by copying from it, but by arranging for it to appear in print under his own name, thus alienating the original author from the rightful credit and proceeds of his labour; the third, meanwhile, is where a publisher arranges for unauthorized publication of an author's work, in which case the author retains the credit for the work but is robbed of the proceeds of its publication. What perplexes our understanding of early modern plagiarism is that for these three categories of trespass we only have at our disposal two terms: 'plagiarism', which nowadays fits the first category, and literary 'piracy', which applies to the third category. In between, however, there is a kind of trespass (the very same as was identified and rebuked by Martial) that accords with modern notions of plagiarism in as much as it alienates a writer from his due credit, but which also approximates to piracy, in that it involves a loss of authorial control over the publication of a work.

Literary piracy could only emerge once the book trade has flourished to an extent sufficient to have spawned its own set of professional malpractices. The *OED* dates the first use of 'pirate', in relation not to a sea-bandit but to a predatory publisher, to 1668. By the turn of the following century, authorial indignation at the activities of pirates was becoming widespread, as reflected in Edward Ward's *A Journey to Hell*: '*Piracy, Piracy*, they cry'd aloud/What made you print my Copy, Sir?'[22] As the new offence of literary piracy became more widely recognized and condemned, there was understandably confusion as to whether or not it could be assimilated into the same category of misdemeanours for which Martial had provided the name 'plagiarism'. It is instructive that when the emerging literary acceptation of the word is first recorded in an English dictionary, the reader is simply directed to the expression neologized by Martial: 'Pirate: one who lives by pillage and robbing on the sea. Also a plagiary.'[23] The separating out of 'piracy' and 'plagiarism', so that they command distinct fields of meaning, comes about during the mid-eighteenth century. Even as late as 1730 we can find Thomas Cooke's *The Candidates for the Bays* (1730) accusing Henry Fielding's play *The Author's Farce* (1730) of having 'pirated' the Goddess of Nonsense from the figure of Dulness in Pope's *Dunciad*.[24] However, when we turn to Samuel Johnson's *Dictionary* of 1755, we find a transparent ruling that piracy is to be considered an offence particular not to authors but to booksellers: 'a bookseller who seizes the copies of other men'.[25] The sharpening distinction between the two terms owes something to a greater specialization of the sense of 'piracy' (as evident in Johnson) but also depends on a corresponding shift in the understanding of 'plagiarism'. Indeed, it is the semantic creep of the term 'plagiarism' that I next wish to explore.

V

The first recorded usage in English of the word 'plagiarism' (or any variant of it) occurs in Bishop Joseph Hall's *Virgidemiae* (1597–8) in a reference to 'a Plagiarie sonnet-wright'.[26] The first nominal form appears in Ben Jonson's *The Poetaster* (1601): 'Why? The ditty's all borrowed! 'Tis Horace's: hang him, plagiary!'[27] Our own 'plagiarism' and 'plagiarist' were slightly later to enter the tongue, in 1621 and 1674 respectively. From an early point, the range of orthographical or morphological variants is broad. The seventeenth century, for example, sees 'plagiarie', 'plagiarian' and 'plagianisme', as well as the more standard forms. Once the term is noticed by the lexicographers, the lemma is usually 'plagiary', which by the mid-seventeenth century was used to refer both to the act of plagiarism and to its perpetrator.[28]

The earliest dictionary gloss of the term of which I am aware occurs not in an English dictionary as such but in Randle Cotgrave's

A Dictionarie of the French and English Tongues (1611), in which the French word 'Plagiaire' is glossed as follows:

> One that steales, or takes free people out of one countrey, & sells them in another for slaues; a stealer, or suborner of mens children, or seruants, for the same, or the like, purpose; [...] also, a booke-stealer, or booke-theefe; one that fathers other mens workes upon himselfe.

The definition is repeated more or less verbatim in the earliest English dictionary to record 'plagiary', Thomas Blount's *Glossographia* (1656), and forms the basis of all lexicographical definitions up until Johnson's *Dictionary* of 1755. The literal meaning is given as a stealer of people, though Cotgrave recognizes an ancillary sense as a person who suborns other men's children. When we proceed to the figurative application, we encounter a cluster of associations already familiar from Martial's complaints about literary theft and from those of his English imitators. In this sense, the 'plagiarie' is a 'booke-stealer' or, more precisely, one who 'fathers other mens workes upon himselfe', presumably by claiming authorial ownership of works actually composed by others. Consistent with invocations of Martial's concept around this time, plagiarism is associated not with an irregularity in how a work has been composed or put together, but with the fabrication of a false claim of ownership over a work.

The definition established by Cotgrave survives unrevised throughout the seventeenth century. John Bullokar's *An English Expositor, or Compleat Dictionary* (1695), for example, describes the plagiarist as 'A Book-thief, one that fathers other mens works upon himself: Also a stealer of mens servants, or children'.[29] All that has happened in the 80 years since Cotgrave's original definition is that the figurative sense, relating to books, has by now all but ousted the literal sense concerning the abduction of 'servants, or children'. Bullokar puts the literary acceptation first, indicating the downgraded status of the non-literary acceptation. In Nathan Bailey's *Dictionarium Britannicum* (1730), the meaning of plagiarism as relating to the stealing of slaves is given as what the word 'originally' signified, and the acceptation is omitted altogether in Johnson's *Dictionary*. Except as relating to this shift, however, Bailey's dictionary endorses the understanding of plagiarism derived from Martial.

Yet, by the early eighteenth century, authors were clearly aware that there existed a literary trespass relating to the unacknowledged copying of parts of authors' works, which was not encompassed by the particular understanding of plagiarism popularized by Martial. What is more, some were even using the very word 'plagiarism' to label this offence, an offence which had never been envisaged by Martial and had never been incorporated into lexicographical glosses in English of the term 'plagiarism'. One author whose usage stretches the term 'plagiarism' in this way is John Dryden, whose criticism touches on the ethics of literary borrowing and imitation on numerous occasions. One such case is in his essay *Of Dramatic Poesy* (1668), in which he remarks that Ben Jonson had not merely been a 'professed imitator of Horace, but a learned plagiary' of several other classical authors.[30] The term, in Dryden's mouth, carries a weaker force of reproof than in the mouths of many other authors, and in his Preface to *An Evening's Love* (1671) he was to find good company for Jonson among Virgil, Terence and Tasso, all of whom he names as having been not unfairly smeared as 'plagiaries'.[31] It is clear from these references that Dryden intended plagiarism to equate to the incorporation into one work of ideas, plotlines or phraseology lifted from another. In other words, the false practice concerns how a work is composed, not how it greets its audience.

By the mid-eighteenth century, prescription needed to catch up with usage, and the first lexicographer in whose work this begins to happen is Samuel Johnson, whose definition runs as follows:

Plagiarism Theft; literary adoption of the thoughts or works of another

Plagiary 1. A thief in literature; one who steals the thoughts or writings of another

Johnson is the first lexicographer to state that plagiarism might involve theft of something less than a work in its entirety: to be specific, it could involve seizure of the 'thoughts' contained in a work. Once the stealing of thoughts becomes an issue, a new nebulousness, the possibility of an equivocality, enters the frame. Johnson is the first lexicographer to use the word 'adoption' to define what a plagiarist does with the material he appropriates. It is true he could mean by 'adoption' the elective parenting of children in line with the old metaphor of plagiarism as a wresting of paternity rights, but I suspect he means it more unspecifically as (in his words) 'taking to one's self what is not native'. This sudden turn to abstraction suggests for the first time a moral havering or reticence, or even the possibility of an ethical neutrality.

Johnson is legislating on a concept that he had had occasion to ponder at some length, and at some pain to himself, in the years prior to the completion of the *Dictionary*. He had found himself sucked into and embarrassed by a controversy (to be explored in Chapter 6) that had arisen from William Lauder's bogus accusations of plagiarism against Milton, which Johnson had unwittingly endorsed.[32] When it became clear that Lauder had been bent all along on fabricating the evidence cited against Milton, Johnson was duly horrified. The episode can only have instructed him of the need for doubt and circumspection in engaging with plagiarism cases.

Though Johnson's definition of the term may be tinctured by personal experience, it does not reflect the most recent consideration of plagiarism available to him. Only two years before the *Dictionary*, Richard Hurd, in his *Discourse on Poetical Imitation* (1753), had argued that the only definite cases of plagiarism related to the copying of phraseology. Thomas Gray, a friend of Hurd's and an habitual verbal borrower, felt so disconcerted by this conclusion that he immediately made a disclosure to a friend of a series of borrowings in 'The Bard', adding resignedly: 'do not wonder therefore, if some Magazine or Review call me Plagiary'.[33] However, Johnson's definition still does not include the stealing of expressions as constitutive of plagiarism and, moreover, it still preserves a place for Martial's old construction of the term (now effectively obsolete) as the appropriation in their entirety of the 'works of another'. His definition, then, closes the gap on, but fails quite to draw abreast with, usage current at the time.

Johnson's ruling on plagiarism is reproduced verbatim by a number of later eighteenth-century lexicographers such as Thomas Sheridan and John Walker, but in 1775, John Ash's *New and Complete Dictionary of the English Language* unveils a powerful new construction of the term, one that heralds the modern sense as enshrined in the *OED*:

Plagiarism A literary theft, the practice of taking thoughts or expressions from another

Plagiary A thief in literature, one that clandestinely borrows the thoughts or expressions of another; literary theft, plagiarism

This is the earliest definition to include theft of expressions as constitutive of plagiarism; it is also the earliest one to omit altogether the sense of plagiarism as book theft that had been engendered by Martial and had remained uppermost in the understanding of the term in England since 1600. Ash's designation of what is plundered by plagiarists, namely 'thoughts or expressions', lies beneath the *OED*'s rendering of 'plagiarism' as 'the wrongful appropriation or purloining, and publication as one's own, of the ideas, or the expression of the ideas [...] of another'.

Ash's definition is inceptive in other respects. It is the earliest one to depart so much from the old construction of plagiarism as theft as to consider it instead a mode of 'borrowing'. Of course, the plagiarist 'borrows' without staying to receive permission, but, even so, the new term suggests a relaxation in the moral disapproval of plagiarism. Furthermore, in Ash's definition the stigma shifts from the verb to the adverb, not so much as a question of what is done but how it is done. The plagiarist 'clandestinely borrows', where the disapprobation inheres in the hugger-mugger, the attempt to conceal. This, should we need to remind ourselves, is how it is for us today, in that the gravity of a plagiarism infringement by a student, for example, will depend on consideration not just of how much has been borrowed, but also of the visibility with which the borrowing has been acknowledged. In earlier definitions of plagiarism, however, the offensiveness of the act was seen as lying instead in its openness, its slack obviousness: in *A Journal from Parnassus*, for instance, the delegation of readers rails at plagiarists partly because their thefts are usually 'so miserably cloath'd, so poorly disguis'd that the meanest capacity may see through the thin Cheat'.

In suggesting that the offence of plagiarism resides in the secretiveness of the borrowing, Ash is reflecting a new sense of plagiarism, not as brazen theft so much as a subtle con, a veiled cheat. These are the grounds on which Matthew Green attacks plagiarists in his poem *The Spleen* (1737):

> A common place, and many friends
> Can serve the plagiary's ends,
> Whose easy vamping talent lies,
> First wit to pilfer, then disguise.[34]

'Vamping' meant repairing or patching up something and is a common conceit in early eighteenth-century descriptions of plagiarists: Colley Cibber, for example, a self-acknowledged serial offender, describes his technique of pilfering from old plays as being similar to how 'a good housewife will mend old linnen'.[35] Green's plagiarist is promiscuous in his attentions ('many friends'), his practice consisting of both thieving from other authors and covering up his thefts: 'First wit to pilfer, then disguise.' Exactly the same attributes are recorded in William Stevenson's *Poetical Characteristics: or An Estimate of the Advantages of Rhyming* (1765), in which the plagiarist is seen as patching up a work while 'meanly the base act conceal[ing]'.[36]

VI

The purpose of this chapter has not been to investigate early modern attitudes towards literary theft in a general way. Instead, I have undertaken a more minor, but still necessary task: that of analysing the history in English up until 1775 of the term 'plagiarism' as received into English culture from the Roman poet Martial. For all the many books that have appeared on literary plagiarism, none, to my knowledge, has ever unpicked in a satisfactory way what the word meant in its different phases of usage, or indeed ever made the obvious point that in early modern England its meaning was altogether different from our understanding of it nowadays, as recorded in *OED* 2. Before 1700, 'plagiarism' meant the unauthorized presentation of one author's work under the name of another: it was a sin of attribution, not of composition. In the eighteenth century, under pressure of actual usage, the word was gradually redefined by lexicographers to mean the copying of ideas and expressions.

While 'plagiarism' has always been a term expressive of disapproval, there can be shades of disapproval, and disapproval of the same thing can be felt for different reasons. Before 1700, plagiarism tends to be figured as a sort of petty theft, the desperate recourse of the creatively poverty-stricken; in the eighteenth century, however, it comes to be seen as a con or deception, a cunning hoodwinking of the unvigilant. Part of this process is a shift of stigma from the act of plagiarism to the properties of the act, to the way in which, and spirit in which, the theft is carried out. Why these changes should have occurred to the understanding of the term 'plagiarism' is a question that the rest of this book will endeavour to answer.

2
Plagiarism, Authorial Fame and Proprietary Authorship

A recognized landmark in the emergence of modern conceptions of authorship is the appearance in 1616 of the monumental folio edition of *The Workes of Beniamin Jonson*. Merely by publishing his plays, Jonson was seeking to rescue them from the evanescence of their theatrical production and to secure his own posterity. But the lavish typographic appearance of the work, as well as the silent editing and reordering of the plays (including the exclusion of some) in ways tending always to enhance the visible integrity of the corpus, also betrays an attempt to confer canonical status on his own career, or at least to put his works into a state fit for their future canonization.[1]

Nowadays our ears are cushioned to the singularity of the term applied by Jonson to his literary productions: his *Workes*. No previous author had employed such an expression to refer to his writings, and the neologism was quickly seized on as a symptom of Jonson's colossal self-assurance. Sir John Suckling's *A Session of the Poets* (1637), composed in the year in which Jonson died, has the playwright blustering that 'he deserv'd the Bays,/For his were call'd Works, where others were but Plays'.[2] 'Works', as used by Jonson, probably equates to *OED* 13: 'A literary or musical composition (viewed in relation to its author).' The parenthesis here is critically constitutive of the term's meaning. 'Works' were literary productions seen specifically as having been realized through the agency of an author. Jonson's *Workes* were accordingly the enshrinement in textual form of his literary 'acts' or 'deeds' (see *OED* 1).

Jonson may be the earliest English author to publicly declare his ownership of the corpus of his own writings, the first, that is, to exemplify the principle of proprietary authorship. In Jonson's case, his entitlement to an indissoluble association with his own writings rests on his agency and labour: his *Workes* comprise the fruits of his toil. Yet such assertions of authorial possession remain rare in this period, one in which even the publication of play-scripts, let alone the preservation of authors' works in collected form, was uncommon. Recently, a powerful argument has been advanced to the effect that the idea of proprietary authorship only fully emerged with the reopening of the theatres after 1660. It is only after the Restoration that theatre companies felt relaxed about the appearance in print of newly performed plays. Moreover, the institution of the third-night benefit for authors, along with the proceeds generated from the publication of play-scripts, made writing for the theatre far more lucrative than any other form of literary activity. Under these conditions, so it has been asserted, authors had a more definite vested interest in asserting ownership of their writings.

It has become something of a truism that 'authorship' should not be equated with the simple act of writing, but instead should be seen as a complex role or function, constructed from a range of institutions and discourses.[3] A writer can only assert his authorship over his works, so it is claimed, at a point when something would be sacrificed by his not doing so, and this 'something' is naturally understood as money, or the commercial return upon his labour. Authorship is accordingly seen as a form of self-identity engendered by the participation of writers in a literary market. It has also been claimed that the modern author only emerges once that role has been invested with a legal personality, especially through copyright legislation capable of protecting writers from unlawful reproduction of their works. The point at which this intellectual safeguard was established in England is 1774, for the 1710 Copyright Act, probably the earliest such legislation passed anywhere in the world, though outlawing the reproduction of works by anyone other than the copyright holder, took no interest in the particular entitlement of a work's originator or author.

Brean Hammond and Paulina Kewes have recently argued that the earliest point at which the protection of authors' ownership of their works became a pressing issue is the Restoration, particularly in connection with the theatre.[4] Nearly all Restoration plays are based on historical or literary sources. Playwrights, in their haste to present texts to the theatre companies, seem to have appropriated and plundered almost with abandon, including reworking the plays of each other. Up until recently, the general assumption has been that authors were happy to take their place at the feast and to collude with the cynical artistic standards of the time. However, both Hammond and Kewes argue that the licence of playwrights to appropriate at will was perhaps more contested than we have been wont to assume. Authors cannot have relished the prospect of their own labours being taken over by others, or of having their slice of the market diminished by other dramatists and theatre companies conspiring to offer 'new' plays to the public that were little more than recyclings of old ones. Yet to what ethical standard could they have recourse in an era before the enshrinement of authorial copyright?

One answer proposed to this question is that they could invoke the allegation of plagiarism. Kewes, for example, sees the plagiarism allegation as rising in dignity and influence between 1660 and 1700: it starts off as part of the normal accusatory jostling between writers in a hectic marketplace but eventually becomes a regulatory principle within the same market. In the process, it forces authors to ponder the legitimacy of their appropriative practices.[5] Both Hammond and Kewes contend that the plagiarism allegation must ensue from, and be posterior to, the emergence of possessive authorship, for it is the seizure of what is perceived to be someone else's rightful possession that prompts the allegation. What follows from this is that the emergence of the modern author function can, to some extent at least, be charted against the incidence of the plagiarism allegation. Where such allegations are rife, as is indisputably the case in the theatrical culture of the Restoration, the principle of possessive authorship can be seen as being most robustly upheld.

It will already be clear that the claims made by Kewes and Hammond conflict with one of the main contentions of this book: namely, that plagiarism allegations should be viewed for the most part as untrustworthy and, even when justified, as very often tainted by some impurity of motive. It is not assumed in this study that any pronounced correlation need exist between allegations of plagiarism and actual incidents of plagiarism, the plagiarism accusation being a literary speech act that might be incited by a range of factors independent of plagiarism itself. The arguments put forward by Kewes and Hammond accordingly seem to me to rest on a number of unevidenced contentions. If their claims were true, we would expect a significantly higher incidence of plagiarism allegations after 1660 than before; we would anticipate a significantly higher incidence in connection with plays than with poems or prose writings, where the commercial returns were lower and the need to assert authorial ownership was less urgent; we would assume that the party perceived to be most directly injured by an instance of plagiarism would be the plundered author or, more generally, the wider cohort of original authors whose market position would be threatened by a proliferation of derivative works; we would expect allegations of plagiarism to be for the most part fair and judicious, as appealing to a set of ethics that emerged directly from the concept of possessive authorship; and finally we would expect such allegations to be effective both as a deterrent and admonition, for if the plagiarism accusation were powerless to shame, deter or change behaviour, in what sense could it be said to be imbued with any cultural authority? These are the issues that I intend to explore in the present chapter.

II

Paulina Kewes's *Authorship and Appropriation* is a work of such fine, measured scholarship that it is easy to forget the startling magnitude of some of her claims. Perhaps the most disarming claims concern Gerard Langbaine (1656–92), whose reputation and achievements Kewes very assiduously seeks to rehabilitate and champion.[6] Langbaine, in spite of being a son of the notable scholar Gerard Langbaine the elder, Provost of Queen's College Oxford, spent a rather reckless and unpromising youth. However, in the early 1680s he began to cultivate an interest in dramatic poetry, which eventually resulted in his publication of a catalogue of plays under the title of *Momus Triumphans* (1687) and a collection of biographies of dramatic poets entitled *An Account of the English Dramatick Poets* (1691). Chiefly remembered now as the scourge of Dryden, Langbaine made a name for himself in his own time as a fine scholar, but also as a rather venomous pedant, who discomfited his enemies by levelling plagiarism allegations at them. To some of his contemporaries he seemed fixated to the point of being unbalanced. Modern scholars, other than Kewes, have also found it difficult to warm to him or to his activities and motives. Tomas Mallon describes his *Momus* as 'a nasty little bibliography' and John Loftis points to the 'ill-tempered' nature of the later *Account*.[7] It is against this inauspicious backdrop that Kewes lionizes Langbaine as nothing less than the father of modern proprietary authorship in England. It was through his attempt to systematize the different sorts of textual appropriation and to distinguish the licensed from the plagiaristic that Langbaine (so Kewes claims) helped foster an appreciation of what we now call intellectual property rights. His work, Kewes believes, is the earliest adumbration in English of the principles of modern copyright law.[8]

Langbaine inevitably bulks large in the history of the plagiarism allegation in England, but is he important for quite the reason that Kewes claims he is? It is certainly true, as she asserts, that his scholarship is both ample and innovative. Kirkman's *Catalogue* of 1671, on which *Momus Triumphans* was based, 'the first ... printed of any worth' as Langbaine notes, had simply listed plays by title with limited reference to authors and with no ancillary information: it was probably never compiled for reasons of scholarship but rather to set out an inventory of Kirkman's own saleable stock.[9] *Momus*, on the other hand, confronts its user with a complex tabulation of detail: plays are listed under the authorial surname, accompanied by information about genre and printed format; separate sections are allocated to '*Supposed* AUTHORS' and '*Unknown* AUTHORS'; and the volume ends with an index of plays arranged alphabetically, so as to allow for cross-referencing. By the standards of the day such fastidiousness was beyond reproach. However, where reproach did subsequently arise was in the final aspect of Langbaine's industry: at the foot of each page of his main authorial listing were a series of footnotes, keyed to the plays above, which identified the principal source of each work. The perception that such information had relevance to a work of this nature seems to have been entirely Langbaine's own.

Langbaine's *Account*, though a work of much greater length than *Momus*, was built upon the same foundations. It combines extensive research inserted into a strong schematic framework. Arranged by authorial surname, each entry consists of a biographical sketch of the authorial life concerned; a list of extended titles of the author's printed plays; a list of non-literary sources for plays based on historical events; and a list of sources for plays based on earlier literary works. Rather than merely recording the fact of derivativeness, Langbaine helped himself to a sufficient wordage to build questions of reliance, borrowing or plagiarism into a more rounded literary critical response to each playwright.

The professionalism of Langbaine's scholarship, on the basis of which his *Account* surpasses previous collections of authorial biographies such as those by Edward Phillips (1675) and William Winstanley (1687), and his innovative appreciation of the potential role of source-criticism distinguish him as a pioneer.[10] This is certainly how Kewes views him, as a man ahead of his time who helps to usher in the modern conception of authorship. Yet to ask not *how* Langbaine proceeds but *why* he proceeds as he does is to be thrown back on answers that conversely make him seem a much more backward-looking figure than is ever proposed in Kewes's account. Crucial to this, moreover, is the idea of 'fame'.

Fame, as invoked by seventeenth-century authors and antiquarians, is a complex notion to which we have no precise equivalent, though it could be seen to compact the modern terms 'renown' and 'posterity'.[11]

It enunciated a conceit that 'worthy' individuals who achieved renown in life could perpetuate themselves through an everlasting remembrance. Nowadays, we are accustomed to the notion that, though we ourselves will not survive, our deeds and achievements, if sufficiently notable, may survive us. Fame, however, predicated instead that we can *ourselves* survive through the recollection of our deeds: that fame, or public remembrance, can confer on us a sort of imperishibility, or as Pope put it a 'second Life in others' Breath'.[12] This unfolding prospect of eternity was also felt to be more within the reach of writers than people of any other occupation, for the medium of print allowed in principle for the indefinite reproduction of an author's works and thus the continuous renewal of his fame. Edmund Waller, for example, believed that the durability of 'lasting' verses could 'so preserve the hero's name,/ They make him live again in fame'.[13] Writing in fact became seen as an activity almost uniquely driven by an appetite for fame.

Fame was not merely a flattering conceit of authors, for from an early point it provides the conceptual framework for attempts to preserve and record the literary past. Literary history begins in England as an attempt to fix and perpetuate the fames of dead authors: it starts as a mortuary discourse, imbued with a strong ethical sense of what is owed to the dead by the living.[14] The idea stands very prominently in the two collections of authorial biography that precede Langbaine's *Account of the English Poets* and that he records having consulted. Phillips's *Theatrum Poetarum* has a lengthy preface deliberating on issues concerning the possession and desert of fame:

> in the State of Learning, among the Writers of all Ages, some deserve Fame & have it, others neither have nor deserve it, some have it, not deserving, others though deserving yet totally miss it, or have it not equall to their deserts.[15]

It is in the context of this dismaying arbitrariness in the distribution of fame that Phillips asserts his own intention of securing for all 'deserving' writers 'a lasting Fame, equal to ... [their] ... merit'.[16]

Winstanley's *Lives of the Most Famous English Poets*, cobbled together from earlier works such as Phillips's *Theatrum Poetrum* and Thomas Fuller's *History of the Worthies of England* (1662), also rationalizes its project in terms of the thematics of fame. His 'Preface' is given over to the issue, containing, as well as some liftings from Phillips's own prefatory essay on the subject, a set of wistful remarks by classical authors on their hope for a lasting renown. A frontispiece engraving allegorizes the bestowal of fame on a number of deceased English and classical authors. The image's centre-ground is occupied by a bust of Shakespeare flanked by twin pyramidical towers, on the top of each of which a cherub is about to set a laurel crown in which is encircled the word 'Imortality'. The cherub at the same time purses its lips to blow through a clarion in order to proclaim the fame of Shakespeare and the other named writers (Chaucer and Cowley being the sole other English writers). This rich iconography of fame conferment was clearly meant to represent Winstanley's own self-appointed task of reuniting numerous less well-known writers with their appropriate share of fame.

Neither Langbaine's *Momus* nor his *Account of the English Dramatick Poets* contains such a well-developed theorization of fame. Yet the idiom of fame and the perception that all acts of literary historical retrieval and documentation are ultimately conducted in service to its governing ethic are persistently on view in the prefatory material of both works. There is, however, one particular ingredient that Langbaine adds to all previous discussions of fame of which I am aware. This is a pronounced sense that what imperils authorial fame is not just neglect or forgetfulness but also a very specific unethical activity: plagiarism. The Preface to *Momus*, for example, defends the notice that Langbaine will take of authorial thefts in the following terms:

> having read most of our English Plays, as well ancient as those of latter date, I found that our modern Writers had made Incursions into the deceas'd Authors Labours, and robb'd them of their Fame ... I know I cannot do a better service to their memory, than by taking notice of the Plagiaries, who have been so free to borrow, and to endeavour to vindicate the Fame of these ancient Authors from whom they took their Spoiles.[17]

Langbaine pledges himself to 'vindicate the Fame' of those earlier authors who have fallen victim to the attentions of modern-day plagiarists. His adherence to this precise idiom of fame is not glib or gestural but considered, and he reiterates the argument on the first page of his brief preface to the *Account*. Here he regrets that he may not in the earlier work have fully achieved what he intended, and he regrets that his powers of execution may not have been equal to 'the Zeal I have for the Memory of those Illustrious Authors, the Classicks, as well as those later writers of our own Nation'. Yet what he still hopes to be able to achieve on behalf of these writers is to do them 'better service, in vindicating *Their* Fame, and in exposing our Modern *Plagiaries*, by detecting *Part* of their Thefts'.[18]

This conjunction of fame and plagiarism is very pronounced, though not all of its aspects are transparent. When Langbaine talks of his zeal to 'vindicate' plagiarized authors, he does not intend its modern sense as to justify something but rather 'to assert or establish possession of (something) *for* oneself or another' (*OED* 5). What he sees himself as doing, in other words, is seizing possession of the bogus fame or credit acquired by the plagiarist and re-endowing the original author with it. The originating author, it should be emphasized, has to be deceased, as if this were not the case, the invocation of fame would be redundant. What plagiarism threatens to desecrate is exactly that literary past that scholars like Langbaine had been reverentially and scrupulously trying to reassemble. The great writers will risk a final and irreversible extinction of their fame if modern plagiarists can simply plunder their works and publish them under their own names.

My sense of Langbaine's significance has little in common with that of Paulina Kewes, yet coincidentally the passage cited from *Momus Triumphans* above is one which Kewes seizes on as proof of her very different case. She notes Langbaine's comment about modern authors making 'Incursions into the deceas'd Authors Labours' and also points out Langbaine's stated determination (cropped from the quote above) to identify such thefts and to bring about 'a restitution to their right Owners'.[19] This, Kewes claims, is an inaugurative idiom: literary works are being endowed with the status of property in a way that foreshadows the invention of intellectual copyright. It is on the basis of such evidence that she later characterizes Langbaine's arguments as 'ethical and commercial' in nature.[20]

This seems to me to misstate Langbaine's real contribution to the theorization of plagiarism. Insofar as there is an economy whose operation is distorted by plagiarism, what circulates in that economy is not money but 'fame' or authorial credit. Though Langbaine sees himself as restoring stolen material to its rightful owners, he is not appealing to some high principle concerning the inalienable nature of individual creativity. What moves him is rather the prospect of the great writers suffering an erosion of their fames, as their credit is embezzled and spirited away by plagiarists. Far from being a pioneer in endowing literary texts with the status of property, Langbaine seems a good deal less engrossed by the notion than, say, his contemporary Samuel Butler, whose ideas I will discuss later. Not only does he not invoke the concept of property or 'propriety', he never considers the affront of plagiarism in monetary terms, in terms of the gains falsely reaped by the plagiarist from the labour of an original author.

That he should not do so betrays Langbaine's indifference to the theatre as an institution. He does not attend to the commercial consequences of plagiarism because he does not think of plays specifically in terms of the market for scripts generated by the Restoration theatre duopoly. Instead, he concerns himself with play-texts as books, his caveats about plagiarism being addressed directly to potential readers of plays and, even more narrowly, to potential collectors of them. It is indicative that he identifies the primary improvement made by his catalogue *Momus Triumphans* on earlier examples as being that these have in some instances referenced plays that have never been printed, an error (if it can be termed as such) that can have caused frustration only to the most zealous category of collector.[21] Where readers of plays and theatregoers are mentioned in the same sentence, the former are invariably cited first, as those whose interests Langbaine is most directly trying to serve and safeguard. When he pronounces the basic rationale for *Momus Triumphans*, for example, he sees this as being 'to prevent my Readers being impos'd on by crafty Booksellers, whose custom is as frequently to vent *old* Plays with new Titles, as it has been the use of the Theatres to dupe the Town, by acting old Plays under new Names'.[22] Langbaine recognizes that the sharp practices of booksellers are matched by those of the patented theatre companies, but it is the injury that plagiarism does to readers (not to playgoers or indeed dramatists) that actuates his project.

III

One of Langbaine's superiorities over earlier cataloguers and biographical compilers is the more orderly way in which he expresses his researches. Yet this is not to say that his invocation of the plagiarism allegation is itself systematic or untouched by what Giles Jacob called his 'private and ungenerous Malice' or, conversely, by occasional spurts of chivalric emollience.[23] Fathoming Langbaine's attitudes towards plagiarism has been made all the harder by the unfortunate publication circumstances of *Momus Triumphans*, which may have motivated the way that his anti-plagiarism campaign unfolded. When the work appeared in 1687, it did so under a title that had never been authorized by the compiler. 'Momus' was a catchword for a carping critic, and purchasers of the initial 500 copies can only have assumed the title was intended to exhibit self-irony. However, Langbaine was not inclined to humour of that sort and was left red-faced and vituperative, desperate that 'my *Friends* may not think me *Lunatick*'.[24] In the Preface to his later *Account* he hints darkly that the spurious title-page had been perpetrated by the 'Malice and poor Designes of some of the *Poets* and their Agents'.[25] A notion has long existed that Langbaine blamed Dryden in particular for his discomfiture, but Dryden's involvement has never been substantiated.

Because the book came into the world under a cod title, it remains unclear how Langbaine had sought at the outset to designate his undertaking. The revised title-page used for the 1688 edition may be the one originally intended or it may alternatively have been drafted specifically in order to scotch the damaging impressions generated by the bogus one. What follow (in edited form) are the title-pages of the volumes published respectively in 1687 and 1688:

Momus Triumphans: or, the Plagiaries of the English Stage; Expos'd in a Catalogue of all the Comedies, Opera's ... &c Both Ancient and Modern, that were ever yet Printed in English. The Names of their Known and Supposed Authors. Their Several Volumes and Editions: with an Account of the various Originals, as well English, French, and Italian, as Greek and Latine; from whence most of them have Stole their Plots. (1687)

A New Catalogue of English Plays, Containing All the Comedies, Tragedies ... &c. Both Ancient and Modern, that have ever yet been Printed ... To which, are Added, The Volumes, and best Editions; with divers Remarks, of the Originals of most Plays; and the Plagiaries of several Authors. (1688)

What stands out is that not just the ludicrous reference to Momus but also that the larger titular reference to the 'Plagiaries of the English Stage' has been excised from the reissued work. In addition, the impression that Langbaine was bent on incriminating the majority of his referenced authors as plagiarists – 'most of them have Stole their Plots' – has also been removed. Instead, the new edition speaks in more restrained terms of 'the Plagiaries of several Authors'.

The impression foisted on to the work by the original title-page was that the exposure of plagiarisms provided the principal rationale for Langbaine's catalogue, whereas the revised title-page makes it only incidental to an essentially bibliographical undertaking. This may be how Langbaine envisaged the project all along, but it may also be that he felt that the spurious title-page had so conclusively turned to jest his interest in plagiarism that it was best to play the matter down. Either way, the episode of the unauthorized title-page complicates our understanding of Langbaine's original motives. Other issues, however, serve to thicken this complication. It is odd that when in the Preface to the work Langbaine describes the ensuing catalogue, this does not tally with what is actually provided. When, for example, he claims that the reader will be presented with 'an Essay towards a more large Account of the Basis on which each play is built', this implies something altogether more substantial than the perfunctory glosses that are actually supplied.[26]

No 'large Account' actually exists: instead Langbaine specifies forms of derivativeness through a series of formulaic expressions: 'Borrow'd from', 'Founded on', 'Plot from', 'Translated from', 'Reviv'd from', 'Taken from' and 'Stollen from'. These categorizations (not discussed by Kewes) matter to any enquiry into the rationale and system of Langbaine's judgements. In spite of the fact that even the muted 1688 title-page leads us to expect the exposure of *some* plagiarisms, that term itself is not used at all throughout the catalogue. The one expression used by Langbaine sufficiently envenomed to indicate plagiarism is 'Stollen from', but even this figures only twice, in connection with Behn's *Emperor of the Moon* and Otway's *Caius Marius*. In this regard, Langbaine's catalogue neither consistently identifies nor indicts plagiarisms, nor does it enforce a systematic distinction between legitimate and culpable forms of appropriation. The impression of a series of spasmodic, unstable discriminations is borne out by the later *Account*, in which neither of the two plays earlier perceived as having been 'Stollen' is branded as plagiaristic. It is even more telling that Dryden, the author singled out for the most virulent denunciations of plagiarism in the *Account,* is given in *Momus* an entirely clean bill of health, without a single insinuation of plagiarism being made against any of his plays.

It matters to Kewes's rehabilitation of Langbaine that his judgements should be seen as studied and temperate, untainted by personal animus. In her view, he unveils for the use of contemporaries a rationale for differentiating between acceptable and illicit forms of literary borrowing, and he tutors them towards an appreciation that literary works constitute a form of property, the exact same intellectual property that copyright legislation is subsequently introduced to protect. Yet the difficulty with this argument is that Langbaine's discriminations are so prone to erraticism and flux. It is true that he appears to uphold a distinction between borrowing plots or narrative ingredients (as acceptable) and appropriating the linguistic content of originals (as not so), but when it comes to either reproving or condoning an author in a particular instance, his decisions can seem almost arbitrary. In the case of Aphra Behn, he is compelled to admit that 'she has borrow'd very much' but finds an unlikely extenuation for this in that 'she has often been forc'd to it through hast: and has borrow'd from others Stores, rather of Choice than for want of a fond of Wit of her own'.[27] Barely more convincing is the excuse for an author's plagiarism in terms of inexperience, as when Langbaine exonerates Robert Baron's borrowings on account of 'the Author's Youth, he being but 17 Years of age' when he composed the offending text.[28]

Such extenuations speak volumes about Langbaine's attitude to plagiarism. They certainly do not indicate that he viewed its offensiveness as resting on the infringement of an author's property rights. The exculpation, for example, that he applies to Behn is not that she did not steal or did not steal very much, but that she was induced to do so by haste rather than by imaginative poverty. Accordingly, no *mens rea*, or culpable intent, attaches to her case. (Think how weak such an extenuation would seem in the context of breach of copyright litigation.) This seems to me typical of what Langbaine responds to in instances or seeming instances of plagiarism: not to the bare alienation of a piece of textual property but to the mental disposition out of which the act has emerged.

The critical test-case, of course, must be Langbaine's censuring of Dryden. Langbaine criticizes Dryden at some length in the Preface to *Momus* and, while no evidence exists of the dramatist's role in the subterfuge concerning the unauthorized title-page, he certainly stood to benefit from the work's reduction to ridicule. No precise allegations of plagiarism were, however, lodged at this stage against Dryden's plays, but things were to be very different in the 48-page denunciation of the dramatist (far and away the longest authorial entry) that appears in the *Account*. Dryden appears in *Momus* at the head of a modern tendency to disown the protocols of borrowing observed by the ancients. Classical borrowing involved the conscious emulation of an esteemed original. The borrower would seize on the most beautiful aspects of the earlier text, attempt to alter and improve them, and insert them seamlessly into the new work. In addition, such imitative authors 'plainly confess'd what they borrow'd'. Dryden, by implication, falls foul of these tenets; in particular he prostitutes himself by filling his plays not with borrowings of earlier texts of sterling worth, but with 'empty French Kickshaws'.[29]

The main case that Langbaine brings against Dryden, however, concerns hypocrisy: this, rather than in theft per se, is where his culpability lies. It is not a new case, of course, but Langbaine does all he can to invigorate it. Dryden (so he asserts) both plagiarizes from other authors (such as from Molière and Shadwell) and issues windy protestations of not having done so, while also having the temerity to impugn other authors of plagiarism, such as Ben Jonson, when ''tis evident that he himself is guilty of the same'. Dryden is not castigated here for having infringed the principle of literary property: rather, he is pilloried for ethical failings that bear upon the act of plagiarism but are not identical with it. It is Dryden's frame of mind that is objectionable to Langbaine, and he urges the dramatist to give up his 'Confidence and self-love' and resort to 'Modesty'.[30]

The entry on Dryden in Langbaine's *Account*, as well as itemizing supposed plagiarisms contained in the plays, renews the assault on Dryden's hypocrisy, as a plagiarist all too willing to asperse others with the same charge. Yet it also unveils a further aspect of Dryden's shamefulness. As well as having demeaned his muse by stealing from French sources, Dryden has attacked the hallowed line of English drama:

> as if the proscription of his Contemporaries Reputation, were not sufficient to satiate his implacable thirst after Fame, endeavouring to demolish the Statues and Monuments of his Ancestors, the Works of those his Illustrious predecessors, *Shakespear, Fletcher*, and *Johnson*: I was resolv'd to endeavour the rescue and preservation of those excellent Trophies of Wit ... to put a stop to his Spoils upon his own Country-men. Therefore I present my self a Champion in the Dead Poets Cause, to vindicate their Fame.[31]

Although this is an invective specifically against Dryden, these comments resonate with Langbaine's larger critical mission. Dryden's crime is not only to have besmirched his contemporaries, but also to have degraded the reputations of those fathers of the English dramatic tradition: Shakespeare, Fletcher and Jonson. What Langbaine's case rests on, of course, are the critical comments on these writers in Dryden's *Essay of Dramatic Poesy* and specifically his identification of Jonson as a 'learned plagiary' from the classics: 'you track him every where in their snow'.[32] Dryden has assaulted the fames of these great writers partly to serve his own 'implacable thirst after Fame'.

The issue here defies reduction to the bare fact that Dryden has borrowed from other writers and by doing so has offended against Langbaine's saintly adherence to the principle of private literary property. Rather, as an asperser of plagiarism against Jonson and as a critical denigrator in general of the great English dramatists, Dryden has set himself against the ethic that motivated Langbaine's entire career as a scholar. This ethic concerned the preservation of the memory of, and the continuing recognition of the credit accruing to, the worthy dead. As Langbaine puts it, 'I present my self a Champion in the Dead Poets Cause, to vindicate their Fame'.[33] The act of restitution that Langbaine saw himself as undertaking does not relate to stolen words, but to the due credit or fame from which the great poets had found themselves exiled by the sly appropriations of modern plagiarists and the grudging words of modern critics. Langbaine's intrinsic interest to the student of plagiarism has more to do, I contend, with the old concept of literary fame than with the new one of literary property.

IV

The most lively and assiduous interrogator of plagiarism in the Restoration era is not Langbaine but Samuel Butler, author of *Hudibras*. That Butler is rarely adduced in this context owes a certain amount to plain oversight, but also perhaps to the fact that his writings on the subject exerted no influence, since none were published in his lifetime, or indeed even before Robert Thyer's edition of his *Works* in 1759.[34] His repertoire of pronouncements on the topic take in several 'Characters', not just that of 'A Plagiary' but also 'A Translater', 'An Imitater', 'A Playwright' and 'A Small Poet', along with a few poems expressly about or touching on plagiarism, supplemented by a few excoriating observations in his miscellaneous prose. Why Butler was so vexed by the subject has remained elusive. His poem *Hudibras* became much imitated, but mainly after his death and not in a way that would evidently have led him to take umbrage, and no evidence is extant showing that he fell victim to the offence.[35] He seems, however, to have viewed plagiarism as an objectionable trespass in relation to several sorts of literary composition: poems, plays and literary criticism.

A good place to begin is with his 'Satyr upon Plagiaries', which is not just his fullest treatment but also a poem that indicts plagiarism while also giving their due to certain arguments that could tend to exculpate the offence. Robert Thyer catches something of this doubleness in referring to the poem as a 'sneering Apology for the Plagiary', where the plagiarist is the one being sneered at, not the moral majority scandalized by his activities.[36] It begins by posing the conundrum:

> WHY should the World be so averse
> To *Plagiary* Privateers,

> That all Mens Sense and Fancy seize,
> And make free Prize of what they please. (1–4)[37]

What follow are a series of extenuations, paraded with Butler's typical rhetorical gusto, occupying all but the final 20 or so lines of the entire poem. Only in these final lines does it become clear that the prior arguments are cited only reprovingly, as forms of ethical laxity and critical abdication that have the ultimate effect of devaluing literary culture.

The first extenuation secretes itself in the very formulation of the issue: for what is it exactly for the plagiarist to 'seize' on the 'Sense and Fancy' of other authors? Such phrases imbue the creative productions of authors with the status of property, but how can such a hollow conceit be maintained? After all, as Butler, puts it: 'no Inditement justly lies,/But where the Theft will bear a Price' (15–16). A literary work cannot be classed as property because it bears no monetary tag; it exists outside the realm of conventional commercial transactions: 'Is neither Moveable, nor Rent,/Nor Chattel, Goods, nor Tenement' (25–6). 'Wit', the rarefied condition of mind from which literary works emerge, can never be chained by the laws of economics:

> So 'tis no more to be engross'd,
> Than Sun-shine, or the Air inclos'd;
> Or to Propriety confin'd,
> Than th'uncontrol'd and scatter'd Wind. (31–4)

By 'Propriety', Butler means 'property': plagiarism can be justified, he claims, because literary works do not count as property. Lacking any determinate value, they cannot be subject to theft, and for this reason an author can neither be legally protected from nor compensated as a result of such an offence.

One reason why writings are insusceptible to hard valuation is that their worth lies not in possession but in dissemination, in being 'Vent' as Butler puts it: a poem 'has no Value of its own,/But as it is divulg'd and known'. Plagiarism, it might be thought, enriches the public domain of texts in the sense that it adds to the churning and circulation of written material. More than this, though, the plagiarist benefits from being a second comer, from being ideally placed to benefit from the exertions of the original author and also to improve on them. The plagiarist winnows and purifies the original 'As Salt, that's made of Salt's more fine,/Than when it first came from the Brine' (83–4).

Butler's final extenuation concerns the relation of plagiarism to labour. When Jonson terms his collected plays his *Workes*, he is suggesting that it is his input of toil that confers on him the ownership of his own productions. The cheat perpetrated by the plagiarist consists of trying to claim ownership of writings in which none of his own labour has been invested. Yet Butler disarmingly stands the whole argument on its head, for is not original creation more like an instantaneous force of nature than an expression of toil? The real labour instead belongs to the plagiarist, who has to select his appropriations, 'What's fit to chuse, and what to leave' (78), and then combine his heterogeneous material together 'by *Mosaic* Art,/In graceful Order, Part to Part' (111–12). Why should such strenuous activities not merit the same regard as is given to writers who lazily fall back on their own 'Mother Wit'?

Only at the end of the poem are these exculpations dismissed as the work of siren voices, for to succumb to such sophistries is to institute a culture of permissiveness in which the worst will ultimately triumph over the best. In these circumstances, barren, scraping poets, whose only recourse is to 'commit/The *Petty-Larceny* of Wit' (169–70), will find themselves regaled as authors of the same merit as original practitioners. This false regard paid to plagiarists has something to do with the confusion between exercising control over property and rightfully owning it. A humble banker can dispose of greater sums than are available even to the richest man, and so equally a plagiarist can garner more credit than might come to an author solely dependent on his own resources. But bankers are not genuinely rich (or did not used to be) and a plagiarist should not be considered as authentically credit-worthy.

The main question that the poem poses is whether we should be the more impressed by the final condemnation of plagiarism or by the seductive plausibility of the arguments mounted along the way in its favour. One of his arguments in particular, namely that plagiarism might be immunized from reproach because literary works, lacking determinate value, cannot be considered as authorial property, is one that Butler ponders elsewhere. Take his prose character of 'A Plagiary':

> [A Plagiary] IS one, that has an inclination to wit and knowledge, but being not born nor bred to it takes evil courses, and will rather steal and pilfer, than appear to want, or be without it. He makes no conscience how he comes by it, but with a felonious intention will take, and bear away any man's goods, he can lay his hands on. He is a wit-sharke, that has nothing of his own, but subsists by shifting, and filching from others ... He knows not what invention means, unless

it be to take whatsoever he finds in his way, which he makes no scruple to do, because very few will enquire, whether he came honestly by it, and no action of *trover* lyes against him. He accounts invention and thievery all one, because *Mercury* is equally Lord of both, and in that he owns him for his ascendant, but in nothing else. As soon as he has lighted upon a purchase, he presently commits it to writing, and to that purpose always carry pen and ink-horn about him, which are his horn-thimble and knife, with which he dispatches matters neatly, and conveys them away without being discover'd ... He steals mens wit, which the law setting no value on, it will not bear an inditement, and so he comes off clear, without putting himself to the hazard of God and his country. He adopts other mens writings for his own, especially orphans, that have no body to look after them, having no issue legitimate of his own. All his works are like instruments in law; what other men write he owns as his own act and deed. He is like a cuckow, that lives by sucking other birds eggs.[38]

The most pronounced feature of the character is that Butler, in line with early lexicographical definitions of the term, views plagiarism as a species of theft, the alienation of another person's property: it is 'shifting', 'filching' and 'thievery'. Given that plagiarism is an educated trespass (and those of his time whom Butler asperses as plagiarists are certainly polite), it is odd that Butler likens the crime exclusively to forms of low-born criminality. The plagiarist is 'not born nor bred' to wit and knowledge but forced into plagiarism as a desperate resort to cover his creative indigence. The specific crime to which plagiarism bears the closest resemblance is petty theft: its tools are metaphorically the horn-thimble and knife, those belonging to the street cutpurse.

To speak of plagiarism as theft is to imply, of course, that literature can fittingly be considered as a form of property and so, in principle, might invite protection under law. But Butler knows only too well that, in this respect, the metaphor is actually misleading, for a particular excruciation of being plagiarized is realizing that in fact no protection or redress exists. Because literary works possess no value intrinsic to themselves, the law omits to comprehend them as property. As Butler puts it, the plagiarist 'steals mens wit, which the law setting no value on, it will not bear an inditement, and so he comes off clear'. The impossibility of mobilizing the law against plagiarism is a regular refrain in Butler's writings on the subject. Much as he portrays the act of plagiarism in the most colourful and explicit terms (as street thievery and highway robbery), his identification of what is removed in the execution of the offence never ceases to be elusively abstract. The plagiarist steals nothing so much as 'mens wit'; he is a 'wit-sharke', a 'wit-caper', guilty of the 'Robbery' and 'Larceny of Wit'. All such phrases carry the knowing stamp of the oxymoron, for what is it for one person to pilfer the genius of another, and how could the law identify and protect a commodity so wispy and vanishing as wit?

Butler explores this conundrum through another conceit, in associating issues concerning plagiarism with the legal instrument of trover. Under law, trover constitutes the act of finding and assuming possession of property that is not originally one's own; as such, bringing an act of trover entails attempting to 'recover the value of personal property illegally converted by another to his own use' (*OED*). The expression cuts two ways in its application to plagiarism. In 'Upon Critics who Judge of Modern Plays', for example, Butler accuses Dryden and others of bringing a *false* action of trover against Corneille as a way of converting to their own use the prescriptions laid down in his critical treatises. The plagiarism, then, consists of mounting the pretence that they are merely seizing back from the French critic what were originally their own perceptions, the true plagiarist being Corneille.[39] Trover, then, is what a plagiarist might falsely assert as well as what an injured author could be driven to claim in order to recover the literary goods stolen by a plagiarist. Yet, for all the attractiveness of comparing plagiarism with other sorts of legal offence, Butler never forgets that part of the affront of plagiarism is that it evades legal sanction or even enquiry. The plagiarist, having pilfered the work of another author, knows that 'very few will enquire, whether he came honestly by it, and no action of *trover* lyes against him'.

V

Butler's general militancy towards plagiarism is coupled with admonitions directed at specific writers. His nasty invective against Denham, 'A Panegyric upon Sir John Denham's Recovery from his Madness', publicly endorses defamatory rumours concerning Denham's originality by referring to 'the bought *Cooper's Hill*, or borrow'd *Sophy*'.[40] His poems and prose writings are also dotted with snide references towards Dryden that seem at odds with the cordiality with which Dryden seems to have viewed him, notwithstanding the rumour that Butler had collaborated in Buckingham's *The Rehearsal*. Butler's 'Upon Critics who Judge of Modern Plays' contains a tart observation about 'our English Plagiarys', a company certainly including Dryden and possibly Thomas Rymer as well, who 'Nim/And steal their farfet Criticismes' from the French critic Corneille.[41] References to the injurious nature of Dryden's criticism appear in veiled forms in several places, sometimes connected with Dryden's own reputation as a leading exponent of the plagiarism allegation. In 'A Small Poet', the eponymous character is described as acting 'like an *Italian* Thief, that never robs, but he murthers, to prevent Discovery; so sure he is to cry down the Man from whom he purloins, that his petty Larceny of Wit may pass unsuspected'.[42] This double indignity of running down an author's works while pilfering from them at the same time was seen as something of a Drydenian trademark. Butler comments sardonically in one of his *Observations* that Dryden 'complayned of B Johnson for stealing 40 Sceanes out of Plautus. —Set a Thief to finde out a Thief'.[43]

However, one figure in particular seems to have aroused Butler's scorn: Edward Benlowes, a royalist poet, chiefly remembered for having brought financial ruin on his own sizeable estate and for having composed a rambling theological poem entitled *Theophilia: or Love's Sacrifice*. Benlowes's verse is distinctive for its florid and ingenious conceits but also for its extensive reliance on the words and images of earlier poets. As the poet's biographer, Harold Jenkins, has pointed out, the recycling of expressions and conceits was standard practice amongst seventeenth-century poets of a metaphysical bent, but Benlowes's technique stands out both because he tends to mine a relatively narrow seam of sources and because his appropriations tend not towards adaptation so much as outright copying.[44] What most catch his roving eye tend also to be the more obtrusive and showy kinds of conceit, such as when he takes over Joshua Sylvester's comparison of snow coating the tops of trees with a periwig set on a bald man's head:

And Perriwig with wooll the bald-pate Woods (Sylvester)

When periwig'd with *Snow*'s each bald-pate Wood (Benlowes).[45]

While such borrowings, taken individually, seem inoffensive, Benlowes sometimes employs the technique so feverishly that his poems turn into a patchwork or mosaic of verse clippings.

Benlowes may be the earliest poet whose essential technique of composition (rather than whose occasional indiscretions) was such as to attract the label of plagiarism. It is certainly stuck on him in the brutal caricature that Butler composed of 'A Small Poet', in which Benlowes's shortcomings are proposed as a model of a more generic kind of literary failure. 'There is no Feat of Activity, nor Gambol of Wit', Butler notes, but Benlowes 'has got the Mastery in it'. Elsewhere, in a remark not aimed directly at Benlowes but which seems an apt summation of his compositional method, Butler remarks that the small poet 'is but a Copier at best, and will never arrive to practise by the Life: For bar him the Imitation of something he has read, and he has no Image in his Thoughts'.[46]

Yet there is a risk that, in raising the cases of Benlowes and Dryden, I am giving a wrong impression, the impression that Butler took exception to the literary malefactions of certain contemporaries and that this leads to his heated crusade against the offence of plagiarism. This, however, is probably not the case. Certainly, in his literary characters, which supply a large number of vituperative comments aimed at derivative writers, Butler was working within an established set of satiric conventions. He seems to have been guided by earlier collections of characters, which would have instructed him that a staple of the satiric defamation of authors was the aspersion that they routinely copy from each other. Take, for example, Thomas Overbury's sketch of 'A Rymer':

> Hee is a juggler with words, yet practises the art of most uncleanely conveyance. He doth boggle very often; and because himselfe winks at it, thinks tis not perceived: the main thing that ever he did was the tune hee sang to.[47]

There is an obscurity here surrounding the neologism 'boggle', but we can still pick out two faults (both incidentally to be epitomized later by Benlowes) that are stated as being generic to poets: they engage in a quibbling type of wordplay and they steal their words from other writers through what Overbury calls 'the art of most uncleanely conveyance'. This expansive equation of authorship in general with plagiarism feeds through into Richard Flecknoe's *Enigmatical Characters* (1658), in which 'a wit' is described as being 'rather a *pump* of other jests, Conceits, and Stories, than a *Fountain* of his own'.[48]

Butler, then, is capitalizing on a cynical tradition of stigmatizing writers as plagiarists, and his trashing of poor Benlowes may be based less on personal resentment than the fact that Benlowes fortuitously seemed to epitomize a satirically derived set of traits. What else might give us pause in drawing conclusions about Butler's attitude to plagiarists are issues of category and differentiation. It is natural to think that any discussion of plagiarism must rest on a secure sense of the boundary between that concept and others contiguous to it. As such, you might assert, for example, that while plagiarism should be outlawed, there remain other types of imitative or allusive practice that might be sanctioned. Butler, however, smears his negativity towards plagiarists across all the relevant categories. His character of 'An Imitater', for example, an author who 'runs a whoring after another Man's Inventions', or of 'A Translater' is scarcely less intemperate than that of 'A Plagiary'.[49] Nor does he allow any distinction between the debased practices of modern literary culture and the higher standards of the classical authors, for a truism that he seems to have particularly relished is that the classical world was infected by all the same barbarities as the modern one: 'The Ancients ... never writ any Thing but what they stole and borrowed from others.'[50]

Butler's preoccupation with plagiarism, something almost entirely overlooked by modern scholars, presents a corrective not to Langbaine, but to certain arguments that have recently been constructed around Langbaine. Fundamental to such arguments is a sense that the plagiarism allegation rises in cachet and influence after the Restoration, at a time when the necessity that authors protect their intellectual property becomes more pressing as the returns on that property increase in a growing commercial market. Protestations of plagiarism become a way in which authors can ward off invasions of their property. However, what Butler tells us is that accusations of plagiarism might be seen as emanations from an older satiric tradition, in which the malefaction was assumed to be more or less endemic to the very practice of writing, regardless of whether authors were deemed to be participating in a developed literary market.

When, in his 'Satyr upon Plagiaries', Butler describes the cultural malaise that will inevitably set in should plagiarism be tolerated and allowed to become rife, this is not that authors will be cheated from the legitimate proceeds of their labour, but rather that they will be stripped of their 'Fame and Credit'. The specific malignity of plagiarism is widely viewed at this time in terms of its desecration of authorial fame. Langbaine's whole ill-tempered crusade on the issue is dedicated to preserving the fames of deserving authors against the twin threats posed by plagiarists and malevolent critics. The same rhetorical collocation of 'plagiarism' and 'fame' appears in other contemporary works confronting the issue, such as Margaret Cavendish's 'Of Poets and their Theft'. Here Cavendish declares that only the authentically original author 'ought to have the *Crowne* of *Praise*, and *Fame*,/In the *long Role* of *Time* to write his *Name*', while 'those that steale it out [are] to blame'.[51]

I am slightly embarrassed that the case made in the previous pages is couched in such negative terms. What this chapter challenges is the view that plagiarism can be seen as a sort of outrider for an emerging concept of intellectual copyright and that, accordingly, a book about plagiarism during this period should be in essence one about the development of the modern notion of literary property. The role that the plagiarism allegation plays in the crystallizing of a sense of literary property seems to me to have been considerably overstated, and the mission of my book is to try to situate plagiarism within a range of contemporary discourses (such as of 'fame' or 'sufficiency') rather than to reduce it to a mere symptom of the onward rush of modernity. Butler seems to me to have a crucial admonitory role in relation to these dilemmas: his writings, much more than those of Langbaine, probe the extent to which literary texts might plausibly be viewed as properties, and also how plagiarism could be seen as an infringement of such property. However, much as he explores such avenues of speculation, he always draws back from them, recalled by a pragmatic sense that 'wit' is something too melting and fugitive ever to accede to the protected status of property.

There is also the question of whose side one sees oneself as being on. For Paulina Kewes, allegations of plagiarism are what keep writers honest; they intimidate and chastise authors into recognizing that principle of literary property on which our own literary culture is dependent. Those who lodge such accusations, like Langbaine, are approved as the watchdogs of the literary republic. Within this framework of assumptions, the erratic and grudge-bearing Langbaine is hailed as an ethical guardian, a champion of the modern concept of authorship, the man who ushers in the new age. My own book, much more so than Kewes's, will be inclined to point up the sourness and mischief that accompany many plagiarism accusations (including Langbaine's), and views the allegation as a literary speech act, loyal only to itself and its own motives, without necessarily being reactive to actual occurrences of plagiarism. In Chapter 5, I will discuss the plagiarism controversy that engulfed Alexander Pope's career: those who so routinely and venomously discharged such allegations against him do not necessarily deserve by their acts to be vindicated as the heralds of the future.

3
Plagiarism and the Burden of Tradition in Dryden and Others

I

Dryden's dedicatory epistle 'To my Dear Friend Mr. Congreve' appeared in 1694, prefixed to the first quarto edition of *The Double-Dealer*. It was composed six years before Dryden's death, an event itself anticipated in the poem. Congreve is tasked with protecting the older poet's posthumous reputation, charged to 'Let not th'insulting foe my fame pursue' (line 74).[1] However, the responsibility conferred on him goes further than this, for the poem is essentially one of filial anointment: 'For only you are lineal to the throne' (line 44). Dryden nominates Congreve as his poetic heir, the one true successor qualified for ascent to the 'throne of wit' after his own death. The two burdens imposed on Congreve, of protecting Dryden's fame and succeeding him in the literary pantheon, were noted by contemporaries. In the same year, Addison predicts that 'Congreve shall still preserve thy fame alive/And Dryden's muse shall in his friend survive'.[2]

Yet Dryden's 'To Mr. Congreve', although a poem about literary futurity, is equally about the poetic past, for to say that Congreve is appointed Dryden's creative legatee requires that something be said about the literary estate that he stands to inherit. This Dryden attends to in the opening lines of the poem:

> Well then, the promised hour is come at last;
> The present age of wit obscures the past.
> Strong were our sires; and as they fought they writ,
> Conquering with force of arms and dint of wit;
> Theirs was the giant race before the flood,
> And thus, when Charles returned, our empire stood.

Like Janus he the stubborn soil manured,
With rules of husbandry the rankness cured;
Tamed us to manners, when the stage was rude,
And boist'rous English wit, with art indued.
Our age was cultivated thus at length,
But what we gained in skill we lost in strength. (1–12)

The passage grapples to reconcile two quite opposite attitudes. True enough, there is a note of triumph in the announcement of Congreve's ascent ('the promised hour is come at last'), but this competes against an anxious sense of modern inadequacy. Dryden, it has been claimed, is one of the earliest English poets to succumb to a sense of literary belatedness, to feel puny and overawed in relation to the achievements of an earlier generation of writers.[3] The 'giant race before the flood' consists in his mind of the pre-Interregnum playwrights, especially the auspicious triumvirate of Shakespeare, Jonson and Fletcher. These he sees as the forbidding 'sires' of the authors of his own day.

Dryden's sense of the *pastness* of earlier authors is particularly pronounced. The metaphor of the 'flood' refers to the closure of the public theatres between 1642 and 1660, which suspended most remunerative literary activity. But the phrase implies an abyss lying between Restoration writers and their predecessors, a suggestion that hardly squares with the fact that Dryden had already turned seven by the time that Jonson, for example, died. The same rather exaggerated sense of temporal removal can also be seen in the title of Thomas Rymer's study of the pre-Interregnum drama *The Tragedies of the Last Age* (1677). In Dryden's case, the exaggeration underscores his conviction that literary distinction will henceforth need to be understood in terms of the relation of modern authors to the 'giant race' inhabiting the pre-Interregnum world. Modern authors, such as Congreve, wanting to establish their canonical credentials will need to undergo a rite of succession.

This understanding of canonization in terms of creative succession accords with the fact that the Restoration is probably the first era in which literary culture had cause to re-awaken to its past, a past from which the shutting down of the theatres had effected an abrupt divorce. They had been closed by force of a resolution passed by the Long Parliament on 2 September 1642: stage plays were henceforth to be banned as 'Spectacles of pleasure, too commonly expressing lascivious Mirth and Levitie' and as being inconsistent with a time of 'publike Calamaties'.[4] Of course, theatrical performances continued to be given in the privacy of the great houses, but the official closure of the theatres still effectively thrust English drama into a state of abeyance. When the Stuart monarchy was restored in the person of Charles II in early 1660, and the theatres could once again fling open their doors, the literary landscape had changed utterly. It was now 44 years since Shakespeare's death and 23 years since that of Jonson. No evidence exists of any Shakespeare play having been staged illicitly during the two decades of closure and, as Gary Taylor has pointed out, not a single one of 26 'Principall Actors' listed as performing his plays in the first folio of 1623 was alive at the time of the Restoration.[5] The revival of the stage accordingly seemed like a fresh start, the inauguration of a new theatrical world, and one aspect of this new world would be the invention of an historical repertory.[6]

The starting up of theatrical activities was immediate with the King's return, with Charles soon moving to legalize formally the emergent theatrical culture by granting duopolistic rights for stage productions to William Davenant and Thomas Killigrew. The immediate dilemma facing the new theatre managers was naturally the dearth of new plays readily available to them. Virtually all pre-Interregnum playwrights, with a few exceptions including Killigrew and Davenant themselves, had perished in the interim, and it would take a while for new play-wrights to emerge to populate the market. Indeed, Robert Hume has noted that not a single author made a living from writing plays between 1660 and 1665, and only Dryden was able to do so before 1670.[7] The only way that the theatre could be supplied in the early years after the Restoration was accordingly through the revival of old plays. In 1660–1, for example, the King's Company staged at least 39 old plays, with the only new plays produced by either the King's or the Duke's Company being the two parts of Davenant's own work, *The Siege of Rhodes*. In the following season, both companies com-bined mounted no more than two conclusively new plays.[8] Gunnar Sorelius has calculated that at least 177 old plays were revived during the Restoration period, either in original or altered form, with some 45 pre-Restoration dramatists being represented, including Webster, Middleton, Shirley, Heywood, Massinger and Brome.[9] Only when the theatres reopened for the 1666–7 season, following closure for the plague in 1665, did both companies embrace the production of new plays as their principal business strategy.

II

The invention of the historical repertory and its domination of the stage in the early years of the Restoration brought home to contemporary writers the full weight of the antecedent tradition. It also precipitated an understanding amongst authors that their very creative identity was bound up with attitudes of rivalry, veneration or condescension towards the pre-Interregnum tradition. Writers of the new generation were in effect the creative heirs and legatees of the generation that had preceded them. Dryden, of all major authors, is the one who is distinctive for grasping this sense of the canon as a nexus of specifically paternal or filial relations. The figure crops up routinely in his critical prose as the way that he expresses the fixity and influence of the great male poets:

> Shakespeare was the Homer, or father of our dramatic poets

> I had often read with pleasure ... those two fathers of our English poetry [Waller and Denham]

> Milton was the poetical son of Spenser, and Mr Waller of Fairfax; for we have our lineal descents and clans as well as other families.[10]

Dryden seems not only to have nursed a sense of his own affiliation to the pre-Restoration literary tradition, but also to have been attracted to the prospect of fathering poetic sons of his own. Both Pope and Charles Churchill were to pride themselves in the eighteenth century on having taken up Dryden's mantle, but Congreve appears to have been the younger poet whom Dryden most coveted as his natural heir. In his dedicatory poem to Congreve, he laments that the laureateship, from which he had been ignominiously removed in 1688, could not have devolved patrilineally to Congreve, for then 'The father had descended for the son;/For only you are lineal to the throne' (lines 43–4).

Dryden's habit of figuring literary influence as a form of paternity, and of viewing the literary tradition as a succession of paternal-filial relations, soon became recognized as one of his critical trademarks. It appears in Swift's *Battle of the Books* (1704), in a passage where Dryden is satirized for seeking to emulate the Roman poet Virgil:

> Dryden in a long Harangue soothed up the good *Antient*, called him *Father*, and by a large deduction of Genealogies, made it plainly appear, that they were nearly related.[11]

Here the claim of a filial relationship registers Dryden's vanity and creative presumption, but the figure was not always invoked to his detriment. When he died, for example, the event was marked by an ode by Alexander Oldys, depicting the poet entering a heavenly pantheon of authors, greeted in particular by Chaucer as '*Thou my Son*, Adopted into *me*'.[12]

This chapter will explore the way in which two sorts of anxiety collocate with each other in Dryden's critical writing: the first being Dryden's 'anxiety of influence', his sense that the creative prospects for poets of his own generation had been curtailed as a result of the achievements of the pre-Restoration writers who, while they may be acknowledged 'our fathers in wit', have 'ruined their estates themselves before they came to their children's hands'; and the second being his sensitivity that his own particular dealings with those earlier writers, especially in the form of theatrical adaptations, could lay himself open to the charge of unoriginality or plagiarism.[13] These two concerns dovetail closely in a number of Dryden's essays and controversies. In some part, the combination of these two issues arises from the particular ways in which Dryden understood sexual generation, especially the possibility that the 'greater gust' of copulation could lead to the biological imprinting of the son in the father's image: so it is, in Dryden's famous poem, with Absalom, whose father David sees his 'youthfull image in his son renewed'.[14] So too with Flecknoe's recognition of the unique physical likeness he bears towards his son Shadwell, who 'alone my perfect image bears'.[15] The same motif, moreover, is taken up in a poem of the following century, Pope's *Dunciad*, which is itself imprinted by Dryden's *Mac Flecknoe*. When the Goddess Dulness envisions an unfolding sequence of city bards, imagined as a succession of father-son relationships, the parent and offspring are conjoined by their shared physical identity: 'Each sire imprest and glaring in his son.'[16] The line usefully summarizes the danger that Dryden was conscious of skirting in his dealings with the older authors, especially Shakespeare. To assume the Shakespearean mantle, to receive creative support through Shakespeare's adoptive parentage might have been amongst the most cherished of Dryden's professional aspirations. But the danger was always that of the father's being 'imprest and glaring in his son': in other words, that the rite of sonship might shrink to mere filial replication of the father in a manner that, in literary terms, would be indistinguishable from plagiarism.

III

The inclination to claim filiation to a strong authorial father, while resisting succumbing to outright dependency, becomes especially acute for Dryden in his adaptation of Shakespeare's plays. Though Shakespeare was in fact less prominent in the historical repertory than either Jonson or the Beaumont-Fletcher partnership, his plays stood out as particularly eligible for, and also as especially requiring, adaptation. His are the most adapted works during the Restoration era. These reworkings of Shakespeare's plays have been largely scorned by critics writing nearer to our own time as mutilations of Shakespeare's genius, necessitated in the Restoration era by a set of dogmatically irrational principles of taste. George Odell, in his study of *Shakespeare from Betterton to Irving* (1920–1), for example, denounces the effect of perusing the altered Shakespearean texts as like the horror of staring at a 'rouged corpse'.[17]

There is no doubt that the adaptation of Shakespeare's plays seemed altogether more reasonable to Restoration dramatists and theatre audiences than it does now. The original patents granted to Killigrew and Davenant had indeed expressly permitted the altering of plays, albeit with a view to expunging 'Prophaneness and Scurrility' rather than to regularizing and improving them. What added to the general lack of compunction when it came to refashioning the works was a sense that Shakespeare's plays could be seen as in some way dramatically inchoate and, when set against the refined standards of the day, as essentially unmediated expressions of nature.[18] They provided merely the raw materials from which more satisfyingly decorous modern plays could be constructed. This attitude fitted with a general cultural narrative about how post-Restoration literary culture had advanced beyond the rudeness and 'rankness' of the pre-Interregnum era. It was under the influence of Charles II that the English theatre had cleansed and refined itself, as Dryden records in 'To Mr. Congreve' and 'Tamed us to manners, when the Stage was rude'. Even Shakespearean adapters themselves could be less than flattering about the original material with which they had to work: in the Preface to his adaptation of *Troilus and Cressida* (1679), for instance, Dryden refers witheringly to Shakespeare's rudimentary play as 'that heap of rubbish under which many excellent thoughts lay wholly buried'.[19]

Although one substantive ground for the alteration of Shakespeare's original texts was to make them speak to the political issues of the post-Restoration era, other categories of 'improvement' were concerned with editing out Shakespeare's linguistic solecisms, purging his plays of their more offensive breeches of decorum, reordering and streamlining his plots, and clarifying the moral fault-lines.[20] In making such alterations, dramatists were colluding in what were understood to be the more highly evolved critical tastes of Restoration theatre audiences. Yet the appropriating of plays in this way still continued to bear an unnerving adjacency to the literary crime of plagiarism. For one thing, no clear demarcation existed between adaptation, as a nominally legitimate dramatic practice, and other more causally opportunistic exploitations of the works of earlier authors. Such practices occupied a common spectrum and could be subject to positive or negative interpretations. Moreover, adapters were generally unabashed in placing their own names on the title-pages of printed editions of adapted plays, a practice seen as being justified on the strength of the labour required to render an old work conformable to the more exacting standards of the current age.[21]

However, anxieties surrounding the ethics of adaptation were never altogether easy to quell. Dryden in particular confronts them in his edgy but diplomatic Preface to *The Enchanted Island* written in late 1669, two years after the first appearance of the play and 20 months after the death of his collaborator in the work, Sir William Davenant. The Preface, written in significant part in homage to Davenant, puts itself to the teasing out of all the lines of filiation and influence that have converged in the making of the adapted play. There is, naturally, Dryden's indebtedness to Davenant as an elder statesman of the theatre and as a literary 'sire' of his own. It was Davenant who, over and above correcting Dryden's contribution to *The Enchanted Island*, first tutored the younger poet in his admiration for Shakespeare's works. However, Davenant is proposed less as an authentic father figure than as a sort of intercessor between Dryden and his true poetic sire, Shakespeare. Dryden could be seen as both uncovering and re-clothing his father's nakedness in revamping Shakespeare's plays for a Restoration audience. Finally, there remains the greatest enigma of filiation: Davenant's own apparent claim to have imbibed the spirit of Shakespeare's art but furthermore to have been his illegitimate, biological son.[22]

Just as the Preface teases apart the different threads of creative influence, so it also grapples with the ethics of appropriation. Dryden takes especial pains to represent the fact that Shakespeare's play has been subject to earlier appropriations, including by Fletcher, who 'thought fit to make use of the same design, not much varied, a second time'.[23] The status of these subsequent versions of the play, however, remains ambiguous, in ways that follow closely from Dryden's suggestive remark that the work 'was originally Shakespeare's'. Adaptation, in other words, involves both the fashioning of a new play based on an old model and also a transfer of property entitlement from the originating author to the adapter. Strangely, in the context of a collaborative adaptation, the literary credential of his friend that Dryden most wants to emphasize is his originality: 'He borrowed not of any other.' Stressing Davenant's originality at this moment feels like a rhetoric of compensation, given that Davenant was chiefly renowned for adaptation, and that Dryden himself had much to gain from a view that the reforming of old plays was as creative an undertaking as the composition of entirely new ones. Dryden's anxiety that adaptation itself could be viewed as a kind of theft seeps outwards into a similar nervousness concerning the need to acknowledge the contribution of his dead collaborator. He notes, to his own credit, that 'It had perhaps been easy enough for me to have arrogated more to my self than was my due in the writing of this play, and to have passed by his name with silence in the publication of it'. This he has disdained to do, so as openly to acknowledge his obligation to two literary sires, in 'joining my imperfections with the merit and name of Shakespeare and Sir William Davenant'.[24]

IV

Dryden's agitation that his appropriations from both Shakespeare and Davenant might be seen as untoward was not entirely baseless. Even at this early stage of his career, his dependency on source-texts was already attracting adverse comment. The very first sentence of the Preface to *Enchanted Love*, with its suggestion that the idea of writing prefaces to plays must have been dreamt up by 'some ape of the French eloquence', makes a twistingly oblique acknowledgement of the debts owed in his *Of Dramatic Poesy* to the French critic Corneille.[25] Dryden stands as the first major English poet to have been routinely goaded with the allegation of plagiarism, an accusation that pursues not just his plays but his poems and critical writings as well.[26]

That Dryden had been open about the derivativeness of his essay *Of Dramatic Poesy*, as a 'discourse in dialogue, for the most part borrowed from the observations of others', failed to indemnify him against unfavourable reflections on his professional conduct.[27] Samuel Butler, a skulking denigrator of Dryden in several compositions only published posthumously, names him as one of 'our English Plagiarys', who 'Nim/And steal their farfet Criticismes' from Corneille.[28] The same condemnation is voiced more vehemently by Martin Clifford, who tasks himself with 'letting the World know how great a Plagiary you are', notwithstanding Dryden's ostensible 'pretences to Wit and Judicious Censure'; and also by the anonymous author of *The Hind and the Panther Transvers'd*, for whom Dryden, in his acute dependence on

Corneille and Rapin, merely reflects 'from afar/The rays he borrowed from a better star'.[29]

The ridicule of Dryden's method of dramatic composition, seen as a mechanical process of stripping and recycling the works of others, probably begins with the Duke of Buckingham's *The Rehearsal*, first performed in 1671, with both Butler and Clifford as possible authorial accomplices. Dryden is represented as the self-intoxicated Bayes who, when asked to articulate his 'Rule for Invention', retorts smugly: 'Why, Sir, when I have any thing to invent, I never trouble me head about it.' What he troubles to do instead is to lift some passages from eminent classical sources, interlard them with a few paltry lines of his own, and as if by magic 'the business is done'.[30] The figure of Bayes compacts two senses of Dryden: as both creatively indigent and as reducing the higher calling of literature to a soulless and grubby professionalism. These two understandings of the particular abomination his case represents also appear in Rochester's 'An Allusion to Horace', where Dryden's plays, 'Embroider'd up and downe,/With Witt, and Learning', are reported as having all the same 'justly pleas'd the Towne'.[31]

The great arraignment of Dryden's credentials as an original playwright would only come in 1691 with Gerard Langbaine's *Account of the English Dramatick Poets*, a work discussed at length in the previous chapter and so passed over here. Dryden, for his own part, could be territorial over his writings: he took exception late in life to Richard Blackmore for supposedly stealing the idea for his epic poem *Prince Arthur* (1695) from a throwaway remark in his own *Original and Progress of Satire* (1693).[32] However, while Langbaine's revelations no doubt caused embarrassment and may even have caused Dryden to quit writing plays altogether after 1693, they probably did not induce any great spasms of penitence. He may well have been of a mind with Sir Samuel Garth, who became a close friend and delivered the poet's funeral oration, in believing that such allegations of plagiarism are the inevitable tribute that minor talents feel compelled to pay to greater ones:

> With all these wondrous Talents, He [Dryden] was Libell'd in his Life-time by the very Men, who had no other Excellencies, but as they were his Imitators. Where he was allow'd to have Sentiments superior to all others, they charged him with Theft: But how did he Steal? no otherwise, than like those, that steal Beggars Children, only to cloath them the better.[33]

V

I have so far set to one side the most celebrated and revealing of all Dryden's plagiarism controversies: that with Thomas Shadwell. Although one tends nowadays to see Shadwell as merely a straw in the wind of Dryden's satire, throughout much of the 1670s Dryden treated him as a respectable associate and professional disputant.[34] He forced Dryden to ponder a number of issues that were to retain a high degree of prominence in his critical prose. Two such issues, which get batted back and forward between Shadwell and Dryden across several essays and responses, are the entitlement of later writers to borrow from earlier writers, and the true estimate of Ben Jonson's literary achievement. What I contend in this chapter is that these issues are inescapably twinned, since they both concern the posture which contemporary writers should adopt towards their literary ancestors. Dryden's dilemma as a dramatist was to maintain an allegiance to past authors that resisted being seen as an illicit form of appropriation; as a critic of earlier literature, he needed to practise objectivity and candour without these being taken for signs of an inherent disrespect towards the authors with whom he was dealing.

The controversy between the two dramatists is ignited by Shadwell's Preface to *The Sullen Lovers, or the Impertinents* (1668), in which he wigs Dryden for having the audacity to state that Jonson 'wrote his best *Playes* without Wit', this being a frugal and tendentious paraphrase of Dryden's actual remark that 'One cannot say he [Jonson] wanted wit, but rather that he was frugal of it'.[35] Yet Shadwell's most pressing concern is not Jonson's reputation but his own, and the damage to it that might result from exposure of the source (Molière's *Les Fascheux*) on which his own play was partially based. He confesses in guarded fashion that 'after it came to my hands, I found so little for my use ... that I have made use of but two short Scenes', and what little he has purloined is made the more excusable, so he concludes, because 'I freely confess my Theft, and am asham'd on it'. It is in respect of such public contrition that his case differs notably from other authors, amongst whom Dryden is implicitly fingered, who 'never yet wrote Play without stealing most of it; And ... at length, by continual Thieving, reckon their stolne goods their own'.[36]

Dryden could scarcely avoid retaliating against such provocative rhetoric, but his better judgement was to do so in a tone less shrill than wounded, and in the context of a measured exposition on the subject of dramatic borrowing. His first duty, however, was to set the record straight relating to Jonson by protesting against having 'been accused as an enemy of his writings; but without any other reason than that I do not admire him blindly'.[37] Dryden believed that the criteria underpinning his appraisal of Jonson were of sufficient consequence to be explored at length, and when he eventually reverts to the allegation of plagiarism ('I am taxed with stealing all my plays') he does so as to a subject with which he is outwardly 'much less concerned'. Interestingly, the grounds of his nonchalance are that he believes that when such accusations stick, they bedaub his reputation as a poet but not his conduct as a man. He admits to having felt himself at liberty wherever he 'liked any story or romance, novel, or foreign play' to have lifted the 'foundation' of it as the basis of a play of his own. Moreover, far from this being a practice deserving of reproach, Dryden argues that he has merely followed in a long tradition of authors, including the likes of Virgil, Terence, Tasso, Shakespeare and Jonson, cannibalizing the works of their predecessors. Indeed, many of these had failed to observe Dryden's own self-denying ordinance of lifting only the basic storyline whilst altering or embellishing the rest.[38]

Dryden's favourite metaphors for explaining the way that a skilful dramatist works with his materials relate to a lapidary setting jewels or to other meticulous craftsmen:

> the employment of a poet is like that of a curious gunsmith or watchmaker: the iron or silver is not his own; but they are the least part of that which gives the value: the price lies wholly in the workmanship.[39]

Dryden's 'workmanship' consists of disposing the actions into scenes, diversifying the characters, adorning the language with descriptions and metaphors, and ensuring that the play as a whole is to the taste of a Restoration audience.

Though Dryden's Preface comprises a measured rebuttal of Shadwell's main points, it failed to exhaust his opponent's appetite for the controversy. Shadwell retorted in his Preface to *The Humorists* (1671), reinstating his wilfully partial understanding of Dryden's view of Jonson ('I cannot be of their opinion who think he wanted wit') while also raking up the subject of the propriety of borrowing.[40] Dryden further responds in his 'Epilogue to the Second Part of Granada' and in its 'Defence', both of which address the relative merits of pre- and post-Restoration writers. At issue once again is the attitude that modern authors should strike when approaching the hallowed members of the 'giant race before the flood'.

For Dryden, the necessity is that modern authors should venerate their creative ancestors without capitulating to them, without on the one hand blinding themselves altogether to their faults and without on the other hand being so cowed by their example as to confine themselves 'to a servile imitation of all they write'.[41]

Dryden's controversy with Shadwell rumbles on through several other dramatic prologues and epilogues until Dryden's definitive satiric salvo with *Mac Flecknoe*, composed in July–August 1676 and circulated soon after in MS copies. The greatness of the poem lies not just in the unflagging dexterity with which it belittles Shadwell's career, but also in the way it exploits different sorts of literary unease experienced at the time.[42] *Mac Flecknoe* is perhaps the first great poem in English to exploit the idea that literary tradition can be imagined as an unfolding process of succession by poetic sons from their poetic fathers. The crushing of poor Shadwell rests in the way its rhetoric constantly orphans him from the father he most craves, Jonson, in order to show him sired ignominiously by Flecknoe. 'Thou art my blood, where Jonson has no part' (line 175), proclaims Flecknoe in process of anointing Shadwell as his 'filial dullness'. Shadwell's election rests on the way he biologically plagiarizes his father ('Shadwell alone my perfect image bears' (line 15)) and the poem's metaphoric preoccupation with inheritance generates the sombre reflection that for every noble act of succession (Congreve from Dryden, for example), there might also be an ignoble one, as the mantle of poetic fecklessness is passed down from one failed hack to another.

One reason, so Dryden suggests, why Shadwell ought not to aspire to Jonson's august paternity is that Jonson himself never stooped to plagiarism: 'When did his Muse from Fletcher scenes purloin,/As thou whole Eth'rege dost transfuse to thine?' (lines 183–4). Nor did he pass off plays as purely his own when they had been interlarded with material scavenged from friends, as Dryden accuses Shadwell as having 'hungrily' done when composing *Epsom-Wells*. The lines are obviously a payback for the insinuations Shadwell had made about Dryden's plagiarism, as well as an exploitation of Shadwell's rhetorical twisting over his own putative plagiarism. These satiric exhortations to give up plagiarism are, however, coupled with a series of intimations that Shadwell's creative nullity destines him forever to be restricted to forms of hapless replication. Just as he replicates the image of Flecknoe, so his stage fools unwittingly replicate him:

> Let 'em be all by thy own model made
> Of dullness, and desire no foreign aid,

> That they to future ages may be known
> Not copies drawn, but issue of thy own. (lines 157–60)

The incitement to 'desire no foreign aid' hints at a reproof about plagiarism, but in this vicinity merely discourages Shadwell from calling on the auxiliaries of sense or imagination. Indeed, the quickest way for Shadwell to fashion a stage fool is to look within his own breast and plagiarize himself.

Shadwell's cruel quandary is to be condemned to uncreative productivity and to plagiaristic iterations of his father in his own self, and himself in his own characters. In metaphoric terms, his plagiarizing tendencies match the weak blood-line from which he has issued, for plagiarism, in Dryden's eyes, is bound up with general depletions of the creative gene pool or with the way that a dominating father can have the effect of enfeebling his progeny. While plagiarism, as well as other related forms of shadowy or ignoble replication, lies at the heart of Dryden's *Mac Flecknoe*, what circumscribes the poem is the larger malaise, to which Dryden in particular was so sensitive, of writing after the flood. How should writers conduct themselves in a context in which creativity itself had become understood as a form of succession? To what extent were writers of the current age capable of bearing up under the burden of precedence established by the giant race that had gone before? And to what extent should they feel at liberty, either through adaptation, appropriation or outright plagiarism, to patch the weakness of their own times with the strength of their forefathers?

4
Plagiarism and Sufficiency in the English 'Battle of the Books'

I

It was his former secretary and literary executor, Jonathan Swift, who said of Sir William Temple's prose style that it 'has advanced our English Tongue, to as great a Perfection as it can well bear'.[1] The compliment is notably handsome but is also in keeping with the general admiration in which Temple's mellifluous and stately writing style was held. Henry Felton, for example, in a work of educational instruction addressed to the young Marquis of Granby, held up Temple as 'the most perfect Pattern of good *Writing* and good *Breeding* this Nation hath produced'.[2] Some observers of the prose, however, noted something other than just its refined cadences: this was Temple's penchant for coining new words. 'Rapport' used to mean 'proportion', 'defense of commerse' for 'prohibition of trade' and 'surintendance' for 'superintendence' were all spotted, as well as numerous gallicisms. William Wotton, an opponent of Temple's in the dispute between the ancients and moderns, mentions these neologisms rather disparagingly as unlikely to 'be commonly received among us in hast', but even he could not deny that one in particular of Temple's verbal inventions had rapidly become influential.[3]

In 'An Essay upon the Ancient and Modern Learning' (1690), Temple describes his indignation at encountering two recent works, Thomas Burnet's *Sacred Theory of the Earth* and Pierre Fontenelle's *Digression sur les anciens et les modernes*, which exalted modern culture above that of the classical world. The mentality that conduced to this unpalatable judgement Temple labels as 'sufficiency', 'the worst composition out of the pride and ignorance of mankind'. In a later passage, he finds 'the sufficient among scholars' to be complicit in the recent 'maim given to learning'.[4] 'Sufficiency' had previously meant an adequate provision of something or the possession of the necessary resources for a particular task, but Temple was intent on stretching its acceptation in a startlingly negative direction. How soon the implications of the coinage were seized on by scholars is hard to say, but the new usage was certainly noted during the 1690s. In an essay published in 1698 under the name of Charles Boyle, for example, Temple is credited as one of those 'Writers of the First Rate' who have earned a special dispensation to create new words: 'Sir *William Temple* may say, *Sufficiency*, and the World will speak after him.'[5]

What exactly did Temple mean by 'sufficiency'? The term seems to engross several aspects of what he believed to be the modern intellectual malaise. It points to a smug self-reliance, the conviction that our own creative resources can see us through any task in hand. Consistent with it is a sullen indifference to the creative example held out to us by earlier writers, especially those of the classical period: to be sufficient is accordingly to be ungrateful to the past. Moreover, the term connotes self-absorption, an entrapment within one's mind that could easily be seen as a form of mania. Crucially, the 'sufficient among scholars' fail to realize that glad cooperation is the essence of all creativity.

The most famous illustration of the principle of sufficiency occurs in Swift's fable of the spider and the bee, inserted in his *Battle of the Books* (1704).[6] A spider has built its web in a high corner of St James' Library, from where it watches out for prey. On a particular day, a bee, entering the building through a broken pane, gets stuck in the web, from which it only extricates itself by rending a big hole in the spider's elaborate fortification. Aroused by the commotion, the spider ventures out to see the full extent of the damage and angrily remonstrates with the bee. When the spider accuses his unwelcome visitor of being disrespectful '*to a Person, whom all the World allows to be so much your Betters*' (p. 230), a debate ensues between the two as to whose lifestyle is intrinsically the superior.

The spider, swollen with self-importance, immediately launches into disparagement of the bee ('*Your Livelihood is an universal Plunder upon Nature ...*' (p. 231)) and portrays his own lifestyle as a model of sturdy self-sufficiency: he has not only built his house but has actually spun it out of his own body. Looking at the nearby ruins of the spider's web, however, the bee finds it easy to retaliate by questioning the practical benefits of the spider's self-reliance. His own lifestyle he justifies as a natural fulfilment of providence, through whose direction he visits '*all the Flowers and Blossoms of the Field*', enriching himself '*without the least Injury to their Beauty, their Smell, or their Taste*' (p. 231). Having upheld his side of the argument, the bee flies off to a bed of roses, and it is left to the character of Aesop to draw out the underlying application of the fable in terms of the relation between the moderns and ancients. The spider's lifestyle is identified as epitomizing the mode of creativity practised by the moderns, in which the materials of composition are spun out of their own entrails, leading to works that are as solid and permanent as cobwebs. Meanwhile, the bee, in the manner of the lovers of the ancients, ranges *'thro' every Corner of Nature'*, fills his hive with honey and wax, and furnishes to mankind both 'Sweetness *and* Light' (pp. 234–5).

Swift's main satiric target was, of course, the classical scholar Richard Bentley, whose role in the ancients and moderns controversy I will discuss later.[7] Although the *Battle* was probably drafted in 1697, the finishing touches seem to have been applied only the following year, a chronology which would have allowed Swift to have been cognizant not only of Bentley's first essay on the *Epistles of Phalaris* (1697) but also of the collaborative attack on that work, *Dr Bentley's Dissertations ... Examin'd* (1698), published under the name of Charles Boyle. Had Swift had any need of prompting, he would have discovered there an incipient characterization of Bentley as an epitome of Temple's notion of sufficiency: 'Dr. *Bentley* is Positive, and Pert; has no regard for what other men have thought or said.'[8]

As the 'battle of the books' controversy rages on, Bentley's standing as a paragon of modern sufficiency is taken for granted by those rallying around the flag of the ancients. William King's *Dialogues of the Dead* (1699) sees Bentley, cast here as the great 'Bentivoglio', turning out works 'full of himself': he 'Amplifies, Expatiates and Comments upon himself'.[9] The exact same condemnation is made in Francis Atterbury's *A Short Review of the Controversy between Mr. Boyle and Dr. Bentley* (1701), where Bentley's huge treatise on Phalaris's *Epistles* is dismissed as containing 'so much of himself, and so little of his Subject in it'.[10] Bentley's monumental self-regard (as it was viewed) and surly indifference to the classical authors he was supposed to be illuminating were seen as graphic illustrations of the modern psyche. Though Temple had coined the idea, it was left to Bentley to actually animate the concept of intellectual sufficiency.

II

The habits of bees, more so than those of spiders, have long been a source of analogy with the creative processes of poets. Aesop, for example, in Swift's *Battle of the Books* characterizes the ancients in general as modest and unpretentious, and, like bees, beholden for their endowments to 'infinite Labor, and search, and ranging thro' every Corner of Nature' (p. 234). The same sentiments had been expressed earlier in Sir William Temple's essay 'Of Poetry' (1690) in which he had described the natural libertinism of poetic creativity in terms of the activity of bees, whose production of honey depends on their free roaming through the blooms:

> They must range through fields, as well as gardens, choose such flowers as they please, and by proprieties and scents they only know and distinguish: they must work up their cells with admirable art, extract their honey with infinite labour, and sever it from the wax, with such distinction and choice as belongs to none but themselves to perform or to judge.[11]

Temple, like Swift, stresses the bees' unceasing industry, the eclectic nature of their visitings and collectings, and the discernment by which they alight on certain flowers and disregard others.

An important text for the classical understanding of the habits of bees, and for the application of their behaviour to styles of poetic imitation, is Seneca's *Epistulae morales* 84.[12] What Seneca makes us aware of is that in his time the actual process through which bees produced honey remained deeply inscrutable, such that natural investigators were unable to resolve whether the bee gathered honey directly from the flowers or converted into honey some other substance on which they fed. This dubiety passes through into Renaissance and eighteenth-century invocations of bees, as is evident for example in Isaac Watts's celebration of the honey bee in his *Divine Songs* of 1715. In the first stanza, Watts describes the female bee busily intent to 'gather honey ... From every opening flow'r!', but in the second he describes her labouring to store the wax 'With the sweet food she makes'.[13] For his part, Swift appears to side with the view that the bee's role is to gather honey and transport it to the hive but not to produce it: it '*brings home Honey and Wax*' (p. 232). Later, the bee describes the function of the species as '*to fill our Hives with Honey and Wax*' (p. 234), where it is clear that the filling is done by judicious acquisition. Swift's insistence that the bees do not manufacture the honey also allows for the contrast which he is at pains to make between them and the spider spinning his web directly from his own juices, these having been enriched by his digestion of dead flies, the previous victims of his web: '*one Insect furnishes you with a share of Poison to destroy another*' (p. 232).

This general puzzlement over bees either gathering or producing honey inevitably had a substantial bearing on any theory of poetic imitation that derived itself from apian behaviour. The belief that bees sipped nectar or some other vaguely conceived nutrition from flowers and then converted this into honey validated a theory of poetic imitation that stressed the transformative nature of the relation between an imitation and an original.[14] However, to suggest, on the other hand, that bees were essentially collectors of the goodness created by another organism implied instead that they were freebooters or aerial plunderers. The imitative practice their behaviour figured was plagiarism.

Much as Swift's allegory is designed to illustrate the superiority of the bee's *ancienneté* over the spider's modernity, he was alert to the unfriendly associations that could attach to the foraging ways of bees. He may have been aware in particular of a passage in John Dunton's *A Voyage Round the World* (1691), in which the narrator talks about himself as a

> *Bee*, nay, a mellifluous Bee, or *Brother* to one who gathers *Sweets* and *Dainties* wherever he comes, without ever hurting the *pretty Pinks*, or tarnishing the fragrant *Roses*, and how ungrateful were that *rustick Boor*, and foolish withal, who would refuse the delicate present that his *little industrious Tenant* would make him forsooth, because he had stoln it from *other folks Gardens*, and not gathered it only out of his *own*, or as the *Spider* spins his Thred drawn from his *own Bowels*.[15]

This passage comprises the closest analogue of which I am aware to Swift's spider and bee fable. We have here the spider spinning 'from his *own Bowels*' like Swift's creature spinning '*out of* ... *[its]* ... *own Entrails*' (p. 234) as well as the bee's protestation not to have hurt the flowers which he invades, just as Swift's bee claims to have sipped the flowers '*without the least Injury to their Beauty, their Smell, or their Taste*'. Where Dunton goes beyond Swift is in his greater candour in owning that the bee's practice is basically that of theft, and so a method of imitation based on apian behaviour would be inherently plagiaristic. This realization is of course not easily reconcilable with Swift's line of argument, but Swift knew full well that the figure of the bee invited associations of plagiarism. Indeed, this is precisely the charge that the spider lays against the bee in his own fable: '*Your Livelihood is an universal Plunder upon Nature; a Freebooter over Fields and Gardens; and for the sake of Stealing, will rob a Nettle as readily as a Violet*' (p. 231).

III

The purpose of this chapter is to explore the larger debate between the spider and the bee, between sufficiency and literary appropriation, as it was conducted around the turn of the eighteenth century. The frame for my discussion is provided by the ancients and moderns debate, one which brought into especially sharp relief the difficulty of reconciling the principle of creative originality with an abiding ethic of deference to the cultural past. It was this quandary or problematic which dictated that shrill accusations of plagiarism were to be a persistent (though previously unexplored) feature of the English 'Querelle'.

The battle between the ancients and moderns (as restricted to the literary field) constellated itself around three main questions: in what spirit, through what techniques and to what end should readers and authors of the present day approach the writings of the classical masters?[16] These general questions are ones with which much of the ensuing discussion will be concerned. One narrower issue, however, seems to have posed itself as a matter of urgency to members of both the ancient and modern camps. How was it possible to exercise deference towards some (if not perhaps all) of the great ancients without this deference tipping over into an incapacitating reverence, without, that is, modern authors lapsing into servile repetition of what their classical forebears had already done? Even so committed an advocate of the ancients as Temple appreciated that this eventuality was definitely to be resisted, since writings that did 'but trace over the paths that have been beaten by the ancients, or comment, critique, and flourish upon them ... are at best but copies after those originals'.[17] For Temple, this was not a matter of creed but of simple practicality: it did not imply any disrespect to the ancients to say that modern authors had to maintain their own creative space.

This caution to admire the ancients without being stifled by them is uppermost in the advice given by Henry Felton in his *Dissertation on Reading the Classics* (1713). Felton, like Temple, is a staunch advocate of the ancients but still instructs his tutee to avoid outright imitation or copying of them. He accepts that modern writers will be hard put to say anything radically new, or indeed to say anything better than the ancients have said it before, but this should not be received as a counsel of creative despair, for modern authors can still make what they say their own so long as they resist raking over the same ground as the ancients. The proper way of reading the classical authors is to imbibe them so subtly that they enter into your own thought processes, so as actually to conspire with your own originality. This is the practice that Felton urges on his tutee, the Marquis of Granby, to 'Mix and incorporate with those ancient Streams' in so discreet a way that what 'shall flow from Your Pen, will be entirely Your Own'.[18]

The unease felt by Temple, Felton and others of their intellectual persuasion is that of staleness or, more specifically, plagiarism. If everything has already been said, and indeed been said better than we can ever hope to emulate, and if furthermore our relation to the ancient texts must always be coloured by the strongest deference, what remains for the modern author but simply to plagiarize them? It was an uncomfortable quandary for lovers of the ancients, one that Swift seems to have been aware of in allowing that his bee, offered to the reader ostensibly as a benign harvester of nature, could also be construed as a serial thief.

What embarrassed the ancients inevitably consoled the moderns. In the Preface he wrote to his response to Temple, his *Reflections upon Ancient and Modern Learning*, William Wotton pointed out where an excess of deference to the ancients could only lead – to a curtailment of creative confidence and to a literary culture built upon sterile repetition:

> He that believes the Ancient *Greeks* and *Romans* to have been the greatest Masters of the *Art of Writing* that have ever yet appeared, will read them as his Instruments, will copy after them.[19]

'Copying' here does not equate to imitation, or at least it means only a debased sort of imitation aesthetically inseparable from plagiarism. Elsewhere, Wotton discounts the idea that writers dedicated to the art of copying can ever outstrip the authors from whom their copies derive: 'all Copiers will ever continue on this side of their Originals'. On another occasion he states more pungently that 'Copying nauseates more in Poetry, than any thing'.[20]

Concerns about servility or plagiarism were endemic to the ancients and moderns debate, for the issue at stake was not merely about the relative merits of classical and modern culture, but how any resolution of that issue would impact on the modern practice of writing. Sir Thomas Pope Blount's essay 'Of the Ancients: The Respect that is due to 'em: That we shou'd not too much enslave our selves to their Opinions', for example, gets to the crux of the matter by stating that the price we pay to follow the ancients is that we inevitably 'break the Force and stunt the Growth of our own Genius'. Blount gruffly asserts that 'For my part, I love to hear a Man speak his own Sense', for 'he who recites another Mans Words, is no more to me than a *Notary*'.[21]

It might be felt that I have taken a licence in my argument so far in that the specific issue about derivativeness from the ancients is perhaps not strictly one of 'plagiarism', a term that I have rather liberally invoked. It might be asserted more strongly that it is not even compatible with plagiarism, in as much as plagiarism is a skulking, ungrateful activity, whereas what is at issue here is a level of grateful deference that becomes creatively inhibiting. Moreover, Wotton's attack on copying is not aimed specifically at *unacknowledged* copying, embracing instead all types of servile duplication. So it is too with Blount, whose particular gripe is not so much with covert plagiarists as with authors who quote a lot. However, these general debates about originality and creative servitude are an essential part of the ancients and moderns debate, a debate that incorporates a very specific, symbolic and rancorous feud about plagiarism (as rather more strictly understood) that I now wish to discuss.

IV

The first exchanges in the ancients and moderns debate were muted and inoffensive. Sir William Temple had published his elegant essay 'Upon Ancient and Modern Learning' (1690) arguing for the supremacy of classical over modern achievements, and this had flushed out, as a riposte, William Wotton's *Reflections upon Ancient and Modern Learning* (1694), in which the author denied the *inevitability* of classical superiority and claimed that in certain areas of learning the moderns might indeed have equalled or surpassed the ancients. It certainly seemed to Wotton that if you were to raise the issue of the comparative status of classical and modern achievements, you needed to pursue it across a wider range of fronts than Temple had exerted himself to do. Yet for those visiting the controversy nowadays, what stands out is rather the high level of unanimity between the squabbling parties. Neither side doubted that the achievements of classical culture were impressive and formed an immediate and indispensable context for modern advances. No modern creativity or discovery could emerge out of a relation of indifference to the classics.

In his essay, Temple had asserted rather absently that his general thesis that the oldest books were the best was demonstrated in particular by two ancient texts, *Aesop's Fables* and the anonymous *Epistles of Phalaris*, the latter of which he claimed had 'more race, more spirit, more force of wit and genius, than any others I have ever seen, either ancient or modern'.[22] This heady praise of the *Epistles*, notwithstanding that Temple had only ever read them in translation, soon led to a new edition being put into preparation. This was to be by Charles Boyle, who undertook it at the invitation of the Dean of Christ Church, Oxford, where he was an undergraduate. The edition duly came out in 1695.

It was from this point on that the controversy became vicious. In the course of his Preface, Boyle had let drop that he felt the production of the edition had been hampered by the unwillingness of Richard Bentley, the royal librarian, to lend a manuscript for collation. The details of Bentley's supposed obstruction were to be wrangled over in print for some time, but Boyle's accusation gave Bentley a particular incentive to pursue a scholarly interest he already entertained in the likely inauthenticity of Phalaris's *Epistles*. It is true that Boyle's edition had not vouched for their authenticity, yet Temple's claims about their greatness were entirely based on that assumption, and both Wotton and Bentley were aware that an exposure of a substantial error of fact underlying Temple's claims would make for a very potent contribution to the ancients and moderns debate.

When a new edition of Wotton's *Reflections* was issued in 1697, it was accompanied by an essay by Bentley which attacked the reputation of the *Epistles of Phalaris* and *Aesop's Fables* as illustrious works of the classical age. Bentley was already employing the apparatus of scholarly techniques that was to make him notorious, especially the use of indexes and lexicons to root out analogies between works. What his scholarly method informed him, first and foremost, was that the *Epistles* were a patchwork of (sometimes flagrant) borrowings or plagiarisms from earlier works. Bentley's discovery of deep plagiarism was, of course, entirely in keeping with his hunch from the start that the *Epistles* had been forged well after the lifetime of Phalaris, their method of composition being entirely disreputable. His conclusions, reinforced by his own hectoring prose style, were horrifying for supporters of Temple and the ancients. It would have been damaging enough for Bentley merely to prove the *Epistles* to be less ancient than Temple had supposed, but he also demonstrated them to be worthless in literary terms. He had debunked not just Temple's scholarship but also his taste.

From this point on, plagiarism becomes fundamental to the battle between the ancients and moderns, and yet (to my knowledge) no previous commentator, including Joseph Levine, has documented its prominence. Bentley himself, it might be thought, had committed an outright theft, in that he had stripped Phalaris of the ownership of his *Epistles* and handed it instead to a sophist. In William King's *Dialogues of the Dead*, Phalaris is actually shown accosting the sophist and voicing his indignation at the theft from him instigated by Bentley: 'Shall a Prince be rifled of his Honour by a Pedant?'[23] It is precisely Bentley's massive self-possession in sitting in judgement on the literary credentials of Phalaris and Aesop that is parodied in Swift's *Battle of the Books*, where Aesop pronounces on the dispute between the bee and the Bentleian spider.

Yet this is not yet to get to the heart of why plagiarism becomes so radical to the ancients and moderns dispute. Perhaps above all, the dispute was concerned with the spirit in which learned people should engage with classical culture. For Temple, it was a matter of breeding and taste. He felt he could intuitively discern the literary quality of Phalaris's writing (even through the intervening screen of translation) and he also seems to have felt a gentlemanly rapport with the kind of person he took Phalaris to be. For a professional philologist like Bentley, this was pure humbug. Temple's gossamer taste was not for him: instead he armed himself with an array of scholarly techniques through which classical culture was to be subdued to his rigorous enquiry. Even before the controversy had erupted, gentlemen of letters were beginning to deplore scholarly methods that seemed to them mechanical and soulless: collecting sententiae in commonplace books, using indexes and dictionaries to search the vocabulary of texts, amassing quotations and parading learning in footnotes.[24] Bentley was seen as the high-priest of this scholarly method. Moreover, what Bentley's opponents quickly grasped was that his revelation of Phalaris's plagiarism was not incidental to wider concerns about his methodology, for Bentley's procedure, especially his use of lexicons, seemed particularly calculated to bring evidence of plagiarism to his notice.

This innate tendency of Bentley's scholarship to issue charges of plagiarism is alluded to in a rather later work by William King, *The Odes of Horace in Latin and English* (1712), which satirizes Bentley's recent edition of Horace. One of King's notes seems to reflect an issue at the heart of the Phalaris controversy:

> Nothing is more common among Criticks, than to hear them comparing great Authors with one another; and if they can but find two or three Words in one, which upon the same or the like Occasion they find in another (a thing easie to be accounted for) presently they cry out, This is *stollen*, this is *borrowed*, this is *imitated*, or the like, and then they run on with a Collection of Scraps and Fragments of Prose and Poetry, with a long Catalogue of bright Names, on purpose to convince the Reader, that they have perused those Classicks, at least their *Indexes*; by which Stratagem it often comes to pass, that they make one Author filch from another, who was not born till perhaps a Century after.[25]

A further spoof note explores the same issue: all writers are borrowers in as much as they inevitably use the same words, sometimes in the same combinations, as earlier authors in the same tongue, but coincidences of this sort should not be allowed to underwrite a charge of plagiarism. For King, the inclination of scholars like Bentley to arraign classical authors with plagiarism constituted a vicious coupling of methodology and ego. What better way to parade the depth of your scholarship than by grubbing up the evidence for an accusation of plagiarism?

Bentley's revelation of Phalaris's plagiarism was, then, a matter of wide import, and for adherents to the ancients' cause it could not remain unanswered. Such an answer eventually came in the form of *Dr. Bentley's Dissertations on the Epistles of Phalaris, and the Fables of Aesop Examin'd* (1698), published under the name of Boyle but probably written by a coalition of pens (the so-called Christ Church wits) under the leadership of Francis Atterbury and including King.[26] Between them, they could muster enough learning to banter with Bentley on points of scholarship, if not exactly to overturn his arguments. However, it is clear that the real objective was not to disprove their opponent but to ridicule him: their main satiric technique is to bring Bentley into the foreground, as if his credentials were those under dispute rather than those of Phalaris.

Crucial to the effectiveness of their reply would be their rebuttal of the plagiarism allegation. As I have already indicated, one riposte was to deny that the duplications of phraseology that Bentley had uncovered really amounted to plagiarism. Instead, these duplications could be explained in terms of gnomic or conventional expressions, for which no single author could claim copyright. Besides, they argued, if Bentley's own treatise were subjected to the same sort of analysis that had been applied to Phalaris's *Epistles*, this in its turn could be found to contain just such duplications.[27] Such arguments did exude a scholarly plausibility and the collaborators were also able to suggest that Bentley's attack on Phalaris's plagiarism, while it may have been undertaken in the spirit of cool-headed enquiry, had become intemperate and vindictive. In doing so, they were able to capitalize on the indisputably surly and *ad hominem* nature of Bentley's scholarly manner: 'Hitherto *Phalaris* has stolen discreetly, and borrow'd Expressions proper for him to use; but now it seems he steals without Decency or Distinction.'[28]

Yet to defend Phalaris was only half the objective, the other half being to impugn Bentley. No way of doing this seemed more appropriate than to level a reciprocal accusation of plagiarism against the great scholar himself, thus demonstrating to their enemy the truth of the fable of *'the Old Woman in the Oven'*.[29] The intention was that Bentley's reputation should be incinerated in the very fire that he himself had set. The main (though not the sole) text from which Bentley is accused of plagiarizing is the edition of *Aesop's Fables* prepared by Isaac Nevelet and published in 1660. In particular, he is charged with the shamelessness of having plundered from Nevelet some of the evidence he then deploys in mounting his plagiarism charge against Phalaris. In order to make Bentley squirm as much as possible, the collaborators compose a dramatic exchange between Nevelet and Bentley, in which the former angrily remonstrates about his treatment:

> You endeavour what You can to disguise what You take from me; but after all, there appears upon You here and there *not only a Sameness of Sense, but a Sameness of Words too, which could not fall out by Accident*: and this is Your Own Way of traducing a Plagiary.[30]

Nevelet's *Aesop* is not alone, so the collaborators claim, as a classical edition rifled by Bentley: they also point to Vizzanius's edition of Iamblichus and even suggest that Bentley stole from Boyle's edition of the *Epistles of Phalaris*, even in the midst of deriding it. The book ends with a cod index, probably compiled by William King, in which various supposedly plundered sources are collected under a single head.[31]

When Nevelet is depicted, in the quote above, protesting at being plagiarized, the response attributed to Bentley is one of querulous denial: '*do you think I'd turn Filcher* my self?'. Supporting this rebuttal, moreover, is a ringing statement of his own sufficiency: 'I tread in No man's Footsteps.'[32] What the collaborators were skilfully establishing was a caricature of Bentley on the basis of which he would be harassed for the remainder of the controversy. In part, he was the puffed up, self-regarding exemplar of intellectual sufficiency, unheeding of and ungrateful to the generosity of past authors. Yet, in another part, he was the skulking plagiarist, helplessly reliant on the texts of others for his evidence and putative insights. It is exactly this ambivalence that we see in Swift's representation of Bentley in the *Battle of the Books*, a work which gives a sort of allegoric validation to the wits' denunciations. Bentley appears as a bloated spider squat within the centre of his web, an image of intellectual sufficiency. However, Swift also cannot resist a satiric thrust of a different sort, for the bee's particular reproach to the spider is as follows:

> *You boast, indeed, of being obliged to no other Creature, but of drawing, and spinning out all from your self ... yet, I doubt you are somewhat obliged ... to a little foreign Assistance.* (p. 232)

This is exactly the wits' case against Bentley: that his front of sufficiency, which is itself objectionable, was in fact a cover for his discreet plundering (his *'little foreign Assistance'*) from the works of other scholars.

Bentley must have been truly vexed by the nature and severity of the attack upon him. Yet it was only in 1699 that he re-entered the fray with his *Dissertation upon the Epistles of Phalaris*, containing an 'Answer' to the Christ Church party. Bentley's main objective was, as Joseph Levine has noted, nothing less than 'to crush the enemy beneath the weight and fury of his scholarship'.[33] He applied his vast knowledge of the history and social customs of the classical period, of philology and of numismatics to arrive at a definitive chronology of the *Epistles'* production. It was a piece of virtuoso scholarship, which effectively put to flight all rational objection to his assertion of the inauthenticity of the *Epistles*. It is true that Bentley carried on being harassed, but his enemies, rather than continuing to wrangle over the dating of the *Epistles*, increasingly shifted ground, suggesting instead that the issue had all along been stuffy and esoteric, and scarcely worth the sustained attention of anyone other than an irredeemable pedant like Bentley.[34]

Yet to defeat his opponents over the matter of chronology was not in itself to drive out the stain of the plagiarism accusation. Bentley felt it incumbent on himself to address this, though without giving it so much space as in any way to validate the allegation. In his *Dissertation*, he responds to the 'calumny' spread by Boyle's party in accusing 'me of *pillaging his* [Boyle's] *poor Notes*, and robbing *Vizzanius* and *Nevelett*'.[35] His defence is that if, by his own research, he has arrived at a textual emendation that happens to reproduce one introduced by an earlier commentator, this duplication should not be considered plagiaristic: 'For a Man would have very hard measure, if because another, whom he knew not of, had lit upon the same thought, he must be traduced as a Plagiary.'[36] Bentley is in effect suggesting that the business of compiling editions and improving texts is one that inevitably lays a scholar open to the charge of plagiarism, an argument that mirrors that of his opponents, who believed that his scholarly method, with its use of indexes and lexicons, was tilted from the outset in the direction of exposing plagiarism between authors.

Bentley's defends himself in particular against the accusation of having plundered Vizzanius's edition of Iamblichus; although he attacks the injustice of the charge relating to Nevelet's *Aesop*, he never actually gets around to refuting it. Yet what would have been the point anyway? The issues were not really about the probity of Bentley's scholarly method: Bentley's enemies, however much they asserted it, probably never really believed his guilt or, if they did believe it, cared about it. The allegation was in reality a way of baiting and stigmatizing Bentley in the context of a controversy that was not directly about plagiarism (though to which plagiarism does have a natural relevance). The Christ Church party must have been gleeful at the success of their original set of allegations, because they soon sought to build on them. *A Short Account of Dr. Bentley's Humanity and Justice to those Authors who have written before him* (1699) repeats the disgraceful fact of Bentley's plagiarism as if it is now commonly received knowledge: it has been 'undeniably demonstrated, that *Vizzani* and *Nevelet* are Authors, whom he has rifled, and prided himself in their Spoils'.[37] Yet more shocking revelations are to come, for it can now be revealed that Bentley has also been found out to have plundered a set of manuscript notes by the scholar Thomas Stanley in preparing his 'Fragments of Callimachus' (1697). The collaborators state that they will prove unanswerably that Stanley's 'Locks were pick'd, and his Trunks rifled', by arranging that the manuscript be made available for public perusal.[38]

It should be noted that Bentley's plagiarism has now ceased to inhere merely in his rebarbative scholarly method and has blossomed into a symptom of his entire intellectual engagement with the cultural past. It conspires with a general spirit of inhumanity and injustice in which he approaches past authors. Bentley is a fascinating figure in the cultural history of plagiarism, and not just because of the vehemence with which his is accused of it. One way of contemplating the historical mutation of a concept such as plagiarism is to consider those concepts that, at any one time, stand in an antonymic relation to it. In the mid-eighteenth century, this position is occupied by 'originality'. In the 1690s, however, the most influential antonym to plagiarism is 'sufficiency', a term (unlike 'originality') invariably used negatively to mean a sort of intellectual insularity or to express a view of creativity as an unwholesome evacuation out of the self. Bentley's particular torment was to find himself pincered between, and derided on account of, both the negative thing that was sufficiency and the equally negative thing that was its opposite: plagiarism. It was on this forked hook that supporters of the ancients ensured he would be made to squirm.

V

I wish to finish this chapter by concentrating on one of those agitators against Bentley, Jonathan Swift, and describing the events by which he himself becomes a victim of the plagiarism controversy. When the *Tale* and *Battle* appeared in 1704, reawakening the slumbering ancients and moderns controversy and reiterating the established slur on Bentley,

Swift could not have suspected that his own literary probity was about to be publicly questioned. Yet in 1705 appeared William Wotton's *A Defense of the Reflections upon Ancient and Modern Learning*, which levelled specific allegations of plagiarism against Swift's *Tale* and *Battle*. What may have emboldened Wotton was his appreciation that the *Tale* actually invited just such an allegation, as a uniquely pertinent form of critical riposte. He would have no doubt noticed the ridiculing in the *Tale* of his own *Reflections*, a work, in Swift's grinning phrase, 'never to be sufficiently valued', and the confession made by the narrator of having plagiarized from it: 'I cannot forbear doing that Author the Justice of my publick Acknowledgments for the great *Helps* and *Liftings* I had out of his incomparable Piece while I was penning this Treatise' (pp. 128–9). Wotton's allegations, though not about plagiarism from his own writings, are simply a translation from irony to literalism, from wit to acrimony.

Wotton broaches his topic by way of the overarching slur that the author's '*Wit* is *not his own*, in many places', though only three precise allegations are made.[39] These have not been granted credibility by Swift scholars and the last in particular is so hedged about with qualifications as to evaporate before any sort of forensic gaze: 'I have been assured that the *Battel in St. James's Library* is *Mutandis Mutandis* [*sic*] taken out of a *French* Book, entituled, *Combat des Livres*, if I misremember not' (p. 328). An unnamed third party has reported to Wotton something of which his recall may not be entirely accurate: namely, that the *Tale*'s author has plagiarized to an indefinite degree from a French book of undisclosed title and authorship. How many ways can there be of dodging responsibility for an allegation?

Swift's precise reaction to the plagiarism slur cast by Wotton is the topic on which I wish to conclude this chapter, but I will approach it only by way of a few more general comments about Swift and plagiarism. The particular channels in which Swift's genius ran have always been seen as peculiar and inimitable, and also by many commentators as inherently non-imitative in nature. Johnson, in his 'Life of Swift', put the matter like this:

It was said, in a Preface to one of the Irish editions, that Swift had never been known to take a single thought from any writer, ancient or modern. This is not literally true; but perhaps no writer can easily be found that has borrowed so little, or that in all his excellences and all his defects has so well maintained his claim to be original.[40]

It would be hard in fact to imagine an author so fresh and neoteric in nature as to avoid borrowing a single thought whatsoever, so Johnson is right to add the caution that such a portrait of Swift 'is not literally true'. Yet perhaps of most interest here is not the characterization of Swift's literary achievement so much as the conviction that Swift had prided himself on, and publicly claimed, his own originality.

Where Swift does this, other than as part of his injured protests at Wotton's plagiarism accusation (which I will discuss in a moment), is not altogether clear. Johnson may be thinking of the famous couplet in 'Verses on the Death of Dr. Swift D.S.P.D.' in which Swift imagines a sympathetic commentator extolling the Dean's literary record after his death:

> To steal a hint was never known,
> But what he writ was all his own.[41]

Yet this self-compliment softly implodes once the reader recognizes it to have been lifted from John Denham's elegy on Abraham Cowley:

> To him no Author was unknown,
> Yet what he wrote was all his own.[42]

We do not know whether Swift expected the joke to be picked up or whether the plagiarism was inserted like a concealed pocket of irony, awaiting the discovery of curious future readers. We also do not know whether the sentiment the lines express conforms exactly to what Swift terms a 'hint', a word that he seems to use to mean a plagiarizable element of a work. It occurs again in a letter written by John Gay to Swift in 1731, ascribing to the latter an aversion to borrowing material from other authors: 'You and I are alike in one particular ... I mean that we hate to write upon other folk's hints. I love to have my own Scheme, and to treat it in my own way.'[43]

Before returning to the *Tale*, it is worth noting another work that reflects interestingly on the topic on plagiarism: *A Letter of Advice to a Young Poet* (1721). It has long been associated with Swift and is included in Davis's edition of the *Prose Works* as an appendix, relegated there because of the editor's unease (justified in my opinion) about its authenticity. In any event, it contains views that some commentators have accepted as Swift's own:

For to speak my private Opinion, I am for every Man's working upon his own Materials, and producing only what he can find within himself, which is commonly a better Stock than the owner knows it to be. I think Flowers of Wit ought to spring, as those in a Garden do, from their own Root and Stem, without Foreign Assistance. I would have a Man's Wit rather like a Fountain that feeds it self invisibly, than a River that is supply'd by several Streams from abroad.[44]

A case against the likelihood of Swift's authorship is that the *Letter* evinces attitudes that are difficult to square with his stated opinions in other places. In a neighbouring passage, for example, the author exhorts young poets not to steal from the classical authors, but instead to 'improve *upon* them', where the prospect of doing so is seen as no greatly exacting challenge for young pretenders. The extract above reads to me like a garbled rendition, with a reversal of intellectual affiliation, of the spider and bee analogy in Swift's *Battle of the Books*. Swift's spider is 'furnished with a native stock' within himself, a resource that is seen as inferior to the creative booty of the bee, gathered from the garden flowers. Here the author argues instead for intellectual sufficiency, for every man, like the spider, 'working upon his own Materials'.[45]

It does not seem likely that Swift would have been so negligent as to pen two works containing treatment of originality and plagiarism whose conclusions so entirely contradict each other. Yet the *Letter*, if not convincing as Swift's work, is instructive in another way. If the author of the *Letter*, in the midst of a general dissuasion from literary copying, can hold up fully sufficient authorship as an ideal to be followed by aspiring writers and as the best antidote to the malady of plagiarism, then it demonstrates just how confused the ethical issues surrounding good writing were. Might not the spider be the better role model after all?

Whatever Swift's exact views about the aesthetic requirement for originality, his infuriation over the allegations of plagiarism made against the *Tale* is not to be doubted. Nor did it console him that these were not discharged against him personally, for Wotton did not know the true identity of the *Tale*'s author and mistakenly assumed it to be Swift's cousin, Thomas Swift, whom, by virtue of a second error grafted on to the first, he believed actually to be Swift's brother. Swift's temper can hardly have been improved when in 1710, shortly before the publication of the *Tale*'s third edition, in which Swift designed to scotch the allegation, Edmund Curll issued *A Complete Key to the Tale of a Tub*, which hinted at Thomas's authorship of the *Tale* and, while noting them, made light of the plagiarism allegations.[46]

The 1710 edition was the first to have a new section, 'An Apology for the Tale of a Tub', stationed at the front. Here Swift addresses and rebuts each charge in turn, reserving his largest measure of outrage for the third charge, in which Wotton had blithely asserted Swift's plagiarism, on the basis of hearsay, from a book that he was unable to identify. Swift was indignant that evidence as threadbare as this could be used to justify a public allegation of plagiarism, especially given, as he says, that '*I know nothing more contemptible in a Writer than the Character of a Plagiary*' (p. 14). In a key section, he questions what exactly Wotton's motives can have been in dreaming up such allegations and whether these must not have had '*some Allay of Personal Animosity*'. Not only are the allegations unfounded, so Swift claims, but they slight the profound originality of the book:

> it indeed touches the Author in a very tender Point, who insists upon it, that through the whole Book he has not borrowed one single Hint from any Writer in the World; and he thought, of all Criticisms, that would never have been one. He conceived it was never disputed to be an Original, whatever Faults it might have. (p. 13)

How we respond to such remarks will depend in part on how we respond to the 'Apology' in general. Some critics view it as discontinuous from the *Tale* itself, as a much later piece of writing, prompted by specific issues concerning the original work's reception.[47] It is the one part of the *Tale*, so it is sometimes suggested, where Swift's prose can be read 'straight', rather than through the customary veils of irony. Yet Swift chose, even at this juncture, not to come clean about his authorship, and the 'Apology', far from being devoid of obscurities, even has a textual problematic not present in the rest of the *Tale*: that is, the exact attitude of the narrator (the older writer revisiting his work) to the young creative pup who had actually composed it '*above thirteen Years since*' (p. 4).

When Swift wrote the *Tale* in the 1690s, he was (by his own admission in 1704) '*young, his Invention at the Height, and his Reading fresh in his Head*'; he determined to proceed in a manner '*altogether new*', the world having long been '*nauseated with endless Repetitions upon every Subject*' (p. 4). In describing the neophyte author he used to be, the narrator assigns to his earlier self the characteristics of a modern. The reference above to '*his reading fresh in his Head*', for example, conjures up the *Tale*'s earlier correlation between 'freshness' and a larger modern 'pertness', as in the '*freshest Modern*' who claims 'Despotick Power' over all authors before him (p. 130). Similarly, references to the nausea induced by copying were (for reasons I have discussed already) a natural extension of the cultural viewpoint of the moderns, as in Wotton's remark cited earlier that 'copying nauseates more in Poetry, than any thing'. Is Swift really being 'straight' when he puts these remarks into the mouth of his earlier self? Even his trenchant declaration about the originality of the *Tale* seems to me to be dusted with stylistic irony. What we are given is a denial so absolute, so manically set upon the elimination of any possible qualifying note, as to become itself a paragon of modern verbosity and over-assertion: 'through the *whole* Book he has not borrowed *one single* Hint from *any* Writer *in the World*' (emphasis added).

The plagiarism allegations were unsettling for Swift (as Wotton may well have appreciated) not because they were true, but because there would always be an awkwardness in Swift wording a strong denial of having committed the offence and denouncing plagiarism in general. To have issued a peremptory disavowal of creative reliance would have been for Swift to cast himself as his own morose spider, spinning his web-creation out of his own entrails. It may be for this reason that there is a rhetorical inflatedness, an elusiveness of tone, in which he couches his denial.

The *Tale* attacks the moderns for having furnished a specious creed of scholarship, that is, the Bentleian method of using '*Indexes*' and '*Compendiums*' so as to practise the '*Art of being Deep-learned and Shallow-read*' (p. 130), but also as apostles of originality. Another aspect of the modern mentality is an irrational and artless novelty, epitomized by the 'ingenious Poet, who solliciting his Brain for something new, compared himself to the *Hangman*, and his Patron to the *Patient*' (p. 43). As well as novelty per se, the *Tale* also scorns writers for whom invention is the sole or paramount faculty involved in composition, 'who deal entirely with *Invention*, and strike all Things out of themselves' or who 'make *Invention* the *Master*' and method and reason 'its *Lacquays*' (pp. 135, 209). As I have said, the consistent hostility of Swift's treatment of modern originality complicated his immediate riposte to Wotton's plagiarism allegation. It left him no positive anti-plagiaristic principle to which he could state his allegiance. When he tried to protest the originality of his methods, he could only do so by reeling off protestations of invention, freshness, his work being 'altogether new', which sound like the mantra of an irredeemable modernist. By conspiring with Temple's attack on 'sufficiency', Swift had inadvertently disarmed himself in the face of Wotton's accusations.

Swift's discomfiture on this point reflects a dilemma felt more widely in his day. How could an attitude of deference to the ancients be reconciled with the principle of creative individuality? If all original endeavour must be impugned as evincing intellectual sufficiency, an introverted disregard for the achievements of the classical past, what was left for authors but servile reiteration? Of course, albeit that reconciliation between the two views was difficult, an intermediate position did remain feasible. Many commentators realized that it was possible to drink deep from the well of classical culture while still preserving a measure of creative independence. Authors could revere the classical originals while still vying with and seeking to outstrip them. But the more polemical you were on one side of the case, the less space for such reconciliation existed.

To some degree Swift had been ensnared in his own spider's web. It was impossible to square a very positive view of creative originality with the image of the ruffian arachnid, ensconced at the centre of its web, spinning a death-trap from its own entrails. If creative individuality were to be considered more favourably than this, a much more obliging metaphoric vehicle was called for. And yet one lay surprisingly close to hand. In *The Medal of John Bayes* (1682), Thomas Shadwell satirizes Dryden's plagiaristic tendencies in the following terms:

> No Piece did ever from thy self begin;
> Thou can'st no web, from thine own bowels, spin.[48]

At first sight these lines might seem to effect a startling re-evaluation of the spider's creed of originality: Dryden is here stigmatized exactly in as much as he fails to spin his works directly from his own bowels. Yet Shadwell was most likely thinking not of the spider, but of another creature, much celebrated and exploited in the Augustan era for the indefatigability and value of its labours: the silkworm.[49] Invocations of the silkworm as a model of irreproachable creativity are common in the English Augustan era. That fervent inculpator of plagiarists, Gerard Langbaine, for example, denounces the playwright Edward Ravenscroft as a 'leech' on other writers, even though 'he would be thought to imitate the Silk-worm, that spins its Web from its own Bowels'.[50] Similarly, in his essay on 'The State of Poetry', Leonard Welsted asserts that what pleases in any writing is never the result of imitation or tuition but a 'Man's own Force': this is his 'proper Wealth, and he draws it out of himself, as the Silk-Worm spins out of her own Bowels that soft ductile Substance'.[51]

It is sometimes assumed that Edward Young's *Conjectures on Original Composition* (1759) invented the concept of literary originality, or at least opened the door to originality being considered as a good thing. Yet critics of an earlier generation, such as Welsted, can be found making observations of the same broad tenor as Young's, though they express them differently in accordance with the different way the originality debate was then structured. Young did not have to contend with the idea of 'sufficiency' as a powerful reproach to aspirations of creative independence. Nor did he have to weigh the claims of the surly spider and the industrious silkworm as rival exemplars of the ethos of original composition. Furthermore, while deference to the classical past remained in Young's day an endemic cultural mentality, the justness and limitations of this mentality were not being so feverishly contested as they had been during the ancients and moderns debate of 60 years earlier. This debate sets the context for understanding attitudes towards literary originality at the turn of the eighteenth century. It also gives rise to a great antihero in the figure of Bentley, the dark epitome both of self-centred originality and, conversely, a malignant plagiarism.

5
Pope and Plagiarism

I

Oliver Goldsmith, in his biography of Thomas Parnell, relates a practical joke played by the poet on his friend Pope. Parnell had happened to be around when Pope was reading out parts of a new, unfinished poem, *The Rape of the Lock*, to Jonathan Swift. Finding reason to leave the room, though not before committing to memory Pope's description of Belinda's toilette, Parnell then set about translating it into Latin verse. The next day, when Pope was reading the poem to another group of friends, Parnell publicly rebuked him for stealing the episode and produced his Latin version as evidence of a prior source. Pope was startled at this public revelation of a detail about the poem's composition so darkly secret as to have escaped the notice even of the author. After a teasing pause, he was put out of his confusion, but the incident is a curious earnest of an issue that was to impact both on Pope's career and on his literary posterity.[1]

The earliest major English poet to have had his peace disturbed and his career significantly tarnished by the issue of plagiarism is not Pope but Dryden. Pope's case resembles and also differs from Dryden's, with a particular difference being that his career and immediate posterity coincide with a shift from plagiarism being viewed mainly as a moral offence to being seen as an aesthetic shortcoming. Such a change has the effect of sparing Pope as a man but incriminating him as a poet. This chapter will concentrate on the following matters: Pope's general sensitivity to the ethics of literary borrowing; the role played by the plagiarism allegation in satiric attacks on him in his lifetime; Pope's use of the same allegation in the conduct of his quarrels; and the way that, in a less overtly tendentious manner, critical writing after Pope's death comes to define the nature of his achievement in terms of an inherently plagiaristic aesthetic.[2]

II

From early in his career, Pope seems to have been alert to the trespass that could be caused by over-reliance on other authors' works: an early letter to his poetic mentor William Walsh, for example, enquires nervously 'how far the liberty of *Borrowing* may extend'.[3] Even as a fledgling author, he was aware of whisperings about the derivative nature of his own compositional practice, although he was reassured that those writers who most wanted to raise the issue were 'such whose writings no man ever borrowed from' and so who had 'the least reason to complain'.[4] He also seems to have reacted with sympathetic annoyance to a plagiarism slur cast on an author for whom in his early years he had the utmost respect: Samuel Garth. Garth and another physician-poet, Richard Blackmore, had found themselves on opposite sides of a controversy in the late 1690s over the founding in London of a charitable dispensary, and Garth had perhaps ill-advisedly lampooned his opponent's poetry in a mock-heroic poem on the subject, *The Dispensary* (1699). Blackmore's counter-attack took the form of *A Satyr against Wit* (1699), the work in which he set out to turn the tables on his enemies. As a preliminary to turning its fire on Garth, the poem sets aside some lines for a general denunciation of plagiarism:

> If in *Parnassus* any *needy Wit*
> Should filch and Petty Larceny commit,
> If he should riffle Books, and Pilferer turn,
> An Inch beside the Nose the *Felon* burn.
> Let him distinguish'd by this Mark appear,
> And in his Cheek a plain *Signetur* wear. (lines 307–12)[5]

Having established the felonious nature of plagiarists, Blackmore then cites Garth as an offender of exactly this kind, a writer who has in fact compounded the obloquy of plagiarism by stealing his poem *The Dispensary* from a specifically French source, Boileau's *Le Lutrin*: 'Felonious *Garth* pursuing this Design,/Smuggles French Wit, as others Silks and Wine' (lines 315–16). This allegation against Garth quickly got around and was endorsed in print two years later in an anonymous work entitled *Letters of Wit, Politicks and Morality* (1701) and echoed some years later in John Lacy's *The Steeleids* (1714): '*G[art]h*'s *a Wit*, for verses not his own.'[6]

Garth had been a friend to Pope's youthful poetic ambitions, a fact recorded in the *Epistle to Arbuthnot* (1735), in which the younger poet remembers how 'Well-natur'd *Garth* inflam'd [him] with early praise', and Pope must have been pained to see Garth's reputation fall victim to such a smear.[7] In the *Essay on Criticism* (1711), as well as a hostile allusion to Blackmore, subsequently edited out of the poem but later reinserted into it, there is a reference to the travails of Garth, cast in the form of the typical opinions maintained by a blockhead critic:

> With *him*, most Authors steal their Works, or buy;
> *Garth* did not write his own *Dispensary*. (lines 618–19)[8]

In the early editions this couplet is left to speak for itself, and only in the year of his death did Pope compose a gloss to it, explaining that charges of literary theft constituted:

> A common slander at that time in prejudice of that deserving author. Our poet did him this justice, when that slander most prevail'd; and it is now (perhaps the sooner for this very verse) dead and forgotten.[9] (*TE*, I. 309)

Pope was evidently pleased to have been put to the trouble of composing this gloss, because the very need for it confirmed that the slander was now out of mind. Looking back to his youthful lines, he is proud that he stood up for Garth and proud that his intervention may have played some part in the restoration of Garth's name. His own role in the affair he characterizes as dispensing justice to Garth, as against the injustice or 'prejudice' of the plagiarism slur. Writing close to the end of his own life, Pope is understandably sensitive to the potential deathliness of such accusations, the fact that life for them can mean death to the authors against whom they are directed. For Garth to accede to an immortal fame requires that the plagiarism stain laid upon him should be 'dead and forgotten'.

III

It was no doubt mainly on Garth's behalf that Pope felt aggrieved, but he may also have been a little discomfited by the supposition that the slur of plagiarism might be inevitable for anyone composing a mock-heroic poem, as Garth had done. Rallying around Garth, Pope might have been trying to discourage in advance accusations that he feared would be brought against his own *The Rape of the Lock*. In bracing himself against such allegations, he would not be taking an undue precaution. As early as 1715, John Harris, in his *Treatise upon the Modes*, lodges against Pope exactly the same accusation that Blackmore had earlier made against Garth, namely his having been guilty of smuggling French wit. In a complex conceit, mischievously applied, Harris describes how writers inspire one another in an endless cycle of metempsychosis, and he includes as an example of such a process the case of 'a certain Poet of this Nation, and a *French* Poet, call'd Despreaux'.[10] The jibe is that Pope has taken the idea of his heroicomical poem from Boileau, exactly as Garth was claimed to have done before him. Metempsychosis (or spiritual transmigration) had by this time a general currency as a metaphor for literary tradition; however, Harris's invocation of it relates not so much to creative descent as to the debt of plagiarism.[11]

Few of Pope's poems over the course of his lifetime were to escape the accusation of plagiarism. The charge is a staple one among the innumerable attacks on him by enemies and detractors, and its occurrence specifically within pamphlet literature has been recorded by J.V. Guerinot.[12] The principal accusation made is that Pope has received unacknowledged assistance from friends or from the writings of contemporaries (or near-contemporaries), though another accusation is that in his works based on classical sources, as the translations from Homer, Pope's method of proceeding could fairly be seen as larcenous and as an attempt to appropriate credit from the original author to himself.

From an early point in Pope's career, a typical allegation is that he has not just plagiarized but plagiarized from intimates, thus violating not just a rule of literature but also a principle of friendship. His *Essay on Criticism*, it was alleged, had been written with the undeclared assistance of his early mentors, William Walsh and William Wycherley. Leonard Welsted's 'Of Dulness and Scandal' (1732), for example, eagerly anticipates a future in which Pope's poetic voice, particularly the grating precocity of the *Essay on Criticism*, will have faded from memory:

> Forgot the self-applauding strain shall be;
> Though own'd by Walsh, or palm'd on Wycherley.[13]

The scandalous origins of the *Essay* are also discussed in a poem of two years later, 'An Epistle to the Egregious Mr. Pope', the author footnoting his lines with reference to the supposedly established fact that Wycherley had written the *Essay on Criticism* and sent it to Pope for revision, only for Pope to publish it under his own name:

> The first gay Colours which thy Muse assum'd,
> Were false – the Jay in Peacock's Beauties plum'd:
> This Work, 'tis true, was nervous, learn'd, polite,
> The Sound an artful Comment to the Wit;
> With *Sheffield* and *Roscommon* claim'd the Prize,
> And justly too – the Piece was WITCHERLEYS.[14]

That Pope has duped his friends by appropriating their words without permission becomes received wisdom amongst those dedicated to slandering his career: Edward Ward, for example, in his *Durgen* of 1729 claims that Pope's success in usurping the 'Throne of Wit' has been achieved through 'fath'ring what [his] trusty Friends have writ'.[15]

Even before he fledged as a poet in his own right, Pope, so his enemies noted, was already donning the plumage of others. In 'An Epistle to the Egregious Mr Pope', he is a 'Jay in Peacock's Beauties plum'd'; in Ward's *Durgen*, a 'Howlet', due to be stripped of his 'Plume' by his injured and indignant friends (line 130). For those who wanted to besmirch Pope's literary achievement through the accusation of plagiarism, one fact about his career stood out as a veritable *trouvaille*: namely, the ironic coincidence that a writer so devoted to stealing the plumage of others should have founded his early reputation on a poem on the subject of a stolen lock of hair. It was as if Pope has secreted in the very subject of the poem the fact of his own general malpractice. This association of Belinda's ravished lock with Pope's own stolen garlands is evident in Thomas Cooke's *Battel of the Poets* (1742), in which Pope is described taking to the battlefield 'In glaring Arms array'd' but also plumed with Belinda's stolen lock:

> The Plume, *Belinda*, was thy ravish'd Hair.[16]

Later in the poem, Cooke describes how the critic John Dennis steals the entire body of Pope's writings so as to perform a sacrifice of them demanded by Apollo and the nine muses. What Pope is stripped of by this act consists largely of what he himself, as a working plagiarist, has already stolen from others:

> Too long the Task, the Toil of Moons, to name,
> His ev'ry guilty Line that fed the Flame,
> How he purloin'd from the immortal dead,
> And in his Thefts converted Gold to Lead. (Canto II, lines 71–4)

The poem's allegory, then, turns Pope into a victim of the same offence that he has perpetrated against others, and when later on the poet impotently calls for his works to be restored to him ('Restore my Arms, restore my plunder'd Lays' (II. 186)), he is made to parody Belinda's indignation at the loss of her ringlet: '*Restore the Lock!*'[17]

Another early work to fall victim to accusations of plagiarism was the Scriblerian collaboration *Three Hours After Marriage*. Here the obliquities of ownership, inevitable to a collaborative project, were especially congenial for those wanting to cry plagiarism. Harris's *Treatise upon the Modes* alleges that Pope had originally tried to claim the entire work as his own before belatedly conceding some recognition to Gay: the poet was prevailed on 'to own the Right of the true Author, after some Contest between his Thirst of Fame, and his Duty to his Neighbour'.[18] The same general claim of Pope's reliance on Gay occurs in 'An Epistle to the Egregious Mr. Pope': 'The Grain of *Wit* was *Gay's*, the Mass of *Scandal* thine'.[19] That the work was also substantially based on a French source, Molière's *The Imaginary Cuckold*, seems to lie behind Harris's teasing reference to 'a genteel Poet, who translated a Play from the *French* to debate, whether he might not call it his own' (p. ii); and the use of Molière among other sources is the basis of a blunt accusation of plagiarism against the play in a pamphlet of 1717, *A Complete Key to the New Farce*.[20]

Pope must have been needled by accusations such as these, but was also aware that they were part and parcel of a satiric rhetoric that had little claim to objectivity. What might have been a greater cause for concern were the aspersions made against his use of classical sources. Probably the most famous of all plagiarism jibes against Pope is that made by Lady Mary Wortley Montagu to Joseph Spence in early 1741: 'I admired Mr. Pope's *Essay on Criticism* at first very much, because I had not then read any of the ancient critics and did not know that it was all stolen.'[21] Pope and Lady Mary had, of course, once been close friends, and though Lady Mary claims that Pope's plagiarism had remained invisible to her before she had read the appropriate sources, a more likely scenario is that she had no cause to cast such a slur until the two had irretrievably fallen out. Yet allegations of this kind, that Pope had capitalized a little too much on the classical sources he regularly used, were ones that were to cast a pall over his poetry, both in his own lifetime and afterwards.

Pope's most substantial literary undertakings, and certainly his biggest money-spinners, were the Homeric translations, and it was inevitable that these should also fall victim to allegations of plagiarism. Edward Ward, for example, after describing Pope as being like a hoyden, rigged up in borrowed fashions, being forced to reassume her own, more humble, attire, warns the poet that even his *Homer* will succumb to the same sort of exposure as the rest of his oeuvre:

> Take care your epick Muse, so bold of late,
> Falls not beneath as scandalous a fate. (lines 137–8)

Similarly, when Cooke accuses Pope of having 'purloin'd from the immortal dead' (II. 73), it is likely that he has the Homeric translations chiefly in view. Of course, the notion that Pope in translating Homer was in some way stealing from him was added to by the suspicion that Pope had also stolen from the efforts of his collaborators, William Broome and Elijah Fenton, to whom much of the translation of the *Odyssey* had been entrusted. Leonard Welsted imagines Pope withdrawing to his seat at Twickenham, this having been funded by the efforts of 'half-paid drudging Broome':

> There to stale, stol'n, stum crambo bid adieu,
> And sneer the fops that thought thy crambo new.[22]

The full resonance of the phrasing here is hard to reconstruct. 'Stum' could refer to flat wine reinvigorated by unfermented grape juice, a pertinent image, Pope's detractors might have thought, of the relation between Pope's own verse and that of his collaborators. 'Stum crambo' however recalls the game 'dumb crambo' in which one team of players has to guess a word on the basis of knowing what it rhymes with. Understood as an anti-Pope jibe, it might mean that in the *Odyssey* and perhaps elsewhere, Pope's collaborators tagged his verses for him.

Shortly after the appearance of Pope's *Odyssey*, two essays appeared in *Applebee's Journal*, both seemingly by Daniel Defoe, debating whether

Pope's translation, in particular its use of contracted labour, could fairly be branded as plagiaristic. The first one begins by drawing attention to the 'Clamour' that accompanied the work's appearance:

> Sir, I suppose, among the rest of your Friends, you have not been ignorant of the Clamour which has been made upon a certain Author, for publishing his Translation, or Version, of your old Friend *Homer*, under his own Name, when it seems he has not been, nay, some have had the hardiness to say, *could not have been*, the real Operator.

The essayist declares himself unable to 'come into all the Resentments of the learned World upon that Subject' and sets out two arguments in defence of Pope's entitlement to lower from sight the extent of his work's indebtedness. The first is that books should not be seen as different from all other manufactures, which are invariably sold under the name of a proprietor, not those of the actual artisans who have produced them. The second is that even if Pope were found guilty of exploiting his collaborators, so might Homer himself have been 'guilty of the same *Plagiarism*', for who can say that Homer did not likewise have his silent helpers and underlings?[23]

The essay argues that Pope should be absolved from any blame, but it does so by reducing literature to the conventions of manufacture and by happily conceding that some duplicity of procedure might be endemic even to the greatest creative talents. A week later, Defoe contributed a rejoinder to his own original essay, once more on Pope's side of the case, but this time even more pointedly reconciled to the inevitability of plagiarism:

> Sir, I wonder much your Friend who wrote you a Letter, published in your last Journal, should make such a serious piece of Work of a little Plagiarism, and one Author borrowing the Labours and Fame of another, as if Mr. *Pope* had been the first of that kind, or the World had never been imposed upon before; whereas I make no difficulty of telling you there are abundant Instances of the like or worse Doings than that; and in Books celebrated for their Wit, Learning and Usefulness.

Defoe then cites instances of plagiarism by a small number of historical figures and one contemporary poet, Sir Richard Blackmore, and draws attention to the practice of clergymen stealing their sermons, thus equipping themselves with 'the borrowed Labours of their Ancestors'.[24] For Defoe, plagiarism is an offence that stabs not so much against writers as against readers. Being taken in by a plagiarized work is like being cuckolded by a book, and what a reader needs to acquire is the philosophy of the wise cuckold: namely, that of putting his horns away rather than brandishing them for the derision of the public. If a reader comes to feel misled by the authorial name supplied on the title-page, he should be the more vigilant on future occasions.

IV

Defoe's defence of Pope is a jokily equivocal one, and not one for which the poet would have been especially thankful, for Pope is not found innocent of plagiarism; rather, he is found guilty of it, but plagiarism itself is exempted from blame. Defoe's observations here are of some general interest, but what matters in the current context is the narrower testimony they offer to the chorus of disapproval that greeted the *Odyssey*. Attacks of this kind must have taken some toll on Pope, yet precisely because he was so sensitive to *any* attacks made on his writings and character, there exists limited evidence of his specific touchiness about the plagiarism accusation. In fact, the strongest evidence of Pope having thought such allegations intrinsically hurtful derives from his preparedness, from the late 1720s onwards, to deploy them as part of his own satiric register as ammunition against his enemies.

One episode that relates to this generalization, though whose interest is not restricted to it, is Pope's quarrel with James Moore-Smythe over a set of verses that, in the course of 12 months, appeared in works authored by each of them. What follows are the lines as they appear in Moore-Smythe's play *The Rival Modes* (1727) and in the relevant version of Pope's verses to Martha Blount 'Sent on Her Birth-Day' (1728):

> 'Tis thus that Vanity Coquettes rewards,
> A Youth of Frolick, an Old Age of Cards;
> Fair to no purpose, Artful to no end,
> Young without Lovers, Old without a Friend.
> A Fool their Aim, their Prize some worn-out Sot;
> Alive ridiculous, when dead, forgot.
> *The Rival Modes*

> Not as the World its pretty Slaves rewards,
> A Youth of Frolicks, an Old-Age of Cards;

> Fair to no Purpose, artful to no End,
> Young without Lovers, old without a Friend;
> A Fop their Passion, but their Prize a Sot;
> Alive, ridiculous; and dead, forgot.
> 'Sent on Her Birth-Day'[25]

As Norman Ault has pointed out, the lines as they appear in the verses to Martha have been interpolated into a work that had previously been published without them; they are also ones that Pope was to auto-plagiarize when he inserted them into his *Epistle to a Lady* (1735).

The uncanniness of a number of lines originally published under Moore-Smythe's name reappearing in a poem by Pope received comment in *The Daily Journal* (18 March 1728), in which a pseudonymous letter accuses Pope of plagiarism. The facts of the case, however, were not as they might easily have seemed. The course of events, as generally understood by Pope scholars, is that Pope authored the six lines but at some point Moore-Smythe had been able to see them in an unpublished manuscript. He asked Pope if he could incorporate them into a work of his own, and Pope appears initially to have consented, only to have withdrawn this consent a month before the play was released. At this point, Moore-Smythe seems to have decided that Pope's lines were of the nature of a gift rather than a loan, and declined to give them up. Norman Ault, who has discussed the episode in a manner that is sympathetic to both parties, suggests that Pope had probably got over his pique at Moore-Smythe's intransigence when he reused the lines in his birthday poem to Martha Blount, though a less charitable hypothesis would be that he republished them simply to flush out the inevitable plagiarism allegation against himself that he could then deflect on to Moore-Smythe.[26]

Whatever the case, Moore-Smythe was to find himself pilloried over the episode in the vicious footnotes of the 1729 *Dunciad*, where he comes into the poem under the guise of 'a Plagiary'. A long note observes that 'our author' felt 'obliged to represent this gentleman as a Plagiary, or to pass for one himself', and he compares Moore-Smythe's case to that of a thief who, caught in the act of taking a handkerchief, allows the rightful owner to repossess it, only then to cry out 'See Gentlemen! what a Thief we have among us! look, he is stealing my handkerchief'.[27]

In the 1720s, Pope increasingly identifies plagiarism as disorder generic among bad writers, and accordingly the plagiarism accusation becomes in his writing a staple form of satiric incrimination. In his *Peri Bathous*

(1727), for example, he identifies a particular species of hapless poets as 'parrots':

> The *Parrots* are they that repeat *another's* words, in such a hoarse odd voice, as makes them seem their *own*. W.B. W.S. C.C. The Reverend D.D.[28]

The initials are fairly cryptic: W.B. is probably Pope's collaborator on the *Odyssey*, William Broome, and D.D. most likely refers to the Rev. Dean of Armagh, Richard Daniel. The initials W.S., however, constitute a revision of an earlier set, W.H., which survived through various reprintings right up until the 1742 text, from which I quote. One possible candidate for the revised initials is William Shippen, and while this attribution is discounted by the work's most recent editor, Rosemary Cowler, it might be worth noting that Shippen had publicly disparaged Pope's mentor, Garth.[29] The penultimate initials, of course, are not at all cryptic, referring unmistakably to the derided Colley Cibber, to whom I will return in a moment.

It is in the *Epistle to Arbuthnot* that Pope next resorts to the plagiarism allegation as a way of tarnishing the reputation of an opponent. The poet in question is Ambrose Philips and the charge relates to a spat between the poets, the events of which are well-known to Popeans, and which by now went back a quarter of a century. In 1709, Jacob Tonson had published a volume of *Poetical Miscellanies* which included pastoral poems by both Pope and Philips. Pope's were influenced by the French critics Rapin and Fontenelle, his conception of the pastoral being that it should produce an 'image of what they call the Golden age'.[30] Stylistically, such poems, he believed, should be marked by simplicity and refinement. This credo was somewhat at odds with that of Philips, whose pastorals, based on the model of Spenser's *Shepheardes Calendar*, were anglicized and packed with quaintly rustic diction. Pope was initially full of praise for Philips's achievement, although noting it was one along different lines from his own, declaring there to be 'no better Eclogs in our Language' than Philips's.[31] However, his attitude soured in April 1713 when a series of essays by Thomas Tickell appeared in the *Guardian*, in which Philips's pastorals were exalted above his own.

Pope may have been riled in particular by Tickell's association of his own kind of pastoral, based on classical models, with actual plagiarism:

> I must in the first place observe, that our Countrymen have so good an Opinion of the Ancients, and think so modestly of themselves, that the generality of Pastoral Writers have either stoln all from

the *Greeks* and *Romans*, or so servilely imitated their Manners and Customs, as makes them very ridiculous.[32]

Pope hit back at both Tickell and Philips by contributing an anonymous *Guardian* essay of his own, in which he heaped ironic praise on Philips's method. As part of this irony, he deprecates his own pastorals as achieving only a desultory copying from the ancients, and instead champions Philips as having taken this sort of plagiarism to a new level. Philips's 'whole third Pastoral is an Instance how well he hath studied the fifth of *Virgil* ... as his Contention of *Colin Clout* and the *Nightingale* shows with what Exactness he hath imitated *Strada*'.[33]

As in other controversies, Pope, while not being wont to pass up the chance for instant retaliation, understood that revenge is best served cold. Accordingly, in payment of the final instalment of his acrimony over the Philips affair, he inserted the following lines into the *Epistle to Arbuthnot* (1735):

The Bard whom pilfer'd Pastorals renown,
Who turns a *Persian* Tale for half a crown,
Just writes to make his barrenness appear,
And strains from hard-boned brains eight lines a-year:
He, who still wanting tho' he lives on theft,
Steals much, spends little, yet has nothing left. (lines 179–84)[34]

The smear against Philips's 'pilfer'd Pastorals' repeats the accusation of derivativeness originally advanced in *Guardian* 40 and, combined with a jibe at Philips's slow rate of composition, produces an image of a poet who 'Steals much, spends little, yet has nothing left'. The feud with Philips is a good example of how plagiarism allegations often figure in the eighteenth century: one accusation simply fuelling a retaliatory accusation inside a closed system of acrimony. Of course, there remains the question of whether either Philips or Pope might be thought culpable of plagiarism by the standards of our own day or, indeed, by the dispassionately applied standards of their own. However, the question of their actual innocence or guilt is importantly different from the question of why the plagiarism accusation comes to be invoked against them.

The metaphor applied to Philips is that of a self-defeating acquisitiveness: he steals and hoards and yet still ends up creatively indigent. In his revised *Dunciad* of 1742, Pope was to apply a very different metaphor to another supposed plagiarist, Colley Cibber. Cibber is depicted, in a scenario originally created for Lewis Theobald, as the

antihero of the first version of the *Dunciad*, sitting in a book-lined
study:

> Next o'er his Books his eyes begin to roll,
> In pleasing memory of all he stole,
> How here he sipp'd, how here he plunder'd snug
> And suck'd all o'er, like an Industrious Bug.
> Here lay poor Fletcher's half-eat scenes, and here
> The Frippery of crucify'd Moliere. (I. 127–32)[35]

Unlike Pope's attack on Philips, the allegations concerning Cibber's plagiarism were in general circulation, and Pope may have come across the
stinging attack on Cibber's compositional methods, especially his use of
Molière, in John Dennis's *Decay and Defects of Dramatick Poetry* (1725):

> For as The wretch who turns Highway man, Footpad or House Breaker,
> bids Defiance at once to all the Laws both of God and His Countrey,
> and supports Himself by plundering others of what They have gott
> by their Honest Industry: soe this outlaw of Parnassus who treats
> with this contempt all the Laws of Apollo, lives by plundering His
> Faithfull subjects of the Riches They have acquird by their Labours
> in their Lawfull callings.[36]

Yet Dennis's remarks, though wounding in their formulation, hardly
amounted to an exposure, for Cibber seems to have been perfectly open
about his methods. Indeed, in his *Apology*, he writes unguardedly about
his way of adapting earlier plays 'whenever I took upon me to make
some dormant play of an old author ... fitter for the stage, it was ... as a
good housewife will mend old linnen': indeed, Pope's reference in the
final line quoted above to the 'Frippery' (*OED* 1 'Old clothes; cast-off
garments. *Obs.*') may be a recollection of Cibber's actual remark.[37] Yet
the metaphor that sticks in the reader's mind is less that of the mend-
ing of garments than of insectival ingestion. Cibber the plagiarist is
like a bug crawling over the work of other playwrights, liquefying
and slurping up textual material, and leaving behind a saliva-trail of
'half-eat scenes'.

V

Given his controversial career as a satirist, Pope was not likely to have
escaped the plagiarism allegation, or indeed to have got by without

using it himself. Ultimately, you feel that he is as much the master as the victim of this line of accusation, just as he had skilfully helped himself to the last word in his contretemps with James Moore-Smythe. Yet, ironically for a writer so adept at wounding the posterities of others, the plagiarism issue was to do more harm to Pope's posthumous 'fame' than he would have felt comfortable in envisaging, as alongside the attack on Pope's supposed plagiarism by outright enemies, a more considered critical reflection emerges in the decades following his death, which categorizes Pope's literary technique on the basis of its proximity to plagiarism.

We can associate this development with John Dennis, not admittedly a fountain of dispassionate commentary on Pope's writings, but even so a critic who is perhaps the first to understand the centrality of imitation to Pope's entire oeuvre: 'for fifteen Years together this Ludicrous Animal has been a constant *Imitator*'. For Dennis, Pope is a little chattering jackanape, mouthing the words of others and producing only 'awkward servile Imitations', the word 'servile' here being a code-word for plagiarism.[38] This accusation flowed in the same current as the malodorous jibe that Pope, a disabled and stooped figure, was himself a work of imitation, that is, a poor approximation to, or 'counterfeit' of, a human being. Dennis, of course, puts the case against Pope as nastily as anyone could, yet worse for him was the fact that this particular accusation broadened into a general regret, felt by critics with no unquenchable personal animosity towards Pope, that he had so much limited himself to the imitative arts. In the year of Pope's death (1744), for example, Samuel Richardson can be found asking: 'Must all be personal Satire, or Imitations of others Temples of Fame, Alexander's Feasts, Cooper's Hills, Mac Flecknoe's?'[39]

Yet it is not until 1753, when Joseph Warton contributes an essay on literary borrowing to *The Adventurer* (no. 63), that the plagiarism issue becomes central to the evaluation of Pope's literary achievement. Warton's essay, it should be said, is quite unflustered by the spectre of literary borrowing or by similarities between works: he argues that, given the invariability of things in the world, the works of authors, dedicated as they are to imitating reality, 'must needs be stamped with a close resemblance'. It would be hard for them to appear as anything other than 'uniform and alike'. Yet, while being relaxed about such similarities, he still manages to develop his argument in a way that was to prove very prejudicial to Pope's reputation. Warton had available to him the established distinction between imitation and plagiarism, in which the latter was considered blameworthy and the former not so, yet this did not provide the principal demarcation upon which he proceeds. Instead, he differentiates between resemblances between books that come about because of the uniform nature of things in the world and those that are caused by specific authorial design, as a result of 'imitation and plagiarism'. While it would be wrong to suggest that Warton sees no difference between imitation and plagiarism, his particular invocation of the two terms is such as to effect a rather too casual elision. When he subsequently identifies Pope as a borrower by design, he assigns him to a category of authors which includes, though is not exclusively comprised of, plagiarists.[40]

Warton is far from indicting Pope as a plagiarist, but the effect of his argument's maladroitness is to end up associating Pope's literary technique with that of plagiarism. It is clear that Warton was quick to realize the unwittingly devastating nature of his comments, and when he reworked the *Adventurer* essay in his *Essay on the Genius and Writings of Pope* (1756), he tried to cover his tracks. Once more, he sets before the reader some 'remarkable coincidences of POPE'S thought and expressions, with those of other writers', these including Jonson and Boileau. Yet, having anthologized these borrowings, Warton, in a passage much extended from the original essay, discourages the reader from enlisting them as evidence of outright plagiarism:

> I should be sensibly touched at the injurious imputation of so ungenerous, and, indeed, impotent a design, as that of attempting to diminish or sully the reputation of so valuable a writer as POPE, by the most distant hint, or accusation of his being a plagiary; a writer to whom the English poesy, and the English language, is everlastingly indebted. But we may say of his imitations, what his poetical father, Dryden, said of another, who deserved not such a panegyric so justly as our author: 'HE INVADES AUTHORS LIKE A MONARCH; AND WHAT WOULD BE THEFT IN OTHER POETS, IS ONLY VICTORY IN HIM.'[41]

Warton then goes on to draw out the particular way that Dryden's remark ought to be applied to Pope: namely that Pope's borrowings can be exonerated because they improve so much on their originals. Given the contortions which Warton gets into in order to dissociate himself from the plagiarism slur, it is a strange paradox that the *Essay* was actually received as a malignant, though largely convincing exposure of Pope's plagiaristic tendencies. One problem was that Warton had again been incautious, in that his comparison of Pope's imitative practice with that of Jonson could only send a confusing signal. In the same vicinity as Dryden describes Jonson as invading authors 'like a monarch', he defines his 'victory' as one of criminal audacity: 'he has done his robberies so openly that one may see he fears not to be taxed by any law'.[42] Elsewhere, he remarks tersely that Jonson was not only 'a professed imitator of Horace, but a learned plagiary of all the others', these others including Horace, Lucan, Petronius, Seneca and Juvenal.[43] The problem for Warton is that he tries to exculpate Pope from the charge of plagiarism on the grounds that he is merely doing what Dryden claimed Jonson had done: unfortunately, the particular thing that Jonson had done is labelled by Dryden as plagiarism.

To appreciate the baleful influence of Warton's book on Pope's reputation, it is necessary to see the larger picture. Warton thinks highly of Pope as a practitioner of a certain kind of poetry, but he retains a low opinion of the value of this kind of work. Pope's poetry (according to Warton) belongs to the '*didactic, moral,* and *satyric* kind', which expresses '*good sense* and *judgment*' rather than '*fancy* and *invention*'.[44] It is the *nature* of his achievement, rather than its quality, that disqualifies him from standing, in the great pantheon of poets, on the same level as Spenser, Shakespeare and Milton. This view that Pope's work was a poetry of creative impairment and that what defined his literary technique was its contiguity to plagiarism becomes for a while an orthodoxy in the reception of his work. This is how Pope is viewed, for example, in Edward Young's *Conjectures on Original Composition* (1759), which tends to elide imitation and plagiarism and which identifies Pope as the standard-bearer for a school of uniformity. Similarly, Edward Capell classifies Pope amongst those writers who are 'indisputably Copiers, the Imitators and small Poets' and who can be deprecated as 'plunderers of Parnassus'.[45] While John Pinkerton is prepared to flatter Pope's 'Imitations of Horace' as 'original and happy', he still does so in the context of a governing assumption that the value of all imitative writing (such as that largely practised by Pope) is 'very minute'.[46]

Warton's comments were received by Pope's admirers as an act of vandalism, as a desecration of the poet's memory. One of the first to challenge them was W.H. Dilworth, in his *Life of Alexander Pope* (1759), who attacked the sneerers, chief amongst them being Warton, 'who have maliciously endeavoured to prove, that Mr. Pope had no invention, fancy or imagination, and that all his merit consisted in being a correct plagiarist'.[47] The neologism 'correct plagiarist' strikes at the heart of the matter. Warton had not proposed Pope to have been guilty of a *moral* offence, and in this sense the poet's conduct can be seen as upright and 'correct'. What Pope is guilty of is rather an *aesthetic* failing, a creative debilitation, and it is this supposed weakness which Warton, to some degree inadvertently, associates with the word 'plagiarism'.

Dilworth's sense of scandal was shared by others: indeed, the most famous put-down of Warton, and the most robust defence of Pope against Warton's school of criticism, is by Johnson, in his 'Life of Pope'. For Johnson, Warton's mistake was to have become a hostage to his own avidity for drawing up categories. Too trusting of his own defini-tions, he is ultimately seduced into conclusions that, when subjected to independent reflection, are revealed as absurd. To ask 'Whether Pope was a poet' is for Johnson an idle speculation, for 'If Pope be not a poet, where is poetry to be found?'. All such constricted definitions can only ever serve to show 'the narrowness of the definer'.[48]

After Pope's death, the debates concerning his supposed plagiarism are different from those kindled during his lifetime. For one thing, they are no longer collaborative with an essentially satiric impulse, no longer being willed by spite and *parti pris*. Another difference, though, is that the plagiarism case against Pope now gets made under the auspices of aesthetics rather than of ethics: what is at stake is not whether Pope pilfered culpably from particular works, but whether the very nature of his artistic achievement is compromised by a radical failure of originality. We can see these issues surfacing in the powerful defence of Pope made by Percival Stockdale. Stockdale takes up Pope's case in *An Inquiry into the Nature, and Genuine Laws of Poetry; including a particular Defence of the Writings and Genius of Pope* (1778), and again in the discussion of the poet, much of it reworked from the earlier book, in his *Lectures* (1807). Stockdale sets out from the premise that 'no great poet has been so severely accused of plagiarism as Pope', a situation that has arisen from a widespread perception that his verse lacks invention, imagination and originality. For all that such accusations could be made just as vocifer-ously against Shakespeare, Milton and Dryden, the ears of the reading public, so Stockdale declares, have been 'stunned with the plagiarisms of Pope'.[49]

Because the issue of Pope's plagiarism is by now received as an aesthetic one, Stockdale can afford a defence that would not have been available to him had the case against Pope been expressed in moral terms. He does not challenge the assertion that Pope takes material from other authors; rather, he accepts it but finds a way of condoning it, as Pope's practice is one of rejuvenating and enhancing the words of others. For Stockdale, the 'true' plagiarist is an author devoid of creativity, bent upon a furtive 'transcription' and 'piracy' of other authors' words.[50] Pope's technique, on the other hand, is one in which the works of earlier authors are smoothly harmonized with his own, and his borrowings are magnanimously open, not skulking, nor are they beset by an anxiety 'that the obligations should be concealed'.[51]

Pope's complex relation to the plagiarism allegation reflects his turbulent working life as a satirist: no author whose career was as controversial and divisive as his could have hoped to have avoided the plagiarism accusation, for in the early eighteenth century such accusations were traded as a currency of literary enmity. Yet his vulnerability to such allegations also speaks of a shift in literary attitudes and aesthetic values during the eighteenth century. At the beginning of the century, the moral demarcation between imitation and plagiarism seemed an obvious one, but over the course of several decades it became smudged and problematic. It was Pope's misfortune to become the most eminent victim of this blurring of categories, a malaise from which his reputation was to be slow to recover. His case remains one of the most illuminating individual cases in relation to the history of literary plagiarism, and allegations of it, in the early modern era.

6
Johnson and the Lauder Affair

I

In spite of being the author of two distinguished Juvenalian Imitation poems, Johnson seems to have taken a dim view of imitation in its general sense of literary borrowing. While conceding that overlap between the works of different authors was perhaps inevitable, his attitude is for the most part disdainful towards writers who fail to get beyond mere dependence on others; indeed, this point of view lies behind his famous intolerance of pastoral poetry, a genre that he believed to be uniquely founded on mechanical duplication.[1] He was wont to discount the prospect of any author of a derivative bent, such as Gray, ever achieving greatness, believing that 'to copy is less than to invent' and that the highest qualification of a genius must always remain 'original invention'.[2] Such general principles are borne out with a high degree of consistency in Johnson's pronouncements on individual writers, as in the critical summations at the end of each of his 'Lives', which nearly always raise questions of derivativeness and originality. His 'Life of Swift', for example, rounds off with the glowing recommendation that 'perhaps no writer can easily be found that has borrowed so little, or that in all his excellences and all his defects has so well maintained his claim to be considered as original', while that of 'Young' concludes with the compliment that the author's 'versification is his own, neither his blank nor his rhyming lines have any resemblance to those of former writers'.[3] Even the bedraggled Savage earns the absolution that his works, more than those of many more celebrated authors, 'have an original air, which has no resemblance of any foregoing work'.[4]

When his eye alights on particular examples of borrowing, Johnson's comments are invariably hostile or at least unappreciative. One author given a particularly disparaging dressing down for crimes of this sort is Richard Broome, of whom 'it cannot be said', so Johnson avers, 'that he was a great poet'. Johnson's reprimand runs as follows:

> His imitations are so apparent, that it is part of his reader's employ-ment to recall the verses of some former poet. Sometimes he copies the most popular writers, for he seems scarcely to endeavour at con-cealment; and sometimes he picks up fragments in obscure corners.[5]

Having cited an inoffensive example of Broome's borrowing from another poet, Johnson concludes that 'To detect his imitations were tedious and useless'. Of course, good poets borrow better than bad ones, but the terms of Johnson's dismissal of Broome make one wonder whether he had *any* capacity to be gratified by borrowing as a poetic technique. Poor Broome certainly gets the worst of it both ways. His imitations are sometimes too glaring ('so apparent'), and yet on other occasions, when they are hidden or veiled, the process of their detection is 'tedious and useless'. No readerly pleasure seems to be permitted to borrowings either conspicuous or obscure. The task that all borrowings impose on the reader of referring backwards and forwards between a present text and an original source is something that Johnson views only as an 'employment', a laborious chore.

Johnson's distaste for Broome's technique reflects his doughty commit-ment to the principle of artistic independence as well as his suspicions concerning one particular category of borrowing: literary allusion. His admonitions in this area were not reserved alone for poets but also touch on critics, for he felt that it was critics who were largely responsible for fuelling the cult of allusion by devoting their energies to spotting or inventing bogus allusions, ones 'too remote to be discovered by the rest of mankind'. Such sleuthing critics pore over texts, trying to disinter 'in every passage some secret meaning, some remote allusion, some artful allegory, or some occult imitation which no other reader ever suspected'.[6] What such a critical method generates are microscopic revelations of the non-existent.

This chapter will address a conundrum concerning Johnson's critical views. Given that he seems to have been so inhospitable towards liter-ary borrowing, it might be expected that he would take an especially dim view of plagiarism, the type of borrowing that is normally seen as the least defensible. Yet Johnson's attitude towards plagiarism is far from being straightforwardly censorious. To state this is partly to sug-gest that he sometimes speaks of plagiarism in ways that seem more conciliatory than we might expect. In *Adventurer* 95, for example, he identifies plagiarism not (it might be noted) as it occupies a place in the entire spectrum of crimes, but simply as it figures in the slim ledger of purely literary offences, as 'one of the most reproachful, though, perhaps, not the most atrocious'.[7] But what exclusively literary act could be deemed more atrocious?[8] We cannot, however, extract Johnson's views about plagiarism merely from how he seems to understand the term, for also of importance are the circumstances in which he chooses to invoke that meaning. It is possible to entertain a very negative view of plagiarism and yet to be all too willing to find practical extenuations when confronted with seeming instances of it. As we will see, Johnson may have been appalled (albeit not horrified) by plagiarism, but he is always concerned not to be incautious in bringing the charge, and is also wary that the greater offence might lie not in plagiarism itself, but in the erroneous and perhaps malignant accusation of it. The position he adopts on the subject is even by Johnson's standards especially pained and painstaking. Moreover, as I will argue in the remainder of this chapter, it is shaped by Johnson's unlucky involvement in the notorious controversy surrounding William Lauder.

II

In January 1747 there appeared in the *Gentleman's Magazine* the first of a series of essays by a contributor signing himself W.L. that claimed to expose the widespread borrowing from neo-Latin authors in Milton's celebrated poem *Paradise Lost*. The aim of the series purported to be modest and inoffensive: W.L. 'adventured to publish' his 'conjecture' that Milton had 'consulted' several modern Latin authors in the process of composing his 'glorious' poem. The author made it plain that it was in no way his intention 'to derogate from the glory or merit of that noble poet': rather, as W.L. equivocally put it, even if it emerged that the greater part of the poem had been borrowed, this should not detract from Milton's entitlement to the 'highest praise'.[9] The first article, and subsequent ones, cited extracts from some of the authors by whom Milton, so it was claimed, had been influenced; in addition, the editors of the *Gentleman's Magazine* encouraged readers to write in with their own English translations of those passages so that it could be gauged publicly how closely they stood to actual lines in *Paradise Lost*.[10]

As the series rolled out, however, the true malignancy of the enterprise became more apparent. The first two contributions had both been entitled levelly 'An Essay on Milton's Imitations of the Moderns', but the second appeared under a running head that registered a sharper tone: 'Milton accused of imitating the Moderns'. By April the fact that Milton was in effect being put on trial was naked in the very title of the piece: 'Further Charge against Milton'. By July of the same year, it had begun to dawn on readers of the magazine's columns that some mischief was afoot, and the first major objection appeared, in a letter initialled R.R. (Richard Richardson), which cast doubt on Milton's supposed borrowings from Masenius.[11] This challenge, however, was met defiantly in the following issue, in which the anonymous author for the first time felt embold-ened to sign with his full name: William Lauder. That he should have done so might suggest a growing confidence if not in the integrity of his case, then in the invulnerability of his position.

Lauder, however, had good cause to be apprehensive, for his whole case against Milton was based on a fiction. While the immediate idea for the essay series derived from an earlier and entirely reputable work that had come out in 1741, *An Essay upon Milton's Imitations of the Ancients in his Paradise Lost*, Lauder's own method of procedure departed from this precursor in some notable respects. Having come upon a Latin translation of *Paradise Lost* by the classical scholar William Hog, Lauder hatched a plot to besmirch Milton by interpolating lines from Hog's translation into a number of earlier Latin works by the likes of Masenius, Grotius, Staphorstius and others, and then accusing Milton of having copied them. The whole project had a cunning circularity about it: Milton's own poem was to provide the lines which, in trans-lated form, he was to be accused of having stolen.

Why Lauder should have launched this campaign of defamation against Milton is not entirely clear and is rendered less so by the fact that his own explanation of his conduct exists in several versions.[12] One of these versions relates to an incident that at first sight seems almost trifling. At the beginning of the 1740s, Lauder had been involved in a controversy concerning the literary merit of the Latin poet Arthur Johnston, whose poems he had edited and championed. Lauder sought to enlist on his side of the argument the eminent voice of Alexander Pope, and he sent for Pope's consultation a copy of his edi-tion of Johnston's work. To this correspondence, Pope, rather shabbily, declined to react, other than in the satiric manner of including in his *Dunciad* of 1742 a couplet in which he compared Johnston unfavour-ably with Milton. Lauder was annoyed with Pope, and some of this annoyance may have been displaced onto Milton, but the incident hardly seems commensurate with the fervour with which he committed himself to his campaign.[13]

What perhaps alone explains Lauder's behaviour is his allegiance to the Jacobite cause. In 1742, he secured the position of Latin master at the Grammar School in Dundee, a post that he had obtained seemingly only after 'prolonged and importunate efforts'. In September 1745, a detachment of Jacobite supporters entered Dundee to rally support, and on 31 October Lauder vacated his post, this being the very day that Charles Edward Stuart left Edinburgh to begin his march into England. The likelihood is that Lauder relinquished his position in order to involve himself in the 'Forty-Five', which fits comfortably with his assumed arrival in London in early 1746 and the beginning of his journalistic campaign against Milton at the beginning of 1747.[14] Moreover, the earliest intimations of Lauder's campaign appear in his correspondence with the classical scholar Thomas Ruddiman that has been preserved in a collection of Jacobite materials.

Lauder clearly felt that a revelation whose effect would be to tarnish the reputation of Milton, the most eminent apologist for the regicide, would count as a worthwhile contribution to the Jacobite cause. It was with this conviction that in 1745 he disclosed his discovery of Milton's 'plagiarism', a condemnatory word that had clearly lodged in Lauder's mind from the outset, to Ruddiman, laying down that 'Milton has taken not only the Plan, or Scheme or Ground-work' of *Paradise Lost* but also 'four or five thousand Lines' from neo-Latin originals without 'acknowledging the same fairly & candidly'. Such a circumstance justified, in Lauder's view, the application to Milton of the character 'of one of the most noted Plagiaries ... that ever wrote'.[15]

Not only did Lauder send his findings to Ruddiman, in pursuit of a scholarly endorsement of them, but he also asked Ruddiman to pass a copy of them to John Murray of Broughton, the Secretary to the Prince, on the inflated assumption that they would be seen as having material relevance to the Jacobite uprising or at least to Jacobite propaganda. However, even at this stage, Lauder's one-eyed zealotry was beginning to unsettle those who might have been his natural allies. Ruddiman's response was lengthy and considered, but in effect little more than a snub. As to the actual charge that Milton had plagiarized from Ramsay and Masenius, Ruddiman dismissed it so summarily as to retort that Lauder had hardly demonstrated that Milton 'has so much as seen or read their Works'. As tactfully as he could, he suggested that Lauder had allowed himself to be distracted by his own bigotry and, as a result of personal hostility, had failed to maintain a spirit of 'Truth and Justice' in approaching Milton's poetry. In addition, he scorned Lauder's conviction that such charges against Milton (even if well-founded) had any particular relevance to the Jacobite campaign.[16]

The letter to Ruddiman provides the clearest evidence of the motivation behind Lauder's campaign against Milton. The wonder is that, given its shameless nature, the imposture remained undetected for so long. That it should have done so, in fact, owes much to the editorial policy of the *Gentleman's Magazine*, which seems to have suppressed or bowdlerized readers' contributions which threatened to bring Lauder's fraudulence into the open. In January 1749, for example, Richard Richardson, who had tried to challenge Lauder's case as early as 1747, wrote to the magazine, pointing out that the lines Milton had supposedly lifted from Masenius and Staphorstius were in fact entirely absent from available printed editions of their work and, moreover, by an uncanny coincidence were traceable to Hog's Latin verse rendering of *Paradise Lost*. The magazine, however, declined to publish Richardson's offering, presumably on the grounds of the sheer implausibility of Lauder having practised an imposture as brazen as Richardson's findings seemed to indicate.[17]

By 1749, then, the chill wind of public scrutiny was beginning to visit Lauder's dishonest claims. Yet in December 1749, almost three years after he had first put these claims abroad, Lauder still felt sufficiently secure in his deceitful allegations to publish them as a book, *An Essay on Milton's Use and Imitation of the Moderns in his Paradise Lost* (1750), both the Preface and Postscript to which were written in significant part by Samuel Johnson. Like the series of magazine articles, the early part of the work is characterized by a deceptive moderation of argument. The allegation that is initially made is that of Milton 'consulting and copying' his sources, but as the book goes on Lauder inexorably cranks up his machinery of defamation. One part of this escalation is the charge of hypocrisy: Milton, so Lauder gets around to asserting, has not merely acquired in a questionable way the words of Masenius and others, but he has also 'concealed his obligations' and accordingly fallen foul of his own 'high pretensions to truth and integrity'.[18] The highly calculated nature of the deceit is evident, moreover, in the poet's disingenuous claim to originality, to having written 'Things unattempted yet in prose or rhyme'.[19] Yet the reader still has to trawl through to page 159 to hear Lauder actually invoke '*Milton*'s plagiarism' as such, though the word's appearance is anticipated earlier (p. 115) when, using a figure of speech which had an understood historical association with the act of plagiarism, Lauder asserts that '*Milton* has plum'd himself' with false feathers drawn from other writers. The argument finally comes to an ebullition on pages 162–3 with a tirade against the nefarious practices that have, and have alone, generated Milton's reputation as the 'BRITISH HOMER'. Lauder prides himself that his own public-spirited offices have now 'reduced [Milton] to his true standard' and have shown him in his true colours as 'the most unlicensed plagiary that ever wrote'.[20]

The accusations made against Milton, then, are actually various. He has copied the words of earlier authors; these appropriations have been 'unlicensed' (though in what ways theft from dead authors could ever be licensed and whether, were it so licensed, it would then count as plagiaristic is not clarified); he has conducted himself hypocritically in stealing from authors while protesting the originality of his methods; and he has exploited the advantage of plagiarism to secure for himself an unjustified priority in the canon of English poetry, to the detriment of more honest practitioners like Cowley, Waller, Denham, Dryden, Prior and Pope. The list of indictments is long and vociferous.

Just as the list of indictments has now grown into a clamour, so the body of Lauder's bogus evidence has also expanded: the number of neo-Latin texts Milton has supposedly pillaged has now grown to 18. By this stage, however, the day of Lauder's debunking was soon to dawn. Michael Marcuse has identified John Bowle of Oriel College, Oxford, whose letter to the *Gentleman's Magazine* of October 1747 was held up from publication for four months and then only appeared in edited form, as the first scholar to start stripping bare Lauder's falsifications. From this point, Bowle busied himself in Lauder's exposure, compiling a lengthy manuscript and arranging to have advertised in the *General Evening Post* of January 1750 a forthcoming 'Critical Examen' of Lauder's recently published book. However, Bowle soon found himself bogged down in the quagmire of Lauder's deviousness. The books from which Lauder was alleging that Milton had pilfered were sufficiently rare that tracking them down in order to disprove his claims was proving a fruitless task. As Bowle sat back to ponder the dilemma, John Douglas, put in touch with Bowle by their mutual friend Roger Watkins, emerged as the candidate to write up the case against Lauder.[21]

Douglas was no further forward than Bowle in being able to *prove* the fraudulence of Lauder's claims about Masenius and Grotius: copies of their works could not easily be procured in order to offer testimony either way. However, by making much of what little he had, he was still able to compose a devastating critique: this was published in November 1750 under the title *Milton Vindicated from the Charge of Plagiarism Brought against him by Mr. Lauder*. Fundamental to Douglas's counter-assault was his subjection of Lauder to an intellectual pincer movement: first, he argued that the extrapolations drawn from Lauder's evidence were unjustified; and second, and *only* second, that the evidence itself was fraudulent. Douglas had noticed that, even if you accepted the evidence put forward at face value, there still remained something disingenuous about the way in which Lauder drifted from claiming that Milton had 'consulted' earlier authors to suggesting that he had actually imitated them, to then alleging that he had directly plagiarized from them. Douglas made clear that there was no inherent incompatibility between creative genius and a preparedness to borrow material from other writers, that 'a Writer may be an Imitator of others without *Plagiarism*'.[22] For Douglas, even if Milton had done exactly what Lauder claimed he had, this would still not warrant a charge as grievous as 'plagiarism'. To be added to this sternly reasonable case, however, was the near-certainty that Milton had *not* in fact done what Lauder claimed he had. It was by now indubitable that, in some instances at least, Lauder had interpolated lines into his sources; moreover, even where the sources (such as works by Masenius and Grotius) were not available for independent consulta- tion, Lauder's citation from them was so inconsistent as to render it improbable that he was really working from any extant texts.[23] Without being able to *prove* the case, Douglas was able to make a convincing case for the likelihood of the entirety of Lauder's claims having been based on forged evidence.

For a while Lauder tried to brazen matters out and to maintain a public front of denial, but his position was hopeless. Under pressure from his booksellers, who publicly disclaimed all connection with the offending book other than 'as a Masterpiece of Fraud', he admitted his falsehood, and in December 1750 there appeared a *Letter to the Reverend Mr Douglas Occasioned by His Vindication of Milton*, an abject, though dignified, apol- ogy written by Johnson to which Lauder was made to put his name.[24] In this work, as part of his rite of contrition, Lauder made disclosure of a further 18 falsifications on which his defamation of Milton had been based.

It might be thought that Lauder would now have retreated from the ruins of his campaign against Milton and from the rubble of his per- sonal reputation, yet astonishingly he was still unready to put aside his feud with Milton. In a Postscript to his *Letter to Douglas*, a part of the work not overseen by Johnson, he planted the seeds of more mischief. Here Lauder claims that the real reason for his actions was not outright hatred of Milton but a desire to expose the cult of Milton idolatry. His reason for inserting Miltonic lines into earlier neo-Latin works was to see if Milton's admirers would recognize them as such; the exercise had been vindicated by the spectacle of such fanatics, when confronted with actual lines of *Paradise Lost* translated into Latin and assigned to known neo-Latin authors, refusing to perceive in them the least connection with Milton's great original, instead arguing that '*Milton* might have written as he had done, supposing he had never seen these Authors, or they had never existed'.[25]

Having managed to adulterate the apology that Johnson had composed for him, Lauder was not long in returning to his old, brazen ways. It is true that in March 1751 he was still intent on salvaging his reputation by releasing *An Apology Addressed to the Archbishop of Canterbury*, in which he sought to excuse his actions while denying any attempt to 'depreciate the just Reputation of Milton'.[26] However, over the next two years, he returns to a project he had envisaged at the height of his campaign against Milton, an edition of Milton's 'sources', the *Delectus Auctorum Sacrorum Miltono Facem Praelucentium*. Here the old charges against Milton are reinstated and the old chicaneries of scholarly method are given another airing.

In 1754, Lauder brought out a further contribution to a campaign that had now come to seem the public expression of an inner frenzy: this was *King Charles I Vindicated from the Charge of Plagiarism brought against him by Milton, and Milton himself Convicted of Forgery, and a gross Imposition on the Public*. The plan was to dress Milton in the same weeds of ignominy that Lauder had had to wear in the aftermath of his own exposure. Once again he revises and updates earlier explanations of his misdemeanours. It is true that he keeps faith with the claim, set down in the Postscript to the *Letter to Douglas*, that one objective was that of triumphing over Milton's admirers by duping them into denying similarities between *Paradise Lost* in its original English and as translated into Latin. However, Lauder now discloses that he never expected or desired to get away with this falsehood. Instead, he had craved to be exposed, and to have the brand of 'forger' fixed upon him, in order to attract public attention to the general evil of literary forgery, as a preliminary to exposing Milton's guiltiness of exactly this offence. For once, Lauder did not need to invent his charge against Milton; rather, he revived one that had enjoyed some former currency and had been endorsed within recent memory in Thomas Birch's edition of Milton's prose in 1738. The charge was that Milton had arranged for the *Eikon Basilike* of Charles I to be printed with a prayer taken from Sidney's *Arcadia* mischievously interpolated into it, which had then become the basis of a plagiarism accusation against the King. The fact that more recent scholarship available to Lauder had dismissed the story proved to be of no concern to him.

The Lauder story is characterized by duplicity and malignancy, but also by a strong mental restlessness and addiction. It starts out from a series of magazine articles in which the rhetoric of inculpation is gradually cranked up; one piece of bogus evidence supplements another until in 1753, in sublime disregard to the exorbitance of the allegation, Lauder can claim that Milton has pilfered from fully 97 different authors; and then when circumstances extort from him a reluctant confession, this proves only a preliminary to further reinstatements of the original falsehood. Lauder's duplicity found expression in the silent editing of Milton's neo-Latin sources, but it subsequently passes into a publicly defiant editing of his own original motivations. He begins by forging texts; he ends by forging himself. Even in 1754, the date of a further set of excuses, he is still frenziedly promising the reader even more allegations, this time accompanied with an unimpugnable standard of proof, leading to the utter vanquishment, in an apocalypse of pure scholarly revelation, of the ranks of Milton's idolators:

> As for his Plagiarisms, I intend shortly, God willing, to extract such genuine Proofs from those Authors, who held forth the lighted Torch to *Milton*, I mean, who illustrated the Subject of *Paradise Lost*, long before that Prince of Plagiaries enter'd upon it, as may be deem'd sufficient not only to replace the few Interpolations, (for which I have been so hideously exclaimed against) but even to reinforce the Charge of Plagiarism against the *English* Poet, and fix it upon him by irrefragable Conviction, in the Face of the whole World, and by the Suffrage of all candid and impartial Judges, while Sun and Moon shall endure, to the everlasting Shame and Confusion of the whole idolatrous Rabble of his numerous Partizans, particularly my vain-glorious Adversary, who will reap only the goodly Harvest of Disappointment and Disgrace, where he expected to gather Laurels.[27]

III

One aspect of the Lauder episode that has teased literary historians has been the precise involvement in it of Samuel Johnson and his true feelings towards Lauder's activities. While these matters have been explored by James Clifford in particular, they are worth summarizing here.[28] It seems now that Johnson had withdrawn from participation in the running of the *Gentleman's Magazine* by the time that Lauder's first communication was received by it and accepted for publication.[29] Yet it is not improbable that he heard about Lauder's contribution on the grapevine, and perhaps had an opportunity to see it before its publication: certainly its contents, an excavation of the working methods of a great poet, could only have interested him. Throughout his later *Lives of the Poets*, Johnson shows himself fascinated by the processes through which great works have come into the world, by the hidden techniques of their compilation and by the psychogenesis of authorial genius. In his 'Life of Milton', for example, having remarked on the origins of *Paradise Lost* from Milton's earlier play *Adam Unparadised*, Johnson reflects on the 'delightful entertainment' arising from tracing how 'great works' are 'suddenly advanced by accidental hints'.[30]

That Johnson was not unsympathetic to the general line of Lauder's 'enquiry' can be discerned from the fact that he was prevailed upon to draft some 'Proposals' for another project of Lauder's, an edition by subscription of Grotius's *Adamus Exsul*, a work that had recently gained scholarly interest as one of those that Milton was alleged to have 'consulted'. In the 'Proposals', Johnson sees Lauder's project as an exercise in scholarly magnanimity and as allowing for:

> a retrospection of the progress of this mighty genius [Milton], in the construction of his work, a view of the fabric gradually rising, perhaps from small beginnings, till its foundation rests in the centre, and its turrets sparkle in the skies; to trace back the structure, thro' all its variations, to the simplicity of its first plan, to find what was first projected, whence the scheme was taken, how it was improved, by what assistance it was executed, and from what stores the materials were collected; whether its founder dug them from the quarries of nature, or demolished other buildings to embellish his own.[31]

It is clear that Johnson believed that this impartial unearthing of Milton's sources would assist public appreciation of his genius, in the sense of clarifying the precise working methods through which that genius expressed itself. Exactly when he was awoken from this complacency remains unclear. We do not know, for example, if he was aware of the sceptical correspondence received by the *Gentleman's Magazine*, or took heed of other printed misgivings about Lauder's scholarly probity. What we can say, however, is that even in late 1749 he was sufficiently at ease in his association with Lauder's project as to allow the material written for the earlier 'Proposals' to be incorporated into the Preface to Lauder's *An Essay on Milton's Use and Imitation of the Moderns*, and to write a Postscript, incongruously soliciting financial support for Milton's indigent surviving granddaughter.

Once Lauder's *Essay* had been published, Johnson was in deep. Moreover, it was probably not long before his eyes began to be opened, for we know that early in 1750 he had the opportunity to discuss some of the finer points of the case with Richard Richardson, one of the earliest suspectors of Lauder's fraudulence.[32] When John Douglas's exposure of Lauder appeared late in the same year, Johnson, though he probably anticipated what was coming, must still have been aghast. There was certainly no possibility of slinking away from the issue, for Johnson had been alluded to personally in Douglas's work as, in effect, the principal gull of Lauder's whole imposture:

> 'Tis to be hoped, nay 'tis *expected*, that the elegant and nervous Writer, whose judicious sentiments, and inimitable Stile, point out the Author of Lauder's Preface and Postscript, will no longer allow one to *plume himself with his Feathers* who appears so little to have deserved his Assistance; an Assistance which, I am persuaded, would never have been communicated, had there been the least Suspicion of those Facts, which I have been the Instrument of conveying to the World in these Sheets ...[33]

For Johnson, the most pressing need was to protect his reputation by publicly dissociating himself from Lauder. The first opportunity to do this arose when he was called on to draft an apology for the publishers in the form of 'A New Preface' to be inserted into unsold copies of Lauder's work. Here Johnson tried to acquit both himself and Lauder's publishers from blame by claiming that it was impossible for anyone to conceive that a man such as Lauder 'could even think of supporting so bold a charge of dishonesty and secret dealing, by actual fraud, and the violation of every duty which an author in his circumstances was obliged to practice'.[34]

Though Johnson may have vindicated himself, this still left Lauder, the villain of the affair, unscathed, and it mattered to Johnson's sense of principle that this situation should not be allowed to continue. Accordingly, he wrote for Lauder, or dictated to him, a formal statement of apology to be published as his *Letter to the Reverend Mr. Douglas*, the work in which the forger comes clean about his textual interpolations. Here Lauder, under duress from Johnson, fashions the first of his extenuations, namely that he had been riled by Pope's ungracious response to his attempt to champion the merits of the Latin poet Arthur Johnston, and in particular by Pope's unfavourable comparison of Johnston with

Milton. It was on account of this that Lauder 'resolved to attack his [Milton's] Fame, and found some passages in cursory Reading, which gave me Hopes of stigmatising him as a Plagiary'.[35]

Johnson's misjudgement was to allow himself to be associated with a book by Lauder without having read the entirety of it. Yet, having succumbed to this error once, he seems to have repeated it in connection with the *Letter to Douglas*, for Lauder added to the work a dissonant Postscript, almost certainly unseen by Johnson, justifying his procedure on the grounds of the facile idolatory lavished on Milton by his admirers. Johnson must have been furious, all the more so because in his final unapproved paragraph, Lauder had talked of electing 'at last to pull off the Mask', implying that the earlier contrite paragraphs overseen by Johnson had been disingenuous. Nonetheless, Johnson seems to have felt the best policy towards Lauder would henceforth be distance and silence. In subsequent writings on plagiarism which seem to have been influenced by the Lauder episode, the fraudster himself goes unnoticed. We do, however, have on record a remark that Johnson made when shown a recent book attacking him for supporting Lauder: 'In the business of Lauder I was deceived, partly by thinking the man too frantic to be fraudulent.'[36]

IV

Lauder's villainy, and Douglas's triumph in exposing it, are celebrated in numerous letters and reviews around the time. Catherine Talbot, for example, writes two letters in close succession to her friend Elizabeth Carter in which she comments on the issue: 'Do you not rejoice in the public infamy of that villainous forger Lauder?'[37] Similarly, in his poem of 1751, *The Progress of Envy: A Poem, in Imitation of Spenser*, Robert Lloyd depicts in allegorical terms Lauder's success in poisoning Milton's reputation before 'DOUGLAS and TRUTH appear, [and] ENVY and LAUDER die'.[38] A more circumspect contemporary view, though, is taken by William Warburton. He had read Lauder's book not long after its publication and concluded it to be 'silly and knavish'. Warburton had spotted that there were gaps in Lauder's case, where the author seemed reluctant to supply the required evidence, and he also felt that at the bottom of Lauder's charge against Milton was an understanding of literary imitation that was woefully limited. Yet, at the same time, he seems to have shared with Lauder himself a happy anticipation that his book would be sure 'to mortify all the silly adorers of Milton'.[39] When Lauder's falsehood was revealed to public execration, Warburton saw the course of events as justifying a cynical view of human nature: people who had been gratified to hear that Milton was a plagiarist were now equally gratified to hear that his accuser was a forger.[40]

Lauder's attack on Milton, and its exposure as fraudulent, were to be very constitutive of attitudes towards plagiarism over the next two or three decades. For one thing, it underscored that allegations of plagiarism should not necessarily be taken at face value, and that there might be a trespass involved in spreading such accusations just as much as one arising from plagiarism itself. Such an appreciation is certainly constitutive of Johnson's position on the subject. His earliest published pronouncements on the issue occur at a time when the Lauder brouhaha was still fresh in his mind. *Rambler* 143 (30 July 1751) begins with what might be interpreted as a moral commentary on the Lauder episode:

> Among the innumerable practices by which interest or envy have taught those who live upon literary fame to disturb each other at their airy banquets, one of the most common is the charge of plagiarism. When the excellence of a new composition can no longer be contested, and malice is compelled to give way to the unanimity of applause, there is yet this one expedient to be tried, by which the author may be degraded, though his work be reverenced; and the excellence which we cannot obscure, may be set at such a distance as not to overpower our fainter lustre.[41]

Johnson sees plagiarism as a charge most often laid against works and writers of established reputation, the effect of which is to call that reputation into question. He believes that what is eroded by such allegations is an author's fame, the halo of renown that sits upon, but also extends beyond, the mortal life of any particular writer. But a second mischief inherent in plagiarism allegations lies in their defiance of, and disdain for, consensus, that 'unanimity of applause' by which the greatness of literary works is both confirmed and rewarded. The allegation of plagiarism is always an enemy of the prevailing consensus, because it is precisely that consensus that it wants to overturn. Animated by envy and subversion, such accounts, so Johnson implies, are unlikely to be trustworthy.

Yet Johnson's suspicious treatment of plagiarism allegations is coupled with a realization of the inevitability of their arising. After all, all writers find themselves cast as latecomers, and to try to write on almost any subject is to discover that everything has already been said, that the 'descriptions and sentiment have been long exhausted' (p. 394). There can be no writing, then, without repetition, and repetitions amongst literary works are inevitably condemned to run the gauntlet of the plagiarism allegation.[42] However, having described the conditions that make accusations of plagiarism unavoidable, Johnson argues that those inclined to make them should proceed with maximum circumspection. Listing a series of coincidences between mainly classical authors, Johnson defends their occurrence on the grounds that the topics addressed could only ever have sustained a limited diversification of treatment, and finds the authors guilty of no more than plucking 'flowers of fiction' that 'may be said to have been planted by the antients in the open road of poetry'. It is these factors that should make the critic hesitate to label a resemblance as an imitation, for no writer should be 'convicted of imitation' (p. 399) unless on the basis of a pattern of resemblances that is demonstrably non-fortuitous. Moreover, just as critics should be backward to invoke the word 'imitation', so they ought to be equally hesitant in translating an imitation into a 'plagiarism'.

Johnson's distinctions are provoking ones. It is odd, for example, that when talking about uncovering imitation, he uses the verb 'convict', defined in the *Dictionary* as 'To prove guilty; to detect in guilt'. The oddness, of course, is that we would normally say that 'guilt' as such only enters the case where 'plagiarism' (not imitation) is what is involved. Thus, we would see the critical distinction as lying between imitation (innocent) and plagiarism (guilty), *not* unwitting resemblance (innocent) and conscious imitation (guilty). Moreover, if Johnson seems to be bearing down hard on imitation, he seems unduly lenient towards plagiarism. At the essay's conclusion, for example, he notes, as the reason why 'not every imitation ought to be stigmatized as plagiarism', that:

> The adoption of a noble sentiment, or the insertion of a borrowed ornament may sometimes display so much judgment as will almost compensate for invention; and an inferior genius may without any imputation of servility pursue the path of the antients, provided he declines to tread in their footsteps. (p. 401)

Sure enough, this sentence divides imitation from plagiarism, but in a way that expresses more tolerance of the latter than might have been expected. Both imitation and plagiarism are seen as forms of discipleship: they have to do with pursuing the path of a predecessor, only the plagiarist treads in his very footsteps. The metaphor implies that all that really differentiates plagiarism from imitation is misplaced zeal.

The nature of Johnson's argument here can be attributed to his familiarity with, and personal discomfiture by, the Lauder controversy. Lauder had used the label of *imitation* (as much as plagiarism) as the basis of his arraignment of Milton, and the effect of the Lauder episode had been to bring all forms of authorial derivativeness into a measure of disrepute. Two years later, Johnson submitted an essay to the *Adventurer* (no. 95) in which he further elaborates on the proprieties that ought to govern the making of plagiarism accusations. Take these examples from the essay:

> The allegation of resemblance between authors is indisputably true; but the charge of plagiarism, which is raised upon it, is not to be allowed with equal readiness.

> It is necessary ... that before an author be charged with plagiarism ... the subject on which he treats should be carefully considered.

> Nothing, therefore, can be more unjust, than to charge an author with plagiarism, merely because he assigns to every cause its natural effect; and makes his personages act, as others in like circumstances have always done.[43]

Johnson's position is noticeably different here from the earlier *Rambler* essay. For one thing, he now takes issue with a general viewpoint that he had endorsed two years before: namely that the occurrences of human life being essentially unchanging, writers can do little else but repeat the same ideas and sentiments. Instead, his new stress is on how the general happenings of life are modulated by changing social configurations, providing authors with a constant fund of new images. On the face of it, this line of argument seems to be less amenable to plagiarism, in the sense of denying the inevitability of authorial repetition, and therefore discounting the very phenomenon which had previously offered plagiarism a certain alibi. Yet, even while arguing for 'a perpetual vicissitude of fashion' and refusing to concede the inevitability of repetition, Johnson remains chary of the plagiarism allegation. It is true that his remarks quoted above do not extenuate plagiarism, but they discourage anything but the most circumspect pressing of the charge. As elsewhere in Johnson's writings, an impression is created that if the subject of plagiarism throws up the possibility of an injury against which we particularly need to guard ourselves, this results not from the act of plagiarism but from its allegation.

How, though, does Johnson deal with plagiarism when it appears before him in incontestable form? The place where an answer can best be sought is his 'Life of Dryden', since Johnson was acutely aware of the notorious allegations of plagiarism made against Dryden nearly a century previously in Gerard Langbaine's *An Account of the English Dramatick Poets* (1691), allegations to which Johnson returns a full five times in his biography.[44] Much as Johnson believed that Langbaine had sensationalized his case, he also accepted that Dryden was, in significant part, guilty of the charges levelled against him. At one point, indeed, he concludes that whatever Dryden's plays had 'of humorous or passionate' they received 'not from nature, but from other poets; if not always as a plagiary, at least as an imitator'; not 'always as a plagiary', but, so it is implied, in very many places so.[45] And it comes as no surprise that Johnson accounts for Dryden's reluctance to challenge Langbaine's accusations on the grounds that he knew his defence against them was weak. Yet whenever Johnson raises the plagiarism allegation and begrudgingly attaches credence to it, he almost immediately retaliates with strong statements of the intrinsic value of the works concerned. Thus, he mentions that Langbaine had indicted *Sir Martin Marall*, 'like most of the rest', as having been contaminated with plagiarism, but then points out that even Langbaine allowed that 'both the sense and measure are exactly observed'.[46] And later, bracketing together six of Dryden's plays, he remarks that even 'though all Langbaine's charges of plagiarism should be allowed', these plays demonstrate 'such facility of composition, such readiness of language, and such copiousness of sentiment, as ... perhaps no other author has possessed'.[47]

One assumption about plagiarism that seems convincing to us nowadays is that both the author and the work are implicated when such as act occurs. Certainly, universities nowadays take the line that a plagiarizing student is morally culpable and that their essay is invalid within the assessment framework. In the eighteenth century, however, on occasions when plagiarism is viewed as a strictly moral offence, there is a tendency to assume that its discovery impugns an author's reputation but not that of a work. In his *Milton Vindicated*, Douglas, for example, at one point suggests that even if Lauder's general allegations against Milton were true, this would 'lessen our Regard to the *Man*, but does not destroy his Reputation as a *Poet*'.[48] This position, which might seem casual in terms of its attitude to the products of plagiarism, is also invariably Johnson's own. In *Rambler* 143, for example, he mentions the activity of plagiarism as an expedient through which an 'author may be degraded, though his work be reverenced'.[49] Similarly, even though he concedes the strength of Langbaine's accusations against Dryden, there is no hint of condemnation, nor is there any suggestion that a natural concomitant of this concession should be that he revise his estimation of Dryden's works.

I am not aware of a case (including that of Lauder) in which Johnson seems to have sided emotionally or rhetorically with the exposure of a plagiarist. The emphasis of his rhetoric is persistently on the high scruple required before such an accusation is brought into the world. Certainly, in the *Lives*, the tendency is for plagiarism allegations to be received in a spirit of mellow scepticism. In his 'Life of Pope', Johnson is dismissive of the case made against the poet in Warton's *Essay on the Life and Genius of Pope*, one part of which had been the general association of Pope's imitative aesthetic with plagiarism.[50] Elsewhere he seems to give credence to the charge of plagiarism levelled against Thomas Parnell ('Of the little that appears still less is his own') while responding warmly to the poet's verses: he 'always delights though he never ravishes'.[51] He also records that David Mallet had been 'envied the reputation' of authorship of the ballad 'William and Margaret' and that 'plagiarism has been boldly charged, but never proved'.[52] In this last instance, several characteristic Johnsonian responses to plagiarism come together: plagiarism allegations are assumed to be bred from a union of envy and audacity, with many likely to fall beneath an acceptable standard of proof.

Johnson's general reluctance to allege plagiarism stretches in one further direction. In 1775, John Wesley published *A Calm Address to our American Colonies*, in which he argued for the legal entitlement of the English government to impose taxes on the American colonies. The pamphlet appears to have been widely distributed, and though well-received in official quarters, it inevitably incensed pro-American readers. A number of pamphlet reprisals appeared against it, the most relevant to the present discussion being one by Caleb Evans. As well as trying to refute Wesley's views on taxation, Evans pointed out that Wesley's recent pamphlet represented an entire turnaround in his previously held position on the predicament of the American colonies. However, he also observed that Wesley's pamphlet had plagiarized, that is, reproduced 'verbatim, without acknowledgement', significant passages from Samuel Johnson's *Taxation No Tyranny*, published in March 1775.[53]

Wesley felt obliged to face up to Evans's charges in the Preface to a new printing of the pamphlet. Here he conceded that it was his acquaintance with Johnson's pamphlet that led him to relinquish his own previously held views about American taxation, and that while he had plagiarized from Johnson, this was done only to impart to the reader the wisdom of Johnson's case. Evans, in his subsequent response, inevitably took Wesley's excuse for his plagiarism as an admission of his guilt of a literary crime that was inherently inexcusable: Wesley had simply been found out as having 'published as his own, what he had pilfered from another'.[54] Wesley must have been embarrassed by his exposure, and not just in relation to Evans but also in relation to Johnson. Yet any anxiety that Wesley might have had about Johnson's indignation was to prove unfounded, for it is clear that Johnson was sympathetic to, and flattered by, Wesley's justification of his plagiarism: namely, that it was a deferential means of disseminating another author's views. On 6 February 1776, Johnson wrote to Wesley, thanking him for 'the addition of your important suffrage to my argument on the American question'.[55] It is true that Johnson may not have been aware of the full extent of Wesley's borrowings, but the equability of his response is not inconsistent with the treatment of plagiarism cases elsewhere in his writing, especially with Johnson's general reluctance to be quickly condemnatory of plagiarism and plagiarists.

Johnson's approach to plagiarism is, as is usually the case with him, the result of powerful processes of reasoning, but nonetheless remains of its time. His sceptical view in general of literary imitation might, in other circumstances, have led him towards a more casually censorious attitude towards plagiarism. However, the effect of the Lauder episode, one of the most embarrassing of Johnson's career, was to chastise him into a painful appreciation of the unreliability of plagiarism allegations and of the fact that even a charge rightly levelled might still be visited by the shadow of an impure motive. For Johnson, the damage done by plagiarists to the republic of letters was potentially less grave than that brought about by those who erroneously accused others of plagiarism. The accusation, not the act, ultimately constituted the greater evil.

7
The Plagiarism Allegation and the Female Author

I

Laura Rosenthal argues in her *Playwrights and Plagiarists in Early Modern England* (1996) that the lowest common denominator in all charges of plagiarism is the alleger's attempt to divest an author of the right to be considered as the legitimate custodian of his or her own literary property. To accuse authors of plagiarism is to deny publicly their literary agency, to impeach their entitlement to exercise ownership over the works associated with their names. Rosenthal's study joins with those published around the same time by Paulina Kewes and Brean Hammond in believing that plagiarism emerges as a concept, or at least fully institutes itself, only in the post-Restoration era, as literature in general (though especially dramatic literature) becomes commodified and increasingly understood as a form of property.

These views, whatever the critical momentum that has developed behind them, seem to me to be unreliable and misleading. While plagiarism was certainly viewed by authors as being pernicious, the idea that what it specifically infringed was an author's property rights seems to have had very little currency in the period itself. Much more common was the idea that plagiarism constituted a rape against an author's credit or fame, the plaudits that should be the exclusive preserve of the literary originator.[1] By the same token, when writers express indignation about unfair accusations of plagiarism, they tend to bemoan not the challenge to their ownership of property but to their entitlement to fame. In the 'Post-Script' to *The Rover*, for example, Aphra Behn confronts the accusation, '*made by some either very Malitious or very Ignorant*', that her play was merely an adaptation of Thomas Killigrew's *Thomaso*. Wronged though she might feel by such a slur, her indignation relates not to lost property but lost credit: '*I will only say in* English *what the famous* Virgil *does in* Latin: I make Verses, and others have the Fame.'[2]

Rosenthal's contention that the allegation of plagiarism comprises an (often unscrupulous) attempt to deny another author's right to own literary property goes hand in hand with the conviction that the accusation is normally propelled by those possessing cultural power against those bereft of it. Which writers get tarred with the plagiarism allegation tends to depend, so she claims, on which individuals, or categories of individuals, the culturally powerful have found reason to dislike. In Rosenthal's study the increasing salience, as she sees it, of the plagiarism allegation is connected with the stratification of literary culture, in which highbrow literature increasingly divorces itself from and pulls rank on popular literary forms. The plagiarism allegation is how the highbrow polices its boundary with the lowbrow: that is, by establishing the particular terms of its stigmatization. Low cultural texts are stale and derivative; high cultural texts are emanations of genius, valued as the individual property of those who conceive them. These views are summed up in Rosenthal's pithy and repeated observation that plagiarism is the Grub Street form of imitation.[3]

One case against Rosenthal's argument might take the form of scepticism that everything simply reduces down to politics, to the exercise of power. To say that 'plagiarism' is only a cipher for the cultural disdain of a canonical elite renders obsolete all those ethical considerations that the issue of textual theft, looked at in other ways, might seem likely to arouse. Yet perhaps a more immediate problem for Rosenthal's argument is the volume of cases, largely neglected in her treatment, in which the plagiarism allegation is directed not against the powerless but against the powerful. Her theory is well-calculated to explain the aspersions of plagiarism tossed by Pope at the Grub Street hacks, but is ill-calculated to explain how Pope himself should have so often fallen victim to the same charge. Equally, her coverage passes silently over the numerous vexatious charges of plagiarism levelled at another eminent canonical poet, Dryden. When in 1751 Dr Johnson tried to formulate the motives underlying plagiarism allegations, he did so entirely oppositely to Rosenthal, seeing the aspersion as normally cast upwards, as an envious attempt to besmirch and unseat authors of established canonical rank: 'there is yet this one expedient to be tried, by which the author may be degraded, though his work be reverenced'.[4]

Rosenthal makes the plagiarism allegation seem, in differing ways, both highly arbitrary and highly strategic. The accusation is arbitrary in its indifference to the empirical facts concerning actual intertextual relationships, but highly strategic in publicly challenging the right of certain categories of writer to occupy the authorial subject-position. While her arguments in general about cultural hierarchy seem to me to be eminently disputable, there exists one particular area in which they ring true: the predicament of female writers subject to plagiarism allegations levelled by men. Tilar Mazzeo, in her recent book *Plagiarism and Literary Property in the Romantic Period* (2007), has noted that during the Romantic era 'it was extremely rare for a male author to be persuasively charged with plagiarism from a female author'.[5] The allegation more commonly flows in the opposite direction, in which cultural power conspires with a male discourse of misogyny. This chapter will address both plagiarism by women and the strategic suppression of women's creativity through the taint of plagiarism. It will question whether women were more prone to forms of cultural deference that might express themselves in plagiarism, and also whether they were inherently more vulnerable to the charge as the male establishment sought to control and stigmatize female literary ambition.

II

I want to begin by reflecting on the different attitudes applied during the eighteenth century to male and female creativity, ones that bear on the susceptibility of writers of either sex to being adjudged to have plagiarized. These attitudes can be seen neatly in evidence in the cases of two sibling literary relationships, those of William and Dorothy Wordsworth and Henry and Sarah Fielding. Since Pamela Woof's 1991 edition of the *Grasmere Journals,* readers have had opportunity to be aware of the nature and scope of William's literary indebtedness to his sister, a relationship manifest in the former's 'Daffodils', composed between 1804 and 1807. William drafted the poem having re-read an entry in Dorothy's journal of two years earlier describing a shared walk near Ullswater in which they had happened on a field of daffodils. The entry captures how the flowers 'tossed & reeled & danced & seemed as if they verily laughed with the wind that blew upon them over the Lake', figurative perceptions that are closely reproduced in her brother's poem:

> The waves beside them danced; but they
> Out-did the sparkling waves in glee:
> A poet could not but be gay,
> In such a jocund company.[6]

William's lines silently appropriate Dorothy's observations, while transmuting a shared pleasure into an isolated self-communion: 'I wandered lonely as a cloud.' The poem dwells not just on the scene itself but also on William's ability to recall it subsequently to his 'inward eye', eliciting a inner colloquium between the poet's past and present selves, not between him and his sister. Dorothy's very presence on the walk to the daffodils, as well as her written description of the scene, are discreetly effaced from the record. William's exploitation of his sister's creativity could easily be viewed as plagiaristic, as an abduction of the creative insights she had stored in her journal. The case against William, however, is not something that I want to investigate here; rather, what I want to claim is that the use to which he puts Dorothy's reflections is entirely consistent with his general attitude towards her mental and creative powers.

The poem in which William records most frankly his sense of companionship with his sister is 'Tintern Abbey', but the principle on which this is based is not, as might have been assumed, a shared apprehension of nature. Dorothy's relationship with the natural world is sharply differentiated in the poem from that of her brother. Hers is a joyous, visual, essentially appetitive rapture, displayed in the 'shooting lights' of her 'wild eyes', and in which William sees imprinted the sensations of his own childhood: 'May I behold in thee what I was once.' The adult William, on the other hand, apprehends nature meditatively, through a language of abstract intellection, which discloses to him nature's inner meaning, 'a sense sublime/Of something far more deeply interfused'.[7]

It is not merely that William and Dorothy engage with nature differently, for the poem clearly ascribes discrepant values to their modes of apprehension. William is able to build his immediate sense impressions into a mature conceptualization of nature, in doing so escaping (as Dorothy is unable to do) from its power to determine his own being. The distinction William insists on between himself and his sister clearly underpins the use he makes of Dorothy's journal entry on the daffodils. She preserves a record of her own sensory experience that William then translates into a reflective poem. To say that Dorothy's description is premeditative is also to say that it is pre-creative, that it constitutes something nascent rather than realized; and, for this reason, to suggest that William's relation to Dorothy's writings might be plagiaristic could be seen as misconstruing their two discourses.[8]

The point of introducing the Wordsworths into a study, as this is, of pre-Romantic writing is that their case is exemplary of a general susceptibility of women's writing to being defined in strictly gendered terms, in terms moreover that have a bearing on the extent to which women could be seen either as plagiarists or as victims of plagiarism. William, for example, can arrogate to himself ownership of Dorothy's journal entries because, as a mere record of sensory experience, these have no creative status of their own. The case of the Wordworths may be a special one and certainly involves writings falling into two distinct categories (private and public), but it is generally indicative of a tendency of male writers to feel empowered to invade and colonize female creative space, to claim women's authorial property as their own. William seizes on Dorothy's imaginings as the rudimentary sense-data that underpins his own deeper imaginings.

The prerogative for male authors to subsume the creativity of the female writers with whom they associate can be seen in the relationship between the earlier literary siblings Henry and Sarah Fielding.[9] Sarah's career probably begins with the evasively acknowledged donation of her labour to projects published by her brother. She is generally credited as having authored the letter from Leonora to Horatio inserted in her brother's *Joseph Andrews* (1742), glossed by Henry with the comment that 'This Letter was written by a young Lady'; and, in the following year, she probably supplied the chapter '*Wherein* Anna Boleyn *relates the History of her Life*' for his *Journey from This World to the Next* (1743).[10] Here Henry teases the reader with the admission that this part of the narrative 'is in the Original writ in a Woman's Hand', which leads him 'to fancy it was really written by one of that Sex'.[11] While Henry may have been disinclined to take the credit for labour not exclusively his own, he was also less than frank in assigning that credit publicly to his sister.

Sarah Fielding's first major work, *The Adventures of David Simple*, appeared anonymously in 1744, the first of a series of works in which she withheld her name or merely indicated her authorship rather than stating it. The immediate effect of her reticence on the reception of the *Adventures* was that her brother Henry was widely suspected of being its true author, a rumour that he sought to quash when he supplied the Preface to a second impression of the book published later in the same year. Henry's Preface exudes a brotherly chivalry while also being suavely condescending and self-absorbed. Sarah's authorship is hinted at rather than positively asserted: a veil of obscurity remains draped over the origins of the work. Moreover, Henry's reasons for distancing himself from the work's authorship are not seen, first and foremost, as having to do with his reluctance to hijack the credit belonging to his sister. The first reason he gives is instead his unease that a work published anonymously should be associated with his own name, when he had foresworn in print ever to publish '*even a Pamphlet, without setting my Name to it*'.[12]

Henry's Preface teases over the problem of ownership of Sarah's writing. One impulse is towards ringing proclamations of her title to possession of the book: '*I believe*', so he asserts, that '*there are few Books in the World so absolutely the Author's own as this*'. Another impulse, however, is for Henry to edge himself into the picture as an accomplice in the work. His own input, while not exactly trumpeted, is still faithfully recorded. Though he is at pains not to overstate '*the Share I have in this Book*', the fact that he owns some share is not allowed to pass unregistered. The abiding feeling is that Henry responds to Sarah's creativity as a kind of adjunct of his own, the rhetorical assignment of authorial ownership to his sister being little more than an act of vacuous chivalry.[13] When Henry saw the novel's second impression through the press, he also corrected it, making whatever stylistic or grammatical corrections appealed to him, feeling no need for them to be authorized by his sister. One category of changes seems designed to dampen down the book's sentimental excitabilities and to align it more closely with the ironic tradition of Cervantes, to which Henry's own fiction belonged.[14]

Of course, sibling relationships should not be used to produce binding generalizations about the relation between male and female creativity. However, the cases of the Fieldings and Wordsworths remain indicative of the ways that male writers can feel emboldened to claim women's authorial property as their own. William reduces Dorothy's description of the daffodils to the level of a rough prototype for his own finished poem; Henry meanwhile (at least in the early 1740s) sees Sarah's creativity as in effect apprenticed to his own. Both male figures seem reluctant to recognize their sisters as fully vested with ownership of their own literary property. Just such an attitude towards women has had a considerable impact on their historical vulnerability to accusations of plagiarism.

III

Women's writing has always been subject to often quite ritualistic forms of denigration by men.[15] The very fact of female authorship, of women's audacity in placing their creative wares in the public domain, and indeed in some cases in living off their proceeds, was routinely vilified in the post-Restoration era as a form of prostitution.[16] Women's writing was viewed by many as unseemly, as a defiance or monstrosity of nature. This sense of abnormality grew from a belief that literary composition sprang from intellectual resources that were inherently masculine, so that women who took up the pen were necessarily engaged in an act of self-unsexing or cross-dressing. We can see this in Dryden's 'To the Pious Memory of Anne Killigrew', in which he accounts for the miraculous genesis of Anne's literary talents on the grounds that 'Thy father was transfused into thy blood', and in his double-edged praise of Elizabeth Thomas's poems as being 'too good to be a woman's'.[17] Even the decorous verses of Katherine Philips attracted praise as being 'manly', and Aphra Behn, partly because of her libertine lifestyle, was routinely characterized in this way: she 'did at once a Masculine wit express'.[18]

What these examples show is the extent to which male authors sought to monopolize creativity, either by denying its existence in women or by requiring that, when it did appear, it be characterized in masculine terms. We can see this mentality persisting late in the eighteenth century in the figure of clergyman critic William Duff. Duff is most well-known for his theorizing of the psychology of human genius in two influential works, his *Essay on Original Genius* (1767) and *Critical Observations on the Writings of the Most Celebrated Original Geniuses in Poetry* (1770), but in later life he returned to the issue in *Letters on the Intellectual and Moral Character of Women* (1807). One of his principal findings in this work was that women, for reasons relating to their psychological make-up, could never aspire to the condition of genius, for genius itself is an expression of an inner masculinity.[19]

How could women write, granted that the attributes necessary for literary success were masculine ones? One answer was that they could cloak their writings in anonymity, perhaps by presenting their wares as authored 'by a Lady', a sobriquet that gathers popularity during the eighteenth century as indicating female authorial reticence. Another strategy through which women could evade the stigma of print and ensure that their writings were restricted to sympathetic circles was through what Harold Love has labelled as 'scribal publication': the distribution of manuscript copies of works. Such a method of circulation seems to have fitted with the social constraints placed on female authors. Love, for example, cites Anne Finch praising Lady Pakington, the supposed author of *The Whole Duty of Man*, as having combined the 'Skill to write' with the 'Modesty to hide'.[20] The inclination to withhold their writings from the full glare of print was powerfully felt, even by authors who were subsequently to become central to the emerging female canon. Katherine Philips, the most revered female poet of the seventeenth century, built her lifetime reputation on just such manuscript transmission and was distraught at the unauthorized publication of her works in 1664.

Women writers seem in general to have been more ready than male writers to be content to find expression in secretive forms such as diaries, journals and commonplace volumes, and in works circulated only amongst a familial group or coterie. Writings of this kind, privately circulated or penned only for the solitary eyes of the composer, stand problematically to the charge of plagiarism. The ambiguity of secret plagiarism raises itself, for example, with the voluminous diaries of Lady Sarah Cowper, whose daily entries amount to some 2,300 pages of text over a 16 year period. Cowper's writings weave original and borrowed passages together almost in disregard of the distinction, though she was not complacent about penning to herself little admonitions or self-justifications about her plagiaristic practice. On one occasion she reconciles herself to her own habits by stating that 'I account Stealing to be when we altogether Transcribe out of any Author'; on another, she remarks more self-critically that 'Like an Errant Plagiary I Cull from Books and Elsewhere what pleases my Fancy'.[21]

Private composition had the double benefit of enabling women to avoid the scandal of being seen to write for money but also of indemnifying them against the charge of plagiarism, the main vehicle through which the male literary establishment could express its incredulity towards, and scorn for, female literary ambitions. The branding of women authors as plagiarists is commonplace in literary culture after 1640 and seems to issue directly from the misogynist dogma that women lacked the intellectual resources to be creative in their own right. Protestations against the plagiarism slur appear in the writings of numerous female authors, of whom Aphra Behn is only the most famous. The New England poet Anne Bradstreet complained about the persistent denigration of her creativity in ways that speak volubly about the predicament of numerous female writers in England:

> I am obnoxious to each carping tongue
> Who says my hand a needle better fits,
> A poet's pen all scorn I should thus wrong,
> For such despite they cast on female wits:
> If what I do prove well, it won't advance,
> They'll say it's stol'n, or else it was by chance.[22]

What Bradstreet sets out is not a single case against women's creativity but a flexible repertoire of arguments. Women's natural bent is towards wielding a needle, not a pen; their attempts at poetry are ill-advised and destined to be unhappy; and, where a female poet has been well-received, this can only be the result of chance or, even worse, of concealed plagiarism.

The same gauntlet of male suspicion is run by nearly all female writers of the time. Jacqueline Pearson names, amongst others, Mary Pix, Delarivière Manley, Jane Wiseman and Mary Davys as having been accused of passing off the writings of men as their own.[23] All were, at least in part, playwrights, but the charge was not confined merely to women who wrote for a living. The feminist intellectual Mary Astell took the opportunity in the Preface to the third edition of her *Reflections upon Marriage* (1706) to bemoan the aspersions made against her own authorship of an earlier version of the same work: 'The World will hardly allow a Woman to say any thing well, unless as she borrows it from Men, or is assisted by them.'[24] The same problems were encountered by the Anglo-Saxon scholar Elizabeth Elstob, who suffered from achieving excellence in a field of learning almost exclusively dominated by men, as well as from predictable insinuations about her indebtedness to her brother William, also a linguist and antiquarian. Elstob addresses these rumblings of suspicion in the Preface to her edition of *An English-Saxon Homily* (1709). She begins by dissenting from what she sees as a prevalent male view that women should have nothing to do with learning. 'If good Learning be one of the Soul's greatest Improvements', she enquires, 'Where is the Fault in Womens seeking after Learning?' Male reluctance to acknowledge women's intellectual capacities brings her inevitably to the charge of plagiarism: 'I have been askt the Question, more than once, whether this Performance was all my own.'[25]

Elstob's case reflects a general assumption that male writers and scholars radiate influence while female writers and scholars receive and absorb it. Jane Brereton captures precisely this assumption when she notes some similarities between some lines by Elizabeth Rowe and lines in Pope's later *Essay on Man*. Had Pope's poem published first, she suggests, Rowe would have been accused of imitating Pope, 'But who dares say, that the great Poet copy'd Mrs *Rowe*?'.[26] Literary association with powerful male figures has a tendency to end up being incriminating for women, who get accused of leeching off the superior intellectual attributes of their patrons.

One female writer to have suffered gravely in this regard is Margaret Cavendish, Duchess of Newcastle. Imputations of plagiarism swirled around Cavendish even in her own day, of which many can no longer be traced other than in her indignant repudiation of them. As well as being reliant on her husband and brother-in-law, it was also claimed she had rifled ideas out of Hobbes and Descartes. The physician Walter Charleton felt the aspersions were sufficiently damaging to write to tell her that:

> among those, who have perused your Writings, I meet with a sort of Infidels, who refuse to believe, that you have always preserved your self so free from the Contagion of Books, and Book-men.[27]

Cavendish never let up in her vehement denial of these claims. In the 1656 edition of *Natures Pictures Drawn by Fancies Pencil*, she asks that if readers 'will not believe my Books are my own, let them search the Author or Authoress' and calls upon her servants as witnesses that she composes with 'none but my own Thoughts, Fancies, and Speculations to assist me'.[28] She also fully understood that such accusations were endemic to her role as a publishing female author, denial of her authorship reflecting a distrust that her books could have been written 'by a Woman'.[29]

However, Cavendish's determination to build a case for her own originality takes the form not just of public disavowals of plagiarism but also of strongly enunciated convictions about the value of originality in general. Her poem 'Of Poets, and their Theft' included in *Poems and Fancies* (1653) is typical in this respect in championing the principle of invention over 'what *Imitation* makes'. She concedes that while poets can sometimes build a reputation through copying the verses of others:

> Yet he that teaches still, hath *Mastery*:
> And ought to have the *Crowne* of *Praise*, and *Fame*,
> In the *long Role* of *Time* to write his *Name*:
> And those that steale it out the blame.[30]

Connected with this disparagement of poets who piece their works together from the writings of others (those who 'take a *Line* or two of *Horace Wit*') is Cavendish's employment of the figure of the spider's or silkworm's web as a metaphor of self-engendered composition. In *Poems and Fancies*, she describes poetry as '*Spinning* with the *braine*', stating her intention to win fame as a writer by weaving a '*Garment* of *Memory*'.[31] This way of conceiving originality as a spinning of matter directly out of the authorial brain was famously to be brought into disrepute by Swift in his *Battle of the Books*, where it is associated with the imperious self-engrossment of modern authors. Yet Cavendish herself knew that the figure was associated with negative connotations: in *Natures Picture Drawn by Fancies Pencil* (1656), she depicts a 'Man' denigrating silkworms and spiders as builders of flimsy monuments, 'As imaginations, when Reason's weak'.[32] Spinning seems to be in her writing a metaphor strictly for female authorship, one that is deliberately provocative insofar as it counters the male notion of women's creativity deriving ultimately from that of men.

The particular difficulties encountered by Cavendish, and the precise nature of her attempts to counteract them, are necessarily unique, but the malaise afflicting women's claims to authorship is a generic one. A writer of a century and a half later to be beset by a not dissimilar set of problems is Charlotte Smith. Smith practised a highly allusive form of poetry in which she made liberal use of poetic models and also individual lines and sentiments culled from earlier poets. Her most recent editor describes her poems as transmitting 'a number of ventriloquized voices'.[33] These voices, it should be noted, are invariably male ones. Some of her early sonnets are based on Petrarch, others seize on incidents in Goethe's *Werther*, and her poems contain regular echoes of Milton, Pope, Collins and perhaps most notably Gray. The novels are also rich in transient allusions to other authors.[34]

These habits of composition are consistent with what has often been noted about Smith's verse in particular: that it is highly preoccupied with forms of identification between self and other. The poems contain descriptions of individuals and of the natural world that seem closely to replicate what Smith viewed as her own personal plight. Moreover, in poems such as 'On being cautioned against walking on an headland ... because it was frequented by a lunatic', the spectating narrator and the contemplated other seem almost to blur into one, as if Smith's personhood flows outwards to dissolve itself within the characters she creates. The emergence in her poems of voices belonging to other poets constitutes another kind of rich sympathy with something external to herself, as if she is dissolving a part of her poetic identity in order to accommodate a secondary voice.

Smith's co-option of other literary voices made her work acutely vulnerable to charges of plagiarism. Her earliest scrape over the issue came in 1785 when she released a translation of Prévost's licentious *Manon L'Escaut*. Smith, at this stage in her career, remained a literary novice and she made the naïve error of asking her publisher to deliver a copy of the work to the irascible critic George Steevens. It is clear that Steevens considered the work to be morally unpalatable, but he chose publicly to vent his disapproval of it through an allegation of plagiarism.

Returning his copy to the publisher, he wrote to the editor of *The Public Advertiser*:

> Sir,
> Literary frauds should be made known as soon as discovered; please to acquaint the public that the novel called *Manon L'Escaut*, just published in two volumes octavo, has been twice before printed in English, once annexed to *The Marquis de Bretagne*, and once by itself, under the title of *The Chevalier de Grieux* – it was written by the Abbé Prévost about 40 or 50 years ago. I am, Sir, your old correspondent
>
> Scourge[35]

The letter was decidedly unfair, in as much as Smith never attempted to disguise her work's status as a translation, but she was embarrassed all the same by Steevens's scholarly revelations about previous translations of *Manon* of which she had been unaware. Under pressure from the book's printer, who felt that his reputation might be injured by suspicion that he had colluded in an imposture on the public, Smith consented to the work being withdrawn from publication.

Steevens hoists his plagiarism charge like a flag of convenience: it provides a swift way of debunking a work to which he probably took exception for other reasons. Plagiarism charges often work in this way, as a generic, spoiling accusation linked to a more particular grudge or objection. We can sense this in the disparagement of Smith's work by Anna Seward, who combines aspersions of plagiarism against the *Elegiac Sonnets* with attacks on their relentlessly maudlin tone. In 1788, she records that the sonnets amounted to little more than a 'flow of melancholy and harmonious numbers, full of notorious plagiarisms, barren of original ideas and poetical imagery'; later, she alludes to the 'hackneyed scraps of dismality' with which Smith's 'memory furnished her from our various poets'.[36]

It is difficult to say how widespread the plagiarism accusations made against *Elegiac Sonnets* were: Seward should not necessarily be trusted in claiming that Smith's thefts were 'notorious'. However, from an early point in her career, Smith seems to have taken pains to anticipate and head off accusations of plagiarism. In 1786 she took advantage of a third edition of the *Sonnets* to supply numerous notes identifying sources for her poetic allusions as well as furnishing some contextual facts. The comment on her procedure she supplies in the Preface suggests that she may have felt coerced into this self-disclosure: 'I have there [at the end of the volume] quoted such lines as I have borrowed; and even where I am conscious the ideas were not my own, I have restored them to the original possessors.'[37] What she means by the latter part of the sentence is hard to discern, but it seems a garbled attempt to suggest that even when she has come to certain ideas independently, she has still felt an obligation to cite earlier sources for them. Such a strategy suggests an extreme degree of apprehension about allegations of plagiarism.

Advance rebuttals of plagiarism are a feature of later works as well. In the Preface to *The Banished Man* (1795), she tries to discourage plagiarism accusations that could stem from her reworking of Gothic materials. In retrospect, she thinks it might have been better, so as 'to avoid the charge of plagiarism', to have set her fable not in a castle but in a subterraneous town. This would have put her under less threat 'of being *again* accused of borrowing'.[38] Anxiety about plagiarism and the damage that its exposure might wreak on her reputation stayed with her until the end. One of her last writings must have been her 'Notes to the Fables', which appeared in *Beachy Head, Fables, and Other Poems* (1807), published by Joseph Johnson three months after her death. The note consists of an agonized justification of the semblance of plagiarism that Smith thought might be apparent in the relation between her own description of a lark and one in James Grahame's *Birds of Scotland*, published the year before (1806). While she accounts the similarity to the fact that descriptions of 'natural objects' will always tend to be similar to each other, she is also at pains to set down that her own verses had not just been composed but actually submitted to the publisher some while before the appearance of Grahame's book. Smith's acute anxiety about putting the record straight is understandable, given that, as she says, 'There is nothing I am more desirous of avoiding, even in a trifle like this, than the charge of plagiarism'.[39]

IV

Of course, Smith is not unique as an allusive writer who felt a need to absolve herself of the imputation of plagiarism: Thomas Gray, a poet whom she particularly admired and modelled herself on, was beset by precisely the same problem. Yet Smith may have been all the more beleaguered over the issue because of being a woman, and so subject to the plagiarism allegation as a denigration that had a specialized application to aspiring female authors. Loraine Fletcher, for example, has noted that when some anonymous copies of Smith's translation of *Manon* were released in 1786, a reviewer in the *Monthly*, while highlighting the same issues that had been of concern for Steevens, was a good deal more temperate. However, he was assuming that the translator was a man.[40]

What I have tried to suggest so far is not exactly that women were more susceptible to plagiarism accusations than men (though that may have been the case), but that allegations made against them tend to spring from a very particular set of motives. Many are tinged by, or flagrantly exude, misogyny. However, to say this much is not to have explored all those senses in which plagiarism might be considered a gendered practice. There is some evidence that women writers did plagiarize more readily than men or, to put it more precisely, that women may not so strongly have identified their own writings and those of others as a form of inalienable property. Plagiarism, or a sort of imaginative sharing and mutuality, may have come more easily to female authors than male authors.

Jane Spencer has suggested that women's response to male authors within the tradition is characterized by 'filial deference'.[41] Certainly, deference is a much stronger theme in women's writing than in men's, and plagiarism sometimes surfaces in women writers as consistent with an aesthetics of deference. We can see this in the anonymous *Essay in Defence of a Female Sex* (1696), probably written by Judith Drake or Mary Astell and addressed to Princess Anne of Denmark. It begins with a ringing statement of social and intellectual obeisance to Anne:

> to let you see how absolutely you may command me, I had rather be your *Eccho*, than be silent when you bid me speak, and beg your Excuse rather for my Failures, than want of Complaisance. I know you will not excuse me for a Plagiary, if I return you nothing but what I have glean'd from you, when you consider that I pretend not to make a Present, but to pay the Interest only of a Debt.[42]

Plagiarism may be glossed here as an inexcusable practice, but the author's compliment consists of saying that in this case it is ultimately unavoidable. Anne's intellectual influence is so overcoming that those falling beneath it can only echo back what she has taught them, paying back the interest on their indebtedness. Of course, book dedications around this time invariably strike a self-abasing posture, but this is the only one of which I know where an author willingly takes on the mantle of plagiarist to express intellectual subordination to a patron.

Although Margaret Cavendish is one female author who mounts a robust, public defence of her own originality, many other women writers did not feel a need to found their authorship on any such claim. Perhaps it is that women writers felt less compromised by influence than male writers, perhaps less attentive to the encrusted boundaries between texts and more to their fluid and porous interfaces. It is interesting that when Elstob, in the Preface to her *An English-Saxon Homily*, reports the suspicious enquiry frequently put to her 'whether this Performance was all my own', the question becomes the pretext not for a ringing statement of her originality but rather for an open confession of the assistance supplied to her. She notes the role of her 'kind Brother', about whose assistance she would expatiate at length but for his desire for reticence on this subject. His injunction alone stops her cataloguing his help and makes her guilty of a 'silence' of unacknowledgement that would otherwise be 'unpardonable'.[43]

Elstob cherishes the influences her own work has received and incorporated. It is as if the cachet of originality is something that she sees as less for keeping than bestowing, in this instance on her brother. She would rather reflect the light than emit it. Something of the same compositional mentality can be seen in a fascinating passage of Sarah Fielding's *The Cry* (1754), in which 'the Cry' itself, a maledictory chorus of sniping voices, tries to impugn the wise observations on life of the central character, Portia:

> They were resolved, if possible, to rob her of any little degree of merit which they had granted to her observation, and fled to that stale common trick of taxing her with picking up all her observations from some favourite of her own acquaintance: nor were they at a loss on whom to confer the honour of being the prompter to all her sentiments; for in full chorus they all agreed, that she had been retailing to them the peculiar notions of Ferdinand.[44]

Ferdinand is the man with whom Portia is in love and to whom she has embraced a kind of intellectual discipleship. In response to the Cry's malignant aspersions that she owes her wise words to him, standing guilty of 'being a plagiarist in all ... [her] ... thoughts', she retaliates not by attesting to her own originality but by refusing to acknowledge any shame in her deference to Ferdinand. She confesses to have heard 'many useful and improving observations' made by Ferdinand and has 'endeavoured to apply them properly, and by the help of my memory to retain them in my own particular service'.[45] What she believes should absolve her practice from the taint of plagiarism is that she takes ownership of Ferdinand's observations through understanding them and applying them in a different context. Far from being like a giant's garb thrown upon a pygmy, his remarks hang naturally on her figure. Her candour and stubborn pride in her intellectual inheritance from Ferdinand baffles the Cry and they leave her to attack Ferdinand instead, whose character they 'mangled and defaced ... into every false form they could invent'.[46]

Portia's readiness to admit and even proclaim Ferdinand's influence on her could be seen as a gendered trait: women embrace influence, while men try to overcome it or are wont publicly to renounce it. Women's authorship, in certain instances at least, seems less predicated on a discourse of monopolistic textual ownership than that of men. Women authors seem to have been more ready to cede ownership of their works to peers or patrons; or, to put this the other way around, male authors seem to have been equipped with greater self-assurance in claiming user rights over writings produced by the opposite sex. It is easy to think of Samuel Richardson's complacent reproduction of Elizabeth Carter's 'Ode to Wisdom' in the second volume of *Clarissa*, or Richard Sheridan's somewhat unscrupulous use of his mother Frances's unpublished writings following her death.[47] However, the same gendered reasons that caused women to fall victim to the appropriation of their works by men also entailed that they would so often run the gauntlet of the plagiarism accusation in relation to their own published works. This book is not so much about the essential nature of plagiarism but about the (sometimes shabby) work that gets done by the allegation of plagiarism. This chapter has tried to show that no small part of that work was the conscious stigmatizing by male authors of female creativity.

8
Plagiarism, Imitation and Originality

The debate between the rival claims of imitation and original invention has been formative for English literature since the fourteenth century. The terms of the debate are to some degree unchanging. The rebuke that original creativity levels against imitation is that of servility, of reducing the act of writing to an unambitious repetition of what has gone before. That which is lodged in turn by imitation against originality has to do with indifference to the past, and with brashness and wilfulness of a kind likely to lead to idiosyncrasy. Occasionally, the argument pivots around some particular historical notion such as 'sufficiency', which informs discussions of originality between about 1690 and 1710. This was the idea, transient in its relation to English literature, that creative self-subsistence, relying on one's own inner resources, makes for an unhealthy model of writing. It is associated in Swift's familiar fable with a spider morosely spinning its web from its own body and compared unfavourably with the activity of bees, who garner their creative nutrition liberally from the blooms of the field.[1]

In the English Augustan era, the debate was conducted in the context of a governing assumption, acquiesced in by both parties, that human experience was essentially immutable and unvarying, the tapestry of life being woven and coloured in much the same way in all places and at all times. This was not, of course, to say that people's lives remained wholly untouched by particularities of time and culture, but the fact that human experience might be pigmented by local and transient factors (as Johnson for example believed) was seen as a qualification, not a negation, of the general principle of immutability.[2] What followed from the principle was that human deeds, dilemmas and emotions were all susceptible to being seen as re-enactments, and the predicament faced by authors was that of being obliged to create original works while being tied to subject matter that could not be anything other than stale and repetitious. The idea that the spectrum of human experience was a finite one connected with the further view that the canonical representation of such experience lay in the classics. The great classical authors, by virtue of chronological priority, had all but exhausted the possibilities for representing human life. The modern author had little choice but to imitate, or unwittingly to duplicate, what they had already conceived.[3]

Belief in an unchanging human experience and resignation to the fact that the classical authors had already patented the best ways of representing it were shared by both camps in the originality debate. It was how best to act in the given circumstances that divided them. For some, the way forward was through study of the classical models and disciplined imitation of them. Modern creativity, it was maintained, could best develop from an abiding relation of submission to the classics; moreover, it was paradoxically through active imitation of classical models that authors could best apprehend and describe their own world, for the reason that, as Pope put it, '*Nature* and *Homer* were ... the *same*'.[4] Yet, though observance of the classics might present itself as the best creative creed, it was attended for many with a sense of cultural defeat. Because the classical authors had gone first, they had used up all the best lines. Accordingly, to imitate could be seen as merely studying to be second best, to follow in the footsteps of, while being resigned always to be outstripped by, the classical writers themselves.

The championing of imitation tended, then, to belong to the pessimistic attitude that modern literary achievements were unlikely to surpass or even rival those of the classical world. Yet the proponents of imitation were not altogether as downcast as this might suggest. For one thing, the actual practice of imitation came to be invested with stronger creative connotations than one might readily suppose, a process in which a crucial role was played by Longinus's influential treatise *On the Sublime*. First translated into English in 1652, and into French by Boileau in 1674, it had become by the early eighteenth century a significant fund of modern critical ideas.[5] Most important in the present context is Longinus's claim that the imitation and emulation of previous poets and writers could be a source of literary sublimity. Longinus imagines the relation between the great poets of earlier ages and their modern imitators in a highly spiritualized way, as a direct communicating of inspiration. Imitation arising from this process is not 'to be look'd upon as a Theft' but rather as a 'beautiful idea ... form'd upon the Morals, the Invention, and the Work of another'.[6] The best kind of imitation is not achieved through mechanical duplication but by capturing the spirit of the original author and exploring new subjects as those earlier authors would have explored them had they attempted to do so.

The influence exerted by Longinus's ideas is both strong and complicated. One legacy is that arguments put forward about originality in the eighteenth century very often issue in the context of discussion of imitation. Originality has something to do with how authors imitate or how they manage their relation to earlier writers: it does not normally imply creation *ex nihilo*. We can see this in the writings of early eighteenth-century commentators on the issue such as Thomas Parnell:

> We are much beholden to *Antiquity* for those excellent Compositions by which Writers at present form their Minds; but it is not so much requir'd of us to adhere meerly to their Fables, as to observe their Manner. For if we preclude or [*sic*] own Invention, Poetry will consist only in Expression, or Simile, or the Application of old Stories; and the utmost Character to which a Genius can arrive, will depend on Imitation, or a borrowing from others, which we must agree together not to call Stealing, because we take it from the Ancients.[7]

There is a temptation to read this as an inceptive statement of a new doctrine of originality, but it is probably better seen instead as an endorsement of Longinus's notion of creative imitation. Authors, Parnell suggests, will naturally be 'beholden' to their predecessors, but adhering 'meerly' (that is, entirely) to the template laid down by classical writers is a recipe for staleness and repetition. What is called for, though, is not that writers simply strike out on their own, but that they construct a relation to the 'excellent Compositions' of 'Antiquity' that does not 'preclude [our] own Invention'. Imitation is not intrinsically bad, but it becomes bad when it constitutes the horizon of creative ambition.

There is undoubtedly much truth in the familiar literary critical narrative that between 1660 and 1760 the aesthetic of imitation is ousted by one of creative originality. Some such thing does happen. However, it is not so much that some wholly new concept is spawned (genius, creative inspiration or whatever) as that a rhetorical momentum builds up behind the case for originality. This has partly to do with a new spin being placed on the real significance of Longinus's ideas. What Longinus had established was that imitation need not be inert and slavish, but could be creatively emulative and touched with inspiration.

Such a line of argument was designed to enlarge what imitation might be seen as doing and accordingly to make a positive case for it. But critics in the eighteenth century increasingly press Longinus's notion into the service of a different cause: that of rebuking and stigmatizing all forms of imitation not deemed to be inventive. Rather than imitation being a broadly unified concept, a sink category is created of unoriginal imitation. It is this debased category, for example, to which Leonard Welsted refers when he states that 'Imitation is the Bane of Writing, nor ever was a good Author, that entirely form'd himself on the Model of another'.[8] This is a ringing declaration but also a hollow one. A writer who 'entirely' worked by the template of another would of course be a poor specimen, but imitation never entailed proceeding so religiously on that basis.

The debate between invention and imitation is one of those squabbles, like the quarrel between the ancients and moderns, in which participants often hold closely allied views while being rhetorically at loggerheads over them. Nearly everyone agreed that writing had to be imitative to some extent, since the burden of literary tradition was simply so heavy; moreover, nearly everyone also agreed that, in the process of imitating, modern authors needed to carve out their own creative space so as to achieve some degree of freshness. But this general consensus allowed some authors to side with imitation (as allowing for creativity within itself) and others to attack imitation, having defined it in terms that excluded the creative. It is telling, for example, that Edward Young in his *Conjectures on Originality* (1759) broadly agrees with Longinus as to what authors should be doing, while advancing the case of originality expressly against that of imitation.

The purpose of this chapter is to spotlight shifting attitudes towards originality and imitation, considering these in relation to the specific issue of plagiarism. During the seventeenth century, as charted in Chapter 1, plagiarism gravitates from being an offence relating to how a work is presented to one relating to how it is composed. It becomes less about stealing another author's writings and putting them into the public domain under one's own name and more about copying as a literary practice. In the process, plagiarism sheds some of its previously strong associations with criminal theft, instead entering into a less noxious alliance with a range of aesthetic techniques dependent on the use of sources, chiefly imitation. Of course, plagiarism, in its relation to imitation, might at first be dismissed as no more than a disreputable, distant cousin, but when imitation becomes shorn of its more creative associations and viewed by many as an expression of servility, then the gap between the concepts inevitably narrows. How does imitation's plight impact on plagiarism?

II

The main sense of 'imitation' current during the eighteenth century was 'To copy; to endeavour to resemble' (Johnson). The word stood more closely to activities such as plagiarism and counterfeiting than we are apt to recollect nowadays. In a passage already cited, Thomas Parnell glosses the term as 'borrowing from others' and suggests that imitation of classical authors is only granted a reprieve from being considered as outright stealing because of the chronological distance separating the parties. What has tended to occlude the generally questionable nature of imitation at this time is the undoubted success of the Augustan Imitation poem. This was a particular post-Restoration form, sometimes seen as having been pioneered by Rochester's 'Allusion to Horace', which reached its apogee in Pope's *Imitations of Horace* (1733–8) and Johnson's *Vanity of Human Wishes* (1749). It fell quickly from fashion, ceasing to be attractive to the leading poets even by the time that its characteristics were first authoritatively defined, in Johnson's *Dictionary* of 1755. The Imitation poem differed from the more general sense of imitation in two main respects: first, such poems consciously adapted and modernized the earlier works on which they were based; and, second, appreciation of them was always understood to require the reader's familiarity with the original.[9]

That classical authors had imitated and borrowed widely from each other was well-known, knowledge of this helping, in one way, to dignify the practice of imitation while also giving rise to some cynical commentary, such as that by Samuel Butler, on the ethics of composition practised in the classical world.[10] What eighteenth-century readers increasingly came to understand was that the canonical English poets had also engaged in such practices, drawing both on classical authors and on their predecessors in the vernacular tradition. The scholarly quarrying for imitations is a characteristic of eighteenth-century historical criticism. The anonymous *Essay upon Milton's Imitations of the Ancients* (1741) had planted the idea in William Lauder's mind for his wholly disreputable study of *Milton's Imitation of the Moderns*; the illumination of Spenser's imitations (including 'of himself') provides for a significant bulk of Thomas Warton's *Observations on the Faerie Queene* (1754); and Shakespeare's imitations were pored over in the name of enquiry into his sources and the origins of his learning.[11]

The phenomenon of imitation posed an even bigger quandary for scholarly editors, who necessarily fell under an onus to bring to light such instances and to account for them. The difficulties that this task posed can be seen from Patrick Hume's *Annotations on Milton's Paradise Lost* (1695), which sets out to identify the 'Parallel Places and Imitations of the Most Excellent Homer and Virgil'. The key word for Hume, as for other scholarly editors, is 'parallel': why should there be parts of Milton's text that parallel or duplicate those of earlier authors? What could be made of such a phenomenon?[12] Hume in fact has several grounds on which he rationalizes the parallels he unearths. Sometimes he cross-references passages in Milton to similar ones in the works of earlier authors in order to confirm the aptness of the poet's observations, though without necessarily claiming that a conscious borrowing has occurred; on other occasions, he reports a parallel as if it were a pure textual coincidence; sometimes he pinpoints passages in which Milton has consciously imitated an earlier poet, but where the intrinsic interest might lie in how much he has surpassed or improved on his original; and in other places he draws attention to Milton's treatment of some common topos, but in a way designed less to illuminate *Paradise Lost* than the working practices of poets in general.

Although Hume is hard put to account for all the parallels he detects, he is not unduly disconcerted by their occurrence. He assumes, like others of his day, that the range of human predicaments changes little over time, so Milton will inevitably find himself depicting the same sort of events and tribulations as occur in the great epics of Homer and Virgil. Certainly, he is not so alarmed as to think that such parallels amount to plagiarism. Having said this, though, his explanation of them remains curiously unsatisfactory. He does not draw a distinction between inadvertent parallelism and conscious imitation, nor does he acknowledge the particular imitative effect that we understand nowadays as an allusion. Accordingly, while he might suggest that a parallel exists because Milton is consciously imitating another poet, he cannot answer the question of *why* he should be imitating.

The word 'allusion' nowadays means 'A covert, implied or indirect reference': an allusion works by bringing to mind something outside the immediate confines of an utterance or its context. Allusions are, by definition, understated and ghostly, heard only as a vibration. Surprisingly, the *OED* acknowledges no specific literary sense, though nowadays the term gets routinely glossed in handbooks of critical terms. The definition cited above comprises the only acceptation of the term still extant (from 1612), with the *OED* recording three others, all long obsolete. These are the meaning of 'illusion', and two senses that hark back to the mid-sixteenth century: sense 2 is 'A play upon words, a word-play, a pun' and 3 is 'A symbolical reference or likening; a metaphor, parable, allegory'. Unnoticed by the great dictionary is that the word also at one point bore a close relation to the poetic Imitation. Rochester's 'An Allusion to Horace' and Oldham's 'Allusion to Martial' are both early Imitation poems and are not allusive at all, in the sense that their literary referential nature is explicit, inscribed in their very titles, and hence is not 'covert or implied'.

Allusion has now become an attractive explanation of borrowings between writers, of the 'parallels' by which eighteenth-century editors found themselves so taxed.[13] We have become comfortable with the idea of an aesthetic pleasure being imparted when a reader registers the chiming between one work and another, and also with the notion that allusions actively enrich the possibilities for interpreting a text, providing a supplementary context against which its meaning can be understood. Principally, we are at ease with the idea that the reader, in detecting allusions and thus importing into a poem a variety of outside contexts, actively participates in the creation of meaning. However, the extent to which these critical conceptions were embraced by eighteenth-century readers remains a matter of debate. My sense is that critics came slowly to entertain them (or something like them) over the course of the century. For the most part, editors and commentators got by without them, and this fact has an important bearing on their ability to explain textual parallels or, indeed, the sort of textual appropriations that might otherwise attract the label of plagiarism.

This is not to say, of course, that allusions, as we understand them, were simply not employed by poets in the eighteenth century or earlier periods: my point is rather about the competence of readers to capture and explicate them. For some genres of Augustan poetry, such as mock-heroic, it makes no sense to imagine that readers failed to respond in the desired way: Pope, in fact, in his own notes supplied to *The Rape of the Lock* and *The Dunciad*, takes the unusual step of actually glossing some of his parallels as 'allusions'.[14] However, the fact that readers might acknowledge the role of allusion in a specialized kind of poem like the mock-heroic gives no assurance that their relevance was understood to all other forms of poetry (or indeed to novels). Another indication that Augustan readers were mainly unconverted to the charms of allusion is the very few clear expositions of the principle evident in critical writing of the time, though one particularly rich passage can be found in Richard Steele's *Guardian* XII, which refers to the 'new Beauty superadded in a happy Imitation of some famous Ancient' and talks about the 'double Delight' conveyed being similar to that of 'observing the Resemblance transmitted from Parents to their Offspring'.[15] For the most part, commentators seem to have been unmoved, none more stonily so than Johnson, who dismisses the detection of borrowings as an affectation belonging to charlatan critics who delight in unearthing bogus allusions 'too remote to be discovered by the rest of mankind'.[16]

The drawn-out process through which allusion gains a critical foothold can be detected from the history of annotation of *Paradise Lost*. In the Richardsons' *Explanatory Notes and Remarks on Milton's Paradise Lost* (1734), the compilers only occasionally apply the term to textual parallels and, when they home in on particular examples, can seem quite brusque in their treatment of them. They insist that effects of this kind should always be circumscribed by a governing principle of relevance and propriety. When, for example, Virgil applies to the petite Queen Dido a simile plucked from Homer, one in which Nausicaa is said to stand out from her maids in the same way that Diana was 'Taller than her Nymphs about her', the Richardsons complain that not only has the simile lost all its beauty in the translation, but it is like 'a Flower cropt from its Native Stalk, 'tis Faded, 'tis Offensive'.[17] It is the misapplication of the allusion that is felt strongly; the intrinsic pleasure of such a chiming between the two poets is hardly felt at all.

Hospitality towards allusion, as an explanation of poetic parallels, does however grow as the century proceeds. It is helped in regard of Milton by the anonymous *An Essay upon Milton's Imitations of the Ancients* (1741), which contains a complex dissection of the pleasures afforded by imitation and allusion. What the author classifies as 'secondary Imitation' occurs somewhere between a 'literal translation' and a 'distant Allusion': it is a way of referencing another text that reconciles imitation and novelty, familiarity and estrangement, in a way that seems to approximate to our own modern sense of what can be achieved through allusion.[18] This way of thinking certainly represents a growing appreciation of allusion as a strategic poetic device, to be differentiated from the coincidental parallels that Hume spends a good deal of his time in recording. It is indeed exactly this discrimination that Thomas Newton promises to enforce in his edition of *Paradise Lost* in 1750, the notes of which he claims will not 'produce every thing that hath any similitude and resemblance, but only such passages as we may suppose the author really alluded to, and had in mind at the time of writing'.[19]

The growing credibility of allusion has some bearing on the history of plagiarism. Controversies over literary appropriation before 1700, while often acrimonious and intemperate, still admitted certain kinds of extenuation: a poet or dramatist might be exculpated, for example, if his borrowing improved on the original or if the fact of reliance was openly acknowledged. However, when no such ground of extenuation could be cited, literary appropriation tended to be frowned on and very often seen, as Langbaine views it, as a means by which lesser writers try to plunder the fame of greater writers. By the mid-eighteenth century, it had become imperative that these issues be looked at differently, especially since the appropriations most under the spotlight were those committed by the recognized canonical poets of the English tradition: chiefly, Spenser and Milton. If these poets had widely borrowed or copied, it required that a more emollient view perhaps be taken towards the practice of imitation in general.

One problem, of course, lay with imitation itself: its standing had for some time been low (except where it dovetailed with the Longinian notion of creative imitation), but another problem was that it delineated a method without specifying a reason. To say that an author had imitated or copied a passage from another simply begged the question: why? What was lacking was a way of apprehending these effects that simultaneously conferred aesthetic value of them, showing why great poets should want to realize them. In this context, allusion promises a more positive approach to authorial borrowing. Yet, even by 1750, the theorization of allusion remains threadbare: allusions were becoming appreciated as an authorial technique, and even by some as a source of poetic felicity, but there appears to have been no consideration of how the phenomenon of allusion actually mobilizes the reader in the creation of a literary work.

A seductive argument has been advanced recently by Christopher Ricks that plagiarism and allusion should be seen historically as twinned, albeit antithetical, concepts. What is reprehensible about plagiarism is that it involves unacknowledged borrowing, thus seeking to hoodwink the reader; allusion, on the other hand, depends for its success on, and indeed actively colludes with, the reader's recognition of the borrowing.[20] Allusion is a child of light and plagiarism an imp of darkness. However, this way of regarding the issue seems to me to be wrong twice over. Certainly, surreptitiousness is something that can be charged against plagiarists, but it has not always been so: before 1700, they were much more likely to be denounced as 'brazen' (a favourite term) and as perpetrating their thefts with unblushing assurance. Similarly, the process by which allusion becomes accepted as an unimpeachable method of literary borrowing is perhaps more laboured than Ricks allows for.

While he may be right that in principle the quickest way of staunching an allegation of plagiarism would be to counter-assert the presence of an allusion, what strikes one most about eighteenth-century interactions between the two terms is the absence of any such line of argument. As we will see, debates about plagiarism, or at least about culpable imitation, are conducted with unusual fervour and pertinacity during the 1750s. Yet no contemporary critic seems to have mounted the case that a questionable borrowing might be reclaimed from opprobrium by being considered instead as an allusion. Even as late as the exposure of Sterne's borrowings in the 1780s and 1790s, it remains a case deafeningly unmade. The disinclination of eighteenth-century critics to summon the explanatory power of allusion inevitably has a significant bearing on the discussion of literary imitation and plagiarism.

III

The 1750s witness a rising volume of critical commentary on the distinction between legitimate and culpable borrowing. Partly incited by Lauder's malignant allegations against Milton, as well as their celebrated exposure by John Douglas, critics wrestled with the problem both of assigning different types of appropriation to a category and of determining the degree of exoneration that could be extended to each of these categories. Douglas's *Milton Vindicated from the Charge of Plagiarism* (1751) takes up the challenge straightaway. The way that he sets out to confound Lauder's aspersions might at first sight seem surprising. Harbouring deep suspicions as to the integrity of his opponent's claims, he begins by accepting most of them at face value, arguing that, even were they to hold true, they would not actually imperil Milton's reputation. The only contention of Lauder's that he firmly rebuffs is that Milton borrowed the '*Plan of his Poem*', but he does not take exception to the suggestion that he borrowed '*particular Sentiments*', for what if he did? Milton was well-read and his reading must have imprinted his mind, giving him 'a Turn of thinking correspondent' with the authors with whom he was acquainted. In this sense, he had an imitative bent, but (as Douglas puts it) there 'may be such a thing as an *original Work* without *Invention*, and a Writer may be an Imitator of others without *Plagiarism*'.[21]

It matters to Douglas that no general slur should be attached to imitation, for by this time it seemed undeniable that Milton had been an avid imitator, of the classical authors at least. Explicitly underpinning his remarks is the doctrine of Longinus that imitation could act as a springboard to the sublime. Douglas is in effect keeping alive the Longinian theory of creative imitation, a way of imitating that depended on writers forming themselves, as Joseph Trapp puts it, on the 'Genius' and 'Way of Writing and Thinking' of earlier authors, and which was entirely disconnected from the practice of transcribing or 'Stealing' other people's words.[22]

In the same year as Douglas's *Vindication of Milton* was published, another disquisition appeared on the topic of legitimate borrowing, Richard Hurd's *Discourse Concerning Poetical Imitation*, printed as an appendix to his edition of Horace's *Epistles*. Hurd investigates whether similarities in idea or expression between works, such as those that could easily be accounted to imitation, can be explained instead in terms of 'our common nature'. Given that the things of the world constitute a 'common stock', is it not inevitable that writers will be hard pressed to avoid repeating each other? What he concludes is that, while the 'objects of imitation' might indeed be universal, writers can still exercise their minds upon these objects in such a way that 'the genius of the poet hath room to show itself'. It is less *what* a writer describes than *how* he describes it that becomes the real test of originality. What he concludes is that, amongst all aspects of writing, only an author's expression offers unequivocal testimony of conscious imitation of another. Other replications, such as those of story or subject matter, are brushed away as evidence only of the immutability of nature.[23]

Hurd's study is not merely an investigation of imitation but a defence of it. He supposes it to be entirely honourable that a later author should revere and be influenced by an earlier author, and he considers it entirely innocent that this influence will inevitably invade the later author's development of his own style and subjects. A high level of background replication between writers is entirely to be expected. This being the case, Hurd encourages his reader to think more positively of 'the class of *imitators*' or at least not 'so hardly, as is usually done'. Indeed, it is the exaggerated 'DREAD OF IMITATION' that he blames for the 'thorough degeneracy of taste' that has overtaken contemporary culture.[24]

Hurd's argument is one of those that works by negatives: it rules out what should *not* count as conscious imitation in order to isolate what might legitimately be counted in that way. In his later *Letter to Mr. Mason on the Marks of Imitation* (1757), he pursues the matter even further, trying to come up with some forensic rules of thumb by which a suspicion of conscious imitation might be converted into a certainty. These rules turn out to be various, some of them relating to the character and circumstances of the author and some to the precise nature of the parallels present in the text. In one sense, Hurd has added to his earlier investigation an attempt, albeit still somewhat undeveloped, to define agency. His earlier study had predicated that the only way to ascertain whether a writer was consciously imitating was to explore the substance of the imitation: parallels of expression were deemed to exude a greater level of deliberation than other sorts. In the *Letter to Mr. Mason*, he tries to rationalize the kinds of external evidence that might substantiate or diminish the likelihood of an 'identity of expression' being the fruits of a deliberate act.[25]

Hurd's whole exercise might be seen as an attempt to stave off the unpalatable. For all its ingenuity in liberating various types of parallel from the suspicion of being conscious imitations, this still left those that could not be eliminated. What could be made of them? For all Hurd's general enthusiasm towards imitation, even he feels that there are some practices that need to be outlawed: a line has to be drawn somewhere. There can be no amnesty in particular for those duplications of expression that have arisen from one author simply lifting words from another. When it comes to labelling instances of this kind, Hurd rather falters. In places, he continues to include them under the rubric of imitation, but elsewhere his phrasing darkens, conjuring up indeed the 'crime of PLAGIARISM'.[26]

Hurd's findings show how far understanding of plagiarism had travelled since the seventeenth century. At that time, the term referred to the stealing of an entire book, in the sense of a book by one writer being presented to an audience as if written by another. We have now moved to an opposite extreme, in which the compass of plagiarism has shrunk down so as to apply merely to borrowings of phraseology. While it is true that Hurd has eliminated a lot from counting as plagiarism, it would have been possible for him to eliminate yet more. For example, in his essay 'On Similarity among Authors' in the *London Magazine* in 1779, James Boswell, in discriminating between plagiarism, coincidence and imitation, reserves the first term for occasions 'where there is a passage of considerable length in one author, which we can discover in the very same words in another author'.[27] This sets the bar of plagiarism very high: the more desultory kind of copying easily creeps in underneath it. Hurd's dictates, on the other hand, were potentially much more incriminating.

Roger Lonsdale pointed out some time ago that one writer who may have been particularly rattled by Hurd's findings was Thomas Gray.[28] Gray was a habitual borrower and must have been dismayed to find his own working method associated so directly with plagiarism. It may have been all the worse that he knew Hurd well and had opportunity to read the *Letter to Mr. Mason* in advance of publication. Whether the *Letter* accounts on its own for the dwindling of Gray's creativity after 1757 can only be surmised, but we know how vulnerable he felt over the issue from a letter to Edward Bedingfield on 27 August 1756. Here he lists some of the allusions embedded in 'The Bard', adding with anxious resignation: 'do not wonder therefore, if some Magazine or Review call me Plagiary'.[29] Nor was Gray alone in being put on the defensive by Hurd. In a letter to Robert Arbuthnot on 18 August 1760, James Beattie comments on finding a line in one of his own poems turning up in exactly the same form in a recently translated work. He resolves to clear himself by dating his own composition (written in 1757), this being 'to obviate the imputation commonly applied in such cases'. Yet, notwithstanding the nuisance of feeling obliged to do this, he can still accept that the 'pamphlet of Mr. Hurd's is ... an ingenious performance'.[30]

IV

Some of the responses to Hurd's efforts were, however, not so admiring as that of Beattie. Edward Gibbon wondered aloud why it was so necessary to convince the reader about resemblances not being the result of conscious imitation, especially (one might add) in a work ostensibly *defending* imitation.[31] Meanwhile, Edward Capell pointed out that the only resemblances that Hurd had categorized as imitations were not really imitations at all, but borrowings or plagiarisms.[32] Capell's observation seems to me to pinpoint a malaise at the heart of Hurd's whole project. At the beginning of his *Discourse*, he had set himself to resolve two key questions, the first to do with the extent to which similarities between authors arise directly from conscious imitation, and the second with how much an author's reputation should be tarnished by the discovery of imitations in his work. This second question is irritatingly left to dangle: Hurd never fully makes up his mind (or at least expresses his mind) as to how reprehensible deliberate imitation should be considered to be. If Gray and Beattie are put on the defensive by him, this is not as a result of what his argument explicitly states but of what might be extrapolated from it.

Hurd's theorizing bears witness to a general trend in the mid-eighteenth century for the categories of imitation and plagiarism to be elided. This is not to say that at this juncture imitation suddenly starts seeming a bad thing, for it had always been susceptible to being considered in a negative way. It was rather that the category of plagiarism had started sliding in imitation's direction. Though 'plagiarism' had been applied to close verbal borrowing for some time, the first English dictionary definition to register this application of the term is Johnson's of 1755. When Hurd flirts with the word 'plagiarism' to name the copying of phraseology, he is assimilating it to an essentially aesthetic nomenclature. In the seventeenth century, plagiarism had comprised a moral offence, occurring when one author dispossessed another of the fruits of his labour. It left a victim, sometimes seen as the wronged author, though on other occasions as the audience or readership of a work who are duped as to its true provenance. However, for Hurd, the trespass is a victimless one. What is wrong with plagiarism equates to what is wrong with all imitation of a servile or unambitious kind: it constitutes bad aesthetics, not bad morals.

From the 1750s onwards there is a noticeable tendency, on occasions where relevant distinctions are being drawn, for imitation and plagiarism to find themselves on the same side of the line. In his *Adventurer* 63 (12 June 1753), for example, Joseph Warton spells out the difficulty of distinguishing 'imitation and plagiarism from necessary resemblance and unavoidable analogy'.[33] Of course, therein lies a distinction eminently worth making, but then, it might also be said, so is that between 'imitation and plagiarism'. However, that one only gets passed over. One senses in addition that hostility towards imitation is stoked up by the very rhetoric in which critical discussion of it is conducted. Hurd's tone is unsparingly forensic, driven by a sense of urgency that readers, suspicious of an imitation, have the tools with which to convert a hunch into a conviction. Though written on the side of imitation, his project feels nowadays like some grand arraignment. Moreover, the same tone is adopted by other commentators, including Johnson. In *Rambler* 143 (30 July 1751), he talks about the need for a thorough survey of the facts to be made before a writer is 'convicted of imitation'.[34]

The turn against imitation is a marked feature of literary criticism of the 1750s. An essay in *The Connoisseur* in May 1755, for example, laments the performance of modern poets who like to 'jingle their bells in the same road with those that went before them' and whose 'whole business is Imitation'; John Armstrong, two years later, declares that the habit of 'imitating another person's manner' is 'always disagreeable'; and in 1760 Robert Lloyd, in his 'Epistle to Mr. Garrick', claims that 'all the art of Imitation,/Is pilf'ring from the first creation'.[35] A letter of November 1783 from William Cowper to Joseph Hill similarly finds the poet berating imitation as a habit 'which I hate and despise most cordially'.[36] Yet for all that this sounds like a unified chorus of deprecation, the attitudes on display here are not necessarily as consistent as they seem.

Notwithstanding the general sharpness of its tone, Armstrong's essay 'Of Imitation', for example, advances arguments that are both bland and dated. He decries writers who set up some model to be 'exactly imitated', for a poet 'that imitates closely will never excel'.[37] But this much had long been conceded, and Armstrong's views are rudimentarily the same as those enunciated by Longinus in his appeal for a creative imitation. Armstrong is merely taking an established position, applying it against imitation rather than in its favour, and expressing it in a rhetoric somewhat more shrill than might seem strictly warranted. We can say much the same about Edward Young's celebrated *Conjectures on Original Composition* of a year later. Despite often being seen as the work that sounds the death-knell of imitation, the *Conjectures* are far from roundly hostile towards it. Indeed, Young thinks of originality in effect as a manner of imitating: you express your originality in the way that you negotiate your relationship with your literary predecessors. In particular, authors should know the classics, admire them, seek to be improved by relation to them, but not capitulate to them: 'let our understanding feed on theirs; they afford the noblest nourishment; But let them nourish, not annihilate, our own'. Writers of the present day should not slavishly follow the pattern of earlier writers, but rather should absorb their spirit. In doing so, they will become less a 'descendant' than a 'collateral'.[38]

Because Young sees originality essentially in terms of creative imitation, he needs to define such a practice against its opposite: servile imitation. As with other critics, the word that falls to his purposes is 'plagiarism'. He stipulates that the way that we can benefit from past authors is not 'by any particular sordid theft' but by a 'noble contagion', by letting our imaginations be kindled by their precedent. And he then asks the reproving question: 'Hope we, from plagiarism, any dominion in literature; as that of *Rome* arose from a nest of thieves?'[39] This application of 'plagiarism' is exactly reproduced in connection with painting in Sir Joshua Reynolds's Royal Academy lecture on 'Imitation' in 1774. For Reynolds, painterly technique must necessarily be founded on imitation, but the only kind of imitation that can be recommended is that which involves a process of 'continual Invention'; that which is to be avoided is contaminated with the 'servility of plagiarism'.[40]

Young's *Conjectures* seem to me more the last flourish of an old way of thinking than the inauguration of a new one: his work preserves, for example, a strong Augustan sense that all creativity (even *original* creativity) must take place under the auspices of the ancients. 'The less we copy the renowned antients', says Young, 'we shall resemble them the more.'[41] Yet as the century proceeds, critics would feel increasingly emboldened in rejecting this pre-supposition, and in thinking of creativity and poetic genius in more radically emancipated terms.[42] However, as the idea of originality enlarges itself beyond merely emulative imitation, it still needs to define itself against an anti-type, some counter-concept that will represent the absence or negation of creativity. The term to which critics would turn in order to express this dark void of the unoriginal increasingly becomes 'plagiarism'.

Only four years after Reynolds's lecture on painterly imitation, Percival Stockdale, the highly irascible essayist and critic, published *An Inquiry into the Nature, and Genuine Laws of Poetry; including a particular Defence of the Writings and Genius of Pope* (1778). As his title intimates, Stockdale was primarily intent on defending Pope against the disparagement meted out by Joseph Warton's *An Essay on the Writings and Genius of Pope* (1756, 1782), especially against the insinuation, mildly made in fact by Warton, that Pope had borrowed from earlier poets. Stockdale's essay is a scattergun of tart observations about plagiarists themselves and about those (like Warton) whose malignancy or inadequacy has led them to make allegations of plagiarism against others. He begins by expressing his determination to silence the 'injudicious' clamour of accusations of plagiarism made against respectable authors, by distinguishing between the 'thievish plagiarist' and writers who merely seek to make 'a judicious, and moderate application of some striking, and expressive sentiments, which They recollect from books, and conversation'.[43] For Stockdale, the plagiarist is a creature of 'sordid spirit' who, conscious of his own shortcomings, still entertains an aspiration to be 'a conspicuous Author'.[44] Yet, notwithstanding the sharpness of tone, Stockdale still declines to recognize plagiarism as a moral wrongdoing. For him it constitutes a creative debilitation: what it affronts is not morality but creativity. The plagiarist in incapable of digesting his acquisitions from others: 'they do not coalesce, they do not incorporate with the little process of his own thoughts'; he fails to use them to ignite his own creativity; and he is at a loss to improve on or embellish what he takes from elsewhere.[45] Moreover, though Stockdale allows that plagiarism has something to do with theft, he does not allow that it is on this ground that it becomes reprehensible. What stands to be condemned in the plagiarist is less that he cheats than that he is unskilled in carrying off the deception:

> The splendid theft of our poetaster is obtruded in too improper a place, and it is too dissimilar from the bad company into which it is

brought, not to discover the cheat: it stands prominent, and glaring from his flat, and inanimate page.[46]

As such, the fault is not to have cheated but rather to have been unable to conceal the fact.

Having decided on what is wrong with plagiarism, Stockdale goes on to delineate the positive type to which the plagiarist stands in diametric opposition: this he finds in 'the true poetical genius'. When he tries to limn this august personage, his lineaments take the form of those of Pope. Certainly, Pope avails himself of the words of others, but these he 'incorporates, and harmonizes ... with his own thoughts' and his acquisitions 'are selected by judgement, and adopted by fancy'.[47] Warton had charged Pope with being uncreative and, by dint of this, with being something less than a 'poet' in the honorific sense of the word; Stockdale's retaliation is to redefine Pope's entitlement to be called a poet by reconstruing what poetry is to consist of. Henceforth, poetry is to be a verbal manifestation of creative originality or 'poetical genius', and 'plagiarism' becomes the antonym, the dark wraith, against which these phenomena can be understood. Just as for Stockdale, originality equates to more than a mere technique (such as that of free imitation), so plagiarism is used as equating to a whole authorial mindset, characterized by creative inhibition and infertility.

The tendency in Stockdale's writing for 'plagiarism' to expand itself into an association with all writing of a weakly derivative nature is also evident in John Pinkerton's *Letters of Literature*, published in 1785 under the pseudonym of Robert Heron. The *Letters* were instantly controversial, causing a spate of aggressive contributions to the *Gentleman's Magazine*, in which the work was given unusually extensive coverage. What caused the furore was the irreligiousness of some of Pinkerton's observations, his hostile attitude towards some Latin authors, especially Virgil, but also the trenchant and unsparing nature of his assault on the principle of literary imitation. Letter XLI, devoted to the topic of imitation, begins with a remark aimed at an interlocutor:

> YOU rightly observe that the fewness of original writers is greatly owing to the unjust esteem in which Imitation is held. Imitation is in fact only a decent and allowed plagiarism. When it appears in a certain degree, it is pronounced literary theft, and justly held infamous: in other degrees, and in certain forms and dresses, it

is called honourable: but in fact it only differs in the degree of disrepute.[48]

The tone here could not be confused with that of Young. Though his work is often read as a rallying cry for originality, Young was happy enough to join in with a wider consensus differentiating between creative and servile forms of imitation. In reality his work makes a case for creative imitation, while expressing that case in deceptively grandiose terms. Pinkerton, however, will have no truck with any kind of imitation. He sees the practice in all its conceivable aspects as so far removed from creativity as to be a mere 'academical occupation'; even the potential for imitative writings sometimes to surpass their originals, which had previously been allowed as one way that an imitation could boast creative credentials, is dismissed as being of no consequence, for 'it is an easy matter to improve on the inventions of others'.[49] On this basis, Pinkerton sallies through the fields of literature, examining both ancients and moderns, insouciantly inculpating some and exonerating others. Pope's 'Imitations of Horace', for example, are held up as an original, whereas Boileau's are 'poor copies'. Similarly, although Milton in his *Paradise Lost* traces, to some degree, the footsteps of Homer, he still deserves to be seen as a glorious original, in contrast to Virgil who has followed Homer 'In every thing' and therefore deserves to be known as 'an infamous plagiary'.[50]

   Pinkerton's treatment of plagiarism in his *Letters of Literature*, along with Stockdale's similar discussion of a few years earlier, bring me to the end of this chapter. What I have tried to recount here is how the idea of plagiarism is drawn into eighteenth-century debates about original-ity and imitation. From the late seventeenth century, critics had been working with a distinction between creative and servile imitation, one acknowledged by advocates of originality and imitation alike. What seems to happen during the course of the century is that the idea of plagiarism, formerly used to describe the moral offence of stealing another author's writings, comes to equate increasingly closely with the derided idea of close or slavish imitation. For a period, arguments about the merits of originality seem to me still to be essentially about imitation, about the spirit of latitude and competitiveness with which authors relate to their notable predecessors, but after a point original-ity, increasingly theorized as a manifestation of an inner authorial gen-ius, sheds this association with creative imitation. Once originality is seen as a facet of mind, it needs to define itself against a countervailing category, a role into which plagiarism once more finds itself promoted.

Plagiarism becomes a generic name for a sort of skulking imaginative dependency, for the very principle of non-creativity. We see this most graphically in Pinkerton's *Letters* in the nomenclature of which plagiarism has actually subsumed imitation: imitation is simply one form in which the unquiet spirit of plagiarism stalks the earth. For Stockdale and Pinkerton, plagiarism has become creativity's dark and implacable Other.

9
Sterne: The Plagiarist as Genius

I

Leo Braudy has described Laurence Sterne as 'the first English author who can be called a celebrity': other earlier writers had certainly been more widely revered, some may have sought more actively to manipulate or groom their reputations, as Pope did when he took the unprecedented step of arranging for the publication of his literary correspondence, but no writer before Sterne seems to have been so much beguiled by the very idea of celebrity or to have measured success in quite such explicit terms.[1] 'I wrote not [to] be *fed*, but to be *famous*', he confided to a friend.[2] Of course, many writers before Sterne might have said the same thing, though perhaps intending something different by it. Before the eighteenth century, fame had generally meant an imperishable renown, outlasting the death of the worthy person, but the sort of fame that Sterne seems to have craved was of the secular sort, which could be enjoyed, and indeed sucked dry, on this side of the grave.[3] Fortunately, *Tristram Shandy*, the first two volumes of which appeared in 1759, was to surpass in this respect even what he might have dared hope for. It came out of the sky like a flaming meteor and Sterne almost immediately found himself warmed by the adulation of fashionable literary society. Few backwater rural parsons can have experienced so sudden and dramatic an apotheosis.

Yet the very immediacy of the book's success can perhaps distract us from thinking about its origins and about the process through which it matured in Sterne's mind. We do not know exactly when he started on its composition, but Melvyn New, Sterne's foremost editor, has suggested that it may have been in January or February 1759.[4] *How* it started, however, is perhaps surprising. It seems that at this time Sterne began writing a prose composition in the style of the French writer Rabelais, an author whom he particularly admired. It was to have been some sort of satire on learning, involving the creation of an encyclopaedia on good preaching. Quickly introduced is the character of Homenas, an unscrupulous clergyman, who is shown beating his brains over the production of his Sunday sermon. Unable to make progress, his mind turns to ways of supplying himself in such an exigency:

> 'Why, may not a Man lawfully call in for Help, in this, as well as any other human Emergency?' So without any more Argumentation, except starting up and nimming down from the Top Shelf but one, the second Volume of Clark tho' without any felonious Intention in so doing, He had begun to clapp me in (making a Joynt first) Five whole Pages, nine round Paragraphs, and a Dozen and a half of good Thoughts all of a Row; and ... was transcribing it away, Like a little black Devil.[5]

What Homenas resorts to is plagiarizing his address from a book of sermons, in this instance those of Samuel Clark, though an earlier, cancelled version of the text had referred instead to the sermons of Dr John Rogers expressly in order to allow for a rude pun (which Sterne eventually thought better of) on the expression 'rogering it'.[6] As the passage proceeds, Homenas is gripped by a spasm of professional shame as he imagines his theft being exposed by his congregation. 'Twil be all over with me before G-d', he acknowledges sorrowfully, '—I may as well shite as shoot.'[7]

Sterne's 'Rabelaisian Fragment' peters out after about 150 lines of prose, but it is here where we can spot the first inklings of what became the comic masterpiece of *Tristram Shandy*. Snippets of the 'Fragment' do turn up later in that novel itself. The idea of a complete repository of sermon-writing artistry and knowledge, the kerukopaedia as Sterne terms it, reappears for instance in the 'Tristrapaedia', the manual of needful knowledge that Walter Shandy seeks to compile for the education of his son. Interestingly at the beginning of it all is a tragically comic clergyman: not Yorick, however, of the later novel, but the creatively challenged, plagiarizing Homenas.

It is poignant to consider that Sterne's path to celebrity (and eventually notoriety) begins with the image of a clergyman guiltily pillaging the writings of others; poignant, of course, because Sterne's own reputation was to be so scarred by the accusation of plagiarism. There is a case against him on this score which, when set down in the most unsparing way, can seem positively damnatory. It is that he, like Homenas, plagiarized freely in the drafting of his sermons; that he exacerbated this particular offence by publishing his sermons for profit; that he plagiarized liberally in the writing of *Tristram Shandy*, including on occasions from his own sermons; that he wrote love letters to his desired mistress that were plagiarisms of letters of the same kind earlier written to his wife; and that having penned a journal of the heart for the eyes solely of his inamorata, he then plagiarized from that in composing his final prose work, *A Sentimental Journey*.[8] Furthermore, virtually all of these lapses from literary grace could be seen as being committed in the service of Sterne's unattractive, overweening lust for celebrity.

This chapter will explore Sterne's putative plagiarism not so much for how it might encroach on how we currently view his literary achievement, but for what the scandal concerning it can tell us about contemporary attitudes to plagiarism in general. As this book should have amply demonstrated, many eighteenth-century authors found themselves spattered by plagiarism accusations: such allegations were part and parcel of a fractious and convulsive literary culture. However, the controversy surrounding Sterne's plagiarism is distinguished by two unparalleled circumstances. For one thing, when Sterne died in 1768 aged 55, his literary (albeit not his personal) reputation remained unstained; moreover, it was only in 1793, the date of a study of the novelist by John Ferriar, that the questionable nature of his compositional methods was first raised. Unlike Pope, for example, who during his lifetime was constantly the subject of plagiarism allegations flung by detractors, Sterne was outed posthumously. Moreover, having been in the grave for a quarter of a century, he was not well placed to rush to the defence of his own beleaguered reputation.

Just as *Tristram Shandy* appeared on the scene like a literary revelation, so too did the news that the book had in fact been plagiarized. Yet part of the shock was not just that of an unforeseen truth seeping out, but of the reading public being faced with evidence of something that seemed so paradoxical and contradictory. Let me explain by turning, once more, to the career of Pope. Pope had been a regular target for accusations of plagiarism just as he was subject to a stream of defamations of other kinds. So much was always to be expected: he was a poet who actively courted controversy and enmity. Moreover, Pope had considerable form of his own when it came to flinging around allegations of plagiarism. Yet his detractors appreciated that there was a special resonance or credibility in accusing him of plagiarism, simply because he did unquestionably practise a brand of poetry that was imitative and hence derivative in nature. To say that it was all plagiarized could be seen as less an outright fabrication and more a strategic overstatement of what was actually the truth. When we come to Sterne, however, the situation is entirely different. Sterne was a creative maverick; he had written a book, *Tristram Shandy*, so breathtakingly singular in nature as to have taken the literary world by storm; he had proved himself a genius of idiosyncratic originality. How could a writer of this kind be a plagiarist? It defied comprehension. Moreover, what does it say about plagiarists that they can at the same time be original geniuses, or about geniuses that their books can be lifted from the writings of others?

II

I want to begin not with the public reception of Sterne's apparent plagiarism, but with some cursory details about his actual handling of sources, beginning with the sermons. Lansing Van der Heyden Hammond's research suggests that as much as 11 per cent of the sentences in Sterne's sermons are lifted from elsewhere.[9] He seems to have read widely amongst mainly post-Restoration sermon writers, including Joseph Hall, John Tillotson, John Rogers, John Norris, Edward Young (father of the poet of that name), Walter Leightonhouse and Jonathan Swift. Indeed, it is in the sermons that Sterne's borrowings tend to be at their laziest and most sustained. We can see evidence of this if we look at one section from his sermon on the 'Eternal Advantages of Religion' compared with its source, John Norris's discourse 'Concerning worldly and divine wisdom' which appeared in his *Practical Discourses upon Divine Subjects: Volume II* (1691). The passage concerns the hold over the human mind that is exercised by forebodings of death and eternal judgement:

> one would think it next to impossible, that a Man who thinks at all, should not consider frequently and thoroughly the vanity and emptiness of all Worldly Good, the shortness and uncertainty of Life, the certainty of Dying, and the uncertainty of the Time when; the Immortality of the Soul, the doubtful and momentous Issues of Eternity, the Terrours of Damnation, and the Glorious things which are spoken, and which cannot be uttered of the City of God. These are Meditations so very obvious, so almost unavoidable, and that so block up a Mans way; and besides they are so very important and

concerning, that for my part I wonder how a Man can think of any thing else. (Norris)[10]

The vanity and emptiness of worldly goods and enjoyments,—the shortness and uncertainty of life,—the unalterable event hanging over our heads,—*that, in a few days, we must all of us go to that place from whence we shall not return;*—the certainty of this,—the uncertainty of the time when,—the immortality of the soul,—the doubtful and momentous issues of eternity,—the terrors of damnation, and the glorious things which are spoken of the city of God, are meditations so obvious, and so naturally check and block up a man's way,—are so very interesting, and, above all, so unavoidable,—that it is astonishing how it was possible, at any time, for mortal man to have his head full of anything else! (Sterne)[11]

Sterne may have been attracted to the passage not just by its religious sentiments but also by its rhythm and structure. It combines two ingredients common in some of his own best passages of writing: a principle of rhetorical accumulation, expressed here through the piling up of all the different causes of spiritual apprehension, and a tendency to lurch between the abstract and the physical. For example, all the eschatological trepidations that Norris comes up with are described as ones that 'block up a Mans way'. What seems almost too lame and redundant to state, of course, is that Sterne's passage has been in large part copied from his predecessor. The surprise is just how little he has bothered to modify it. What perhaps has chiefly been added is a note of jabbing immediacy: Sterne, unlike Norris, draws fearful attention to 'the unalterable event hanging over our heads', this being that 'in a few days, we must all of us go to that place from whence we shall not return'.

There are innumerable instances in Sterne's sermons where he borrows in a similar way and to a similar extent: occurrences are simply too many for it to be practical to cite them. In the passage quoted above, the few changes that are introduced by Sterne seem designed to make the sermon more effective in its oral delivery: they do not seem to indicate any conscious attempt to camouflage the plagiarism or put pursuers off its trail. Perhaps Sterne would have felt no need to obscure the plagiarism since it was common practice in the eighteenth century for clerics to borrow their sermon materials. In this respect, sermon writing was like lexicography, another writing practice that appears not to have been subject to the protocol outlawing linguistic theft. This general laxity about the originality of sermons was one that Dr Johnson was happy to collude in and benefit from. He appears to have written sermons, for which he received payment, for a number of clergymen and did not take exception to seeing them published under the names of their purchasers.[12] Johnson's letter to the Reverend Charles Lawrence in 1780, in which he urges that a clergyman should now and then attempt an original sermon, implicitly endorses a state of affairs in which most of the time sermons were cribbed.[13]

Yet to leave the matter here, by saying that Sterne plagiarizes in a genre in which plagiarism was in fact permissible, would be to do an injustice to the complexities of the issue. After all, I began this chapter with Sterne's portrayal in his 'Rabelaisan Fragment' of the plagiarizing clergyman Homenas, who we find sweating with apprehension that his thefts might be discovered: 'if I am found out, there will be the Deuce & all to pay'. He even imagines the bells of his own church being rung backwards, this being the most frank demonstration of a congregation's rejection of its spiritual leader.[14] It would be hard to understand the point of depicting Homenas in this way if there were no stigma at all attached to the stealing of sermons.

What we can certainly say is that Sterne took a wry interest in moral issues surrounding the provenance of sermons. In Volume II of *Tristram Shandy*, for example, the company discovers an unautographed sermon in Uncle Toby's copy of Stevinus, the sixteenth-century scientist of mechanics and Toby's favourite author. On the subject of having a good conscience, it is read out, with some interruptions, by Corporal Trim. The question that inevitably poses itself is to whom this sermon actually belongs, this being a conundrum that invites two distinct answers. One of these is to say that the real author is Jonathan Swift, Sterne's own sermon being closely modelled on one of Swift's on the same topic. The other one, however, is provided in the text itself by Walter Shandy, who recognizes the distinctive style of the local clergyman, Yorick. What then follows is a rather self-indulgent intrusion by the author, Sterne himself, who, suspending the narrative flow, reports that a 'certain prebendary' of York Minster has recently delivered this very same sermon of Yorick's and, what is more, has had it printed and distributed. What Sterne is up to here is flagrantly puffing his own two volume collection of sermons published in May 1760, using Yorick's fictional sermon on good conscience as an advert for this larger set of wares. What is most interesting, though, is the use that Sterne makes of the conceit of clerical plagiarism. What the story pretends is that the unnamed prebendary has plagiarized his sermon from Yorick, but this act can be exonerated, so we are told, because the offender has 'printed but a few copies to give away' and besides 'he could moreover have made as good a one himself'.[15]

The latter sentiment might well correspond to Sterne's feelings on the subject: that so long as a clergyman was capable of producing a passable sermon of his own, there was little harm in periodic pilfering from those of other people. Besides, Christian doctrine did not lend itself to endless diversification and, accordingly, all preachers were necessarily involved in reiterating a relatively small body of pulpit sentiments. He touches on this issue in the Preface to the 1760 sermons:

> I have nothing to add, but that the reader, upon old and beaten subjects, must not look for many new thoughts,—'tis well if he has new language; in three of four passages, where he has neither the one nor the other, I have quoted the author I made free with—there are some other passages, where I suspect I may have taken the same liberty,—but 'tis only suspicion, for I do not remember it is so, otherwise I should have restored them to their proper owners, so that I put it in here more as a general saving, than from a consciousness of having much to answer for upon that score.[16]

The apology here for 'old and beaten subjects' is something of an Augustan commonplace, arising out of the belief in the immutability of nature: the idea, that is, that human experience is essentially unchanging and accordingly the ways of describing this experience are finite and exhausted. But it is not so much that he has repeated the sentiments of other sermon writers that Sterne feels obliged to justify as that he has borrowed from them without acknowledgement. His comments here are deliciously evasive: 'I suspect I may have taken the same liberty, —but 'tis only suspicion, for I do not remember it is so.' Further on he suggests that such self-indemnifying remarks should not be taken as evidence of his 'having much to answer for upon that score'.

Sterne evidently felt that some aspects of his handling of sources did require justification. That they should do so owes virtually everything to his decision to publish his sermons and, moreover, to publish them in such a singular manner. They appeared under the title of *Sermons of Mr. Yorick* (though a second title-page confirmed Sterne's authorship) and were a blatant attempt to capitalize on the critical and financial success of his unfolding novel. His profiteering over them did reap its reward, in that the sermons, passing through eight editions during his lifetime, were more commercially successful even than *Tristram Shandy*, but the vulgarity of the sales ruse inevitably attracted condemnation. The *Monthly Review* 22 (May 1760), for example, referred to it somewhat hyperbolically as 'the greatest outrage against Sense and Decency, that has been offered since the first establishment of Christianity'.[17] The fact of publication had put an onus on Sterne to acknowledge his sources, but this he fails to do with any regularity. Whether this is because he was reluctant that the full scale of his borrowing should become evident or whether he had merely forgotten what his sources had actually been is impossible to know. However, had he not compounded the felony by exercising such opportunism in marketing his sermons, some of the opprobrium cast on him might have been avoided.

III

Sterne's most famous 'plagiarisms', of course, are those of which he was to be found guilty in *Tristram Shandy*. In composing the novel, he seems to have worked with a number of favourite sources that he plunders on a regular basis, such as Rabelais's *Gargantua and Pantagruel*, Locke's *Essay Concerning Human Understanding* and Ephraim Chambers's *Cyclopaedia* (second edn 1738). Robert Burton's *Anatomy of Melancholy* meanwhile features as what Melvyn New calls a 'frequent, unannounced presence', mainly in volumes V and VI.[18] A further set of sources is used to supply very specific categories of subject matter. The conduct of the siege of Namur, for example, comes fairly directly from Paul Rapin de Thoyras's *The History of England*, a source for the novel only discovered in 1936, while the obstetrical matters discussed in connection with Tristram's extremely fraught arrival into the world are lifted from John Burton's *Letter to William Smellie, M.D.* (1753).[19]

Sterne's use of Burton's *Letter* is comically revealing about the uses in general to which *Tristram Shandy* puts its sources. What follows is a passage in which Walter Shandy frets over the nearly insuperable danger to an infant's skull, and thus to the realization of its entire mental faculties, posed by the process of childbirth, preceded by a passage from Burton to which it is closely related:

> when the Head is large, and has been any Time in passing betwixt the Sacrum and Pubes ... the Head is moulded in an oblong Form ... the more the Head is squeezed, or resisted by the Bones of the Pelvis, the more the Brain is forced towards the Cerebellum, and consequently, the Mischiefs abovementioned will ensue. (Burton)[20]

My father ... had found out, That the lax and pliable state of a child's head in parturition ... was such,—that by force of the woman's efforts, which, in strong labour-pains, was equal, upon an average, to a weight of 470 pounds averdupoise acting perpendicularly upon it;—it so happened that, in 49 instances out of 50, the said head was compressed and moulded into the shape of an oblong conical piece of dough, such as a pastry-cook generally rolls up in order to make a pye of ... But how great was his apprehension, when he further understood, that this force, acting upon the very vertex of the head, not only injured the brain itself or cerebrum,—but that it necessarily squeez'd and propell'd the cerebrum towards the cerebellum, which was the immediate seat of the understanding.—Angels and Ministers of grace defend us! cried my father,—can any soul withstand this shock? (Sterne)[21]

There is slightly more to Sterne's borrowing than can be indicated through a single quote: the unusual expression 'vertex of the head' (meaning the crown), for example, has been absorbed from Burton's text, albeit as one originally coined by his rival in midwifery, William Smellie.[22]

However, what stands out immediately is the extent to which Sterne has embroidered the bare ideas found in Burton. All that Burton has to say is that the pressure exerted by the mother's cervix on the baby's head can be of sufficient force to compress the cranium, this observation being used to advance the case instead for podalic delivery: that is, feet first. To this Sterne has added the exaggerated and alarmist idea that the cervix exerts a pressure of fully 470 pounds (ten times what is probably the case) and the fantastical notion that the baby's skull, so crushed, resembles not just an oblong, as mentioned by Burton, but an oblong 'piece of dough' suitable for being rolled up by a pastry cook and turned into a pie. He has further added Walter's near-hysterical conviction that such an untoward event will certainly have the effect of permanently addling the child's mental faculties.

Most of the borrowings in *Tristram Shandy* are of this nature, with the incidence of continuous copying being very much lower than in the sermons, indeed to my mind being virtually nil. While it would be an exaggeration perhaps to say that the novel practises a thematics of plagiarism, the presence of borrowed material does seem to be keyed into some of the preoccupations of the book. Sterne, for example, regularly figures literary or textual creation in terms of sexual reproduction.[23] Walter Shandy's undelivered discourse on female anatomy is described as having been 'engendered in the womb of speculation', and Sterne talks about the advancement of his own novel in terms of progress through a pregnancy: 'I am going to ly in of another child of the Shandaick procreation, in town—I hope you wish me a swift delivery.'[24] Plagiarizing texts concerned with obstetrics puts the reader in mind of the connection between biological reproduction and a literary technique itself constituted by reproduction. Throughout the book a correlation is faintly hinted at between the unpredictable influences that shape Tristram Shandy the individual and the enigmatic intertexts out of which *Tristram Shandy* the novel is assembled.

Similarly, in an influential article of some years ago, Douglas Jefferson claimed that *Tristram Shandy* belongs to a tradition of learned wit, a tradition which perhaps begins with Rabelais and to which more modern authors like Swift and Pope could be seen as being affiliated.[25] The tradition involves using learned means to satirize the culture of learning. Its adherents are respectful of knowledge but scornful of the self-absorption, pride, pettiness and eccentricity that sometimes accompany learning, and certainly that kind of learning that craves a totality of understanding. Walter and Toby are both characters whose mental lives are shaped, in slightly tragic and self-defeating ways, by their acquaintance with bodies of specialized knowledge. Plagiarism indeed tends to rear its head as an issue in the novel, if not necessarily as a reality of its composition, where characters find themselves grappling with, and perhaps being undermined by, such unwieldy accretions of knowledge: Toby's knowledge of the siege of Namur, for example, and Walter's unmanageable acquaintance with a host of subjects. This incapacity to assimilate knowledge, to end up being not its master so much as its victim, is also a characteristic of hapless plagiarism.

Tristram Shandy does contain some strictly *literary* borrowings, in the form, for example, of parodies of Sterne's favourite author Rabelais and verbal echoes of Pope's *Dunciad*.[26] Yet, for the most part, the passages that were to be impugned as having been plagiarized involve Sterne's dipping into non-literary sources (those of history, philosophy, mechanics and medicine) or sources that, while literary in nature, also presented themselves as repositories of learning, such as Burton's *Anatomy of Melancholy*. For all the critical hullabaloo that was to blow up in the 1790s around Sterne's putative thefts, borrowings of this kind had not previously been thought to evidence plagiarism. One reason for this was that the kind of plagiarism that tended to be most reviled was where a competitive relation existed between the perpetrator and the victim, or where the offence was seen as aiding an author in securing a market advantage. But neither of these factors could provide a meaningful context for understanding Sterne's pilferings from, say, midwifery textbooks. Such circumstances could be seen as working partly in Sterne's favour and partly against him. They offered in principle one sort of exoneration but ruled out another. For example, the exculpation that sometimes came from a plagiarist being seen as having actually improved on the original text could hardly relate to texts that were scholarly rather than literary in nature.

The problem of Sterne's plagiarism is really one of category rather than amount. What is to be made of borrowings drawn from such esoteric sources? The conundrum of what Sterne was actually doing and why would be one that would tease and confound critics in equal measure during the 50 years or so after the author's death, but it has occupied modern critics as well.[27] In an essay of 1975, H.J. Jackson sets out the first strong case for Sterne's defence by claiming that the borrowings from the *Anatomy of Melancholy*, generally considered the most notorious, should be considered as witty allusions and as part of an elaborate prank played by Sterne on the reader.[28] But to what extent is such an argument really plausible?

Most of the borrowings from the *Anatomy* are confined to the first three chapters of Volume V (published 1761). Although the title-page displays epigraphs from Horace and Erasmus, their immediate source of origin lies in a passage of Burton's introductory 'Democritus Junior to the Reader'. Of the liftings from Burton, one has received far more comment than the others. It occurs in the first chapter when Tristram, watching the London coach being hauled up a hill by the 'main strength' of the horses, finds himself visited by a sudden revelation as to the futility of all scholarly or imitative activities:

> Tell me, ye learned, shall we for ever be adding so much to the *bulk*—so little to the *stock*?
> Shall we for ever make new books, as apothecaries make new mixtures, by pouring only out of one vessel into another?
> Are we for ever to be twisting, and untwisting the same rope? for ever in the same track—for ever at the same pace?[29]

John Ferriar was the first to point out that this denunciation of derivative composition was itself closely derived from the following passage in the *Anatomy*:

> As apothecaries we make new mixtures every day, pour out of one vessel into another; and as those old Romans robbed all the cities of

the world to set out their bad-sited Rome, we skim off the cream of other men's wits, pick the choice flowers of their tilled gardens to set out our own sterile plots ... [W]e weave the same web still, twist the same rope again and again.[30]

This trick of using an act of plagiarism as a means of disavowing plagiarism was an old one, earlier exploited by Swift, but to point this out detracts only a little from the joke.[31] Jackson's view is that Sterne scatters enough clues about his borrowings to alert a wakeful reader, and that the technique of private allusion is one by which 'both the novel and the reader should have something to gain'.[32]

Jackson's defence of the novel has come under attack in particular from Thomas Mallon, in his book *Stolen Words* (1989), who sees the plagiarism from Rabelais cited above as less a 'whimsical literary in-joke' and more a 'colossal, gold-medal case of belletristic chutzpah'.[33] Drawing attention to a contradiction that resides uncomfortably in Jackson's article, he points out that the likelihood of any readers spotting allusions to the *Anatomy* would have been seriously diminished by the book's absence from print for nearly a century before the appearance of Volume V of *Tristram Shandy*. It was in reality a book that belonged to scholars, yet Sterne chooses to seed references to it into a work of his own that was intended for a much wider reading public. Even Christopher Ricks, a critic almost unnaturally alert and sympathetic to literary echoes between writers, finds Sterne's case stubbornly resistant to being explained through allusion.[34]

As well as needing to convince us that Sterne's readership had the means of detecting his supposed allusions, Jackson's article, in order for it to make a clinching case, would also need to provide an assurance that Sterne himself understood what it was to allude. While it is clear that eighteenth-century authors and critics appreciated that allusion had a role to play in certain poetic genres, such as epic, mock-epic and the Imitation poem, its relevance to other forms of literary composition had not necessarily been granted. When Sterne sows in his novel occult references to Burton's *Anatomy*, it is not self-evident that he thought he was doing precisely what Pope does, for example, when his *The Rape of the Lock* refers to the epics of Homer. The main argument indeed against Jackson is how little his arguments are voiced by critics writing nearer to Sterne's time: no precedent exists in the 30 years after Ferriar's uncovering of Sterne's plagiarisms for these to be exonerated on the particular ground of their being allusions.

Thomas Keymer has recently referred to the plagiarism aspersions dogging Sterne as a 'tedious old scandal'.[35] The subtext is that we ought now to be able to muster enough critical sophistication to see through the misplaced zealotry of Sterne's deprecators. Certainly, the allegations concerning the sermons relate to a compositional form in which plagiarism was endemic, though there exists evidence that Sterne was made anxious, if not exactly haunted, by the fear that his technique breached a certain protocol. The supposed plagiarisms in *Tristram Shandy* seem defensible by our own standards, in that the author invariably transmogrifies his materials or at least reorients them so that they catch the light in a different way. However, even if we think that the accusations are now a wearisome irrelevance to considerations of Sterne's achievement, they remain of considerable interest to the study of plagiarism allegations in general during the eighteenth century.

IV

When *Tristram Shandy* first appeared, Horace Walpole declared that nothing else 'is talked of, nothing admired'.[36] Although denigrators were quick to castigate the book's oddness and eccentricity, its admirers saw instead only freshness and novelty, praising its author as a man of 'original and uncommon abilities'.[37] Published at a time of lively critical interest in the rival merits of imitation and originality, the work appeared to many to epitomize the rewards, though also the pitfalls, of original genius. This wide acceptance of Sterne's pretensions to originality, however, did not preclude a recognition that *Tristram Shandy* was strongly affiliated to an earlier vein of comic writing associated with Cervantes and Rabelais. Walpole reports, for example, that Warburton had paid Sterne the paradoxical compliment that his book 'was quite an original composition, and in the true Cervantic vein'.[38] To state the book to be original was to make a claim about its uncommon manner rather than necessarily its avoidance of using sources. Sterne himself viewed the conundrum of originality in exactly this way. In a letter of 1759 he talks of the 'air and originality' belonging to 'My Book', which, he says, 'must resemble the Author'; he also suggests that what vests a work with singularity is the 'slighter touches' which 'Mark this resemblance & Identify it from all Others of the [same] Stamp'.[39] While the phrasing is particularly knotted, the main point seems to be that the manner of the novel, not necessarily its subject matter, is in what its uniqueness most inheres.

However, it was not long before mutterings began that Sterne's relation to his sources might not be entirely reputable. Mrs Piozzi, for example, browsing in a bookshop in Derby and picking up a copy of *The Life and*

Memoirs of Corporal Bates (1756), triumphantly proclaimed having found 'the very Novel from which Sterne took his first Idea'.[40] Piozzi's comment relates, of course, to *Tristram Shandy*, but as early as 1768 we can also discover the first dark hints regarding the non-originality of *A Sentimental Journey*: an unsigned piece in the *Critical Review* draws attention in this year to how the character of La Fleur has been 'barbarously cut out and unskilfully put together from other novels'.[41]

Yet it was only in the 1790s that for the first time a body of evidence was provided that was sufficient to the task of judging Sterne's dealings with other writers. It was compiled by Dr John Ferriar, who had been first drawn to *Tristram Shandy* by an interest in the derivation of the obstetrical theorizing that Sterne had introduced in connection with Tristram's perilous delivery.[42] Having discovered Sterne's cribbing from John Burton, he had then pressed on to explore his dippings into a much wider range of sources, including the *Anatomy of Melancholy*. In doing this, Ferriar compiled the first source-study of an English novelist, an enterprise very much along the same lines, albeit probably inadvertently, as investigations earlier in the century of the sources used by the canonical poets, Spenser and Milton. Ferriar's presentation of his findings took the form of a paper delivered to the Literary and Philosophical Society of Manchester, printed in 1793, and a more developed study, his *Illustrations of Sterne* (1798). As scholars have pointed out, Ferriar's attitude towards Sterne's borrowings hardens considerably between his publications.[43] In 1793, for example, he had been at pains to assure that 'I do not mean to treat him as a Plagiarist; I wish to illustrate not to degrade him. If some instances of copying be proved against him, they will detract nothing from his genius'.[44] The only thing he permitted to be said against Sterne was that it no longer remained possible to collude in the pretence of his 'unparellelled originality', though he added that such a quality is one which ignorance alone 'can ascribe to any polished writer'.[45]

Ferriar had compiled the ammunition against Sterne but elected not to ignite it. By the time he revisited the issue in the 1798 *Illustrations*, however, he had made himself acquainted with a significantly expanded range of sources. Moreover, as Alan Howes has observed, he appears to have been influenced by critical reviewers of his earlier *Comments* who had congratulated him on his findings but had chosen to view them in a much more damning light than Ferriar had done himself.[46] It is in the *Illustrations* that Ferriar, as if under pressure from wider critical opinion, for the first time introduces the word 'plagiarism' as aptly descriptive of Sterne's clandestine practices. While he continues to uphold Sterne's claim to be considered a powerful writer in the pathetic style, he dismisses or at least marks down his credentials as a humourist: as he says, 'in the ludicrous, he is generally a copyist'.[47]

Sterne's fiction always had detractors because of its idiosyncrasy and smuttiness, while his lifestyle, especially the separation from his wife and the appearance he gave of milking the celebrity that *Tristram Shandy* had bestowed on him, had also attracted hostility. It is not surprising then that there should be many who were happy to receive Ferriar's revelations about Sterne's borrowings as a conclusive debunking of the author's pretensions to literary merit. A reviewer in the *Analytical Review* (December 1794), for example, concludes that Sterne's merits 'have been too highly estimated' since so many of his best passages 'have been almost servilely copied'; a correspondent to the *Gentleman's Magazine* in 1794, writing under the name of 'Eboracensis', notes that Ferriar's discoveries have left Sterne 'in possession of ... little eminence as a writer' and that his works are on 'the level with the lowest of all literary larcenies'; and a correspondent to the same magazine four years later, signing himself 'R.F.', records that Sterne's 'far-famed originality and wit have shrunk from the test of enquiry' and no longer allow him to be a 'celebrated author'.[48]

Yet this does not present the full picture, for there were other critics who were much less ready to receive news of Sterne's borrowings as being significantly to his detriment. One defence that was predictably mounted was that in fact Sterne had for the most part improved on his sources and this fact ought to indemnify him from allegations of plagiarism. However, there was another kind of defence that seems quite new as applied to high-profile allegations of plagiarism and that grows out of changing conceptions of literary originality and plagiarism during the later eighteenth century. In the early part of the century, there is a tendency for originality to be understood in negative terms, as occurring when an author deliberately refrains from imitating other writers. As the century progresses, however, the concept becomes invested with a much more positive set of connotations: works become originals when their composition is charged with a force of creative genius. As originality acquires this stretched, more strongly honorific denotation, it spawns a sense of what would be its own opposite: namely, a kind of writing characterized by a supine dependency and inspirational famine. And increasingly, for critics such as Percival Stockdale and John Pinkerton, the word 'plagiarism' is the name given to this generic principle of non-creativity.[49]

The rather narrow arraignment of Sterne as a plagiarist on account of his several borrowings from other authors actually ran counter to the way that general debates about originality were increasingly being conducted. Even those who thought the worst of Sterne's discreet copyings could hardly claim that his work as a whole embodied a thoroughgoing principle of sterile non-creativity. To claim that would border on the preposterous. Indeed, Sterne, notwithstanding the exposure of his pilferings, becomes closely identified with one particular sub-theory of originality current in the latter part of the century. This was that originality is conferred on a work by the unique constitution of an author's mind, revealing itself as a distinctive style or mannerism as opposed to any particular reticence as regards imitation or borrowing.[50] It was a theory that had the effect of reclaiming singularity, a quality that *Tristram Shandy* possessed in abundance but which had often been seen as a symptom of pertness or eccentricity, as a positive literary merit.

The more considered responses to Sterne's borrowing after the 1790s show signs of grappling with the different possibilities for understanding what originality might in his case consist of. Anna Seward, for example, in a letter to the Reverend George Gregory takes opposition to her correspondent's dismissal of Sterne as an author 'who has borrowed from others all the tolerable thoughts which are thinly scattered through his writings'.[51] But her attempt to rebut such criticisms does not lie so much in any systematic refutation of the claims about Sterne's borrowing as in a removal of the whole debate about originality to a different ground. It is rather in Sterne's 'colouring', 'penetration' and his 'thrice happy, mixture of the humorous and the pathetic' that his originality stands confirmed.[52]

The singularity of Sterne's manner was also seen as allowing him another highly specific qualification to be considered as original: that of being inimitable. After the publication of Ferriar's research, such a claim is regularly made as a rebuff to the notion that Sterne's claims to originality had been debunked by the revelation of his imitativeness. For Isaac D'Israeli, Sterne belongs to the category of writers 'who imitate, but are inimitable!'.[53] In 1810 Matthew Carey, while accepting that Ferriar's investigations appear *'prima facie*, to afford evidence of the literary piracy of Sterne' and that, damagingly for Sterne, 'In every age and in every country contempt has been the fate of the plagiarist', still protests that there is 'an extraordinary singularity in the case of Sterne'. Moreover, as much as the writings of 'any other man that ever lived', Sterne's bear the 'most infallible stamp of sterling merit': that of being inimitable in spite of the 'numberless attempts' to imitate them.[54]

This paradox of Sterne being an inimitable imitator is explored most richly in Sir Walter Scott's essay on him in 1823, an essay in which Scott veers between extremely stern repudiation of Sterne as a serial literary thief and generous praise of him as an individualistic and inimitable literary talent. Scott had no doubts that Ferriar's findings had exposed Sterne as 'the most unhesitating plagiarist who ever cribbed from his predecessors in order to garnish his own pages', though the skill with which the borrowed materials are woven within his larger fictional tapestry is such that 'in most cases we are disposed to pardon the want of originality'. As his essay unfolds, it testifies to the new conception of originality, as a transcendent creative force capable of subsuming and covering over untidy facts about literary borrowing and derivativeness. Sterne's style, for example, is deemed to be 'full of that animation and force which can only be derived by an intimate acquaintance with the early English prose-writers'. The derivativeness, in other words, is precisely what fuels the peculiar creative vitality of Sterne's writing. It serves to make Sterne's achievement seem a paradoxical one, brought about by a mysterious alchemizing of the borrowed into the original. It is this process that makes Sterne into, as Scott puts it, 'one of the greatest plagiarists, and one of the most original geniuses, whom England has produced'.[55]

Epilogue

Plagiarism is a research topic likely to incite the prospector's worst anxiety, that of suspecting you are toiling away in barren ground while the tracts of land on either side promise much richer pickings. Plagiarism studies abuts nowadays on the larger field of 'crimes of writing', including literary transgressions such as forgery, impersonation and general hoaxing, while being hemmed in on its other flank by copyright studies, which investigates the way that creativity has been circumscribed by the legal construction of authorial property. My policy has been to acknowledge the boundary pressure exerted by these adjacent territories, but at the same time to insist that these patches of ground fall outside the pale of my immediate interests. I have resisted, in particular, the line of argument that sees the plagiarism allegation in history as a premonition of, or a sort of conceptual outrider for, the advancing idea of copyright. My book has understood the charge of plagiarism as tapping into concerns that belong in the first instance to both morality and aesthetics, and it has not viewed such scruples as merely a cover for underlying considerations of an economic nature.

Insofar as plagiarism studies are divided into rival camps, I feel apprehensive that both of them might want to train their critical weaponry on aspects of this book, albeit on different aspects. I have argued here neither (*pace* Ricks) that plagiarism has always existed as an understood and vilified unitary concept nor, conversely, that it came into being at some particular historical point, especially (*pace* Kewes and Hammond) as a result of the professionalization of authorship in the post-Restoration era. Instead, I argue that the unsanctioned appropriation of the writings of other authors has always been liable for moral reproof (as well as aesthetic suspicion), but that questions of what precisely plagiarism is an offence *of*, or what exact ethical principle it offends *against*, have elicited different responses at different historical moments. I have argued across several chapters that the working idea of plagiarism is 'bent' by the local gravity of a range of neighbouring concepts. These include, before 1700, the idea of fame, an ethical discourse concerning the entitlements of the literary dead; the idea, especially in evidence in Dryden and other post-Restoration commentators, that creativity could be viewed as an act of succession or filiation, where plagiarism could arise from a weak son's inability to resist the dominating influence of his literary father; and the concept of 'sufficiency', one that for a period provides a strong rebuff to the attempt to make a virtue out of creativity *ex nihilo*, or from the author's inner resources alone.

This book is the first major study of plagiarism specifically in the period between Butler and Sterne, one that might at first sight seem especially eligible for treatment, given the critical debate rumbling through much of it between the merits of derivative and original composition. However, another distinctive feature of the work rests on its focus primarily on the plagiarism *allegation*. Throughout my study I have tried to view all apparent cases of plagiarism as ones brought to light by the moral or mischievous offices of some accusation, and a major task of the book has been to explore issues relating to the rhetoric, timing and context of allegations of this nature. As I have emphasized, the book has remained sceptical of the grand narratives around plagiarism and I have tended to see the bulk of plagiarism allegations as tactical and opportunistic, many of them indeed rooted in a longstanding satiri-aggressive rhetoric bandied between authors. The book's own moral presumption might indeed be thought to be in favour of plagiarists (that is, those falling victim to the slur) rather than in favour of those levelling the accusation. Gerard Langbaine, for example, who is lionized as a hero of modern proprietary authorship in Paulina Kewes's influential study of plagiarism in Restoration plays, appears in reduced circumstances here as a vindictive and haphazard denigrator of authorial reputations. Though this book does not try to recommend itself specifically as a contribution to the 'crimes of writing' school, it still keeps firmly in view that self-serving accusations of plagiarism do constitute a transgression unto themselves, one potentially as deleterious as plagiarism itself.

Though I have trawled widely for examples, the book has returned repeatedly to the great canonical figures of the age. Dryden and Pope are the first canonical authors not, of course, to have been accused of plagiarism, but to have had to run the gauntlet of the accusation throughout much of their careers. Both also became expert in redirecting the allegation against their detractors, Dryden raising this kind of retaliatory defamation into a satiric artform in his *Mac Flecknoe*. Dr Johnson, whose prodigious memory, so Boswell asserted, rendered him virtually immune to casual plagiarism by always alerting him to the true ownership of any thought, was acutely discomfited by having been misled into endorsing William Lauder's fraudulent allegations of plagiarism against Milton. Meanwhile, the posthumous reputations of both Pope and Sterne were scarred as a result of plagiarism scare stories that emerged after their deaths. In Pope's case, these resulted not from fresh revelations about his purloining of sources but from a new climate of suspicion about imitation and a redrawing of aesthetic boundaries that had the effect of all too easily collapsing the imitative into the plagiaristic. In Sterne's case, startling fresh revelations about the manner of composition of *Tristram Shandy* did lie at the heart of the controversy, but the stoking of that controversy owed much to the wider deprecation of Sterne's character and lifestyle. While the pragmatics of individual plagiarism accusations are always liable to prove more complex than they might immediately seem, it remains indubitable that such allegations in general formed a staple element of interactions between writers in the century following the Restoration.

Notes

Introduction

1. *A Complete Collection of Genteel and Ingenious Conversation* (1738), in Herbert Davis *et al.* (eds) *The Prose Works of Jonathan Swift*, 14 vols. (Oxford: Clarendon Press, 1939–68), 4: 102.
2. *OED* 2.
3. See Ricks's essay on 'Plagiarism', originally published in *Proceedings of the British Academy 97*, reprinted in his *Allusion to the Poets* (Oxford University Press, 2002), pp. 219–40, 220.
4. See Chapter 1 for more detail on the lexicographical history.
5. Martial, *Epigrams*, I. 52.
6. See Stockdale's *An Inquiry into the Nature and Genuine Laws of Poetry* (1778). Stockdale's ideas about plagiarism are discussed in Chapter 8.
7. On modern 'plagiarism studies', see my 'Plagiarism and Plagiarism Studies', *English Subject Centre Newsletter*, 13 (October 2007): 6–8. The explosion of studies in this area can be deduced from two major studies published in 2007 alone: Tilar J. Mazzeo's *Plagiarism and Literary Property in the Romantic Period* (Philadelphia: University of Pennsylvania Press, 2007) and Robert Macfarlane's *Original Copy: Plagiarism and Originality in Nineteenth-Century Literature* (Oxford University Press, 2007).
8. My methodology is indebted to Quentin Skinner, 'The Idea of a Cultural Lexicon', *Essays in Criticism*, 29 (1979): 205–24.
9. It is worth stressing here that this book does not propose itself as a contribution to the debate about the development of copyright. My general view is that no necessary relation exists between issues of literary originality and those concerning the definition of literary property as enshrined in eighteenth-century copyright legislation. See Simon Stern's lucid analysis of these issues in 'Copyright, Originality, and the Public Domain in Eighteenth-Century England', in Reginald McGinnis (ed.) *Originality and Intellectual Property in the French and English Enlightenment* (London: Routledge, 2008), pp. 69–101. See in particular his remark that 'there is little reason to conclude that in the eighteenth century, originality (understood as novelty or creativity) played even a tacit role in the definition of literary property' (p. 70). I am grateful to Dr Stern for allowing me to see his essay prior to publication. For other recent treatments of the relation between copyright legislation and literary creativity, see Paul K. Saint-Amour, *The Copywrights: Intellectual Property and the Literary Imagination* (Ithaca: Cornell University Press, 2003) and Jody Greene, *The Trouble with Ownership: Literary Property and Authorial Liability in England, 1660–1730* (Philadelphia: University of Pennsylvania Press, 2005).
10. *Allusion to the Poets*, p. 231.

1 'Plagiarism': The Emergence of a Literary Concept

1. For an overview of the concept in the classical period, see the *Oxford Classical Dictionary* (Simon Hornblower and Antony Spawforth (eds)), third edn. revised (Oxford University Press, 2003), 'plagiarism'. See also David West and Tony Woodman (eds) *Creative Imitation and Latin Literature* (Cambridge University Press, 1979).
2. For discussions of literary theft in early modern England, see H.M. Paull, *Literary Ethics: A Study of the Growth of the Literary Conscience* (London: Thornton Butterworth Ltd, 1928); Harold Ogden White, *Plagiarism and Imitation During the English Renaissance* (Cambridge, Mass.: Harvard University Press, 1935); Stephen Orgel, 'The Renaissance Artist as Plagiarist', *ELH* 48 (1981): 476–95; Laura J. Rosenthal, *Playwrights and Plagiarists in Early Modern England: Gender, Authorship, Literary Property* (Ithaca: Cornell University Press, 1996); Brean S. Hammond, *Professional Imaginative Writing in England 1670–1740: 'Hackney for Bread'* (Oxford: Clarendon Press, 1997), pp. 83–104; Paulina Kewes, *Authorship and Appropriation: Writing for the Stage in England, 1660–1710* (Oxford: Clarendon Press, 1998); and Paulina Kewes (ed.) *Plagiarism in Early Modern England* (Basingstoke: Palgrave Macmillan, 2003).
3. Cited from Martial, *Epigrams*, Loeb Classical Library edition (D.R. Shackleton Bailey (ed. and trans.)), three vols. (Cambridge, Mass.: Harvard University Press, 1993), 1: 79–81. Poems concerned with plagiarism are indexed.
4. Several epigrams, though not the one just quoted, name Martial's plagiarizing rival as Fidentius. I use the name here, with licence, as a generic cognomen for the plagiarist.
5. See *Epigrams* X. 100: 'Fool, why do you mix your verses with mine? What do you want, wretch, with a book at odds with itself?' Loeb edn, 3: 415.
6. See Loeb edn, 1: 89–91. This epigram is cited, and its implications discussed, in Christopher Ricks's 1997 British Academy lecture on 'Plagiarism', subsequently reprinted in Kewes (ed.), pp. 21–40, and in Ricks's *Allusion to the Poets*, pp. 219–40.
7. *Epigrams* I. 29, in Loeb edn, 1: 61.
8. For Martial's influence on English poets, see J.P. Sullivan and A.J. Boyle (eds) *Martial in English* (London: Penguin Books, 1996).
9. *The Proverbs and Epigrams of John Heywood*, reprinted from the original edition of 1562 for the Spenser Society (1867), p. 130.
10. *Flowers and Epigrammes of Timothe Kendall*, reprinted from the original edition of 1577 for the Spenser Society (1874), p. 22. See also pp. 25, 26.
11. See Harington, *Epigrams, 1618* (Menston: Scolar Press, 1970), 'Of Don Pedro and his Poetry'.
12. For Jonson's relation to the plagiarism issue, see Ian Donaldson '"The Fripperie of Wit": Jonson and Plagiarism', in Kewes (ed.), pp. 119–33.
13. Cited from Jonson, *The Complete Poems* (George Parfitt (ed.)) (Harmondsworth: Penguin Classics, 1975), p. 60.

14. Ben Jonson, *Poetaster* (Tom Cain (ed.)) (Manchester University Press, 1995), p. 181.

15. *Sir Thomas Browne's Pseudodoxia Epidemica* (Robin Robbins (ed.)), two vols. (Oxford: Clarendon Press), 1: 34–5.

16. See Samuel Butler's *Contradictions*: 'There is no one Originall Author of any one Science among the Antients known to the world, ... for the old Philosophers stole all their Doctrines from some others that were before them, as Plato from Epicharmus and as Diognes Laertius say's, Homer stole his Poems out of the Temple of Vulcan in Ægypt where they were kept, and sayd to have been written by a woman, and from him and Ennius, Virgill is sayd to have stole his.' Cited from Samuel Butler, *Characters and Passages from Note-books* (A.R. Waller (ed.)) (Cambridge University Press, 1908), p. 429. See also Dryden, Preface to *An Evening's Love* (1671): 'Virgil has evidently translated Theocritus, Hesiod, and Homer, in many places; besides what he has taken from Ennius in his own language.' Cited from John Dryden, *Of Dramatic Poesy and other Critical Essays* (George Watson (ed.)), two vols. (London: J.M. Dent & Sons Ltd, 1962), 1: 154.

17. Langbaine, *Momus Triumphans: or, The Plagiaries of the English Stage* (1688), sig. A4ᵛ.

18. Hugh Macdonald (ed.) *A Journal from Parnassus* (London: P.J. Dobell, 1937), pp. 44–5.

19. For the relation of allusion to plagiarism, see Ricks, 'Plagiarism', in Kewes (ed.), pp. 31–3.

20. *The Life and Death of Mrs. Mary Frith. Commonly Called Mal Cutpurse.* (1662), in Janet Todd and Elizabeth Spearing (eds) *Counterfeit Ladies* (London: William Pickering, 1994), p. 33.

21. For an historical view of literary piracy, see John Feather, *Publishing, Piracy and Politics: An Historical Study of Copyright in Britain* (London: Mansell Publishing Ltd, 1994).

22. Edward Ward, *A Journey to Hell Part II* (1700), Canto VII, 11–12; cited from http://lion.chadwyck.co.uk.

23. Nathan Bailey, *Dictionarium Britannicum* (1730), 'pirate'.

24. Thomas Cooke, *The Candidates for the Bays. A Poem.* (1730), fn to line 154.

25. Samuel Johnson, *Dictionary of the English Language* (1755), 'Pirate 2'.

26. Book IV, Satire ii, line 84; cited from A. Davenport (ed.) *The Collected Poems of Joseph Hall* (Liverpool University Press, 1949), p. 57. See also I. vii. 11; VI. i. 251–2; and editorial note (pp. 259–60).

27. Cain (ed.), p. 181.

28. For the general development of English lexicography, see De Witt T. Starnes and Gertrude E. Noyes, *The English Dictionary from Cawdrey to Johnson, 1604–1755* (1946), rev. Gabrielle Stein (Amsterdam: J. Benjamin Pub. Co., 1991). For verification of the absence of 'plagiarism' (or any variant) as a lemma in pre-1640 dictionaries, see Jürgen Schäfer, *Early Modern English Lexicography*, two vols. (Oxford: Clarendon Press, 1989). Schäfer surveys all lemmas in printed glossaries and dictionaries between 1475 and 1640.

29. John Bullokar, *An English Expositor, or Compleat English Dictionary* (1695), 'Plagiary'.

30. Dryden, *Of Dramatic Poesy*, 1: 31.

31. Dryden, *Of Dramatic Poesy*, 1: 154. See also Dryden's Preface to his translation of Fresnoy's *De Arte Graphica: The Art of Painting* (1695): 'Without invention a painter is but a copier, and a poet but a plagiary of others.' Dryden, *Of Dramatic Poesy*, 2: 195.

32. For a concise overview of the Lauder affair, see Michael J. Marcuse, 'Miltonoklastes: The Lauder Affair Reconsidered', *Eighteenth-Century Life* 4 (1978): 86–91.

33. Letter of 27 August 1756, in Paget Toynbee and Leonard Whibley (eds) *Correspondence of Thomas Gray* (with corrections and additions by H.W. Starr), three vols. (Oxford: Clarendon Press, 1971), 2: 477. See Roger Lonsdale, 'Gray and "Allusion": the Poet as Debtor', in R.F. Brissenden and J.C. Eade (eds) *Studies in the Eighteenth Century IV* (Canberra: Australian National University Press, 1979), pp. 31–55.

34. Matthew Green, *The Spleen: An Epistle*, second edn corrected (1737), lines 524–7 (pp. 29–30). See also lines 11–32 (pp. 2–3) for a discussion of the difference between stealing from living authors and from dead ones.

35. Colley Cibber, *An Apology for his Life* (London: J.M. Dent & Sons, 1938), p. 138.

36. *Poetical Characteristics*, Canto I, line 250, published in Stevenson, *Original Poems on Several Subjects. Volume II. Satires* (1765). Cited from http://lion.chadwyck.co.uk.

2   Plagiarism, Authorial Fame and Proprietary Authorship

1. See Richard C. Newton, 'Jonson and the (Re)-Invention of the Book', in Claude J. Summers and Ted-Larry Pebworth (eds) *Classic and Cavalier: Essays on Jonson and the Sons of Ben* (University of Pittsburgh Press, 1982), pp. 31–55; and Richard Helgerson, *Self-Crowned Laureates: Spenser, Jonson, Milton and the Literary System* (Berkeley and Los Angeles: California University Press, 1983), pp. 101–84. See also my own *Poetry and the Making of the English Literary Past 1660–1781* (Oxford University Press, 2001), pp. 63–5.

2. *The Works of Sir John Suckling* (1709), p. 4.

3. See Martha Woodmansee, 'The Genius and the Copyright: Economic and Legal Conditions of the Emergence of the "Author"', *Eighteenth Century Studies* 17 (1984): 425–48. See also David Saunders, *Authorship and Copyright* (London: Routledge, 1992). For a discussion of literature as property in this era, see Laura Rosenthal, '(Re)Writing Lear: Literary Property and Dramatic Authorship', in John Brewer and Susan Staves (eds) *Early Modern Conceptions of Property* (London: Routledge, 1995), pp. 323–38. See also the editors' introductory comments on pp. 8–10.

4. See Hammond, *Professional Imaginative Writing*, pp. 83–104; and Kewes, *Authorship and Appropriation*.

5. Kewes, *Authorship and Appropriation*, p. 5: 'At first the charge of theft was merely one of many accusations tossed to and fro by writers eager to discredit one another. In time, the legitimacy of the practice of appropriation came to be questioned.'

6. See Kewes, pp. 96–129. See also Kevin Pask, 'Plagiarism and the Originality of National Literature: Gerard Langbaine', *ELH* 69 (2002): 727–47.

7. Thomas Mallon, *Stolen Words: Forays in the Origins and Ravages of Plagiarism* (New York: Ticknor & Fields, 1989), p. 8; John Loftis, 'Dryden's Comedies', in Earl Miner (ed.) *John Dryden* (London: Bell, 1972), p. 29. See Kewes, p. 98.

8. Kewes, p. 129. For a sceptical view about the relevance of the idea of originality to the definition of literary property, see Stern, 'Copyright, Originality, and the Public Domain in Eighteenth-Century England'.

9. For a comparison of Kirkman's and Langbaine's works, see the Introduction to *Momus Triumphans* (David Stuart Rodes (ed.)). Augustan Reprint Society, v. 150 (1971), p. iii.

10. For discussion of early collections of authorial biography, see Terry, *Poetry and the Making of the English Literary Past*, pp. 63–92.

11. See Leo Braudy, *The Frenzy of Renown: Fame and its History* (New York: Oxford University Press, 1986).

12. *The Temple of Fame* (1715), line 505, in *Twickenham Edition of the Poems of Alexander Pope* (John Butt (gen. ed.)), 11 vols. (London: Methuen, 1939–69), vol. 2 (Geoffrey Tillotson (ed.)), p. 268.

13. 'Of an Elegy Made by Mrs. Wharton on the Earl of Rochester', in Robert Bell (ed.) *Poetical Works of Edmund Waller* (London: John W. Parker & Son, 1854), p. 208.

14. See Terry, p. 87.

15. Cited from J.E. Spingarn (ed.) *Critical Essays of the Seventeenth Century*, three vols. (Oxford: Clarendon Press, 1908), 2: 258.

16. Ibid., 2: 272.

17. *Momus Triumphans*,(1688), Preface, unpaginated.

18. *An Account of the English Dramatick Poets* (1691), Preface, sig. a⁴.

19. Kewes, p. 111.

20. Ibid., p. 125.

21. *Momus Triumphans*, 'Preface'.

22. Ibid.

23. Giles Jacob, *The Poetical Register or the Lives and Characters of the English Dramatick Poets*, two vols. (1723), 2: 73.

24. See the 'Advertisement' to the corrected edition. Cited from Rodes (ed.), p. ix.

25. *Account of the English Dramatick Poets*, 'Preface', sig. a⁴.

26. *Momus Triumphans*, 'Preface'.

27. *Account of the English Dramatick Poets*, pp. 17–18.

28. Ibid., p. 11.

29. *Momus Triumphans*, 'Preface'.

30. Ibid.

31. *Account of the English Dramatick Poets*, p. 133.

32. John Dryden, *Of Dramatic Poesy and other Critical Essays*, 1: 31.

33. *Account of the English Dramatick Poets*, p. 133

34. For the complex issues surrounding the date of composition of Butler's prose writings discussed here, see A.H. de Quehen, 'An Account of Works Attributed to Samuel Butler', *RES* NS 33 (1982): 262–77. See also George R. Wasserman, *Samuel "Hudibras" Butler* (Boston, Mass.: Twayne, 1989), p. 22.

35. For imitations of Butler's most famous poem, see E.A. Richards, *Hudibras in the Burlesque Tradition* (New York: Columbia University Press, 1937).

36. See the note to the poem in R. Thyer (ed.) *The Genuine Remains in Verse and Prose of Mr. Samuel Butler*, two vols. (1759), 1: 168.
37. Butler's poetry is cited from René Lamar (ed.) *Satires and Miscellaneous Poetry and Prose* (Cambridge University Press, 1928). The poem occupies pp. 63–7.
38. A.R. Waller (ed.) *Characters and Passages from Note-books* (Cambridge University Press, 1908), pp. 247–8.
39. For Dryden's use of Corneille, see John M. Aden, 'Dryden, Corneille, and the *Essay of Dramatic Poesy*', *RES* NS 6 (1955): 147–56.
40. See Lamar (ed.), p. 120. The rumour concerning 'Cooper's Hill' was in broad circulation. See the anonymous 'The Session of the Poets' (1668), lines 127–8, which states 'That *Cooper's Hill*, so much bragg'd on before,/Was writ by a vicar who had forty pounds for't'. Cited from *Poems on Affairs of State: Augustan Verse Satire, 1660–1714*, Vol. I: 1660–78 (George DeF. Lord (ed.)) (New Haven: Yale University Press, 1963), p. 334.
41. Lamar (ed.), p. 62
42. Waller (ed.), p. 49.
43. Samuel Butler, *Prose Observations* (Hugh de Quehen (ed.)) (Oxford: Clarendon Press, 1979), p. 159.
44. Harold Jenkins, *Edward Benlowes (1602–1676): Biography of a Minor Poet* (London: Athlone Press, 1952), pp. 111–14. See also the comments on Benlowes in Douglas Bush, *English Literature in the Earlier Seventeenth Century 1600–1660*, second edn (Oxford: Clarendon Press, 1962), p. 159: 'One of Benlowes' marked characteristics is the "conveying", with little or no change, of phrases and longer bits from other writers.'
45. Both lines are quoted from Jenkins, p. 113.
46. Waller (ed.), pp. 53, 49.
47. Cited from Thomas Overbury, *The Miscellaneous Works in Prose and Verse* (Edward F. Rimbault (ed.)) (London: Reeves & Turner, 1890), p. 151.
48. Cited from *Samuel Butler 1612–1680: Characters* (Charles W. Daves (ed.)) (Cleveland: The Press of Case Western Reserve University, 1970), 'Introduction', p. 18.
49. See Waller (ed.), pp. 94, 170–1.
50. 'A Translator', in ibid., p. 171.
51. Margaret Cavendish, *Poems and Fancies written by the Right Honorable, the Lady Margaret Newcastle* (1653), p. 123.

3   Plagiarism and the Burden of Tradition in Dryden and Others

1. The poem is cited from Paul Hammond and David Hopkins (eds) *Dryden: Selected Poems* (Harlow: Pearson Educational Ltd, 2007), pp. 571–81. Its language, especially its strong Saxon line, is discussed in Eric Griffiths, 'Dryden's Past', in *Proceedings of the British Academy 84: 1993 Lectures and Memoirs*, pp. 113–49.
2. 'An Account of the Greatest English Poets', in Richard Hurd (ed.) *The Works of the Right Honourable Joseph Addison*, six vols. (1811), 1: 33. See Harold Weber, '"A Double Portion of his Father's Art": Congreve, Dryden, Jonson and the Drama of Theatrical Succession', *Criticism* 39 (1997): 359–82.

3. On the pressures of literary belatedness, see W. Jackson Bate, *The Burden of the Past and the English Poet* (London: Chatto & Windus, 1971); and Harold Bloom, *The Anxiety of Influence* (New York: Oxford University Press, 1973).

4. See Gary Taylor, *Reinventing Shakespeare: A Cultural History from the Restoration to the Present* (London: Hogarth Press, 1989), p. 7.

5. Ibid., p. 11.

6. On the establishment of the new repertory, see Robert D. Hume, 'Securing a Repertory: Plays on the London Stage 1660–5', in Antony Coleman and Antony Hammond (eds) *Poetry and Drama 1570–1700: Essays in Honour of Harold F. Brooks* (London: Methuen, 1981), pp. 156–72.

7. Ibid., p. 168.

8. Ibid., p. 161–3.

9. Gunnar Sorelius, *'The Giant Race Before the Flood': Pre-Restoration Drama on the Stage and in the Criticism of the Restoration* (Uppsala: Studia anglistica upsaliensia, 1966), pp. 71–2.

10. Passages cited respectively from *Of Dramatic Poesy*, *Discourse Concerning Satire*, and 'Preface to *Fables Ancient and Modern*', in Watson (ed.), 1: 70; 2: 150; 2: 270. The passages are noted in Christopher Ricks's illuminating discussion of Dryden's use of paternity metaphors: see his 'Allusion: The Poet as Heir', in R.F. Brissenden and J.C. Eade (eds) *Studies in the Eighteenth Century III* (University of Toronto Press, 1976), pp. 209–40.

11. *Prose Works*, 1: 157.

12. Alexander Oldys, *An Ode on the Death of Mr Dryden* (1700), Stanza 6.

13. Watson (ed.), 1: 85. For a recent treatment of these issues, see Robert W. McHenry, Jr., 'Plagiarism and Paternity in Dryden's Adaptations', in McGinnis (ed.), *Originality and Intellectual Property*, pp. 1–21.

14. Paul Hammond and David Hopkins (eds) *Poems of John Dryden*, five vols. (Harlow: Pearson Education Ltd, 1995–2005), Vol. 1 (Hammond (ed.)), pp. 456–7 (lines 20, 32).

15. Ibid., 1: 315 (line 15).

16. *Dunciad Variorum* (1729), line 98, in Butt (ed.), 5: 71.

17. Odell cited from Michael Dobson, *The Making of the National Poet: Shakespeare, Adaptation and Authorship, 1660–1769* (Oxford: Clarendon Press, 1992), p. 9.

18. The point is made by Dobson: see pp. 31–32.

19. Watson (ed.), 1: 240.

20. On the politics of Shakespearean adaptation, see Dobson, pp. 62–98. For a useful discussion of several adaptations, including Davenant's *Macbeth*, Tate's *King Lear* and the Dryden-Davenant version of *The Tempest*, see Barbara Murray, *Restoration Shakespeare: Viewing the Voice* (London: Associated University Presses, 2001).

21. For a discussion in particular of Dryden's attempts to forestall plagiarism accusations against his adaptations, see Kewes, *Authorship and Appropriation*, pp. 54–63.

22. On Davenant's claim, see Samuel Schoenbaum, *William Shakespeare: A Compact Documentary Life* (Oxford University Press, 1975), pp. 224–7.

23. Dryden's 'Preface' is cited from Watson (ed.), 1: 133–6: here p. 134. The Preface is discussed in McHenry, Jr., pp. 6–9.

24. Watson (ed.), 1: 134–6.
25. Ibid., 1: 133.
26. For a recent discussion of plagiarism allegations levelled against Dryden, see Hammond, *Professional Imaginative Writing*, pp. 96–104.
27. 'A Defence of *An Essay on Dramatic Poesy*', in Watson (ed.), 1: 112.
28. 'Upon Critics who Judge of Modern Plays', in Lamar (ed.), p. 62.
29. Clifford's *Notes upon Mr. Dryden's Poems in Four Letters* (1687) is cited from James Kinsley and Helen Kinsley (eds) *Dryden: The Critical Heritage* (London: Routledge & Kegan Paul, 1971): see p. 175; *Hind and the Panther Transvers'd*, cited from Edward Pechter, *Dryden's Classical Theory of Literature* (Cambridge: Cambridge University Press, 1975), p. 93. On the plagiarism controversy surrounding the *Essay*, see Frank Livingstone Huntley, *On Dryden's 'Essay of Dramatic Poesy'* (Michigan: Archon Books, 1968), pp. 3–8. See also John M. Aden, 'Dryden, Corneille and the *Essay of Dramatic Poesy*', *Review of English Studies* NS 6 (1955): 147–56.
30. D.E.L. Crane (ed.) *The Rehearsal* (Durham: University of Durham Publications, 1976), p. 6.
31. Cited from Frank H. Ellis (ed.) *The Complete Works* (London: Penguin, 1994), p. 98 (lines 5–6).
32. Dryden responded to Blackmore in *Fables Ancient and Modern* (1700), in Watson (ed.), 2: 292–3.
33. Cited from *Dryden: The Critical Heritage*, pp. 261–2.
34. For the relationship between the two writers, see R. Jack Smith, 'Shadwell's Impact upon John Dryden', *Review of English Studies* 20 (1944): 29–44. The relevant texts are assembled in Richard L. Oden (ed.) *Dryden and Shadwell: The Literary Controversy and 'Mac Flecknoe'* (Delmar, NY: Scholars Facsimiles and Reprints, 1977).
35. Shadwell's prefaces are cited from Spingarn (ed.): here 2: 147–52, 150. For Dryden's original comment on Jonson, see Watson (ed.), 1: 69.
36. Spingarn (ed.), 2: 148.
37. 'Preface' to *An Evening's Love* (1671), in Watson (ed.), 1: 144–55, 148.
38. See ibid., 1: 153–4.
39. Ibid., 1: 155.
40. Spingarn (ed.), 2: 152–62, 158.
41. Watson (ed.), 1: 182–3.
42. The context of the poem, including Dryden's relationship with Shadwell and Flecknoe, is glossed succinctly in Hammond's editorial headnote: see *Poems*, 1: 307–12.

4 Plagiarism and Sufficiency in the English 'Battle of the Books'

1. Preface to Temple's posthumous *Letters* (1699), 1. sig. A2^v–A3^r; cited from A.C. Elias, Jr., *Swift and Moor Park* (Philadelphia: University of Pennsylvania Press, 1982), p. 71.
2. Henry Felton, *A Dissertation on Reading the Classics, and Forming a Just Style*, third edn (1718), p. 57.
3. William Wotton, *A Defense of the Reflections upon Ancient and Modern Learning ... with Observations upon The Tale of a Tub* (1705), p. 13.

4. Samuel Holt Monk (ed.) *Five Miscellaneous Essays by Sir William Temple* (Ann Arbor: University of Michigan Press, 1963), pp. 38, 69.
5. *Dr. Bentley's Dissertations on the Epistles of Phalaris, and the Fables of AEsop Examin'd. By the Honourable Charles Boyle, Esq.* (1698), p. 286. Authorship was in fact collaborative and may not have involved Boyle.
6. Swift's *Battle* and *Tale* are cited throughout from A.C. Guthkelch and D. Nichol Smith (eds) *A Tale of a Tub &c*, second edn (Oxford: Clarendon Press, 1958). Certain other material not by Swift, such as Wotton's plagiarism allegations, are for reasons of convenience cited from the same source. The fable covers pp. 228–35. Precise page references will henceforth be given in the text. For a discussion of the meaning of the fable, see Irvin Ehrenpreis, *Swift: The Man, his Works and the Age*, three vols. (London: Methuen, 1962–83), 1: 231–7; Roberta F. Sarfatt Borkat, 'The Spider and the Bee: Jonathan Swift's Reversal of Tradition in *The Battle of the Books*', *Eighteenth-Century Life* 3, 2 (December 1976): 44–6; and Deborah Baker Wyrick, *Jonathan Swift and the Vested Word* (Chapel Hill: University of North Carolina Press, 1988), pp. 60–2.
7. Not only Bentley and his accomplice William Wotton but also Temple himself may have been satirized in the fable. See Elias, pp. 191–5.
8. *Dr. Bentley's Dissertations ... Examin'd*, pp. 24–5.
9. William King, *Dialogues of the Dead. Relating to the present Controversy Concerning the Epistles of Phalaris* (1699), pp. 21–2. For King's substantial role in the dispute, see Colin J. Horne, 'The Phalaris Controversy: King *versus* Bentley', *Review of English Studies* 22 (1946): 289–303.
10. Francis Atterbury, *A Short Review of the Controversy between Mr. Boyle and Dr. Bentley* (1701), p. 2.
11. *Five Miscellaneous Essays*, p. 182. See Homer E. Woodbridge, *Sir William Temple: The Man and his Work* (New York: MLA of America, 1940), p. 294.
12. For a discussion of apian behaviour as an influence on imitation theory, see G.W. Pigman III, 'Versions of Imitation in the Renaissance', *Renaissance Quarterly* 33, 1 (Spring, 1980): 1–32. See also James W. Johnson, 'That Neo-Classical Bee', *Journal of the History of Ideas* 22, 2 (1961): 262–6.
13. The poem is entitled 'Against Idleness and Mischief' and appeared in *Divine Songs ... for the Use of Children* (1715). It is cited here from Roger Lonsdale (ed.) *The New Oxford Book of Eighteenth Century Verse* (Oxford University Press, 1984), p. 74.
14. See Pigman, pp. 4–7.
15. John Dunton, *A Voyage Round the World; or a Pocket Library* (1691), I. 'Introduction'. Cited from http://lion.chadwyck.co.uk, accessed 31 January 2006. Swift did not own a copy of the work, but Brean Hammond has suggested that Dunton's zany narrative style might have provided a model for the garrulous, self-fixated narrator of the *Tale*. See his 'Swift's Reading', in Christopher Fox (ed.) *A Cambridge Companion to Jonathan Swift* (Cambridge University Press, 2003), p. 81.
16. The best narrative of the 'Querelle', which I have followed here, is Joseph M. Levine, *The Battle of the Books: History and Literature in the Augustan Age* (Ithaca, NY: Cornell University Press, 1991), pp. 13–120. See also John F. Tinkler, 'The Splitting of Humanism: Bentley, Swift, and the English Battle of the Books', *Journal of the History of Ideas* 49, 3 (1988): 453–72. An older

account more concerned with science is R.F. Jones, *Ancients and Moderns* (St Louis: Washington University Press, 1961).

17. 'An Essay upon the Ancient and Modern Learning', in *Five Miscellaneous Essays*, p. 37.

18. *Dissertation on Reading the Classics*, pp. 34–5.

19. William Wotton, *Reflections upon Ancient and Modern Learning* (1694), Preface, p. ii.

20. Ibid., pp. 31, 29.

21. Sir Thomas Pope Blount, *Essays on Several Subjects*, third edn (1697), pp. 132, 134–5.

22. *Five Miscellaneous Essays*, p. 64.

23. *Dialogues of the Dead*, p. 9.

24. See Samuel Butler's character of 'A Pedant', in Daves (ed.), pp. 187–8. Blount associates 'frequent *Quotations* out of *Authors*' with '*Pedants*, and the Vulgar sort of *Scholars*': see *Essays on Several Subjects*, pp. 134–5.

25. William King, *The Odes of Horace in Latin and English; With a Translation of Dr. Bentley's Notes. To which are added, Notes upon Notes; Done in the Bentleian Stile and Manner* (1712), Part III, p. 22.

26. On the question of authorship, see Horne (pp. 290–1) and Levine (pp. 58–9).

27. See *Dr. Bentley's Dissertations ... Examin'd*, p. 138: 'Many *Proverbial Gnomae ...* are to be met with in the Dr's Dissertation; but No-body will allow this Way of Arguing from 'em: Either these *Gnomae* are Dr. *Bentley*'s own, or else he is a *Sorry Plagiary*.'

28. Ibid., p. 143.

29. Ibid.

30. Ibid., p. 248.

31. For theft from Boyle, see ibid., p. 143. Bentley's 'plagiarisms' from various authors are indexed at the back of the volume under '*His Ingenuity in – transcribing and plundering Notes and Prefaces*'.

32. Ibid., p. 250.

33. Levine, p. 73.

34. See Atterbury, *A Short Review*, pp. 4–5.

35. Richard Bentley, *A Dissertation upon the Epistles of Phalaris. With an Answer to the Objections of the Honourable Charles Boyle* (1699), p. 187.

36. Ibid., p. 333.

37. *A Short Account of Dr. Bentley's Humanity and Justice to those Authors who have written before him. With an Honest Vindication of Tho. Stanley, Esquire; and his Notes on Callimachus* (1699), pp. 26–7.

38. Ibid., p. 32.

39. For the sake of the reader's convenience, Wotton's allegations are cited from the portion of his book reproduced in *A Tale of a Tub &c*. Here, p. 327. The charges are considered, along with the general issue of Swift's use of sources in the *Tale* and *Battle*, in the 'Introduction', pp. xxxi–li.

40. Cited from Samuel Johnson, *The Lives of the English Poets* (Roger Lonsdale (ed.)), four vols. (Oxford: Clarendon Press, 2006), 3: 214. Johnson refers to the 'Advertisement' to Swift's *Works* (Dublin, 1735). See Lonsdale's note on 3: 462.

41. Cited from Pat Rogers (ed.) *Jonathan Swift: The Complete Poems* (Harmondsworth: Penguin, 1983), p. 493, lines 317–18.

42. Cited from Theodore Howard Banks, Jr. (ed.) *The Poetical Works of Sir John Denham* (New Haven: Yale University Press, 1928), p. 150.
43. Letter of 18 July 1731 in C.F. Burgess (ed.) *The Letters of John Gay* (Oxford: Clarendon Press, 1966), p. 113.
44. Cited from *Prose Works*, 9: 325–45, 333.
45. Swift's attitude towards literary originality is too broad a topic to be pursued here. However, see Michael G. Devine, 'Disputing the "Original" in Swift's *Tale of a Tub*', *Swift Studies* 18 (2003): 26–33.
46. See *A Tale of a Tub &c*, p. 347. Thomas Swift's relation to the *Tale* has been a vexed question. See Robert Martin Adams, 'Jonathan Swift, Thomas Swift, and the Authorship of *A Tale of a Tub*', *Modern Philology* 64 (1967): 198–232.
47. See Judith C. Mueller, 'Writing under Constraint: Swift's "Apology" for *A Tale of a Tub*', *ELH* 60 (1993): 101–15; and Frank H. Ellis, 'No Apologies, Dr. Swift!', *Eighteenth-Century Life* 21, 3 (1997): 71–6.
48. Cited from *Dryden: The Critical Heritage*, p. 145.
49. For a discussion of contemporary attitudes towards the silkworm, see Louis Landa, 'Pope's Belinda, The General Emporie of the World, and the Wondrous Worm', in his *Essays in Eighteenth-Century Literature* (Princeton University Press, 1980), pp. 178–98.
50. *An Account of the English Dramatick Poets*, p. 418.
51. Leonard Welsted, 'Dissertation concerning the Perfection of the English Language etc', (1724), in W.H. Durham (ed.) *Critical Essays of the Eighteenth Century* (New Haven: Yale University Press, 1915), p. 376.

5   Pope and Plagiarism

1. 'The Life of Dr. Parnell', in Oliver Goldsmith, *Collected Works* (Arthur Friedman (ed.)), five vols. (Oxford: Clarendon Press, 1966), 3: 425–6.
2. Pope's imitative practices are discussed sympathetically in Reuben Brower, *Alexander Pope: the Poetry of Allusion* (Oxford: Clarendon Press, 1959) and censoriously in James Reeves, *The Reputation and Writings of Alexander Pope* (London: Heinemann, 1976). I am grateful to Claude Rawson for drawing Reeves's book to my attention. A valuable recent consideration of Pope's relation to plagiarism is Paul Baines, 'Theft and Poetry and Pope', in Kewes (ed.), pp. 166–80. Baines's essay is focused on the Moore-Smythe controversy and does not seek to track the issue through Pope's full career and his immediate posterity. One issue I will not discuss here is whether Pope's lambasting of his enemies in *The Dunciad* contains actual plagiarism from them. That Pope had plagiarized from the dunces was a charge made during his lifetime. Jonathan Smedley in his *Gulliveriana* of 1728, for example, sneers that 'the Gentleman might have scorn'd to rob *those* Persons he had libell'd for their *Poverty*'. Cited from J.V. Guerinot, *Pamphlet Attacks on Alexander Pope 1711–1744: A Descriptive Bibliography* (London: Methuen & Co Ltd, 1969), p. 147. On this issue, see Roger D. Lund, 'From Oblivion to Dulness: Pope and the Poetics of Appropriation', *British Journal for Eighteenth-Century Studies* 14 (1991): 171–89.
3. Letter of 2 July 1706, in George Sherburn (ed.) *The Correspondence of Alexander Pope*, five vols. (Oxford: Clarendon Press, 1956), 1: 19.

4. To John Caryll, 5 December 1712, in ibid., 1: 161.
5. Cited from George deF. Lord *et al.* (eds) *Poems on Affairs of State: Augustan Satirical Verse, 1660–1714*, 7 vols. (New Haven: Yale University Press, 1963–75), vol. 6: 1697–1704 (Frank H. Ellis (ed.)), p. 150.
6. Cited from John F. Sena, *The Best Natur'd Man: Sir Samuel Garth, Physician and Poet* (New York, AMS Press, 1986), p. 84.
7. *Twickenham Edition*, 4: 105.
8. Ibid., 1: 309. Pope's relationship with Blackmore is discussed in Norman Ault, *New Light on Pope* (London: Methuen & Co, 1949), pp. 248–58.
9. See ibid.
10. John Harris, *A Treatise upon the Modes: or, A Farewell to French Kicks* (1715), p. 40.
11. For a discussion of the use of metempsychosis as a metaphor for literary tradition, see my *Poetry and the Making of the English Literary Past*, pp. 156–68.
12. See *Pamphlet Attacks*. Another useful anthology of early critical responses to Pope's poetry is John Barnard (ed.) *Pope: The Critical Heritage* (London: Routledge & Kegan Paul, 1973).
13. Leonard Welsted, 'Of Dulness and Scandal Occasioned by the Character of Lord Timon in Mr. Pope's Epistle to the Earl of Burlington', lines 81–2, in *Works* (1787). Cited from http://lion.chadwyck.co.uk, accessed 6 January 2006.
14. The poem appeared under the name 'Gerard' in the *London Evening Post*, 14 February 1734. Cited from *Pamphlet Attacks*, p. 246.
15. Edward Ward, *Durgen. Or, A Plain Satyr upon a Pompous Satyrist.* (1729), lines 123–4. Cited from http://lion.chadwyck.co.uk, accessed 6 January 2006.
16. Thomas Cooke, 'The Battel of the Poets', Canto 1, lines 65, 67, in *Poems* (1742). The poem originally appeared in 1725. Cited from http://lion.chadwyck.co.uk, accessed 6 January 2006.
17. *Rape of the Lock* (1714), V. 103–4, in *Twickenham Edition*, 2: 208.
18. *A Treatise upon the Modes*, p. ii.
19. *Pamphlet Attacks*, p. 246.
20. See ibid., p. 51.
21. Joseph Spence, *Observations, Anecdotes, and Characters of Books and Men* (J.M. Osborn (ed.)), two vols. (Oxford: Clarendon Press, 1966), no. 745, 1: 304.
22. Leonard Welsted, 'One Epistle to Mr. A. Pope, Occasioned by Two Epistles lately published', lines 150, 152–3, in *Works* (1787). Cited from http://lion.chadwyck.co.uk, accessed 6 January 2006. The collaborative agreement was a shabby one and reflects poorly on all concerned. Broome and Fenton were initially happy to collude in the fiction, designed to boost sales, that the translation had been undertaken by Pope unaided. However, Broome, who had literary aspirations of his own, seems to have become disenchanted with the deception. In any event, the actual process of composition soon became common knowledge.
23. 'On Pope's Translation of Homer', in *Applebee's Journal*, 31 July 1725, in William Lee (ed.) *Daniel Defoe: His Life and Recently Discovered Writings*, three vols. (1869), 3: 409–12. Defoe's extensive involvement in *Applebee's Journal* is assumed by recent biographers. However, for a comment on the attribution issue, see P.N. Furbank and W.R. Owens, *The Canonisation of Daniel Defoe* (New Haven: Yale University Press, 1988), pp. 72–4.
24. 7 August 1725, 'The Same, and on Literary Frauds', in ibid., 3: 412–14.

25. Both sets of verses are cited from Ault, p. 198.
26. Ault's discussion occupies pp. 195–206; for a more recent consideration, see Baines, 'Theft and Poetry and Pope', in Kewes (ed.), pp. 166–71.
27. *Twickenham Edition*, 5: 101.
28. Cited from Rosemary Cowler (ed.) *The Prose Works of Alexander Pope: Vol. II: The Major Works, 1725–1744* (Oxford: Basil Blackwell, 1986), p. 197.
29. See Sena, p. 180. For Cowler's deliberations, see pp. 251–2.
30. 'A Discourse on Pastoral Poetry', in *Twickenham Edition*, 1: 25.
31. *Correspondence*, 1: 101.
32. *Guardian* 30, 15 April 1713, in John Calhoun Stephens (ed.) *The Guardian* (Lexington: University Press of Kentucky, 1982), p. 128. That Pope was conscious that he might have borrowed to excess in his pastorals is clear from his early letter to Walsh on the subject: 'tell me sincerely, if I have not stretch'd this Licence too far'. *Correspondence*, 1: 20.
33. *Guardian* 40, 27 April 1713, in ibid., p. 161.
34. *Twickenham Edition*, 4: 109.
35. Ibid., 5: 278–9.
36. From *The Causes of the Decay and Defects of Dramatick Poetry*, in John Dennis, *Critical Works* (E.N. Hooker (ed.)), two vols. (Baltimore: The Johns Hopkins Press, 1939–43), 2: 281.
37. Cibber, *An Apology for his Life*, p. 138.
38. Dennis, *A True Character of Mr. Pope, and His Writings* (1716), in Hooker (ed.), 2: 104.
39. John Carroll (ed.) *Selected Letters of Samuel Richardson* (Oxford: Clarendon Press, 1964), p. 60.
40. No. 63, 12 June 1753, in *The Adventurer*, third edn, four vols. (1756), 2: 227–35.
41. Warton, *Essay*, vol. I (1756), cited from *Essay on the Genius and Writings of Pope*, fifth edn, two vols. (1806), I. 91, 94–5.
42. *Of Dramatic Poesy: An Essay* (1668), in Watson (ed.), 1: 69.
43. Ibid., 1: 31.
44. *Essay on the Genius and Writings of Pope* (1806), 2: 402.
45. *Reflections on Originality in Authors: Being Remarks on A Letter to Mr. Mason on the Marks of Imitation ... with a word or two on the Characters of Ben. Johnson and Pope* (1766), p. 63. Authorship is probably by Capell.
46. John Pinkerton [Robert Heron], *Letters of Literature* (1785), p. 359.
47. Dilworth cited from Barnard (ed.), p. 424.
48. Lonsdale (ed.), 4: 79–80.
49. *Lectures on the Truly Eminent English Poets*, two vols. (1807), 1: 427–9.
50. *Inquiry into the Nature, and Genuine Laws of Poetry*, p. 76.
51. *Lectures*, 1: 433.

6 Johnson and the Lauder Affair

1. See *Rambler* 36 (21 July 1750).
2. Lives of 'Gray' and 'Milton' in Lonsdale (ed.), 4: 182, 1: 294. For general discussion of Johnson's attitude to borrowing, see Lonsdale, 1: 331–2; Howard Weinbrot, *The Formal Strain: Studies in Augustan Imitation and Satire* (University of Chicago Press, 1969), esp. pp. 82–5; and James Engell,

'Johnson on Novelty and Originality', *Modern Philology* 75 (February 1978): 273–9.

3. *Lives of the Poets*, 3: 214, 4: 166.

4. Ibid., 3: 188.

5. Ibid., 3: 217.

6. *Rambler* 176 (23 November 1751), in W.J. Bate and Albrecht B. Strauss (eds) *The Rambler* (1969), in *The Yale Edition of the Works of Samuel Johnson* (New Haven: Yale University Press, 1958), 5: 167.

7. *Adventurer* 95 (2 October 1753), in W.J. Bate, John M. Bullitt and L.F. Powell (eds) *The Idler and The Adventurer* (1963), in *Yale Edition*, 2: 425.

8. While Johnson does not define these more atrocious offences, they may have included literary forgery (this is discussed elsewhere in this chapter) and the acts of identity theft perpetrated against writers such as Mark Akenside and Henry Mackenzie which he would some time later discuss with Boswell. See *Boswell's Life of Johnson* (George Birkbeck Hill (ed.), rev. L.F. Powell), six vols. (Oxford: Clarendon Press, 1934–50), 1: 359–61. For Johnson's views about various cases of literary deception, see Jack Lynch, *Deception and Detection in Eighteenth-Century Britain* (Aldershot: Ashgate, 2008).

9. *Gentleman's Magazine* (henceforth *GM*) 17 (1747): 24–6, 24.

10. Lauder brought his charges in four further contributions to *GM*. See February, 82–6; April, 189; June, 285–6; and August, 363–4.

11. *GM* 17 (1747): 322–4.

12. Lauder's disreputable campaign against Milton, the process of its exposure and the general public controversy that resulted have all been researched in detail by Michael J. Marcuse. See his 'The Lauder Controversy and the Jacobite Cause', *Studies in Burke and his Time* 18 (1977): 27–47, and '"The Scourge of Impostors, the Terror of Quacks": John Douglas and the Exposé of William Lauder', *Huntington Library Quarterly* 42 (1978–9): 231–61. An abbreviated overview of the whole matter is provided by the same author's 'Miltonoklastes: The Lauder Affair Reconsidered'. For a view of the way that Lauder's campaign fits within the 'cultural politics' of the Jacobite rebellion, see J.C.D. Clark, *Samuel Johnson: Literature, Religion and English Cultural Politics from the Restoration to Romanticism* (Cambridge University Press, 1994), pp. 59–66.

13. See *The Dunciad* (1743), IV. 112. Lauder's resentment at Pope's snub is expressed in his *Letter to the Reverend Mr. Douglas, occasion'd by his Vindication of Milton* (1751), pp. 12–13.

14. See Marcuse, 'The Lauder Controversy and the Jacobite Cause', p. 30.

15. Letter from Lauder to Ruddiman, Dundee, dated 4 September 1745; cited from Douglas Duncan, *Thomas Ruddiman: A Study in Scottish Scholarship of the Early Eighteenth Century* (Oliver & Boyd: Edinburgh, 1965), p. 159.

16. Draft reply from Ruddiman to Lauder, 5 November 1745; cited from ibid., p. 164.

17. The letter eventually appeared in *GM* 20 (1750): 535–6. For a discussion of its delayed passage into print, see Marcuse, 'Scourge of Impostors', p. 237.

18. William Lauder, *An Essay on Milton's Use and Imitation of the Moderns* (1750), pp. 37, 71.

19. Ibid., p. 74.

20. Ibid., p. 163.
21. See Marcuse, 'Scourge of Impostors', pp. 235–48.
22. *Milton Vindicated from the Charge of Plagiarism* (1751), p. 8.
23. Lauder had carelessly allowed inconsistencies between the neo-Latin texts cited in the *Essay* and in the *GM* articles.
24. Lauder's booksellers, John Payne and Joseph Bouquet, placed an advertisement in the *London Gazeteer*. See Allan T. Hazen, *Samuel Johnson's Prefaces & Dedications* (New Haven: Yale University Press, 1937), p. 79.
25. *Letter to Douglas*, p. 24.
26. See James L. Clifford, 'Johnson and Lauder', *Philological Quarterly* 54 (1975): 342–56, 352.
27. *King Charles I Vindicated from the Charge of Plagiarism* (1754), p. 64.
28. See 'Johnson and Lauder'. See also Paul Baines's chapter on 'Lauder, Johnson and Literary Crime' in his *The House of Forgery in Eighteenth-Century Britain* (Aldershot: Ashgate, 1999); and Bertrand A. Goldgar, 'Imitation and Plagiarism: The Lauder Affair and its Critical Aftermath', *Studies in the Literary Imagination* 34 (2001): 1–16.
29. See 'Johnson and Lauder', p. 343.
30. *Lives of the Poets*, 1: 261.
31. Cited from *GM* 17 (1747): 404. The *Proposals* were also published separately in early September 1747. See also Hazen, pp. 77–84.
32. See 'Johnson and Lauder', p. 346.
33. *Milton Vindicated*, p. 77.
34. Cited from 'Johnson and Lauder', p. 347. See Hazen, p. 79.
35. *Letter to Douglas*, p. 13.
36. See George Birkbeck Hill (ed.) *Johnsonian Miscellanies*, two vols. (Oxford: Clarendon Press, 1897), 1: 398.
37. Montagu Pennington (ed.) *A Series of Letters between Mrs. Elizabeth Carter and Miss Catherine Talbot, from the year 1741 to 1770*, two vols. (1808), 1: 245. See also 1: 248.
38. 'The Scourge of Impostors', p. 233.
39. Letter from Warburton to Richard Hurd, 23 December 1749; cited from *Letters from a Late Eminent Prelate to one of his Friends* (1809), p. 22.
40. See John Nichols, *Illustrations of the Literary History of the Eighteenth Century*, eight vols. (1817–58), 2: 177. A particularly interesting contemporary relation of the Lauder affair is given in the 'Postscript' (dated 5 December 1750) to Thomas Newton's variorum edition of *Paradise Lost: A Poem in Twelve Books*, two vols. (second edn 1751), 2: 449–56.
41. *Yale Edition*, 4: 394.
42. However, Boswell noted that Johnson's prodigious memory which 'at once detected the real owner of any thought, made him less liable to the imputation of plagiarism than, perhaps, any of our writers'. See *Life of Johnson*, 1: 334.
43. *Adventurer* 95, 2 October 1753, in *Yale Edition*, 2: 424–9, esp. 425–7.
44. For discussion of Langbaine's view of plagiarism, see Kewes, *Authorship and Appropriation*, and Chapter 2 of this book.
45. *Lives of the Poets*, 2: 149.
46. Ibid., 2: 83.
47. Ibid., 2: 98.
48. *Milton Vindicated*, p. 14.

49. *Yale Edition*, 4: 394.
50. See Chapter 4.
51. 'Life of Parnell', in *Lives of the Poets*, 2: 194.
52. 'Life of Mallet', in ibid., 4: 167. See also the 'Life of Yalden', which begins by relating how a baseless suspicion of plagiarism was generated by an excellent declamation delivered by the poet: ibid., 3: 109.
53. See Henry Abelove, 'John Wesley's Plagiarism of Samuel Johnson and its Contemporary Reception', *Huntington Library Quarterly* 59 (1997): 73–9, 74.
54. Ibid., p. 75.
55. Letter from Johnson to Wesley, in Bruce Redford (ed.) *The Letters of Samuel Johnson*, five vols. (Oxford: Clarendon Press, 1992–4), 2: 290.

7   The Plagiarism Allegation and the Female Author

1. See Chapter 2 for an exploration of the relation between plagiarism and fame.
2. Cited from Janet Todd (ed.) *The Works of Aphra Behn*, seven vols. (London: William Pickering, 1996), 5: 521.
3. See Rosenthal, *Playwrights and Plagiarists*, p. 13.
4. *Rambler* 143, 30 July 1751, in *Yale Edition*, 4: 394.
5. See Mazzeo, p. 49.
6. See entry of 15 April 1802, in Dorothy Wordsworth, *The Grasmere and Alfoxden Journals* (Pamela Woof (ed.)) (Oxford University Press, 2002), p. 85; Wordsworth's poem is cited from E. De Selincourt (ed.) *The Poetical Works of William Wordsworth*, second edn, five vols. (Oxford: Clarendon Press, 1952), 2: 216.
7. Ibid., 2: 262–3.
8. For a discussion of issues of creative ownership in the relationship between William and Dorothy, see 'The Uses of Dorothy: "The Language of the Sense' in "Tintern Abbey"', in John Barrell, *Poetry, Language and Politics* (Manchester University Press, 1988); Jane Spencer, *Literary Relations: Kinship and the Canon 1660–1830* (Oxford University Press, 2005), pp. 164–87; and Mazzeo, pp. 62–70.
9. The relationship is discussed in Spencer, pp. 137–64.
10. See Martin C. Battestin (ed.) *Joseph Andrews* (Oxford: Clarendon Press, 1967), p. 106; and Ian A. Bell and Andrew Varney (eds) *A Journey from This World to the Next and The Journal of a Voyage to Lisbon* (Oxford: World's Classics, 1997), pp. 102–17. See pp. xvii–xix for discussion of the attribution issue.
11. *A Journey from This World*, p. 101.
12. Henry's Preface is cited as Appendix I to Sarah Fielding, *The Adventures of David Simple and Volume the Last* (Peter Sabor (ed.)) (Lexington: University Press of Kentucky, 1998), pp. 343–9, p. 343.
13. Ibid., p. 345.
14. See Jane Barchas, 'Sarah Fielding's Dashing Style and Eighteenth-Century Print Culture', *ELH* 63 (1996): 633–56.
15. See Joanna Russ, *How to Suppress Women's Writing* (London: Women's Press, 1983), esp. Chapter 3, 'Denial Of Agency', pp. 20–4; Felicity A. Nussbaum, *The Brink of All We Hate: English Satires on Women, 1660–1750* (Lexington: University

of Kentucky Press, 1984); and Margaret Ezell, *Writing Women's Literary History* (Baltimore: Johns Hopkins University Press, 1993). Germaine Greer notes that when a female poet 'begins to express herself in verse, she delivers herself up to the best and worst of which the masculine literary establishment is capable': see her *Slip-Shod Sibyls: Recognition, Rejection and the Woman Poet* (London: Viking, 1995), p. xi.

16. See Jacqueline Pearson, *The Prostituted Muse: Images of Women and Women Dramatists, 1642–1737* (London: Harvester Wheatsheaf, 1988).

17. 'To the Pious Memory', cited from Dryden, *Selected Poems*, p. 361; Charles E. Ward (ed.) *The Letters of John Dryden* (Durham, NC: Duke University Press, 1942), p. 126.

18. Anonymous, 'A Pindarick To Mrs *Behn*', cited from Germaine Greer *et al.* (eds) *Kissing the Rod: An Anthology of 17*th *Century Women's Verse* (London: Virago, 1988), p. 261. For a discussion of the positive connotations of 'manly' as used in a literary context, see Laura L. Runge, *Gender and Language in British Literary Criticism 1660–1790* (Cambridge University Press, 1997), pp. 1–39.

19. See Christine Battersby, *Gender and Genius: Towards a Feminist Aesthetics* (London: Women's Press, 1989).

20. 'On the death of the honourable Mr James Thynne', l. 41, in Myra Reynolds (ed.) *The Poems of Anne, Countess of Winchilsea* (University of Chicago Press, 1903), pp. 56–9: cited from Harold Love, *Scribal Publication in Seventeenth-Century England* (Oxford: Clarendon Press, 1993), p. 54.

21. Cited from Anne Kugler, *Errant Plagiary: The Life and Writings of Lady Sarah Cowper 1644–1720* (Stanford University Press, 2002), p. 3.

22. Jeannine Hensley (ed.) *Works of Anne Bradstreet* (Cambridge, Mass.: Harvard University Press, 1967), p. 16.

23. Pearson, p. 9.

24. Cited from Patricia Springborg (ed.) *Astell: Political Writings* (Cambridge University Press, 1996), p. 23.

25. Elizabeth Elstob, *An English-Saxon Homily on the Birth-day of St. Gregory* (1709), pp. ii, lvii–lviii.

26. *Poems on Several Occasions: By Mrs. Jane Brereton* (1744), p. xxxii: cited from Spencer, p. 117.

27. *Letters and Poems in Honour of ... Margaret, Duchess of Newcastle* (1676), p. 146. For the controversy over Cavendish's originality, see Rosenthal, pp. 58–104, and Jeffery Masten's chapter on Cavendish in his *Textual Intercourse: Collaboration, Authorship, and Sexualities in Renaissance Drama* (Cambridge University Press, 1997).

28. *Nature's Pictures Drawn by Fancies Pencil to the Life* (1665), p. 367: cited from Rosenthal, p. 58; *Life of William Cavendishe*, second edn (1675), dedicatory epistle 'To his Grace the Duke of Newcastle'.

29. *Life of William Cavendishe*, dedicatory epistle.

30. *Poems and Fancies*, p. 123.

31. Ibid., 'The Epsitle Dedicatory'.

32. *Natures Picture Drawn by Fancies Pencil to the Life* (1656), p. 126. See Sylvia Bowerbank, 'The Spider's Delight: Margaret Cavendish and the "Female" Imagination', *English Literary Renaissance* 14 (Winter 1984): 392–408.

33. Stuart Curran (ed.) *The Poems of Charlotte Smith* (Oxford University Press, 1993), p. xxvi.

34. On Smith's borrowing, see Judith Hawley, 'Charlotte Smith's *Elegiac Sonnets*: Losses and Gains', in Isobel Armstrong and Virginia Blain (eds) *Women's Poetry in the Enlightenment: The Making of a Canon, 1730–1820* (Basingstoke: Macmillan, 1999), pp. 184–98; Kathryn Pratt, 'Charlotte Smith's Melancholia on the Page and Stage', *SEL* 41 (2001): 563–81; and Paula R. Backscheider, *Eighteenth-Century Women Poets and their Poetry: Inventing Agency, Inventing Genre* (Baltimore: Johns Hopkins University Press, 2005), pp. 332–8. Backscheider points out that Smith's borrowing has been read traditionally as a means by which she acquired cultural capital (see p. 457).

35. Cited from Loraine Fletcher, *Charlotte Smith: A Critical Biography* (Basingstoke: Palgrave, 2001), p. 82.

36. *Letters of Anna Seward, written between the years 1784 and 1807*, six vols. (1811), 2: 162, 2: 287.

37. Curran (ed.), p. 4.

38. See 'Avis au lecteur' in the second edition of *The Banished Man* (1795): cited from Stuart Curran (gen. ed.)) *The Works of Charlotte Smith*, 14 vols. (London: Pickering & Chatto, 2005), Vol. 7 (M.O. Grenby (ed.)), p. 193.

39. Curran (ed.), p. 251.

40. See Fletcher, p. 84.

41. Spencer, p. 189.

42. *An Essay in Defence of the Female Sex*, fifth edn (1721), p. 2.

43. *An English-Saxon Homily*, p. lviii.

44. Sarah Fielding, *The Cry: A New Dramatic Fable*, three vols. (1754), 1: 186.

45. Ibid., 1: 187.

46. Ibid., 1: 188.

47. See T.C. Duncan Eaves and Ben D. Kimpel, *Samuel Richardson: A Biography* (Oxford: Clarendon Press, 1971), pp. 214–16. For Richard Sheridan's debt to his mother, see Spencer, pp. 107–10.

8   Plagiarism, Imitation and Originality

1. For an historical interview, see White, *Plagiarism and Imitation During the English Renaissance*; Harold F. Brooks, 'The "Imitation" in English Poetry, especially in Formal Satire, before the Age of Pope', *RES* 25 (1949): 124–40; and Weinbrot, *The Formal Strain*.

2. See *Adventurer* 95, 2 October 1753, in *Yale Edition* 2, pp. 424–9, 425–7.

3. See Chapter 4 for a discussion of such attitudes as part of the ancients vs. moderns debate.

4. *Essay on Criticism*, line 135, in Butt (ed.), 1: 255

5. See Elizabeth Nitchie, 'Longinus and the Theory of Poetic Imitation in Seventeenth and Eighteenth Century England', *Studies in Philology* 32 (1935): 580–97.

6. *The Works of Dionysius Longinus, On the Sublime ... Translated from the Greek ... By Mr. Welsted* (1712), p. 48.

7. 'Preface' to 'An Essay on the Different Stiles of Poetry', in Claude Rawson and F.P. Lock (eds) *Collected Poems of Thomas Parnell* (Newark: University of Delaware Press, 1989), p. 48.

8. Welsted, 'Dissertation concerning the Perfection of the English Language etc.' (1724), in Durham (ed.), p. 377.

9. See Weinbrot, *The Formal Strain*, p. 56.

10. See Butler's remark that 'The Ancients ... never writ any Thing but what they stole and borrowed from others': Waller (ed.), p. 171.

11. For a contemporary account of the scope of Shakespeare's imitations, see Richard Farmer, *An Essay on the Learning of Shakespeare* (1767).

12. For parallelism as a poetic technique, see Frederick Keener, 'Parallelism and the Poets' Secret: Eighteenth-Century Commentary on *Paradise Lost*', *Essays in Criticism* 37 (1987): 281–302. See also Marcus Walsh, *Shakespeare, Milton and Eighteenth-Century Literary Editing: The Beginnings of Interpretive Scholarship* (Cambridge University Press, 1997).

13. For a modern discussion of the phenomenon of allusion, see Earl R. Wasserman, 'The Limits of Allusion in *The Rape of the Lock*', *Journal of English and Germanic Philology* 65 (1966): 425–44; Irvin Ehrenpreis, *Literary Meaning and Augustan Values* (Charlottesville: University of Virginia Press, 1974); Harold Bloom, *A Map of Misreading* (New York: Oxford University Press, 1975); John Hollander, *The Figure of Echo: A Mode of Allusion in Milton and After* (Berkeley: California University Press, 1981); Robert Folkenflik, '"Homo Alludens" in the Eighteenth Century', *Criticism* 24 (1982): 218–32; and Lucy Newlyn, *Coleridge, Wordsworth and the Language of Allusion* (Oxford: Clarendon Press, 1986), Preface.

14. See Pope's notes to *Rape* (1714), IV. 133, and *Dunciad* (1729), I. 6, in Butt (ed.), 2: 195, 5: 61.

15. 25 March 1714; cited from Durham (ed.), pp. 295–6.

16. *Rambler* 176, 23 November 1751, in *Yale Edition*, 5: 167.

17. *Explanatory Notes and Remarks on Milton's Paradise Lost. By J. Richardson, Father and Son* (1734), cl.

18. Cited from J.T. Shawcross (ed.) *Milton: The Critical Heritage* (London: Routledge & Kegan Paul, 1970), p. 122.

19. Thomas Newton (ed.) *Paradise Lost: A Poem in Twelve Books*, second edn, two vols. (1750), 1: sig. B³.

20. See *Allusion to the Poets*, pp. 231–2.

21. *Milton Vindicated from the Charge of Plagiarism*, pp. 7–8, 21.

22. Joseph Trapp, *Lectures on Poetry: Read in the Schools of Natural Philosophy at Oxford* (1742), p. 351.

23. Richard Hurd, *Q. Horatii Flacci Epistolae ad Pisones, et Augustum: with an English commentary and notes*, third edn, two vols. (1751), 2: 105.

24. Ibid., 2: 200, 206–7.

25. Richard Hurd, *A Letter to Mr. Mason; On the Marks of Imitation* (1757), p. 62.

26. *Epistolae ad Pisones et Augustum*, 2: 189.

27. No. XXII, July 1779, in Margery Bailey (ed.) *Boswell's Column* (London: William Kimber, 1951), p. 134.

28. See his 'Gray and "Allusion": The Poet as Debtor'.

29. *Correspondence*, 2: 477.

30. Cited from Sir William Forbes (ed.) *An Account of the Life and Writings of James Beattie* (1806), reprinted with introduction by Roger Robinson, two vols. (London: Thoemmes Press, 1976), 1: 54–5.

31. See Patricia Craddock (ed.) *The English Essays of Edward Gibbon* (Oxford: Clarendon Press, 1972), pp. 46–53.
32. *Reflections on Originality in Authors*, pp. 43–6.
33. Cited from *The Adventurer*, four vols. (third edn, 1756), 2: 227–35, 229.
34. *Rambler* 143, in *Yale Edition*, 4: 399.
35. *The Connoisseur* 67, 8 May 1755, in *The Connoisseur; By Mr. Town, Critic and Censor-General*, second edn (1755), p. 242; Armstrong, 'Of Imitation', cited from *Miscellanies*, two vols. (1770), 2: 167; Lloyd, cited from David Nichol Smith (ed.) *The Oxford Book of Eighteenth Century Verse* (Oxford: Clarendon Press, 1926), p. 411.
36. Letter of 23 November 1783, in James King and Charles Ryskamp (ed.) *The Letters and Prose Writings of William Cowper*, five vols. (Oxford: Clarendon Press, 1979–86), 2: 183.
37. *Miscellanies*, 2: 167–8.
38. Edward Young, *Conjectures on Original Composition* (Edith J. Morley (ed.)) (Manchester University Press, 1918), pp. 10–11.
39. Ibid., p. 12.
40. Lecture delivered on 10 December 1774, in Reynolds, *Discourses Delivered to the Students of the Royal Academy* (Roger Fry (ed.)) (London: Seeley & Co., 1905), p. 165.
41. *Conjectures*, p. 11.
42. See Elizabeth L. Mann, 'The Problem of Originality in English Literary Criticism, 1750–1800', *Philological Quarterly* 18 (1939): 97–118. On the valorizing of originality, see Patricia Phillips, *The Adventurous Muse: Theories of Originality in English Poetics 1650–1760* (Uppsala: Almqvist & Wiskell, 1984).
43. *Inquiry into the Nature and Genuine Laws of Poetry*, pp. 74, 85. Stockdale's discussion of plagiarism is reproduced virtually verbatim in his essay on Pope in his later *Lectures on the Truly Eminent English Poets*, 2: 425–37. A good recent treatment of the eccentric Stockdale is Howard D. Weinbrot, 'Samuel Johnson, Percival Stockdale, and Brick-bats from Grubstreet: Some Later Response to the *Lives of the Poets*', *Huntington Library Quarterly* 56 (1993): 105–34.
44. *Inquiry into the Nature and Genuine Laws of Poetry*, p. 74.
45. Ibid., pp. 75–6.
46. Ibid., p. 77.
47. Ibid., pp. 77–9.
48. John Pinkerton, *Letters of Literature* (1785), p. 356.
49. Ibid.
50. Ibid., pp. 357–8.

9   Sterne: The Plagiarist as Genius

1. Braudy, *The Frenzy of Renown*, p. 13.
2. Letter to Dr Noah Thomas (?), 30 January 1760, in Lewis Perry Curtis (ed.) *Letters of Laurence Sterne* (Oxford: Clarendon Press, 1935), p. 90. The comment parodies Colley Cibber, *A Letter from Mr. Cibber to Mr. Pope* (1742), p. 9: 'I wrote more to be Fed, than to be Famous.' See Peter M. Briggs, 'Laurence Sterne and Literary Celebrity in 1760', *Age of Johnson* 4 (1991): 251–80. Sterne's cultivation

of his own fame is emphasized in Ian Campbell Ross's biography, *Laurence Sterne: A Life* (Oxford University Press, 2001); see pp. 1–19.

3. For a broad view of the concept, see Braudy and also Terry, *Poetry and Making of the English Literary Past*, pp. 63–92.

4. See Melvyn New, 'Sterne's Rabelaisian Fragment: A Text from the Holograph Manuscript', *PMLA* 87 (1972): 1083–92, 1085.

5. Ibid., p. 1089, lines 59–68.

6. See ibid., p. 1092, fn. 16.

7. Ibid., p. 1090, lines 90–1.

8. The issue of Sterne's possible plagiarism from letters to his wife-to-be, Elizabeth Lumley, is vexed. See Curtis's discussion in *Letters*, pp. 10–16. For comments on the relation between the *Journal to Eliza* and *A Sentimental Journey*, see Gardner D. Stout, Jr. (ed.) *A Sentimental Journey through France and Italy by Mr. Yorick* (Berkeley and Los Angeles: University of California Press, 1967), p. 323.

9. This extrapolation is made by Arthur Cash using parallel passages cited by Hammond. Cash thinks this figure not inconsistent with general clerical practice. See Arthur H. Cash, *Laurence Sterne: The Later Years* (London: Routledge, 1986), p. 40. For the original evidence, see Lansing Van der Heyden Hammond, *Laurence Sterne's 'Sermons of Mr. Yorick'* (New Haven, Conn.: Yale University Press, 1948). This has been supplemented by James Downey, 'The Sermons of Mr. Yorick: A Reassessment of Hammond', *English Studies in Canada* IV (1978): 193–211. See also Christopher Fanning, '"The Things Themselves": Origins and Originality in Sterne's Sermons', *The Eighteenth Century* 40, 1 (1999): 29–45. The definitive *Florida Edition* of Sterne's works now allows for a more comprehensive understanding of Sterne's sources than was available to earlier scholars.

10. John Norris, *Practical Discourses upon Several Divine Subjects: Volume II* (1691), p. 9; cited from Melvyn New (ed.) *The Sermons of Laurence Sterne* (1996), vols. 4 and 5 of the *Florida Edition of the Works of Laurence Sterne* (Gainsville, Florida: University Press of Florida, 1978), 5: 400.

11. *Florida Edition*, 4: 372.

12. See the account of Johnson's practices by the Revd Thomas Hussey, in *Life of Johnson*, 3: 507.

13. Letter to the Revd Charles Lawrence, 30 August 1780, in Bruce Redford (ed.) *The Letters of Samuel Johnson*, 5 vols. (Oxford: Clarendon Press, 1992–4), 3: 311. For an extenuatory discussion of the plagiarizing of sermons, see Hammond, pp. 74–89.

14. 'Sterne's Rabelaisian Fragment', p. 1089 (lines 70–1).

15. *The Life and Opinions of Tristram Shandy*, in the *Florida Edition*, vol. 1 (Melvyn New and Joan New (eds)), pp. 126–67, esp. 166–7.

16. *Florida Edition*, 4: 2.

17. The author of the remark is Owen Ruffhead. Cited from Alan B. Howes (ed.) *Sterne: The Critical Heritage* (London and Boston: Routledge & Kegan Paul, 1974), p. 77.

18. Cited from *Florida Edition*, vol. 3 (Melvyn New (ed.)), with Richard A. Davies and W.G. Day), p. 336. For an overview of Sterne's main sources, see pp. 12–24.

19. Sterne consulted Thoyras in the translation and continuation by N. Tindal. The source was unearthed in Theodore Baird, 'The Time-Scheme of *Tristram Shandy* and a Source', *PMLA* 51 (1936): 803–20. For the obstetrical background of Tristram's fraught arrival into the world, see Arthur H. Cash, 'The Birth of Tristram Shandy: Sterne and Dr. Burton', in R.F. Brissenden (ed.) *Studies in the Eighteenth Century* (Canberra: Australian National University Press, 1968), pp. 133–54.

20. Burton cited from *Florida Edition*, 3: 201.

21. Ibid., 1: 175–6.

22. *Florida Edition*, 3: 201. See Donna Landry and Gerald MacLean, 'Of Forceps, Patents, and Paternity: *Tristram Shandy*', *Eighteenth Century Studies* 23 (1989–90): 522–43.

23. I benefited greatly from seeing in advance of its publication Vike Plock's work on plagiarism and biological reproduction in Sterne and Joyce. See her *Joyce, Medicine, and Modernity* (Gainesville: University Press of Florida, 2010).

24. *Florida Edition*, 1: 118; Curtis (ed.) *Letters*, p. 290. These passages are referred to by Plock: see p. 83.

25. D.W. Jefferson, '*Tristram Shandy* and the Tradition of Learned Wit', *Essays in Criticism* 1 (1951): 225–48. For a more recent treatment of the same issue, see J.T. Parnell, 'Swift, Sterne, and the Skeptical Tradition', *Studies in Eighteenth-Century Culture* 23 (1994): 220–42.

26. See, for example, echoes of *The Dunciad* ('majesty of mud', 'obstetrick hand') in *Florida Edition*, 1: 124, 126. For a borrowing from Rabelais, see the discussion of the cause of long noses in ibid., 1: 284. The sources are referenced at 3: 156–8, 277–8.

27. The critical literature on Sterne's putative plagiarism is extensive. See J.M. Stedmond, 'Sterne as Plagiarist', *English Studies* 41 (1960): 308–12; Henri Fluchère, *Laurence Sterne: From Tristram to Yorick: An Interpretation of Tristram Shandy*, translated and abridged by Barbara Bray (London: Oxford University Press, 1965), pp. 165–74; Graham Petrie, 'A Rhetorical Topic in *Tristram Shandy*', *Modern Language Review* 65 (1970): 201–6; and Jonathan Lamb, 'Sterne's System of Imitation', *Modern Language Review* 76 (1981): 794–810.

28. H.J. Jackson, 'Sterne, Burton, and Ferriar: Allusions to the *Anatomy of Melancholy* in Volumes V to IX of *Tristram Shandy*', *Philological Quarterly* 54 (1975): 457–70; reprinted in Marcus Walsh (ed.) *Laurence Sterne* (Harlow: Longman, 2002), pp. 123–37.

29. *Florida Edition*, 1: 408.

30. Cited from Robert Burton, *The Anatomy of Melancholy* (Holbrook Jackson (ed.)), three vols. (London: Dent, 1932, 1968), 1: 23–4.

31. See 'Verses on the Death of Dr. Swift D.S.P.D', lines 317–18 in Rogers (ed.), p. 493 for Swift's defence of his poetic originality in a couplet plagiarized from Denham.

32. Walsh (ed.), p. 126.

33. Thomas Mallon, *Stolen Words* (New York: Harcourt, Inc., 2001), p. 17.

34. Ricks, *Allusion to the Poets*, p. 231.

35. Thomas Keymer, *Sterne, the Moderns, and the Novel* (Oxford University Press, 2002), p. 33.

36. From a letter to Sir David Dalrymple: cited in *Sterne: The Critical Heritage*, p. 55.
37. Letter to the *Universal Magazine of Knowledge and Pleasure* (1760): cited in ibid., p. 63.
38. Ibid., p. 56.
39. Letter of summer 1759, in *Letters*, p. 76. Correspondent unknown.
40. *Thraliana*, I. 23–4. Cited from Alan B. Howes, *Yorick and the Critics: Sterne's Reputation in England, 1760–1868* (New Haven: Yale University Press, 1958), p. 81.
41. *Sterne: The Critical Heritage*, p. 198.
42. On Ferriar's varied career, see Edward M. Brockbank, *John Ferriar: Public Health Work: Tristram Shandy: Other Essays and Verses* (London: William Heinemann, 1950).
43. See *Yorick and the Critics*, pp. 81–7.
44. 'Comments on Sterne' cited from *Sterne: The Critical Heritage*, p. 284.
45. Ibid., p. 286.
46. *Yorick and the Critics*, p. 86.
47. John Ferriar, *Illustrations of Sterne with other Essays and Verses* (1798), p. 7. On page 68, Ferriar accuses Sterne of 'plagiarism' (as so expressed) from Burton's *Anatomy of Melancholy*.
48. *Analytical Review* 20 (December 1794), 415; *GM* 64, Pt 1 (May 1794): 406; and 68, Pt 1 (June 1798): 471.
49. See Chapter 8 for a discussion of Stockdale and Pinkerton.
50. See Mann, 'The Problem of Originality in English Literary Criticism 1750–1800', pp. 109–10.
51. For Gregory's remarks, see *Sterne: The Critical Heritage*, p. 265.
52. For Seward's letter of 5 December 1787, see ibid., p. 268.
53. From *Miscellanies, or Literary Recreations* (1796): cited from ibid., p. 295.
54. 'Remarks on the Charge of Plagiarism Alleged Against Sterne', in *Port Folio*, 3rd Series iv (October 1810); cited from ibid., pp. 335, 337.
55. Ibid., pp. 373–4.

Bibliography

Primary sources

Addison, Joseph, *Works* (Richard Hurd (ed.)), six vols. (1811).

Anon., *An Essay in Defence of the Female Sex*, fifth edn (1721). Authorship is probably by Judith Drake or Mary Astell.

Anon., *Reflections on Originality in Authors: Being Remarks on A Letter to Mr. Mason on the Marks of Imitation ... with a word or two on the Characters of Ben. Johnson and Pope* (1766). Authorship is probably by Edward Capell.

Anon., *A Journal from Parnassus* (Hugh Macdonald (ed.)) (London: P.J. Dobell, 1937).

Anon., *The Life and Death of Mrs. Mary Frith. Commonly Called Mal Cutpurse.* (1662), in Janet Todd and Elizabeth Spearing (eds) *Counterfeit Ladies* (London: William Pickering, 1994).

Astell, Mary, *Political Writings* (Patricia Springborg (ed.)) (Cambridge University Press, 1996).

Atterbury, Francis, *A Short Review of the Controversy between Mr. Boyle and Dr. Bentley* (1701).

Bailey, Margery (ed.) *Boswell's Column* (London: William Kimber, 1951).

Bailey, Nathan, *Dictionarium Britannicum* (1730).

Barnard, John (ed.) *Pope: The Critical Heritage* (London: Routledge & Kegan Paul, 1973).

Behn, Aphra, *Works* (Janet Todd (ed.)), seven vols. (London: William Pickering, 1996).

Bentley, Richard, *A Dissertation upon the Epistles of Phalaris. With an Answer to the Objections of the Honourable Charles Boyle* (1699).

Blount, Sir Thomas Pope, *Essays on Several Subjects*, third edn (1697).

Boyle, Charles, *Dr. Bentley's Dissertations on the Epistles of Phalaris, and the Fables of AEsop Examin'd* (1698).

Bradstreet, Anne, *Works* (Jeannine Hensley (ed.)) (Cambridge, Mass.: Harvard University Press, 1967).

Browne, Sir Thomas, *Pseudodoxia Epidemica* (Robin Robbins (ed.)), two vols. (Oxford: Clarendon Press, 1981).

Bullokar, John, *An English Expositor, or Compleat English Dictionary* (1695).

Burton, Robert, *The Anatomy of Melancholy* (Holbrook Jackson (ed.)), three vols. (London: Dent, 1932, 1968).

Butler, Samuel, *Genuine Remains in Verse and Prose* (R. Thyer (ed.)) two vols. (1759).

Butler, Samuel, *Characters and Passages from Note-books* (A.R. Waller (ed.)) (Cambridge University Press, 1908).

Butler, Samuel, *Satires and Miscellaneous Poetry and Prose* (René Lamar (ed.)) (Cambridge University Press, 1928).

Butler, Samuel, *Characters* (Charles W. Daves (ed.)) (Cleveland: The Press of Case Western Reserve University, 1970).

Butler, Samuel, *Prose Observations* (Hugh de Quehen (ed.)) (Oxford: Clarendon Press, 1979).

Cavendish, Margaret, *Poems and Fancies written by the Right Honorable, the Lady Margaret Newcastle* (1653).

Cavendish, Margaret, *Natures Picture Drawn by Fancies Pencil to the Life* (1656).

Cavendish, Margaret, *Life of William Cavendishe*, second edn (1675).

Cibber, Colley, *A Letter from Mr. Cibber to Mr. Pope* (1742).

Cibber, Colley, *An Apology for his Life* (London: J.M. Dent & Sons, 1938).

Connoisseur, The; By Mr. Town, Critic and Censor-General, second edn (1755).

Cooke, Thomas, *The Candidates for the Bays. A Poem* (1730).

Cowper, William, *Letters and Prose Writings* (James King and Charles Ryskamp (eds)), five vols. (Oxford: Clarendon Press, 1979–86).

Denham, Sir John, *Poetical Works* (Theodore Howard Banks, Jr. (ed.)) (New Haven: Yale University Press, 1928).

Dennis John, *Critical Works* (E.N. Hooker (ed.)), two vols. (Baltimore: Johns Hopkins Press, 1939–43).

Douglas, John, *Milton Vindicated from the Charge of Plagiarism, brought against him by Mr. Lauder* (1751).

Dryden, John, *Letters* (Charles E. Ward (ed.)) (Durham, NC: Duke University Press, 1942).

Dryden, John, *Of Dramatic Poesy and other Critical Essays* (George Watson (ed.)), two vols. (London: J.M. Dent & Sons Ltd, 1962).

Dryden, John, *Poems* (Paul Hammond and David Hopkins (eds)), five vols. (Harlow: Pearson Education Ltd, 1995–2005).

Dryden, John, *Selected Poems* (Paul Hammond and David Hopkins (eds)) (Harlow: Pearson Educational Ltd, 2007).

Dunton, John, *A Voyage Round the World; or a Pocket Library* (1691).

Durham, W.H. (ed.) *Critical Essays of the Eighteenth Century 1700–1725* (New York: Russell and Russell, 1961).

Elstob, Elizabeth, *An English-Saxon Homily on the Birth-day of St. Gregory* (1709).

Farmer, Richard, *An Essay on the Learning of Shakespeare* (1767).

Felton, Henry, *A Dissertation on Reading the Classics, and Forming a Just Style*, third edn (1718).

Ferriar, John, *Illustrations of Sterne with other Essays and Verses* (1798).

Fielding, Henry, *Joseph Andrews* (Martin C. Battestin (ed.)) (Oxford: Clarendon Press, 1967).

Fielding, Henry, *A Journey from This World to the Next and The Journal of a Voyage to Lisbon* (Ian A. Bell and Andrew Varney (eds)) (Oxford: World's Classics, 1997).

Fielding, Sarah, *The Cry: A New Dramatic Fable*, three vols. (1754).

Fielding, Sarah, *The Adventures of David Simple and Volume the Last* (Peter Sabor (ed.)) (Lexington: University Press of Kentucky, 1998).

Finch, Anne, *The Poems of Anne, Countess of Winchilsea* (Myra Reynolds (ed.)) (University of Chicago Press, 1903).

Forbes, Sir William (ed.) *An Account of the Life and Writings of James Beattie* (1806), reprinted with introduction by Roger Robinson, two vols. (London: Thoemmes Press, 1976).

Gay, John, *Letters* (C.F. Burgess (ed.)) (Oxford: Clarendon Press, 1966).

Gibbon, Edward, *English Essays* (Patricia Craddock (ed.)) (Oxford: Clarendon Press, 1972).

Goldsmith, Oliver, *Collected Works* (Arthur Friedman (ed.)), five vols. (Oxford: Clarendon Press, 1966).

Gray, Thomas, *Correspondence* (Paget Toynbee and Leonard Whibley (eds), with corrections and additions by H.W. Starr), three vols. (Oxford: Clarendon Press, 1971).

Green, Matthew, *The Spleen: An Epistle*, second edn corrected (1737).

Greer, Germaine *et al.* (eds) *Kissing the Rod: An Anthology of 17th Century Women's Verse* (London: Virago, 1988).

Guerinot, J.V., *Pamphlet Attacks on Alexander Pope 1711-1744: A Descriptive Bibliography* (London: Methuen & Co Ltd, 1969).

Hall, Joseph, *Collected Poems* (A. Davenport (ed.)) (Liverpool University Press, 1949).

Harington, Sir John, *Epigrams, 1618* (Menston: Scolar Press, 1970).

Harris, John, *A Treatise upon the Modes: or, A Farewell to French Kicks* (1715).

Heywood, John, *Proverbs and Epigrams*, reprinted from the original edition of 1562 for the Spenser Society (1867).

Hill, George Birkbeck (ed.) *Johnsonian Miscellanies*, two vols. (Oxford: Clarendon Press, 1897).

Howes, Alan B. (ed.) *Sterne: The Critical Heritage* (London and Boston: Routledge & Kegan Paul, 1974).

Hurd, Richard, *Q. Horatii Flacci Epistolae ad Pisones, et Augustum: with an English commentary and notes*, third edn, two vols. (1751).

Hurd, Richard, *A Letter to Mr. Mason; On the Marks of Imitation* (1757).

Jacob, Giles, *The Poetical Register or the Lives and Characters of the English Dramatick Poets*, two vols. (1723).

Johnson, Samuel, *Dictionary of the English Language* (1755).

Johnson Samuel, *The Yale Edition of the Works* (New Haven: Yale University Press, 1958).

Johnson, Samuel, *Letters* (Bruce Redford (ed.)), five vols. (Oxford: Clarendon Press, 1992-4).

Johnson, Samuel, *The Lives of the English Poets* (Roger Lonsdale (ed.)), four vols. (Oxford: Clarendon Press, 2006).

Jonson, Ben, *The Complete Poems* (George Parfitt (ed.)) (Harmondsworth: Penguin Classics, 1975).

Jonson, Ben, *Poetaster* (Tom Cain (ed.)) (Manchester University Press, 1995).

Kendall, Timothe, *Flowers and Epigrammes*, reprinted from the original edition of 1577 for the Spenser Society (1874).

King, William, *Dialogues of the Dead. Relating to the present Controversy Concerning the Epistles of Phalaris* (1699).

King, William, *The Odes of Horace in Latin and English; With a Translation of Dr. Bentley's Notes. To which are added, Notes upon Notes; Done in the Bentleian Stile and Manner* (1712).

Kinsley, James and Kinsley, Helen (eds) *Dryden: The Critical Heritage* (London: Routledge & Kegan Paul, 1971).

Langbaine, Gerard, *Momus Triumphans or the Plagiaries of the English Stage Expos'd in a Catalogue* (1688).

Langbaine, Gerard, *Momus Triumphans* (David Stuart Rodes (ed.)), Augustan Reprint Society, v. 150 (1971).

Langbaine, Gerard, *An Account of the English Dramatick Poets* (1691).

Lauder, William, *An Essay on Milton's Use and Imitation of the Moderns* (1750).

Lauder, William, *Letter to the Reverend Mr. Douglas, occasion'd by his Vindication of Milton* (1751).

Lauder, William, *King Charles I Vindicated from the Charge of Plagiarism* (1754).

Lee, William (ed.) *Daniel Defoe: His Life and Recently Discovered Writings*, three vols. (1869).

Longinus, Dionysius, *The Works of Dionysius Longinus, On the Sublime ... Translated from the Greek ... By Mr. Welsted* (1712).

Lonsdale, Roger (ed.) *The New Oxford Book of Eighteenth Century Verse* (Oxford University Press, 1984).

Lord, George deF *et al.*, *Poems on Affairs of State: Augustan Satirical Verse, 1660–1714*, seven vols. (New Haven: Yale University Press, 1963–75).

Martial, *Epigrams*, Loeb Classical Library edition (D.R. Shackleton Bailey (ed.) and trans.), three vols. (Cambridge, Mass.: Harvard University Press, 1993).

Milton, John, *Paradise Lost: A Poem in Twelve Books* (Thomas Newton (ed.)), second edn, two vols. (1751).

Nichols, John, *Illustrations of the Literary History of the Eighteenth Century*, eight vols. (1817–58).

Oden, Richard (ed.) *Dryden and Shadwell: The Literary Controversy and 'Mac Flecknoe'* (Delmar, NY: Scholars Facsimiles and Reprints, 1977).

Oldys, Alexander, *An Ode on the Death of Mr Dryden* (1700).

Overbury, Thomas, *Miscellaneous Works in Prose and Verse* (Edward F. Rimbault (ed.)) (London: Reeves & Turner, 1890).

Parnell, Thomas, *Collected Poems of Thomas Parnell* (Claude Rawson and F.P. Lock (eds)) (Newark: University of Delaware Press, 1989).

Pennington, Montagu, *A Series of Letters between Mrs. Elizabeth Carter and Miss Catherine Talbot, from the year 1741 to 1770*, two vols. (1808).

Pinkerton, John [Robert Heron], *Letters of Literature* (1785).

Pope, Alexander, *Poems* (J. Butt *et al.* (eds)), 11 vols. (London: Methuen, 1939–69).

Pope, Alexander, *Correspondence* (George Sherburn (ed.)), five vols. (Oxford: Clarendon Press, 1956).

Pope, Alexander, *Prose Works: Vol. II: The Major Works, 1725–1744* (Rosemary Cowler (ed.)) (Oxford: Basil Blackwell, 1986).

Reynolds, Joshua, *Discourses Delivered to the Students of the Royal Academy* (Roger Fry (ed.)) (London: Seeley & Co., 1905).

Richardson, J. [father and son], *Explanatory Notes and Remarks on Milton's Paradise Lost* (1734).

Richardson, Samuel, *Selected Letters* (John Carroll (ed.)) (Oxford: Clarendon Press, 1964).

Seward, Anna, *Letters ... written between the years 1784 and 1807*, six vols. (1811).

Shawcross, J.T. (ed.) *Milton: The Critical Heritage* (London: Routledge & Kegan Paul, 1970).

Smith, Charlotte, *Poems* (Stuart Curran (ed.)) (Oxford University Press, 1993).

Smith, Charlotte, *Works* (Stuart Curran (gen. ed.)), 14 vols. (London: Pickering & Chatto, 2005).

Smith, David Nichol (ed.) *The Oxford Book of Eighteenth Century Verse* (Oxford: Clarendon Press, 1926).

Spence, Joseph, *Observations, Anecdotes, and Characters of Books and Men* (J.M. Osborn (ed.)), two vols. (Oxford: Clarendon Press, 1966).

Spingarn, J.E. (ed.) *Critical Essays of the Seventeenth Century*, three vols. (Oxford: Clarendon Press, 1908).

Stephens, John Calhoun (ed.) *The Guardian* (Lexington: University Press of Kentucky, 1982).

Sterne, Laurence, *Letters* (Lewis Perry Curtis (ed.)) (Oxford: Clarendon Press, 1935).

Sterne, Laurence, *A Sentimental Journey through France and Italy by Mr. Yorick* (Gardner D. Stout, Jr. (ed.)) (Berkeley and Los Angeles: University of California Press, 1967).

Sterne, Laurence, *Florida Edition of the Works* (Melvyn New *et al.* (eds)) (Gainsville, Florida: University Press of Florida, 1978).

Stockdale, Percival, *An Inquiry into the Nature and Genuine Laws of Poetry* (1778).

Stockdale, Percival, *Lectures on the Truly Eminent English Poets*, two vols. (1807).

Suckling, Sir John, *Works* (1709).

Sullivan, J.P. and Boyle, A.J. (eds) *Martial in English* (London: Penguin, 1996).

Swift, Jonathan, *Prose Works* (Herbert Davis *et al.* (eds)), 14 vols. (Oxford: Clarendon Press, 1939–68).

Swift, Jonathan, *A Tale of a Tub &c* (A.C. Guthkelch and D. Nichol Smith (eds)), second edn (Oxford: Clarendon Press, 1958).

Swift, Jonathan, *Complete Poems* (Pat Rogers (ed.)) (Harmondsworth: Penguin, 1983).

Temple, Sir William, *Five Miscellaneous Essays* (Samuel Holt Monk (ed.)) (Ann Arbor: University of Michigan Press, 1963).

Trapp, Joseph, *Lectures on Poetry: Read in the Schools of Natural Philosophy at Oxford* (1742).

Villiers, George, 2nd Duke of Buckingham, *The Rehearsal* (D.E.L. Crane (ed.)) (Durham: University of Durham Publications, 1976).

Waller, Edmund, *Poetical Works* (Robert Bell (ed.)) (London: John W. Parker & Son, 1854).

Warburton, William, *Letters from a Late Eminent Prelate to one of his Friends* (1809).

Ward, Edward, *A Journey to Hell Part II* (1700).

Ward, Edward, *Durgen. Or, A Plain Satyr upon a Pompous Satyrist* (1729).

Warton, Joseph, *Essay on the Genius and Writings of Pope*, fifth edn, two vols. (1806).

Welsted, Leonard, 'The State of Poetry' (1724), in W.H. Durham (ed.) *Critical Essays of the Eighteenth Century* (New Haven: Yale University Press, 1915).

Wordsworth, Dorothy, *The Grasmere and Alfoxden Journals* (Pamela Woof (ed.)) (Oxford University Press, 2002).

Wordsworth, William, *Poetical Works* (E. De Selincourt (ed.)), second edn, five vols. (Oxford: Clarendon Press, 1952).

Wotton, William, *Reflections upon Ancient and Modern Learning* (1694).

Wotton, William, *A Defense of the Reflections upon Ancient and Modern Learning ... with Observations upon The Tale of a Tub* (1705).

Young, Edward, *Conjectures on Original Composition* (Edith J. Morley (ed.)) (Manchester University Press, 1918).

Secondary sources

Abelove, Henry, 'John Wesley's Plagiarism of Samuel Johnson and its Contemporary Reception', *Huntington Library Quarterly* 59 (1997): 73–9.

Adams, Robert Martin, 'Jonathan Swift, Thomas Swift, and the Authorship of *A Tale of a Tub*', *Modern Philology* 64 (1967): 198–232.

Aden, John M., 'Dryden, Corneille and the *Essay of Dramatic Poesy*', *Review of English Studies* NS 6 (1955): 147–56.

Ault, Norman, *New Light on Pope* (London: Methuen & Co, 1949).

Backscheider, Paula R., *Eighteenth-Century Women Poets and their Poetry: Inventing Agency, Inventing Genre* (Baltimore: Johns Hopkins University Press, 2005).

Baines, Paul, *The House of Forgery in Eighteenth-Century Britain* (Aldershot: Ashgate Press, 1999).

Baines, Paul, 'Theft and Poetry and Pope', in Kewes, Paulina (ed.) *Plagiarism in Early Modern England* (Basingstoke: Palgrave Macmillan, 2003), pp. 166–80.

Baird, Theodore, 'The Time-Scheme of *Tristram Shandy* and a Source', *PMLA* 51 (1936): 803–20.

Barchas, Jane, 'Sarah Fielding's Dashing Style and Eighteenth-Century Print Culture', *ELH* 63 (1996): 633–56.

Barrell, John, 'The Uses of Dorothy: "The Language of the Sense" in "Tintern Abbey"', in his *Poetry, Language and Politics* (Manchester University Press, 1988).

Bate, W. Jackson, *The Burden of the Past and the English Poet* (London: Chatto & Windus, 1971).

Battersby, Christine, *Gender and Genius: Towards a Feminist Aesthetics* (London: Women's Press, 1989).

Bloom, Harold, *The Anxiety of Influence* (New York: Oxford University Press, 1973).

Bloom, Harold, *A Map of Misreading* (New York: Oxford University Press, 1975).

Borkat, Roberta F. Sarfatt, 'The Spider and the Bee: Jonathan Swift's Reversal of Tradition in *The Battle of the Books*', *Eighteenth-Century Life* 3, 2 (December 1976): 44–6.

Bowerbank, Sylvia, 'The Spider's Delight: Margaret Cavendish and the "Female" Imagination', *English Literary Renaissance* 14 (Winter 1984): 392–408.

Braudy, Leo, *The Frenzy of Renown: Fame and its History* (New York: Oxford University Press, 1986).

Briggs, Peter M., 'Laurence Sterne and Literary Celebrity in 1760', *Age of Johnson* 4 (1991): 251–80.

Brockbank, Edward M., *John Ferriar: Public Health Work: Tristram Shandy: Other Essays and Verses* (London: William Heinemann, 1950).

Brooks, Harold F., 'The "Imitation" in English Poetry, especially in Formal Satire, before the Age of Pope', *Review of English Studies* 25 (1949): 124–40.

Brower, Reuben, *Alexander Pope: the Poetry of Allusion* (Oxford: Clarendon Press, 1959).

Bush, Douglas, *English Literature in the Earlier Seventeenth Century 1600–1660*, second edn (Oxford: Clarendon Press, 1962).

Cash, Arthur H., 'The Birth of Tristram Shandy: Sterne and Dr. Burton', in R.F. Brissenden (ed.) *Studies in the Eighteenth Century* (Canberra: Australian National University Press, 1968), pp. 133–54.

Cash, Arthur H., *Laurence Sterne: The Later Years* (London: Routledge, 1986).

Clark, J.C.D., *Samuel Johnson: Literature, Religion and English Cultural Politics from the Restoration to Romanticism* (Cambridge University Press, 1994).

Clifford, James L., 'Johnson and Lauder', *Philological Quarterly* 54 (1975): 342–56.

Devine, Michael G., 'Disputing the "Original" in Swift's *Tale of a Tub*', *Swift Studies* 18 (2003): 26–33.

Dobson, Michael, *The Making of the National Poet: Shakespeare, Adaptation and Authorship, 1660–1769* (Oxford: Clarendon Press, 1992).

Donaldson, Ian, '"The Fripperie of Wit": Jonson and Plagiarism', in Paulina Kewes (ed.) *Plagiarism in Early Modern England* (Basingstoke: Palgrave Macmillan, 2003), pp. 119–33.

Downey, James, 'The Sermons of Mr. Yorick: A Reassessment of Hammond', *English Studies in Canada* IV (1978): 193–211.

Duncan, Douglas, *Thomas Ruddiman: A Study in Scottish Scholarship of the Early Eighteenth Century* (Oliver & Boyd: Edinburgh, 1965).

Eaves, T.C. Duncan and Kimpel, Ben D., *Samuel Richardson: A Biography* (Oxford: Clarendon Press, 1971).

Ehrenpreis, Irvin, *Swift: The Man, his Works and the Age*, three vols. (London: Methuen, 1962–83).

Ehrenpreis, Irvin, *Literary Meaning and Augustan Values* (Charlottesville: University of Virginia Press, 1974).

Elias, Jr., A.C., *Swift and Moor Park* (Philadelphia: University of Pennsylvania Press, 1982).

Ellis, Frank H., 'No Apologies, Dr. Swift!', *Eighteenth-Century Life* 21, 3 (1997): 71–6.

Engell, James, 'Johnson on Novelty and Originality', *Modern Philology* 75 (February 1978): 273–9.

Ezell, Margaret, *Writing Women's Literary History* (Baltimore: Johns Hopkins University Press, 1993).

Fanning, Christopher, '"The Things Themselves": Origins and Originality in Sterne's Sermons', *The Eighteenth Century* 40, 1 (1999): 29–45.

Feather, John, *Publishing, Piracy and Politics: An Historical Study of Copyright in Britain* (London: Mansell Publishing Limited, 1994).

Fletcher, Loraine, *Charlotte Smith: A Critical Biography* (Basingstoke: Palgrave, 2001).

Fluchère, Henri, *Laurence Sterne: From Tristram to Yorick: An Interpretation of Tristram Shandy*, translated and abridged by Barbara Bray (London: Oxford University Press, 1965).

Folkenflik, Robert, '"Homo Alludens" in the Eighteenth Century', *Criticism* 24 (1982): 218–32.

Furbank, P.N., and Owens, W.R., *The Canonisation of Daniel Defoe* (New Haven: Yale University Press, 1988).

Goldgar, Bertrand A., 'Imitation and Plagiarism: The Lauder Affair and its Critical Aftermath', *Studies in the Literary Imagination* 34 (2001): 1–16.

Greene, Jody, *The Trouble with Ownership: Literary Property and Authorial Liability in England, 1660–1730* (Philadelphia: University of Pennsylvania Press, 2005).

Greer, Germaine, *Slop-Shod Sibyls: Recognition, Rejection and the Woman Poet* (London: Viking, 1995).

Griffiths, Eric, 'Dryden's Past', in *Proceedings of the British Academy 84: 1993 Lectures and Memoirs*, 113–49.

Hammond, Brean S., *Professional Imaginative Writing in England 1670–1740: 'Hackney for Bread'* (Oxford: Clarendon Press, 1997).

Hammond, Brean, 'Swift's Reading', in Christopher Fox (ed.) *A Cambridge Companion to Jonathan Swift* (Cambridge University Press, 2003).

Hammond, Lansing Van der Heyden, *Laurence Sterne's 'Sermons of Mr. Yorick'* (New Haven: Yale University Press, 1948).

Hawley, Judith, 'Charlotte Smith's *Elegiac Sonnets*: Losses and Gains', in Isobel Armstrong and Virginia Blain (eds) *Women's Poetry in the Enlightenment: the Making of a Canon, 1730–1820* (Basingstoke: Macmillan, 1999), pp. 184–98.

Hazen, Allan T., *Samuel Johnson's Prefaces & Dedications* (New Haven: Yale University Press, 1937).

Helgerson, Richard, *Self-Crowned Laureates: Spenser, Jonson, Milton and the Literary System* (Berkeley and Los Angeles: California University Press, 1983).

Hollander, John, *The Figure of Echo: A Mode of Allusion in Milton and After* (Berkeley: California University Press, 1981).

Hornblower, Simon and Spawforth, Antony (eds) *Oxford Classical Dictionary*, third edn revised (Oxford University Press, 2003).

Horne, Colin J., 'The Phalaris Controversy: King *versus* Bentley', *Review of English Studies* 22 (1946): 289–303.

Howes, Alan B., *Yorick and the Critics: Sterne's Reputation in England, 1760–1868* (New Haven: Yale University Press, 1958).

Hume, Robert D., 'Securing a Repertory: Plays on the London Stage 1660–5', in Antony Coleman and Antony Hammond (eds) *Poetry and Drama 1570–1700: Essays in Honour of Harold F. Brooks* (London: Methuen, 1981), pp. 156–72.

Huntley, Frank Livingstone, *On Dryden's 'Essay of Dramatic Poesy'* (Michigan: Archon Books, 1968).

Jackson, H.J., 'Sterne, Burton, and Ferriar: Allusions to the *Anatomy of Melancholy* in Volumes V to IX of *Tristram Shandy*', *Philological Quarterly* 54 (1975): 457–70.

Jefferson, D.W., '*Tristram Shandy* and the Tradition of Learned Wit', *Essays in Criticism* 1 (1951): 225–48.

Jenkins, Harold, *Edward Benlowes (1602–1676): Biography of a Minor Poet* (London: Athlone Press, 1952).

Johnson, James W., 'That Neo-Classical Bee', *Journal of the History of Ideas* 22, 2 (1961): 262–6.

Jones, R.F., *Ancients and Moderns* (St Louis: Washington University, 1961).

Keener, Frederick, 'Parallelism and the Poets' Secret: Eighteenth-Century Commentary on *Paradise Lost*', *Essays in Criticism* 37 (1987): 281–302.

Kewes, Paulina, *Authorship and Appropriation: Writing for the Stage in England, 1660–1710* (Oxford: Clarendon Press, 1998).

Kewes, Paulina (ed.) *Plagiarism in Early Modern England* (Basingstoke: Palgrave Macmillan, 2003).

Keymer, Thomas, *Sterne, the Moderns, and the Novel* (Oxford University Press, 2002).

Kugler, Anne, *Errant Plagiary: The Life and Writings of Lady Sarah Cowper 1644–1720* (Stanford, California: Stanford University Press, 2002).

Lamb, Jonathan, 'Sterne's System of Imitation', *Modern Language Review* 76 (1981): 794–810.

Landa, Louis, 'Pope's Belinda, The General Emporie of the World, and the Wondrous Worm', in *Essays in Eighteenth-Century Literature* (Princeton University Press, 1980), pp. 178–98.

Landry, Donna and MacLean, Gerald, 'Of Forceps, Patents, and Paternity: *Tristram Shandy*', *Eighteenth Century Studies* 23 (1989–90): 522–43.

Levine, Joseph M., *The Battle of the Books: History and Literature in the Augustan Age* (Ithaca, NY: Cornell University Press, 1991).

Loftis, John, 'Dryden's Comedies', in Earl Miner (ed.) *John Dryden* (London: Bell, 1972).

Lonsdale, Roger, 'Gray and "Allusion": The Poet as Debtor', in R.F. Brissenden and J.C. Eade (eds) *Studies in the Eighteenth Century IV* (Canberra: Australian National University Press, 1979), pp. 31–55.

Love, Harold, *Scribal Publication in Seventeenth-Century England* (Oxford: Clarendon Press, 1993).

Lund, Roger D., 'From Oblivion to Dulness: Pope and the Poetics of Appropriation', *British Journal for Eighteenth-Century Studies* 14 (1991): 171–89.

Lynch, Jack, *Deception and Detection in Eighteenth-Century Britain* (Aldershot: Ashgate, 2008).

Macfarlane, Robert, *Original Copy: Plagiarism and Originality in Nineteenth-Century Literature* (Oxford University Press, 2007).

Mallon, Thomas, *Stolen Words: Forays in the Origins and Ravages of Plagiarism* (New York: Ticknor & Fields, 1989).

Mann, Elizabeth L., 'The Problem of Originality in English Literary Criticism, 1750-1800', *Philological Quarterly* 18 (1939): 97–118.

Marcuse, Michael J., 'The Lauder Controversy and the Jacobite Cause', *Studies in Burke and his Time* 18 (1977): 27–47.

Marcuse, Michael J., 'Miltonoklastes: The Lauder Affair Reconsidered', *Eighteenth-Century Life* 4 (1978): 86–91.

Marcuse, Michael J., "The Scourge of Impostors, the Terror of Quacks": John Douglas and the Exposé of William Lauder', *Huntington Library Quarterly* 42 (1978–9): 231–61.

Masten, Jeffery, *Textual Intercourse: Collaboration, Authorship, and Sexualities in Renaissance Drama* (Cambridge University Press, 1997).

Mazzeo, Tilar J., *Plagiarism and Literary Property in the Romantic Period* (Philadelphia: University of Pennsylvania Press, 2007).

McGinnis, Reginald (ed.) *Originality and Intellectual Property in the French and English Enlightenment* (London: Routledge, 2008).

McHenry, Robert W. Jr., 'Plagiarism and Paternity in Dryden's Adaptations', in McGinnis, Reginald (ed.) *Originality and Intellectual Property in the French and English Enlightenment* (London: Routledge, 2008), pp. 1–21.

Mueller, Judith C., 'Writing under Constraint: Swift's 'Apology' for *A Tale of a Tub*', *ELH* 60 (1993): 101–15.

Murray, Barbara, *Restoration Shakespeare: Viewing the Voice* (London: Associated University Presses, 2001).

New, Melvyn, 'Sterne's Rabelaisian Fragment: A Text from the Holograph Manuscript', *PMLA* 87 (1972): 1083–92.

Newlyn, Lucy, *Coleridge, Wordsworth and the Language of Allusion* (Oxford: Clarendon Press, 1986).

Newton, Richard C., 'Jonson and the (Re)-Invention of the Book', in Claude J. Summers and Ted-Larry Pebworth (eds) *Classic and Cavalier: Essays on Jonson and the Sons of Ben* (Pittsburgh: University of Pittsburgh Press, 1982), pp. 31–55.

Nitchie, Elizabeth, 'Longinus and the Theory of Poetic Imitation in Seventeenth and Eighteenth Century England', *Studies in Philology* 32 (1935): 580–97.

Nussbaum, Felicity A., *The Brink of All We Hate: English Satires on Women, 1660–1750* (Lexington: University of Kentucky Press, 1984).

Orgel, Stephen, 'The Renaissance Artist as Plagiarist', *ELH* 48 (1981): 476–95.

Parnell, J.T., 'Swift, Sterne, and the Skeptical Tradition', *Studies in Eighteenth-Century Culture* 23 (1994): 220–42.

Pask, Kevin, 'Plagiarism and the Originality of National Literature: Gerard Langbaine', *ELH* 69 (2002): 727–47.

Paull, H.M., *Literary Ethics: A Study of the Growth of the Literary Conscience* (London: Thornton Butterworth Ltd, 1928).

Pearson, Jacqueline, *The Prostituted Muse: Images of Women and Women Dramatists, 1642–1737* (London: Harvester Wheatsheaf, 1988).

Pechter, Edward, *Dryden's Classical Theory of Literature* (Cambridge University Press, 1975).

Petrie, Graham, 'A Rhetorical Topic in *Tristram Shandy*', *Modern Language Review* 65 (1970): 201–6.

Phillips, Patricia, *The Adventurous Muse: Theories of Originality in English Poetics 1650–1760* (Uppsala: Almqvist & Wiskell, 1984).

Pigman III, G.W., 'Versions of Imitation in the Renaissance', *Renaissance Quarterly* 33, 1 (Spring 1980): 1–32.

Plock, Vike, *Joyce, Medicine, and Modernity* (Gainesville: University Press of Florida, 2010).

Pratt, Kathryn, 'Charlotte Smith's Melancholia on the Page and Stage', *Studies in English Literature* 41 (2001): 563–81.

Quehen, A.H. de, 'An Account of Works Attributed to Samuel Butler', *Review of English Studies* NS 33 (1982): 262–77.

Reeves, James, *The Reputation and Writings of Alexander Pope* (London: Heinemann, 1976).

Richards, E.A., *Hudibras in the Burlesque Tradition* (New York: Columbia University Press, 1937).

Ricks, Christopher, 'Allusion: The Poet as Heir', in R.F. Brissenden and J.C. Eade (eds) *Studies in the Eighteenth Century III* (University of Toronto Press, 1976), pp. 209–40.

Ricks, Christopher, 'Plagiarism', originally published in *Proceedings of the British Academy 97*, reprinted in *Allusion to the Poets* (Oxford University Press, 2002), pp. 219–40.

Rosenthal, Laura, '(Re)Writing Lear: Literary Property and Dramatic Authorship', in John Brewer and Susan Staves (eds) *Early Modern Conceptions of Property* (London: Routledge, 1995), pp. 323–38.

Rosenthal, Laura J., *Playwrights and Plagiarists in Early Modern England: Gender, Authorship, Literary Property* (Ithaca: Cornell University Press, 1996).

Ross, Ian Campbell Ross, *Laurence Sterne: A Life* (Oxford University Press, 2001).

Runge, Laura L., *Gender and Language in British Literary Criticism 1660–1790* (Cambridge University Press, 1997).

Russ, Joanna, *How to Suppress Women's Writing* (London: Women's Press, 1983).

Saint-Amour, Paul K., *The Copywrights: Intellectual Property and the Literary Imagination* (Ithaca: Cornell University Press, 2003).

Saunders, David, *Authorship and Copyright* (London: Routledge, 1992).

Schäfer, Jürgen, *Early Modern English Lexicography*, two vols. (Oxford: Clarendon Press, 1989).

Sena, John F., *The Best Natur'd Man: Sir Samuel Garth, Physician and Poet* (New York: AMS Press, 1986).

Skinner, Quentin, 'The Idea of a Cultural Lexicon', *Essays in Criticism*, 29 (1979): 205–24.

Smith, R. Jack, 'Shadwell's Impact upon John Dryden', *Review of English Studies* 20 (1944): 29–44.

Sorelius, Gunnar, '*The Giant Race Before the Flood': Pre-Restoration Drama on the Stage and in the Criticism of the Restoration* (Uppsala: Studia anglistica upsaliensia, 1966).

Spencer, Jane, *Literary Relations: Kinship and the Canon 1660–1830* (Oxford University Press, 2005).

Starnes, De Witt T. and Noyes, Gertrude E., *The English Dictionary from Cawdrey to Johnson, 1604–1755* (1946), rev. Gabrielle Stein (Amsterdam: J. Benjamin Pub. Co., 1991).

Stedmond, J.M., 'Sterne as Plagiarist', *English Studies* 41 (1960): 308–12.

Stern, Simon, 'Copyright, Originality, and the Public Domain in Eighteenth-Century England', in McGinnis, Reginald (ed.) *Originality and Intellectual Property in the French and English Enlightenment* (London: Routledge, 2008), pp. 69–101.

Taylor, Gary, *Reinventing Shakespeare: A Cultural History from the Restoration to the Present* (London: Hogarth Press, 1989).

Terry, Richard, *Poetry and the Making of the English Literary Past 1660–1781* (Oxford University Press, 2001).

Terry, Richard, 'Plagiarism and Plagiarism Studies', *English Subject Centre Newsletter* 13 (October 2007): 6–8.

Tinkler, John F., 'The Splitting of Humanism: Bentley, Swift, and the English Battle of the Books', *Journal of the History of Ideas* 49, 3 (1988): 453–72.

Walsh, Marcus, *Shakespeare, Milton and Eighteenth-Century Literary Editing: The Beginnings of Interpretive Scholarship* (Cambridge University Press, 1997).

Wasserman, Earl R., 'The Limits of Allusion in *The Rape of the Lock'*, *Journal of English and Germanic Philology* 65 (1966): 425–44.

Wasserman, George R, *Samuel "Hudibras" Butler* (Boston, Mass.: Twayne, 1989).

Weber, Harold, '"A Double Portion of his Father's Art": Congreve, Dryden, Jonson and the Drama of Theatrical Succession', *Criticism* 39 (1997): 359–82.

Weinbrot, Howard, *The Formal Strain: Studies in Augustan Imitation and Satire* (University of Chicago Press, 1969).

Weinbrot, Howard D., 'Samuel Johnson, Percival Stockdale, and Brick-bats from Grubstreet: Some Later Response to the *Lives of the Poets'*, *Huntington Library Quarterly* 56 (1993): 105–34.

Weinsheimer, Joel, *Imitation* (London: Routledge & Kegan Paul, 1984).

West, David, and Woodman, Tony (eds) *Creative Imitation and Latin Literature* (Cambridge University Press, 1979).

White, Harold Ogden, *Plagiarism and Imitation During the English Renaissance* (Cambridge, Mass.: Harvard University Press, 1935).

Woodbridge, Homer E., *Sir William Temple: The Man and his Work* (New York: MLA of America, 1940).

Woodmansee, Martha, 'The Genius and the Copyright: Economic and Legal Conditions of the Emergence of the "Author"', *Eighteenth Century Studies* 17 (1984): 425–48.

Wyrick, Deborah Baker, *Jonathan Swift and the Vested Word* (Chapel Hill: University of North Carolina Press, 1988).

Index